SHADOW OF THE BEAST
A Tale of Theseus, Hero of Athens

Jeffrey Peter Clarke

SHADOW OF THE BEAST
A Tale of Theseus, Hero of Athens

FICTION4ALL

Chapter 1
The BLACK SAIL

A clatter of pottery bells broke the calm of a hot, pine-scented afternoon as the mop-haired, bare-footed peasant boy in ragged linen kilt appeared over the rise to hesitate for a moment against a boundless blue sky. Swishing his stick, he called out to urge his small herd of bleating goats down the so familiar path. To him the fates had allotted the tracks, the fields and the pinewoods as compass of his days. Seldom did he find an opportunity to venture outside a world bounded by the labours of each day. Yet when darkness came, even this might become a forbidden realm.

Through clustered pine trees he now and then glimpsed the sea, a cauldron of liquid metal above which hovered a lowering sun. Some way past the point where his path turned inland the ground sloped away gently toward the southern end of a wide bay. The boy stopped, not to rest, though his long day was coming to an end, but to gaze out across the water with a hand raised to protect his eyes from the harsh glare. Greeted by a welcoming sea breeze he remained a while longer, imagining what wonders might be found beyond a distant horizon that was for him a place of wild and youthful dreams.

He would have continued on his way except that below the horizon, almost lost amidst the water's dazzle, something moved as an insect crawling on beaten silver. It was not, of course, the first vessel the boy had seen. Fishing boats plied the waters daily, as did the larger boats from distant places; lands of hearsay, lands people in the city talked about, lands he could never hope to know.

To his keen eye there was something different about this boat, though what it was he could not be certain. Perhaps it was her steady progress - the progress of a larger vessel. One thing he could be quite sure of, however; the now deserted bay across which he gazed was her destination. He was also sure that the sun would be kissing the horizon before she arrived at the meagre straggle of irregular stone buildings that clung to the edge of the bay to form the small port of Phaleron. Uppermost in his mind was the belief he and everyone in Athens and hereabouts shared, that some day a ship would arrive bearing news of great importance. An occasional comment overheard in the marketplace on those rare visits to the city as well as remarks from the mouths of his own parents; these had convinced him that this long-awaited vessel would eventually arrive. His curiosity was much aroused. Could this be the one?

As he watched, a veil of cloud drifted across to haze the sun, so enabling him to make out the ship in more detail. The boy peered harder into the distance then letting out a whistle he threw aside his stick, gathered up his kilt and started in haste along the path. The goats pranced then scattered aside to a cacophony of bleating as he rushed headlong through their midst calling out, 'I'll be first to tell them! Yes, I will! I'll be the first!'

The journey would take him some time, bounding over rough, open pastures toward the woodlands where the broader path leading from the harbour to Athens' western gate crossed open ground. His shadow dancing eagerly ahead, he would follow this well-trodden route to the city. He would not reach the gate before the sun went down but he would deliver his message before the boat arrived in the harbour even though the wind at present looked to be in her favour. But if she did not have a skilled Athenian crew, if she was one of those deep-keeled Cretan vessels that could not easily be beached or would need to be moored at the jetty in the dead of night, she might stand out in the bay until dawn for safety's sake, sheltered by the headland to her south. And what of the reward? Yes, they had spoken of a reward for the one who brought first news of the vessel. And it had to be the right vessel because the boy had abandoned his flock and would otherwise be punished. It *had* to be the right vessel.

Approaching the city, he hurried on with shortening breath, passing by vineyards, olive groves and orchards. On he went toward the massive double gate, on toward the frowning stone tower of coarse Cyclopean blocks that it seemed only the time-shrouded giants of old could have laboured to construct. Citizens and traders were passing to and fro about their business, ignoring the wretched beggars who squatted in the shadows. Oxen, asses and men hauled farm produce and oil jars packed in straw to safety within the city wall, though on this occasion there was little sign of the armed guards who were so often in evidence. On he hurried through white-plastered timber dwellings that pressed upon narrow, crowded streets, through the tantalising odour of cooking, through the acrid

7

smoke of forges until reaching the rough-hewn stairs carved into the rock wall that wound upward to the acropolis.

The boy stopped long enough to calm his breathing then clambered nimbly, but was again quite breathless by the time he reached the top. There he rested to gaze across the open courtyard where arose the royal residence. This was the palace of Aegeus the king, an imposing three storey, stone and timber building topped by a palisade of stone-carved bulls' horns. Glancing about, anxious in case someone else should hurry past him to deliver the message first, he trotted across the courtyard then scrambled awkwardly up the steps leading to the great, bronze-clad doors of the main entrance. Almost there he was challenged by a brusque, 'Oi - where d'you think you're off to?'

'I bring news for our great King Aegeus!' he yelled as the pair of burly, surly guards with bronze-tipped spears and boiled hide corselets closed in to bar his progress. The guards had found little to do that day other than pass time in idle conversation. Here was something to break the monotony. Something trivial but perhaps enough to offer modest entertainment.

'What's this news you've got, then?' one of the guards demanded, eyeing the bedraggled intruder with an exaggerated frown that changed to a bristled, broken-toothed grin as the boy peered up wide-eyed. 'Well – what's an urchin like you got to say that could possibly interest Lord Aegeus?'

'There's a ship entering the bay,' he blurted. 'It's a fine ship – not a fishing boat – not a trader. It's got a royal symbol on its sail.'

An alabaster throne with tall, scalloped back stood at the far side of the hearth. On it, cushioned by a lamb's wool fleece, sat a gaunt faced man with well-trimmed moustache and beard. His long fair hair was held in place by a headband of gold-studded leather, his stooped form clothed in a belted white tunic of finely embroidered linen. In his hand rested a goblet of beaten gold, newly replenished by one of the female slaves who ladled from the wine jar carried awkwardly between two of her male children.

The boy knew he was in the presence of King Aegeus, the man who ruled his land.

Seated or standing close by were the king's richly attired kinsmen and companions, likewise attended by female slaves, whilst at the far side of the hearth sat chattering the red-lipped noblewomen, their faces white-glazed beneath long, elaborately crinkled hair. Adorned in narrow-waisted, long, flounced dresses with short-sleeved bodice cut away to leave their rouged breasts exposed, they were bejewelled in a manner the boy found incomprehensible.

First to notice him enter with the two guards had been three courtly-dressed children who stood chattering among themselves close by. They made no effort to convey their observation to anyone else but continued as before with frequent glances at the newcomer who felt utterly crushed in the presence of such opulence. The strumming continued and he saw that it came from the hands of a grey-haired, almost toothless, long-bearded old man in blue tunic who sat to the king's left and whose attention he held. From time to time the player raised a hand

11

from the lyre in order to recite in deep, sonorous tones the verses of some ancient epic whose meaning was totally lost on the boy. Perhaps nobody would acknowledge his presence until the bard had finished.

Staring about the hall, he was awed by the upward tapering, russet-painted columns that supported a heavily beamed ceiling, this latter blackened by years of rising smoke. About the walls, alternating with bronze-tipped spears, hung boiled-hide, metal-edged shields, some light and circular, hardly an arm's length across, others almost as tall as a man. All were gilded, all elaborately decorated. Here was something the boy found reassuringly familiar. Much plainer versions of these shields he had seen borne by men passing to and from the city on those occasions when the drums of war caused him and his family to gather their livestock and retreat within the sanctuary of Athens' defensive wall or to the more distant rural sanctuary of their kinfolk.

It was the lyre player who next noticed the boy. Finishing his verse, he laid aside his instrument and indicated to Aegeus that a stranger awaited his attention. The king and those about him turned aside as one of the guards stepped forward, bowed and announced above a descending silence, 'Lord Aegeus, we beg forgiveness at our intrusion, but this boy says 'e's observed a ship. He says it's got a royal device on its sail.'

'Does he indeed,' replied Aegeus, rising slowly from his throne to approach the boy.

Shaking visibly, the goatherd fell to his knees, stared hard at the floor and stammered, 'N-noble king, I saw – saw it – yes. A ship with – with -.'

Aegeus peered down at him to ask solemnly, 'It bore a device, you say - what device? And what else? Did you see the colour of the sail?'

'I did, mightiness, yes,' replied the boy at last summoning enough courage to look upward into the king's eyes; eyes that spoke of more than just weariness. 'I saw it clearly, sire. The device was a – a -.'

'A double axe?' interjected the king.

'Yes, lord, that's what it was - a double axe.' This statement was a guess but probably, or so he hoped, not a bad one. As for the second there was no doubt at all as he exclaimed, 'And the sail, master – the sail was black!'

Aegeus did not at first respond, though several of those close to him nodded their heads glumly then fixed their gaze upon the stone floor. The silence, growing more profound, was broken by wood spitting from the fire then by one of the children coughing. Tension grew as Aegeus continued to stare down at the boy, who in turn began to fidget uncontrollably.

When the king at last spoke, his voice was bland in the manner of one whose emotions, whilst kindled, must at all costs conceal his true feelings, though his expression was clouded with pain. 'A black sail. Very well. When what you tell us is confirmed, you shall have the promised reward. No doubt it will change your life as your message is to change mine.' Bidding the boy rise, he turned to the gathering then declared, 'Our entertainment is

13

ended. There are other matters to which I must attend.'

Their heads bowed, people began to leave, glancing at Aegeus in sympathy or not looking at him at all. Saying nothing to him or to one another. Some of the women wept as they followed the men. As he, too, was ushered from the hall, the boy turned to see Aegeus in the act of instructing a young slave boy who, no doubt, would run to the headland then report back to him over the ship. The king, stooped as if carrying an invisible burden about his shoulders then walked slowly, accompanied by his aged lyre player, toward a door at the far side where both vanished into darkness. The boy was taken to wait in the anteroom.

The great hall was deserted. In the fire within the circle, logs settled, life breathed. In the embers eyes watched. In the smoke whispers gathered. Emerging from gaps in the floor close by the hearth, black beetles stole about the deity of heat that was the centre of a realm they could for a time claim as their own.

***

Oil lamps on stands of twisted bronze cast a feeble light over the stone walls. Aegeus sat in pensive quiet. The air hung close and oppressive. Nearby waited the old man, his lyre propped by the side of his chair. When the king at last spoke, his was a voice of sad resignation.

'Haemon, my dear friend, we need not await confirmation of the sail. A simple goatherd would not make such a statement if it were false since he would not know its meaning. Theseus, my son, did not survive the ordeal. Those hopes I held for our future are scattered as chaff to the wind.'

The old man said nothing as Aegeus continued. 'He was the staunchest champion of our land. He shone as the brightest star in our heavens. Now, that light is extinguished, and we are condemned to darkness as are the blind.'

'He should never have sailed to Crete,' muttered the lyre player. 'I should have tried to persuade him. I failed you in not doing so.'

'Ah,' sighed Aegeus, 'I doubt the gods themselves could have prevented his making the journey there - I certainly could not. He would often listen to you when he dismissed the advice of others as a passing breeze but this time he was beyond persuasion. Perhaps he saw glory in that venture though no man could ever claim he was tainted by vanity or greed.'

'He was burdened by neither,' agreed Haemon. 'But I say again, had I tried to stop him joining the rest when the envoys came, perhaps he would be here with us now.'

Aegeus rose up and turned to face the window, saying, 'No, had he stayed when others were sent out to confront unknown danger, he could never have lived with himself. Now the people look at me in anger for allowing him to go on that final voyage. The anger of some will turn to hatred when they learn he has shared the fate of those young people of ours who sailed to Crete before him. Yet I thought that he of all people might have – no, the will of the gods has prevailed. And still my so-called brother Pallas waits in the south and will not rest until Athens writhes defeated in his grasp. My son would have stood against him. By the light of his valour Theseus would have driven back the shadows cast by Pallas. Once news of the ship reaches Pallas' ears, he will uncover the chalice of poison he has been fermenting.' Turning once more to Haemon he declared, 'It is a poison for which we have no antidote, my friend. There are no strong allies on whom we can call. There is no man in the city who might rally the people sufficiently to prevail against our enemy. Metion, the captain of my palace guard would gather his men to Athens' cause but great a warrior though he is, he does not possess those other skills needed to capture the hearts of the people. He is at the forefront in battle but sets himself aside in times of peace.'

'Lord Aegeus!' responded the old man, standing up quickly despite his aching bones. 'Why do we not send over the water to Troizen? King Pittheus surely would cross the gulf to stand with us. He has every reason to despise Pallas.'

'Pittheus,' sighed the king, 'is too busy watching his own back. He will not dare leave Troizen, not until matters are settled there. Pallas controls the supply of silver from the mines at Laurion and together with Cretan gold uses it now to fund intrigues at Troizen just as he has in the past here in Athens.'

Aegeus relapsed into pensive silence.

Eventually Haemon asked, 'Shall I call for wine?'

'No – no more wine,' breathed Aegeus. 'My grief would sail large even on a sea of wine.' Aegeus sighed, pressed hands to his face then fixed his gaze on the window whose leather blind was held rolled up above. The sky was darkening. 'Just now, my friend, I would prefer to be alone.'

Haemon got up, stepped to the door but turned briefly with a tear in his eye as Aegeus added, 'Whatever happens, never doubt that any man could have a truer friend than you have been to your king.'

The old man left but crossing the great hall in near darkness to the echo of his own footsteps he hesitated as if about to retrace his steps, shook his head, then continued on.

Aegeus sat in silence. The first stars would soon begin to appear as he gazed out at the sky, and with those stars would return memories of the long life he had lived and his term of kingship in Athens.

Chapter 2
The KING THAT WAS

The sun was low on that fine spring day those many years before when Aegeus rode into Corinth accompanied by the captain of his guard and a group of armed companions. There they intended to refresh themselves, dine and rest until the following day when they would head southward along the peninsula of Argolis on their way to Troizen, Athens' oldest ally. At Troizen reigned Pittheus, a good and trusted friend, with whom Aegeus wished to confer. It was part of a long journey, taking them originally from Athens when they had travelled north-west to the famed oracle at mountainous Delphi.

The journey to Delphi had been crucial. It had been a journey of discovery. A journey undertaken because Aegeus had needed reassurance over the future of Athens and its king in these times of uncertainty and danger. No longer in the first bloom of youth, he had failed to produce an heir when at the same time another, claiming rights to his throne, denying the legitimacy of his kingship, hovered like a vulture awaiting its chance to swoop.

Aegeus was a son of Pandion, one-time king of Athens who had been driven from the city by his enemies. After Pandion's death his four sons had reconquered Athens and all of Attica with Aegeus, by a short measure the eldest, claiming the throne of Athens. Nisos had taken the throne of Megara, always afterwards a firm ally of Athens. Lycos became ruler of Euboea whilst the ever-resentful

Pallas, all the time maintaining Athens should have been his, had acquired the territories of southern Attica with Thorikos as his capital.

Not long afterwards, Lycos and Pallas had conspired against Aegeus, alleging he was not a true son of Pandion. Nisos had remained a reluctant ally of Athens but with his untimely death Lycos saw an opportunity to lay plans against his elder brother. As a result, Aegeus had found it necessary to drive Lycos from his kingdom and banish him far to the east where he might do no further harm. But it was ruthless Pallas, wealthiest of the three brothers of Aegeus who bore the strongest grudge. Pallas, backed by Cretan gold was fired by visions of conquest. He and his many sons were intent upon the removal of Aegeus by whatever means – after which they would impose their yoke upon a defeated Athens.

***

'Who is that sitting by the fountain?' Aegeus asked the old priest of Poseidon who accompanied him through the bustle of the town square that evening. 'She looks forlorn yet she is well dressed and strikes me as a woman of high breeding.'

The two stopped. The priest ran a tongue over the few remaining teeth his puckered mouth possessed, tapped his gnarled stick on the ground then grinned up at Aegeus. 'The woman we see over there, sir, is the Lady Medea. As for high breeding, I understand she is the daughter of a king – one Aietes of Colchis.'

'Colchis?' said Aegeus. 'I know little about the city or its ruler other than the gossip traders bring.'

'I believe, sir, it is at the far end of the Euxine Sea - a very long way to the east of us so I cannot tell you much about it, either. It would surprise me, though, if you were unaware of the many rumours about that woman. I hear she is regarded by some as a witch.'

'Medea – yes, I've heard people talk about her, but there are tales and there are tales. I know only what others say yet from what I have heard I imagined her as being older by some years than the woman I see over there.'

'I cannot tell you her age,' remarked the priest, 'but I personally am of the opinion she is no older than we perceive her to be, unless her alleged powers are employed to retain a semblance of youth.'

'Hmm,' responded Aegeus, narrowing his eyes, 'I would describe her as reasonably young. And she's certainly beautiful - if a little care worn. She appears quite abandoned in this noisy square. D'you have any idea why that should be?'

'Well, sir, her presence here in Corinth has been and still is – how may I put this – controversial. She was accused of plotting with others against Creon, our own king. The whole matter was very confused so no action was taken other than to exclude her altogether from the palace and its affairs. What she will eventually do with herself only the gods can say and so far they are keeping quiet.'

A cart drawn by two oxen rumbled across the square, obscuring the fountain and the low wall upon which the woman rested. When it had passed by Aegeus asked the priest, 'Do I take it she may be in some danger?'

'Who can say, Lord Aegeus. The people do not like her. Indeed, some of them fear her very reputation. You may have heard tales of the lady's skill in the black arts, of her use of poisons and potions to gain the things she wants. These may be seen as groundless rumours in some parts but are regarded here in Corinth as established fact. That is why people avoid her. Still, she seems to lack for nothing other than company – or so the jewellery she wears would suggest. And that she may well risk losing if she remains here alone after dark.'

'Then I'll enliven her day with my company,' smiled Aegeus, adjusting his tunic, belt and scabbard. Left hand resting on his sword hilt, as was his habit, he stepped across the dusty square to approach the fountain.

Her long hair, gleaming as polished obsidian, was held back at either side by golden clasps from where it tumbled loosely about her shoulders. Precious stones glinted from the rings on her fingers. A crimson gown of finest linen adorned her slim form, heavily embroidered at bodice, sleeve and hem with entwined geometrical forms and held in place by a black sash. To Aegeus' eye it was a style as foreign in appearance as its wearer. She turned her head aside as the well-built, fair-haired figure in pale tunic drew close. Light from the setting sun fell on her prominent dark eyes and high cheek-boned face. There was no sign of apprehension as his shadow fell across her.

'Lady Medea,' he smiled, 'forgive my intrusion but I saw you sitting here alone. I am Aegeus of Athens. Are you waiting for someone?'

'Ah, *the* Aegeus,' she said, not answering his question but adding, 'You are Aegeus the king.'

'The same,' he responded. 'May I speak with you a while?'

'My pleasure,' she replied, eyeing him intently, though her manner otherwise was one of relaxed familiarity, as if she had expected him to walk over and converse with her. 'I heard you left Athens some time ago to visit Delphi.'

'Did you now,' he responded, sitting down next to her. 'And there was I thinking such information had never been put about for reasons of security – my security, that is.'

He was aware of her perfume - exotic and enticing; strong enough to hold at bay the odours of the square, of ox and ass, of cooking and other sources less pleasant.

'We all need security,' she remarked.

'That's so, but I believe mine may be less pressing than yours in the short term. In my case it is concern over the succession in Athens. It's a matter of great importance to myself and my people. It will, I hope, be resolved in time, though the priestess at Delphi was not at all clear in her message.'

'It will be resolved in time,' she assured him. 'The fates will have it so.'

'Really - I wish I had your confidence yet I wonder how it will be resolved. But I understand you yourself are in a difficult situation.' Aegeus looked about the square and its complement of

22

haggling tradesmen, hurrying slaves and yapping dogs, then added, 'Sitting here by the fountain is pleasant enough but it will soon be dark. Will you join me for a cup of wine? My men and I must leave for Troizen by first light tomorrow.'

'Wine?' she smiled, coolly. 'You'll not get wine fit for a king hereabouts except in Creon's palace and since I am forbidden to enter I regret I'm unable accept your offer.'

'Oh, so it's true what I heard - but the palace is where I shortly have to go.'

Medea leant a little closer. Aegeus gazed into her eyes. Her breath seared his cheek. Feelings arose within him; feelings unlike any he had experienced. As they sat there his passions were stirred. He wished to touch and hold her closely. 'Now, look,' he continued, 'perhaps I may be of help here. Tell me why you find yourself in this situation. Are the rumours of a conspiracy true?'

Her eyes shone, seeming to grow larger as she spoke. 'Conspiracy? I'll tell you what is true if you care to hear it.'

He reached out a hand to rest on hers, saying, 'Yes, tell me as much as you wish.'

'Then you should know,' Medea continued, 'I was married to the great Jason, the man everyone's doubtless heard about. I was little more than a child when he landed in Colchis but I was besotted from the very beginning. I travelled with him and his Argonaut friends when he set out against my father's wishes to find the Golden Fleece. I used all the secret arts of our land, all those forbidden spells handed down through our family to help him gain it. We were later chased out of Colchis and ended up travelling half the known world. Still I thought of him as the ideal husband. I used my powers to help him even when I should have known better. King Aegeus – if you care to dig for further rumours, you will doubtless hear of the so-called evil deeds ascribed to me when with Jason, but I'd rather you did not.'

'If true,' asked Aegeus, 'are they deeds you regret?

'Lies and truth entwine like serpents but whatever I did I thought necessary at the time. It is too late for regret. In due course we ended up here in Corinth where Jason met that little tart, Creusa - Creon's blue-eyed daughter. They lodge here at the palace. He dares not face my father and imagines Creon will protect him from the many enemies he's made, including me.' Her eyes blazed, her features set hard. 'He no longer cares a damn about me or our three children but I'll have my revenge when the time is right. Believe me, I will.'

'But you yourself may suffer harm,' responded Aegeus. 'Return with me to Athens. There I'll give you sanctuary. That I promise.'

'No, not yet. There's much I have to do here in Corinth.' She placed a hand on his cheek. The chatter of people, the bustle around them, seemed to recede. Her touch burned deeply as she spoke again. 'But there are two things I will say. Firstly, I will come to you in Athens when I'm done here in Corinth. Secondly, I foretell you will have the son and heir you so desire.'

'But lady,' he breathed, rising to his feet, 'How can you be certain of that?'

Medea stood to face him. Her words echoed in his mind as she spoke. 'King Aegeus, of that I am certain.' She arose, turned about and was gone, hurrying across the darkening square to vanish as a wraith in the shadows.

***

The air was cool, the sun not yet risen when Aegeus and his men rode out beneath the great lintel of the southern gate, plumed bronze helmets gleaming, swords buckled at their sides. Later that day would see them greeted by King Pittheus of Troizen. There they would discuss the dangers faced by both, the state of their respective defences and reports from the south of Attica regarding the situation with Pallas and his Cretan allies.

During his journey the encounter with Medea dominated his thoughts. More than once he felt compelled to turn aside with the oddest of impressions that she was riding close by. It was an illusion, of course. He and his men had drunk strong wine more freely than they ought that previous evening and his head still ached. That must account for it.

***

It was late afternoon when they passed through the fortified city gate to arrive before the gaunt stone palace of Troizen. There they were greeted by Pittheus himself. His drawn features, long hair embellished by a jewelled headband, the abundant grey beard and plain white long gown well matched his reputation for wisdom and sound advice. Few people would guess he was not much older than the far younger looking Aegeus.

King Pittheus stepped forward with his small entourage as Aegeus and his men dismounted. 'Greetings, my friend. Was your journey fruitful? D'you have good news from Delphi?'

'I was given a message by the priestess,' replied Aegeus, grasping the other's hand in friendship, 'but I've not the slightest idea what it meant. You may wish to hear it later but I can tell you that so far no one else has.'

Pittheus' attendants escorted Aegeus' companions to their lodgings, their horses to the palace stables. Aegeus accompanied the king into the great hall of the palace where musicians played and a central fire cracked brightly beneath rising smoke.

'I'll hear about your journey and your message over a goblet of wine,' said Pittheus as they sat together, 'but let me give you my news now since it is brief and uncomplicated. Traders of ours returning from the south report no signs of hostility toward us from your dear brother, Pallas. On the contrary, it seems he's had a minor rebellion to deal with in one of the towns subject to the rule of Thorikos and that has taken his mind off other things. Knowing there's no immediate danger to Athens or to Troizen, I invite you, friend Aegeus, and your men, to stay here in our city for longer than you may have intended. And there are our forthcoming celebrations to be considered.'

'Celebrations?' queried Aegeus as Pittheus gestured for wine.

'Perhaps you had forgotten, my friend – we make sacrifices before the temple of Poseidon in three days' time. He is so important to the people of

Troizen that even I as king refer to him as, "King." Let me be frank with you, sir – you worry more than you ought. Relax with us and let other matters lie for a time. I seldom indulge in any kind of sport myself but you must join my men in the hunt.'

'I thank you for your offer,' Aegeus responded.

'There's much sport to be had in these parts,' Pittheus smiled, raising his goblet, 'even lions - unless they get you first! And well defended as she is, Troizen does not boast walls quite so high or gates quite as massive as those of Athens but, if I may say so, my city does not present so forbidding an aspect indoors or out. There are other, more private entertainments to be had here that I believe are less readily available within the fortress your city has become.'

'Athens has become a fortress out of necessity as you well know,' said Aegeus, 'but I'll stay a while – two, maybe three more days, perhaps.'

***

Later that evening they sat upon cushions of gold-threaded maroon in the ornately draped chamber that was Pittheus' private retreat. Two bare-breasted servant girls were summoned to bring goblets and flagons of wine. Each eyed Aegeus as they filled the goblets but on this occasion they made less impression upon him than they otherwise might. The image of dark-eyed Medea was never quite obscured.

'Now, sir, tell me all about your journey and that mysterious Delphic prophesy,' said Pittheus after dismissing the girls.

Ah, yes,' sighed Aegeus, 'the prophesy. What the priestess said - and I swear I relate this word for word because it is now chiselled into my mind: "Loose not the jutting neck of the wineskin, great leader of your people, until you return to Athens." Now then, what if anything d'you make of that?'

Pittheus lowered his goblet, gazed upward then proceeded to smooth his beard before answering. 'Hmm, what do I make of it. Er, well yes – it is a mystery. Yes – at least for the time being, it's a mystery. But are not most of their pronouncements designed to confuse. My own experience has taught me that and I'm sure many others would agree.'

Aegeus related his encounter with Medea and at the end of it Pittheus mused, 'Very strange. I've heard rumours about her – who hasn't, but I had no idea the woman was in Corinth. Oh, well, if she turned down your offer of help she cannot have been in too much danger.'

'Maybe so, but the effect she had on me –! I tell you no woman ever impressed me quite that way at a first encounter. She's only a memory now – though a damned persistent one.'

Pittheus relapsed once again into deep thought then smiled, 'Well there could be other diversions, you know. I have ordered a banquet prepared in your honour. The seals will be broken on the jars of some of our oldest and best wines and afterwards, when you retire to your bed, you must enjoy the company of one of our girls. I will send one well versed in the arts of love. She will serve you for as long as you wish.

She will put a new face to those memories of yours and should you desire it one of her sisters will also be present for your entertainment.'

***

Aegeus entered the curtained chamber to discover her seated on the bed. Moonlight fell though the arched window to illuminate a soft face, full lips and innocent blue eyes framed by long golden hair. Pulled about her was a plain linen sheet, beneath which she was quite naked.

'My name is Aethra,' smiled the girl, easing aside the sheet as Aegeus stood gazing down at her. 'There is clean water and good wine,' she continued. 'If I do not please you, I will go and you must report this to the king.'

As Aegeus regarded Aethra's beauty, as her seductive voice caressed his ear, the image of Medea retreated from his thoughts. 'Please me?' he breathed. 'Why, I'm honoured by the presence of such a desirable young woman. Please, you must stay.'

Meanwhile, in the privacy of his own chamber, Pittheus considered the words delivered to Aegeus by the Delphian priestess, "Loose not the jutting neck of the wineskin, great leader of your people, until you return to Athens." He voiced those words twice over to himself then he began to laugh.

***

In the company of Pittheus, Aegeus attended the feast in honour of Poseidon then continued three more days of leisure at Troizen, his nights spent in the arms of Aethra.

When further news arrived from the south of Attica, Pittheus said, 'It seems your brother Pallas is still in some difficulty with the uprising on his doorstep. Doubtless his brutal methods will prevail in the end but at least we are spared the need for armed readiness.'

'You're right,' responded Aegeus, 'his methods will be brutal, nor will he spare woman and child. But as you say, the pressure is off ourselves and our allies for a time.'

'Then there's no reason you cannot stay yet longer with us. Yes, my friend, stay until you have exhausted the pleasures of Troizen, though I doubt any man could.'

'It's a prospect I find difficult to resist,' smiled Aegeus, 'and the days pass quickly enough. Oh, yes – and the nights. Yes, the nights. I assume the girl you sent me is a courtesan. She well knows how to satisfy a man's needs.'

At his last comment Pittheus smiled, stroked his beard and said, 'Then I take it she's ousted from your thoughts the woman you encountered in Corinth.'

'Indeed she has – or almost. I must confess there are still times when I see Medea's face and hear her voice, though they occur to me now as cold and distant.'

'Well your description of her when you arrived was vivid enough to make a lasting impression even on me. In fact only the other night I dreamt I saw her in our own market place – large as life and staring directly at me! Hm, very odd indeed. But let me ask you once again – are you content to spend further time with us?'

'I'll gladly accept your offer – but it cannot be for many days longer. One of my men will leave for Athens at sunrise tomorrow to assure our council all is well here in your kingdom and with myself.'

'Then let matters run on as long as it suits you,' said Pittheus. No one will be the worse for it.'

***

The main source of illumination in the darkened chamber was a small oil lamp situated on a wall bracket opposite the covered window. Its flame burned steadily in the warm air. In deepest shadows two incense pots revealed their presence by the faintest of glows and a sweet aroma that pervaded the room. From beyond the window drifted the buzz of night-time insects and the occasional yapping of distant dogs.

'I must leave with my men in two days,' he told her as they lay together. 'Pittheus has used all his powers of persuasion to prolong my stay beyond anything I'd planned – not the least being the pleasure of your company. I must return to prepare for our own festival and games. And the messenger who arrived from Athens this morning, well - he brought news I was not happy to hear.'

'Is there some danger?' she asked, running fingers over his shoulder with sensual delicacy.

'There may be,' sighed Aegeus. 'The Cretans have sent a group of their own men to participate in the games. I believe there's more to it than any desire to gain glory on the field of sport. The Cretans support our worst enemy – the enemy of Athens and of Troizen. They aid my brother Pallas with arms and gold. And in spite of his troubles, Pallas will doubtless have spies here as well as in Athens. I suspect they and the Cretans will get together and connive on how best to gain advantage over us.'

'I'm unhappy because you're going to leave Troizen,' she whispered, squeezing his arm. 'Our time together has for me been a delight. You are thoughtful and kind. Lord Aegeus, I – I wish only to be with you and no other man.'

Aegeus raised up on one arm to stare down at her. 'Oh, but - then ride with me to Athens. Why should Pittheus object? He handed you into my charge the day I arrived here. Even when out hunting he encouraged me to retain your company – though I tell you he had no need to do that since your company and yours alone is all I would have wanted.'

'Returning with you may not be possible,' she answered, the flame of the lamp reflecting brightly in her eyes.

'But you must,' he insisted, 'What if you were to bear my child?'

'I believe I am already with child. Your child.'

'What – but how could you possibly know after only a few -? Then – then why refuse? Athens lies within easy reach of Troizen.'

'Aegeus – I have to make a confession. You need to know the truth here and now.'

'A confession?' he asked. 'A confession about what?'

After some heartbeats of silence she replied, 'I am – I am the King of Troizen's daughter.

'You - you're what?' he exclaimed, sitting upright. 'By the gods, you – a daughter of Pittheus!'

'It's true, but he meant no ill by this arrangement, only – only -.'

'Only what? Why the deception when I would have been honoured all along to know it?'

Aethra sat up to place a hand on his. 'Like yourself, my father has no male heir. He reasoned that – that if I bore a son as our own oracles had already predicted then the boy would be of benefit to both our houses. He hoped that perhaps one day the new king would unite Athens and Troizen under a single rule.'

Sinking back against the pillow, Aegeus said, 'Well, what am I to make of this? You – the king's daughter! This means we should marry. But - but what if the oracles proved to be wrong and you instead gave me a daughter? That would place us in a difficult situation. I would still need an heir but if you as my third wife failed to produce a son, if I had to seek elsewhere, it might jeopardise my relationship with your father, my dear friend and Athens' closest ally.'

'But the oracle may be right,' she responded. 'Then what? Should he be born in Troizen and pronounced sole heir to my father he could be in grave danger from some of our own kin. My father tells me that Pallas has in the past bought off several members of our house with Cretan gold. It was and may still be his intention to damage Troizen's relations with Athens in order to gain a foothold here.'

'And the same might apply if he was to be born in Athens as sole heir to me. The danger from Pallas, as my brother, may be all the greater once the prospect of a son and future king of Athens has arisen. He would need an armed guard present throughout his entire childhood.'

'We live in such dreadful times,' she whispered, rising to press a soft cheek to his shoulder.

***

'No,' declared Pittheus as he sat with Aegeus, 'there was no oracle, at least none relevant to what has happened between you and my daughter.' Morning sunlight bathed the olive trees close to where they sat in the palace courtyard. 'It was the woman I spoke of seeing in my dreams – the image you described of the one you met in Corinth.'

'Of Medea – that's what you're saying?'

'Yes, it was her. It's as though her very image preceded you into Troizen then found me when asleep at night. The dream I first described was true but it occurred before you arrived and not after, as I first told you. She spoke to me in my sleep. The purpose of her message was to ensure the advice you were given at Delphi was *not* followed. Now I see why and so must you if you think about it. Aegeus, I hope you will forgive me; I thought what I did was for the best.'

'That strange woman has placed me in her debt – or so it would seem,' remarked Aegeus. 'I promised her sanctuary if she ever needed it though I now regret having done that.'

'It seems the rumours we hear about Lady Medea's gifts are true,' said Pittheus. 'I feel she has already cast her spell over us – at least she has over me.'

'Be that as it may,' responded Aegeus, 'but for now your daughter seems convinced she will bear my son. If that is so you and I must decide upon measures to protect him from harm until he reaches manhood. I'll speak with Aethra when you and I are done.'

***

'I thought you would have returned earlier,' she said as Aegeus entered the chamber. 'I watched you in the courtyard with my father this morning then you were gone. Now you are with me but the afternoon shadows are lengthening.'

'Aethra,' he replied, placing hands gently on her soft cheeks, 'we must go outside the city wall – beyond the orchards at the south gate.'

She gazed into his eyes then asked, 'Outside the city – now? But why?'

'I have discussed with your father measures we have to take. Measures necessary to protect both yourself and our child. It will be dark soon. I leave Troizen in the morning so we must go outside now. And we must go dressed as peasants of the fields so as not to attract attention.'

In cowled gowns of course, toil-stained linen they threaded their way through the melee of farmers and traders until clear of the gate. A warm, afternoon breeze caressed the land as they passed beyond the orchards to where the ground rose, rocky and uncultivated. By the side of the track stood a carved stone pillar, the height of a man, adorned with the symbols of a long-forgotten god. Here they hesitated. Aegeus led her a few steps away from the track to where lay a tilted slab of rock.

'Remember this place and this stone,' said Aegeus. 'The future of our child may depend upon it.'

'I don't understand,' said Aethra. She clutched her gown, staring at the rock as the breeze ruffled her golden hair.

Aegeus held and kissed her. 'If our child is a boy, and we both are certain he will be, you are to place him in care as an orphan with a trusted farming family; a family outside the city who have no surviving children of their own. Your father agrees to this and assures me he knows of such a family; their two sons died fighting for Troizen some years past. He assures me also that they have served him well since then and that they may be relied upon. Our son must know you only as a friend and protector of this family. He must not know the true identity of his parents but you must ensure the family, poor as they may be, never lack the means to offer him a healthy upbringing. He will have his farm work but as soon as the boy is old enough he will be given duties within the palace so as to avoid suspicion.'

'But why?' pleaded Aethra. 'Why must our son be forced to -?'

'No, let me finish. He will be more than a just labourer - he will be educated by your trusted courtiers and by your priests. He will be taught the habits of the court without ever expecting to be a part of it. But above all he will learn the art of war. Pittheus' captains and best fighting men will see to it that he is trained and fit to take on any man in combat. He should be noble in mind, strong of limb yet humble in his expectations. Other than that he will be prepared to serve as a leader of men in battle. This being so, he may not be regarded as a threat by anyone of evil intent within the palace and ought therefore to be free of danger.'

'And utterly confused,' she breathed. 'He will not know who he is and, possibly, neither will I.

Aegeus, I take it we are not to be married and must soon be parted.'

'I regret that must be so for the sake of the boy,' continued Aegeus. 'Yes, I deeply regret it, but it's a risk we have to take. I'm sure you and your father will manage that. Indeed you must for all our sakes. All being well, when the boy comes of age Pittheus will have you send him to Delphi. As is our custom he will offer clippings of his hair at the shrine of Apollo. When he returns you must bring him in secret to this exact spot and reveal to him the truth of who he is. Keep nothing from him but let no other be party to what you say. Once that is done, have him lift this stone. If he is able to do that, and I must tell you I myself was barely able to move the thing, then he will discover hidden what I have left for him and him alone.'

'Am I to know what is hidden there?' she asked.

'Of course - I obtained a pair of stout sandals fit for the roughest country tracks and picked out the finest sword from your father's armoury. The sword is a splendid piece of workmanship and of great value. It is suited for a hero - no a prince, to hang at his belt. That is what awaits our son. And when he possesses them, tell him he must journey by sea alone and incognito to Athens. Once there he must make his way to the palace, wait for my appearance and make himself known to me carrying the sword at his side. I will then know him also and I will receive him as my son and my true heir. Promise you will do as I ask.'

'I will follow your every wish for our sake and his. But what are we to call him?'

'I leave that to you. When he is born, you must make that decision.'

'No – I have a name. It came to me now as though another spoke it. We must call him Theseus!'

'Theseus - yes, that's a fine name – a name worthy of a hero. Let's keep it for him. But you must speak to no one of our plans. You must not send any messages to me. Nor will I ask after him in case my words, in case my very thoughts are overheard. I will carry on with life and assume nothing has come of this. Nothing at all. I have suffered disappointment for too many years.'

'And now disappointment is to be mine,' she sighed. 'We may never meet again.'

'I – I feel most sorrowful because of that,' he said, placing a hand on her arm and gazing down.

Aethra glanced back toward the city. 'Look - there are people coming this way.'

'Yes and we must return. The day will soon end and your father is preparing another feast. But tonight,' he added, slipping an arm affectionately about her waist, 'tonight I will be with you.'

***

Aethra watched from her window as Aegeus and his men rode through the north gate, passing from the city into morning sunlight and a tear welled in her eye. She placed a hand on her stomach. She thought now that Aegeus had never really loved her as she had loved him. Perhaps if there had been more time. Perhaps. Yet he had left her with a purpose in life beyond anything she could ever have envisaged.

***

Aegeus returned to an Athens for a time strong and well defended, but subsequent years brought unforeseen calamity to his city. Athens had witnessed war, famine and dishonour. And though Aegeus' throne remained for the time being secure, the consequences of misfortune had left him burdened by care.

It was a warm afternoon in the sixth year after his departure from Troizen and a brooding Aegeus sat in the great hall listening to the consoling melody of the lyre. The few male and female courtiers seated close by shared his thoughts and spoke only in low voices. A palace attendant walked in, stopping to bow a short distance from the king. 'Lord Aegeus, there is one of high status arrived who wishes to appear before you. She waits outside.'

Haemon ceased playing and set aside his lyre.

'She?' queried Aegeus. 'She? A woman from where? Has she no name? Has she not stated her business, if she has business here at all?'

'Forgive me, Sire,' the man replied uncomfortably, 'the lady insisted you would know and welcome her without question so I did not consider it my duty to turn her away. She looks to be of noble birth.'

'Does she, now – then have her enter so I can see who interrupts my day.'

The attendant retreated to the main door. There were voices. He reappeared with the newcomer following close behind. Still unable to reveal the woman's identity or the purpose of her visit, the man stood awkwardly aside as she announced, 'Lord Aegeus, I come here to claim the sanctuary you so generously offered when we met in Corinth some years ago.'

'Lady Medea,' he began, rising from the throne, 'I well recall our meeting as I do my offer but your name was not announced.'

All eyes were on her as they waited for Aegeus' next move. She was dressed in gaudy palace fashion with the close fitted bodice that left her firm breasts exposed. Below her constricted waist the tiered, flounced skirt fell to part conceal her short boots of soft leather. Her raven hair was not as he recalled but, held in place by jewelled bands, it hung crinkled at the sides of her rouged face and reddened, sensual lips. Aegeus stared hard at her as she informed him, 'I came to Athens by wagon in disguise with two other women. When I arrived, the women of Aphrodite's temple allowed me to bathe and to dress before meeting you.'

'But why travel in disguise? And why now do you ask me for sanctuary? Athens has suffered much these past years. More than I care to speak about.'

'Much of Greece has suffered,' she responded, peering about at the courtiers who had remained silent since her entering the megaron. Aegeus raised a hand and the courtiers, followed by Haemon, arose and filed quietly from the hall.

When they had gone Medea, in response to his gesture, sat close to the king, saying, 'Lord Aegeus, you will recall what I told you when we met in Corinth. You will recall how I had been abandoned by Jason for Creusa, Creon's daughter, that same Jason to whom I had been married.'

'Yes, *everything* you told me,' nodded Aegeus. 'You were treated badly.' He regarded her closely, breathing her perfume, thinking no more than days might have passed since he last set eyes upon a youthful beauty that remained unsullied by time. His fascination for her was renewed. He recalled the fire she had ignited within him at their first meeting. It burned again now as a subtle flame.

'I begged him not to marry that girl,' she went on, her dark eyes ablaze with anger. 'I demeaned myself before him but all he would offer in return was cold silver with – with no more sentiment than some farmer tendering payment for a farm beast! No one cared about that since in Corinth he was their shining hero – though no longer a hero to me.' Medea lowered her head for some moments then continued, 'In the night, in my dreaming, the spirits of my ancestors came to me. I called to them for vengeance the way my ancestors did and they told me what to do. In the light of day I had a gown made for Creusa as a wedding gift and sent anonymously. Think what you will of this but the day she wore it the gown caught fire and she was burned to death where she stood.'

'Burned to death,' breathed Aegeus, turning away from her with a frown. 'By the gods, burned to death. And you would have me believe that was your doing?'

'As I said, Lord Aegeus, think what you will. The Corinthians certainly did. Some of them set out as a drunken mob to find me and my children. I had sent the children to the temple of Hera for sanctuary but they were dragged away from the altar and stoned to death outside. When I heard what had

41

happened I took up my possessions and escaped to Thebes. I later heard the Corinthians had seen sense and expelled dear Jason from their city. All might have settled down but when troubles came to Thebes, whether plague or fire, they needed someone to blame – that someone being me. My reputation for casting spells had followed me to Thebes and though I had done nothing to offend them, nothing at all, I again had to flee. Now I am here to claim the pledge you made to me. I can offer you much, Lord Aegeus. I can offer you a son – and I know a son is what you desire above all.'

Her eyes smouldered. She reached out to touch him.

'And what might the people of Athens make of your reputation?' asked Aegeus, placing a hand on hers. 'It seems to spread with the winds.'

'Athens is over the worst of her troubles,' Medea replied, 'and none of what has happened can be ascribed to me. Whatever I do here will be for the good of yourself and the city.'

'No, Athens is far from over the worst of times but that greatest of tragedies I will not discuss though all the city and beyond knows about it, as will you if you don't already. All mention of it is forbidden in Athens but whispers are whispers and, like smoke they will seep through the strongest walls.'

'Yes, I am aware of what has happened, but they are events spread too wide afield and involve the gods themselves. There is nothing within my power to alter such affairs.'

Aegeus gazed at her and felt the cares of recent times fall from him. Medea was alluring. She was irresistible. They arose, they stood to face one another and Aegeus took her in his arms.

***

Aegeus married Medea with great ceremony. In the spring of the following year she bore a son she insisted must be named Medeus.

'At last there is an heir to the throne of Athens,' said Haemon as late one evening he and Aegeus sat alone by the circular fire in the great hall.

'Yes, an heir,' breathed the king. 'And Medea is convinced he will take the throne after me. Yet I still think of -.' Aegeus sighed and gazed into the fire. 'Often of late I think about the girl I left in Troizen. I have been there since but neither Pittheus nor I have mentioned her because we agreed we would not. Nor have I set eyes on her. Yet somehow I feel I should set greater store by a future that is unknown rather than by the one that seems so clear to Medea.'

The fire cracked. Glowing embers showered across the stone floor as Haemon spoke. 'The risks that concerned you in the event of Pittheus' daughter bearing a son – surely such risks hold true for Medeus?'

'Something tells me they do not. I feel there is more than the palace guard looking out for his safety even though the boy is not as well liked by the people as I would have hoped. And, Haemon, as always I confide in you. What I'm about to say I have hinted at to no one else. Though she serves me well in bed, I'm inclined of late to think Medea was carrying her child when she arrived in Athens. I doubt he is really my son.'

Haemon looked into the fire for a while before speaking. 'I doubt it also, Lord Aegeus. The boy is pleasing enough in appearance yet he possesses none of your own features. But – but may I speak more freely with you than my situation would otherwise permit?'

'Haemon, you will always have my ear. Speak freely.'

'Lord Aegeus, the people dislike Medeus because they do not trust Lady Medea. They say it is she who rules in Athens as well as yourself because you are enchanted by her. They talk of how she sits enthroned next to you as an equal and about how she commands her own staff. They see this as a sign of weakness within yourself even if everyone knows how, on the field of battle, you have been fired by the gods and carried all before you.'

'Hmm – it's true I allow the queen a free hand in running palace affairs but that in turn lifts the burden from me. It also keeps at bay others who may not be so dependable. And whilst you are the first to express the people's feelings to me directly, this is something I have sensed. For the time being, however, I see no alternative but to carry on as we are.'

'Shall I send for wine?' asked Haemon. 'It will help soothe those cares that seem to haunt you nowadays.'

'Yes, my friend – we shall have wine and I'll try to find more light in our present lives.'

Chapter 3
The BOY from TROIZEN

A group of farm labourers strolled by as he emerged from the humble stone and thatch dwelling into cool morning air, attired in belted tunic of plain linen and countryman's sandals.

'Off into town our lucky lad goes again,' remarked one of the men directly to him.

The young man acknowledged them with a broad smile and a circular wave of his hand.

'Aye, 'is mother reckons 'e's trainin' to serve in the palace guard,' added another as they went on their way. 'That's no bad thing for one of our lot.'

'One of our lot?' smirked the first man. 'His mother's not 'is real mother if you ask me. I say like I always said – the lad's someone's bastard – maybe someone 'igh up they want to keep quiet about.'

Shadows from a glowing horizon spilled across his path and he strode on, a small black and white, tail wagging, ear flapping mongrel yapping playfully at his heels. Vaguely aware of the men's further comments, a smile once again crossed the youth's clean-shaven face, a fresh breeze ruffled his curly, fair hair. A gleam of anticipation shone in his blue eyes as, confident in his step, slim, agile and of powerful build, he trotted over rough ground where sheep grazed, then by the olive groves on the track leading to the city gate. 'Come along, Skipper,' he called as the dog circled about. 'We're not off to the city this morning. No, we're going to meet that nice lady who calls around to see us so you've got to be on your best behaviour.'

Today would be different. There would be no training with sword and spear, no strenuous exercise, no drilling for those aggressive skills needed to cut down the enemy they expected he would one day meet, though his commitment was total. Two days earlier he had returned from Delphi. He, a country dweller of little importance in the grand affairs on humanity, had been sent to offer a lock of his hair at Apollo's shrine. It had been an adventure he always yearned for – to set out with only his dog for company, to prove himself, to demonstrate his independence to the rest of the world. And there was a world out there – a greater world he was determined he would one day see.

But it was she who had summoned him. She who came from the city now and again to visit his home. She who had arranged for his training and sometimes, though always discreetly, offered his family the modest material benefits few of their country companions knew. She had given him silver for his journey to Delphi. Silver to pay for food and a degree of comfort in lands where he was a stranger. He understood little other than that the woman was a wealthy relative of his rustic family. He recalled how her hands, pale and unblemished, bore no evidence of toil. He had never known her real name. His parents, kindly, simple people he had always taken for granted were his own, referred to her only as, 'Your aunt.'

He had long ago been advised, 'She is a lady of the city and deserves our highest respect. Speak to her only when you are spoken to.' In growing older he had come to suspect there was more to the woman than he had been told, and more than once had said as much, but his parents had always insisted there were no hidden secrets.

Before sunset the previous evening, when his parents were absent in the fields, she had visited the dwelling where the young man had grown up. He had been cleaving wood outside when she found him. She had taken him aside saying, 'Theseus, now you're returned from Delphi there are matters of great importance I must reveal to you.' He had never known her eyes so bright and intense, never heard her sound so serious. He had gazed at her puzzled as she continued, 'That old monument you walk by on the road to Troizen – I want you to meet me there shortly before sunrise tomorrow. Say nothing about this to anyone, not even to your parents, but set out as you usually do when you go into the city.'

'But why must I -.' He had started to ask.

'Tomorrow at sunrise,' was all she would say before leaving.

He was mystified over her summons yet certain this was not to be an occasion for idle chatter. His parents, readying themselves for toil about the farm that day, had assumed the city was to be his destination.

Followed by his dog, he observed her from a distance seated on a rock slab close to the roadside stone pillar. She was dressed in a plain woollen gown with her head covered as it always had been when visiting his home. As he approached she looked up, raising a hand to push away the hood that shadowed her face, letting hair, as light as his own, fall in abundance across her shoulders. He had

47

seldom seen her head uncovered. She was, though considerably older than him, a beautiful woman.

'Theseus,' she smiled, 'come and sit by me.'

Sitting awkwardly in the silence that followed he was aware of buzzing insects, bleating goats and the clatter of pottery bells from the fields. The dog circled busily, his tail a constant blur, before settling down at their feet. Theseus felt it would be inappropriate to say anything because the woman appeared deep in thought.

As the first rays of sunlight spilled across the land she turned to look him in the eye. Placing a hand on his she said, 'Theseus, I have something to reveal to you, something that is going to change your life. I had originally thought to speak with you after sunset so we could sit here under the stars with less risk of others passing by. I changed my mind because you would, I'm quite sure, have been unable to sleep afterwards. If I say what I have to say now you will at least have the day ahead to consider my words.'

'Well I'm intrigued,' he smiled. 'I'm even now trying to decide what in this world might hold so much importance for me. You are a person of wealth. My small household has enjoyed your benevolence – myself in particular, but my future is set out as is theirs.'

'Yes, Theseus, you have led a simple life without the luxuries of the city yet you have trained as a warrior and leader in battle with the best of men. And though you have never attended the royal court of Troizen, you have been taught to appreciate its ways and manners.'

'Yes, I've often wondered what use any of it might be.'

'And just as importantly,' she continued, 'you have learned discretion. Unlike the others of your village you have also learned to read and write. I'm told you have now and again asked your - your parents why this was so and I fully understand why.'

'That's true, but I was brought up to believe it was wrong to ask about or even discuss such things. As a child I was questioned – often chided, often picked upon by those who considered me privileged, though I took on any who thought himself better than me.'

'And you usually came out on top as I well remember. But now you are in the early years of manhood you must have considered what your future might bring.'

'I – I believe I'm expected to maintain our livelihood on the farm, though it's not a future I ever felt ought to be mine. I'd sooner believe I will serve if not lead in the defence of Troizen on the field of battle. I believe I will one day bring up my own sons to do the same. I believe this in part because when that greatest of all heroes, Heracles, came to Troizen he approached me in the marketplace. He singled me out from others and placed a hand on my shoulder. He told me I should be true to myself.'

'Yes, I know of that. I watched him in conversation with you there. When you fought with sword and spear in mock battle, I watched your skills improve until you equalled the very best. Always I have followed your progress.'

49

He opened his mouth to ask her what was the reason for her confessed and long-standing interest in his life then decided it would be better to have her go on.

'What you are now to learn has been kept a secret from all but three mortals, most of it even from those you consider to be your parents.'

Her last remark startled him but he said nothing.

The woman closed her eyes, breathed deeply then said, 'I am not your aunt. My name is Aethra. I am the daughter of Pittheus, our king and - and Theseus, you are my son. Your true father is King Aegeus of Athens.'

The dog watched intently, his gaze shifting in anticipation from one to the other as Theseus stared at her, shook his head then began to laugh. 'Me, son of a –!' What's all this about? Why are you -?'

'Listen to me!' she snapped. 'I did *not* invite you here on a fool's errand. Once you begin to understand what I'm saying I will show you the proof you need.'

'But – but me? I'm sorry but I don't understand any of this.'

'Then sit quietly, listen and you will. No, you must!'

Aethra began the account of her meeting with Aegeus but held back for a time mention of what had been decided before his departure from Troizen. She explained slowly and clearly to Theseus the reasons for his exclusion from the court after his birth, his false identity and his relegation to the simple life with a rural couple. He listened intently, though quite perplexed, as she reiterated the dangers

50

faced by Troizen and Athens by forces to their south and beyond the mainland shores. She avoided altogether mention of another matter about which she had considerable knowledge; namely the onerous burden imposed upon Aegeus and Athens by others. She expected, however, this would come to light for Theseus sooner or later.

The shadow cast by the pillar had shortened and had moved around a little when Aethra finished what she had set out to tell him. With tail wagging furiously, the dog jumped up then began to chase back and forth, stopping now and again to rummage in the ground. Theseus gazed into the distance, hands clasped to his cheeks, then turned to Aethra. 'So - so this is why I have had the privilege of learning what I imagined could be of little use - and my training in the skills of combat whilst others toiled in the fields. It's because you claim that I - yes I, am son of a king. How can I believe it? No, I cannot! The proof you claim you have – where is it? Show me before I wake up to find this has been no more than a dream.'

'We are sitting on the proof,' she replied, rising to her feet.

Theseus stood and looked down. 'It's just a slab of stone. What else is there to see?'

'Lift it,' Aethra replied, stepping back from the rock. 'It took all your father's strength - now you have to try. It won't have become any lighter.'

Theseus glanced at her, bent, gripped the edge of the slab and heaved. Nothing happened so again he heaved. The slab scraped, it moved, soil fell away from the sides, it tilted up as he grunted aloud, 'There!' Then it fell aside with a thump. With bright-eyed enthusiasm the dog was about to jump into the newly exposed hollow when Theseus brushed him aside with a cry of, 'Out you go!'

The dog circled then crouched close, tail quivering, eager as his master to see what lay there. Theseus and Aethra stared into the space. Tiny creatures of darkness scampered glistening from the light of day. Discoloured and part soil covered, the object newly exposed might have been mistaken in its appearance for the recently interred carcass of a pig. Aethra held her breath as Theseus reached down to grasp what proved to be a plain terracotta vessel little longer than a man's arm, which, shedding dirt, he dragged clear.

'It is the vase your father left for you all those years ago,' said Aethra, stooping closer.

'And there's something in it!' declared Theseus, pulling the vessel upright. 'The top is sealed with clay. I'll break it open shall I – yes, I will.' The seal crumbled as he wrenched away the pottery lid. Then resting the vase at an angle close to where it had lain he thrust a hand inside. 'It's full of straw and – ah, here's -,' he withdrew his hand, 'just a pair of sandals joined by a leather thong! Is this what I -?'

'There has to be more!' she interrupted, gesturing for him to continue.

Again he reached into the vessel, this time extracting a leather scabbard and finely tooled belt, the former embellished with ornate metal bands. 'Now then,' he breathed. 'What have we here?'

From the scabbard protruded a sword hilt. Theseus withdrew the sword, holding it up between himself and wide-eyed Aethra. Gleaming in the sun, its blade was of keenest bronze gripped by gilded serpents springing from a gilded hilt inlaid with ivory and small coloured gems that sparkled sunlight. He studied it closely before addressing Aethra.

'And this is really mine?' he asked, turning the blade about in admiration then testing its balance with a repeated flexing of his wrist.

'Yes, it is yours. It has lain there all these years waiting for you and you alone. Your father, Aegeus, will know you by that sword as soon as he sees it.'

'It's a fine weapon. One intended for a man far greater than I.'

'It is a sword fit for a prince,' Aethra declared. 'I am as proud of you as will be your father. Then you'll have no need of modesty.'

'But the sandals,' asked Theseus, easing the blade back into its scabbard. 'Why did he leave something so humble with so valuable a gift, though they appear stout and strong?'

'It was a gesture of encouragement – a sign that you must travel to Athens. He intended them to serve you in their own way as will that sword.'

Theseus stared in bemused silence for a time at Aethra, at the sword then at the sandals. 'It's as well you did reveal this at the start of the day,' he said at last. 'It will give me time to consider everything you've told me. I need to go where I can be alone to think about all of this – about everything. There are so many questions but – but if I'm convinced it was no dream when I wake up tomorrow, I will thank my parents – no, my guardians for all they've done for me. Do they know anything of what you've told me?'

'They know nothing of what Aegeus left for you,' replied Aethra. 'What they do know – what they have always known – is that you were to leave them soon after your return from Delphi.'

'Then if I still believe it all by the end of today I will ready myself and leave for Athens at sunrise tomorrow. And you, if you are my true mother, I will surely see you again.' He laid aside the sword, kissed and held Aethra tightly, saying, 'Yes, your eyes – they are the eyes I see when I look into a bronze mirror.'

'Perhaps,' she whispered, 'and when you're gone I will explain to those who have cared for you over the years what happened here. But think of them still as your parents for they will always regard you as their son. My father and I will ensure they never fall into hardship. As for you - you will find it not so difficult a journey to Athens if you go by sea,'

'By sea!' exclaimed Theseus, stepping back to buckle the sword at his waist. 'If I go it will not be by sea. I walked with little company other than my dog from here to Delphi and back so I'll walk to Athens. That way I'll see for myself the land and the people. But Skipper I must leave behind.' The dog tilted his head aside, yapped, then began to scamper about.

'Theseus, if you go by land you must not travel alone. My father would be adamant about that. Delphi is a well-trodden route but even close to Corinth and other towns the deserted tracks between here and Athens are unsafe for a lone traveller. Pirates may come ashore. There are bandits, brigands and worse. Sometimes lions prowl the land. My father will provide an escort for you. You must speak with him today. He will arrange it.'

'No - Heracles faced greater dangers by far and I hear he still goes about his business. Any man barring my way with ill intent will eat cold metal. If my sword is to be sullied by the blood of others then so be it. Yes, if this is as you say then I have to prove myself worthy of you, of the father I have yet to meet and of the people he rules over!'

'I feel I should cry though I do not wish it,' she responded, squeezing his arm. 'I cannot say if I'm happy or sad at the prospect of what may lie ahead for you – for any of us. I will leave you now. I will pray to the gods in the hope of your reaching Athens safely and of seeing you again here in Troizen.'

Aethra turned and left him, her eyes welling tears. She did not look back.

When she had disappeared from view, Theseus returned the now empty jar to the pit and hauled the stone slab back into its former position. Then he walked away from the track, sandals swinging at his side, the dog scampering at his heels, until reaching a boulder-strewn rise where only goats ventured. With the dog sitting close by, he rested on a grassy slope to ponder over what had happened.

'Well, boy,' he breathed, gazing at the dog who stared back in tail wagging anticipation, 'it's not every day you discover you're the son of a king. Whatever next? If it wasn't for this fine sword of mine I'd think some kind of madness had taken me over – really I would.'

The place where he sat offered a fine view of Troizen, its gaunt wall and towers catching the morning sun. He withdrew the precious sword and studied it in silence as Aethra's words flooded through his mind – washing back and forth as a tide to reveal with greater import at each passage the enormity of her message.

'Did you understand what she said, Skipper?' he sighed tickling the dog's ear affectionately. 'No, I don't suppose you did. Me, son of a king. Me! But it isn't a dream is it? No it isn't – no more than this sword is a dream. And after today you'll no longer be running at my side to keep me company. No, you must stay and help guard the house where I lived.'

His thoughts were dispelled when the dog began to bark. There were distant voices. In the valley below trudged two farmers – a gnarled old man with twisted stick and a youth hardly older than Theseus himself - a youth whose future he might have shared. His own humble sandals he shook from his feet. There were better, sturdier ones to be worn for the long journey ahead.

Chapter 4
The NEW PRINCE

It was late afternoon on the twelfth day of his journey when Theseus, leather bag slung over his shoulder, sword concealed beneath his tunic, approached Athens from the north. During his journey he had inquired and learned more about the world. He had rested a short time at Epidaurus and there had been told much about Asclepius the renowned healer. He had remained longer at Corinth where he was well received and there found time to admire its many fountains and speak to its people. Lastly he was to take in the sights of Athens' close ally, Megara, a town noted for its great halls. There he learned of Aegeus' brother, Nisos, and of how, during his reign, the town had been sacked by Minos, king of distant Crete. Minos – a name that until then had meant little but in time would mean more than he ever could have believed.

In between, in the wild country where others travelled in armed groups for safety, he had encountered the dangers predicted by Aethra – and more. But these are diversions to be recounted elsewhere, deeds that were destined to become the stuff of legend in their own right when magnified and retold by others.

For now he was tired, dishevelled and hungry. He intended to find a tavern in the city offering food and rest, an opportunity to wash away the dust of travel and replace his begrimed tunic before presenting himself next day at the palace of Aegeus. Pausing to appraise the great walls then passing through the bustle of the city gate, past oxen and carts, past traders and citizens about their business, he peered along a narrow, darkening street. He saw it led to the marketplace with the acropolis rising high above the far side, topped by the palace where he would find Aegeus.

Some way along to his right there was an alleyway down which he spotted a tavern whose entrance lay beneath a painted sign bearing Poseidon's trident. A dim light shone from within. The fitfully rendered notes of a flute emerged from the entrance, overwhelmed now and again by the clash of a cymbal. Raucous chatter accompanied the voice of a woman singing in shrilly discordant voice. Dipping his head to avoid the stone lintel, Theseus stepped inside. Acrid smoke, the tang of cooking fish and another odour akin to that of the cattle pen assailed him as he paused to survey the small, dim area. This was occupied by eight people sprawled about wooden benches, five men and three women. A hunched, bearded man, evidently the tavern keeper, discharged rough wine from a slender vessel into the upraised earthenware cups of his uncouth guests. At the far end of the beamed room a cooking vessel hung above an open fire, the main source of illumination apart from a small window high up in the wall that admitted pale light from the alleyway. Against the wall, to one side of the fire, lay a low stone bench bearing dishes that included mutton, fish, figs and almonds.

The flute died. The one who had been singing, a stout, straggle-haired, hook-nosed woman swathed in layers of course linen, also stopped to peer up at the newcomer. Elbows prodded. The chatter ceased.

Heads turned. The heavily bearded, gap-toothed mouths of the men grinned from beneath matted hair and drink-glazed eyes. The women grinned at one another then turned to ogle Theseus.

Acknowledging them with a nod and a smile, Theseus pushed by the benches until reaching the hunched man. 'I seek a clean lodging for the night, a flask of oil and a pitcher of good water. Will I find them here?'

The figure peered hard from under bushy eyebrows, then glancing uneasily at his ominously silent customers, grunted, 'Yeah, there's a room above this'un. Got yer silver?'

Before Theseus was able to reply, a woman amidst the odious gathering shrieked, 'Fetch the pretty boy a mirror to tart up 'is face.'

Her remark prompted a spate of raucous laughter and further animated elbow digging. Theseus turned to look at them. Shadows swayed across rough stone walls. Their eyes, reflecting the fire, gleamed addled amusement. Mouths twisted into grins as one of the men smirked, 'And some dainty ribbons for 'is curly 'air.' More laughter. Some coughing. More prodding.

Theseus slipped the leather bag from his shoulder and smiled broadly at the man who had just spoken. 'It seems I amuse you, my friend. Perhaps you'd care to step over and see how entertaining I can be at close hand.'

For several heartbeats they continued to stare, then, 'He's callin' you out, Dolon,' sniggered one of the women. 'Give the snooty bugger what for!'

'We'll 'ave no trouble!' called the hunched man with hands raised but the leering Dolon was not to be deterred. He rose up to push by the benches, brushing aside a cup of wine that toppled to splash its contents across the bench before rolling off to shatter on the floor. He was a balding, broad bear of a man with shaggy beard and small, pale eyes that fixed intently upon Theseus as he lumbered closer, punching a fist of one hand repeatedly into the palm of the other. 'Well now, pretty boy,' he growled, 'what 'ave we to say for ourselves before we fly like a dainty little bird out through the -.'

Dolon never finished his sentence. Theseus delivered a hard, left-hand blow to the man's ribs followed by an equally powerful strike with his right to the side of his jaw. Gasping aloud, eyes starting wildly about, Dolon reeled back to collapse with a clatter of goblets amidst his unsavoury company, all of whom struggled up with two drawing knives from their belts. 'Let's 'ave the bastard!' cried one of them. 'I'll slit 'is fuckin' throat!' exclaimed another.

Theseus leapt onto a low bench, reached beneath his tunic, drew his sword and declared, 'This blade has cut down far better men than any of you but meat is meat and it hardly cares who it cleaves!' He leaned forward as they fell silent, gesturing with a hand for any to approach, his shadow looming large across wall and ceiling. 'Tell me now, who'll be first to choke on his own blood?'

There was a charged silence, then they began to shuffle uneasily, glancing from one to the other, the women murmuring words of caution.

'Very well,' continued Theseus, levelling the sword 'then get yourselves out of here now or I'll cut you men down where you stand then feed you to the street dogs!'

Muttering amongst themselves they dragged the semi-conscious Dolon to his feet then began to push awkwardly through the door and into the darkening alleyway. As the last of them disappeared, the hunched man scuttled across the room, slammed the door shut then thrust a heavy wooden bar across to secure it from the outside world. Turning to Theseus he said, 'Don't know who you are, sir, but the likes of them don't belong in 'ere. They're ruffians, maybe traders or sailors from some other town – not men of Athens.'

'And the air is a great deal sweeter without them,' responded Theseus, returning the sword to its scabbard. 'Now, my friend, do I still have my lodging?'

'Aye sir, that you do. You shall 'ave the very best and whatever else I'm able to offer.'

'Then,' responded Theseus with a reassuring smile, 'I'll pay you extra silver to make up for the custom you may have lost, though I doubt it was worth much. Then at first light tomorrow I'll have you go out and fetch for me a clean tunic – one that befits a townsman of Athens. As for now, if you'd care to show me the way and provide what I ask, I'd prefer to be left with my thoughts.'

***

She sat poised alone in the silence of a sparsely furnished chamber, raven hair cast loosely about her shoulders, her expression intense, her hands clasped together on her lap, her back to the window that framed a crescent moon pale as a newly a stripped rib-bone against the night sky. Before her on a stand of twisted copper rested a cup of smouldering incense from which wraiths of spectral smoke unfurled before coiling upward into obscurity. Medea gazed into the smoke. Her eyes widened. 'Ah, I see you' she hissed. 'You have travelled far on your journey. I know you. Oh, yes, yes, yes, I know who you are and why you have come to Athens and I must be prepared.'

**

Theseus stepped fresh-faced into morning light, skin oiled and cleansed, a band of blue linen about his head, bag over his shoulder, sword buckled clearly on view about a plain new tunic of scallop-edged linen. The alleyway thronged with people, dogs careered yapping here and there, but of the merry crew he had encountered that previous evening there was no sign. He walked to the wider street where ahead lay the busy marketplace and the acropolis with steps leading up to the king's palace. Theseus suppressed an urge to hurry, instead strolling casually as though he knew the town and was confident of his business there.

He was familiar enough with the markets of Troizen but in Athens there seemed to be more of everything, more traders and more produce of field and town. Apart from the usual vendors of fruit, vegetables, fish and other seafoods there were men selling exotic goods and just as intriguing, animals he had never before set eyes upon. On reaching the steps he looked about the lively scene and listened to the calling of farmers, fishermen and artisans. Then he began the long ascent.

The paved area before the palace was almost deserted. Those few people in evidence appeared by their dress to be officials of the palace or priests going about their duties. At the top of the steps, guarding the palace entrance, stood two short-bearded, armed and armoured men wearing red-plumed bronze helmets. These Theseus approached only to have them cross their spears to block the threshold.

What's your business?' demanded one.

'I wish an audience with King Aegeus,' replied Theseus.

'The king has guests and will see no one except by arrangement,' replied the guard.

Both gripped their spears. Their expressions hardened.

Theseus stepped to one side, continued up until level with the two men then said, 'I think Lord Aegeus will wish to see me. I ask you to allow me through.'

The guards turned, lowered their spears threateningly and advanced a step forward, one of them saying, 'Think what you like. We've orders to admit no one! Now go!'

Theseus' hand flew to his sword as the guards closed on him. The blade swished clear of its scabbard, flashed upward then fell with a crack, severing the head from the spear of the closer man who staggered back against his companion, throwing him off balance. The blade flashed again to likewise disarm the second guard as his spearhead clattered down the steps.

The pair reached for their own swords but Theseus sprang forward, knocked the first man to the ground with the sword hilt against his jaw then placed the point of his blade to the throat of the second. 'Now, my friends, you are doing your duty well enough so I wish you no harm – but I *will* see Aegeus! He has waited long for this day!'

Backing off, the two men glanced at one another, uncertain over what to do next.

'I swear to you,' Theseus assured them, 'I'll not approach the king closely until he summons me. Follow me if you will and if I'm dismissed then I'll leave the way I came.'

The pair remained silent as Theseus continued by then, hands firm upon his sword hilt, they followed him cautiously across the anteroom and into the megaron, the great hall. Several of the courtiers standing close by the entrance noted Theseus' and the guards' arrival and drew back to stare at them.

Theseus gazed about the hall, a larger more opulent hall than that of Troizen. He was impressed by the weapons and shields suspended on the walls above milling courtiers and others of lesser rank who pressed about their business. He found most pleasant the sound of a strummed lyre that sweetened the general chatter.

To his left, to one side of the circular hearth where a small fire danced sparks amid a rising veil of smoke, stood a pair of thrones. In the larger, a high-backed seat of scalloped alabaster, sat the blue-gowned figure of the man who ruled Athens. He was deep in conversation with someone of apparent nobility and remained quite unaware of the youth who approached resolutely with two guards a few paces behind.

To the right of the king's throne stood a gaudily draped and cushioned high wooden chair. Upon it was seated a bejewelled, dark-eyed, raven-haired woman attired in a richly coloured gown of fine wool that left her firm, rouged breasts exposed in the manner of courtly custom. Theseus' attention was fixed upon the king but he was well aware of how the woman watched him intently as he suspected she had been from the moment he entered. When he looked directly at her a smile played upon her full, crimson lips. She acknowledged his presence with a discreetly raised hand then turned briefly aside, gesturing to her rear. A slave boy appeared carrying an ornate gold goblet upon a bronze tray. This she indicated should be offered to Theseus who stood now only four paces from the two thrones.

Theseus had listened to others whilst on his journey and had heard much about Medea. He assumed she must know of his father's arrangement with Aethra and so concluded she now recognised him as Aegeus' anticipated son. He lifted the goblet from the tray expecting she would at last alert the distracted king to his presence. She made no attempt to do so but at that point Aegeus turned and seeing Theseus, asked, 'Who stands there looking at us? How did this man gain entry, unannounced?' All eyes were upon Theseus. Voices were lowered. Haemon put aside his lyre whilst the two guards, part drawing their swords, readied themselves to act.

Medea leant close to the king, the smile departing her lips as she hissed, 'He is an intruder sent by your brother Pallas to harm us both. In the night I foresaw his coming. He managed to slip past the guards but they're waiting to cut him down. We want no blood on the floor but once he drinks from the cup he will no longer be a danger to us. Let him drink.'

Aegeus began, 'Then why did you not warn -?' then his gaze fell to the sword at the intruder's side. 'Wait!' he called aloud. 'What are you offering him?' He looked hard at the young man then rose promptly from his throne to demand, 'Name yourself!'

With goblet raised the newcomer declared boldly, 'Lord Aegeus, I am Theseus. I have journeyed from Troizen to find you as my mother Aethra said I must. I drink the wine the Lady Medea has offered me in greeting!'

'Don't drink that!' cried Aegeus, striding forward, arm outstretched to dash the goblet spinning from Theseus' hand. The goblet rang on the flagstones to roll aside in a pool of spreading liquid while Theseus stood in mute confusion. Aegeus stared down at the sword hilt, reached to run fingers over it, glanced at the countryman's sandals then, very slowly, he placed his hands on the young man's shoulders. In the charged moments that followed, few noticed the expression of deep anger that briefly darkened Medea's face.

'At last it is you,' breathed Aegeus, gazing hard at him. 'At last, my son. You have Aethra's eyes and her hair. There is no mistaking it, no, not even after all these years.' He turned to the bewildered courtiers and cried aloud, 'My son is arrived! Theseus – the son I have waited for is with us! I thank almighty Zeus; I thank all the gods!'

The courtiers glanced at one another then at Theseus. They began to chatter, all the time pressing closer to see for themselves the handsome, youthful figure who stared about bemused.

Aegeus glanced aside at Medea who, her face a mask of stone, hands clutched about her lifted skirts, was in the act of departing. 'Stay where you are!' he ordered, then with a gesture to the guards who had followed Theseus he called, 'Seize her! Get that damned woman out of my sight! Lock her away - and her son with her!' He returned his attention to Theseus. Tears welled in his eyes as he spoke. 'Long ago I dismissed all hope of seeing you because I so feared disappointment. Yet deep down a flame of hope still burned. Now you are here, that flame is arisen to fill my house, my world, with light!'

Cries of protest from Medea echoed about the megaron as the enraged woman was hauled away into the shadows. Aegeus drew Theseus across to stand by his side before the two thrones then declared to all present, 'This day we are blessed especially by Athena, defender of heroes and protectress of our city. See now - I have a true heir! Athens has a prince of my own blood!' He raised a hand then continued, 'All Athens will celebrate - this I promise! But for now I must take my son aside and speak with him in private.'

***

They sat alone by a window high in the palace with a late morning view of clear skies and the sea beyond the woodlands. Each held a golden cup of Aegeus' best wine.

Aegeus held up his goblet, smiling broadly, an expression to which his face had for some years been unaccustomed, 'Theseus, my son, your arrival

67

here today has for me made this contentious world of ours a better place by far. Athens will bask in your presence and I consider myself the most fortunate of men now you have made the journey.'

'Whereas I am still at a loss to know quite what the future may reveal,' said Theseus, 'though my feet reminded me of how far I walked until I found overnight rest at the tavern.'

'Tell me now,' said Aegeus, 'is Aethra, is your mother well? I forbade all communication between us because it seemed the best way of ensuring your safety. Her well-being weighed much on my mind in spite of the perils our city has suffered and the fact that I felt it wise to later remarry.'

'Well, Troizen escaped much of the perils it seems Athens has faced but I had too little time to learn much before leaving. I know she's well but has remained alone and unmarried. It seems she spends much of her time within the palace sitting at the loom but also helping those who were my guardians and others who suffer misfortune. Surely now you can send word to her. Surely you will speak with her again.'

'Perhaps, but I'll make sure she learns you have arrived here safely. But there are other matters I have to consider and – and, yes, Medea is not the least of them though she will soon be gone from here.' Aegeus went on to explain much about the affairs of Athens after his final meeting with Aethra, though he did not touch upon the matter that ever filled him with remorse; the matter he hoped beyond all likelihood would remain concealed from his son until enough time had passed. The matter from which even his delinquent queen had all the time distanced herself.

At one point Theseus said, 'I grew up feeling somewhere beyond Pittheus' kingdom another world waited but I never could have explained why unless it was some rare insight. I wonder if it might have been an unguarded remark by my mother.'

'Maybe you somehow read Aethra's thoughts,' offered Aegeus. 'Or perhaps when you were a child she spoke of me in the night while she slept. But at the Delphic oracle – did the priestess of Apollo give no clue as to your origin or destiny when you made your offering? You did go to Delphi did you not?'

'Yes, I made my way to the oracle at Delphi and I listened to the priestess' pronouncement, but I fear in the end her message was lost on me. There were words about my fate and that of Athens being decided within halls of stone but this is a city with halls of stone as are Troizen, Megara and others. The rest was rather confusing so I have all but forgotten most of it. Anyhow, never could I have believed I would become heir to a kingdom or that my father could be so great a man.' Theseus grinned widely then added, 'or that his queen might try to poison me as soon as I walked through the door. She must have known I was coming - but how?'

'Yes, how did she,' breathed Aegeus, though his own smile was somewhat reserved as he continued, 'But seeing you at last here in Athens and speaking with you now, I feel I could not have asked the gods for a better son or a more worthy successor. Our priesthood and our people were much concerned that I had no heir although Medea, the woman I took as my wife, had a son already.

69

And yes, she had a reputation for soothsaying, for concocting potions and poisons – and well-founded it turned out to be. I didn't realise until you appeared before me how she had clouded my mind with her spells. Even so, these last few years I sensed no one close to me felt entirely at ease when Medea was present, though they dared not express their fears. As for her son, Medeus - well, no one seemed to know who his father was, including her. She told everyone when it suited her that I was, which I very much doubted since he was born weeks too soon after her arrival in our city. I dare say he'd have made a good enough son but neither he nor his mother, especially his mother, were popular with the people – no, that was clear from the beginning.'

'You were very lenient with her, father I doubt Pittheus would have been so. He'd have ordered her flogged and beheaded. I'm sure of that from what I know of him.'

'Quite so, after that foolish attempt on your life I should have her put to death at once. But that would leave behind a vengeful son who at present is young and innocent of any crime. He, too, would have to die. No, I will instead banish them both from Greece. There's a trading vessel from Italy berthed close to Phaleron. It leaves at dawn and returns to its homeport. Directly before it sails I'll have her and the boy escorted out of Athens by armed men and placed on board with all of their possessions the vessel's captain will allow. That should be the last of her as far as we're concerned. But there is still Pallas and others of my own kin who consider themselves as having greater claim to the throne than I. Others who expect to seize it on my death – a death they'll gladly hasten if they're able. I dare say they'll pursue such matters with greater zeal now they know Athens has a true successor to her king.'

'And they'll feel this successor's cold blade as a reward for that zeal.'

'Theseus, don't think yet of bloodshed. We have ahead of us the celebrations I promised. I will offer a special sacrifice at the temple of Athena then our city will enjoy feasting and wine in your name. The gods above will know our pleasure.'

'Nevertheless,' breathed Theseus, 'One day I'll meet this man, Pallas, and when I do only one of us will leave the field of battle alive. From what I have learned of him, it must be so.'

Chapter 5
The ASSASSINS

It was a clear morning when, later that summer, Theseus and Aegeus stood by the parapet surrounding the upper section of the acropolis' south-eastern guard house. From there they observed bright Helios already ascended above the rugged hills to the east.

'The people of Athens have accepted you with great enthusiasm,' said Aegeus. 'Certainly with more confidence than they've had in me of late.'

The cloud of anxiety that seemed to hover about Aegeus, even at times of relaxation and entertainment, lifted for a while as he continued. 'Today our people are gathering for the greatest of the season's markets. The city will be host to traders from many lands. They will bring copper ingots from Cyprus, much valued tin from lands to the far west, amber from cold lands far to our north, ivory and precious stones from the east, fine cotton, grain, gold and alabaster from Egypt. Yes, all will come here to trade with each other and for our manufactured goods, our olive oil, our wines, our own textiles, our fine quality arms.'

'Well,' reflected Theseus, 'the markets of Troizen were always busy but never quite so cosmopolitan. It will be interesting.'

'But we must be on our guard,' warned Aegeus. 'Now more than ever when there are so many strangers in the city. I say it with a heavy heart because so few months have passed since the day you crossed my threshold.'

***

Mid-morning heat was infused with an odour of cooking vegetables and fish. The air hung oppressive over a crowded Athens whilst a tide of people ebbed and flowed about the vendors' and merchants' stalls that had sprouted throughout the town as well as over rocky ground outside the city wall. To the cries of tradesmen, to the constant hammering of craftsmen in their oven-like workshops, the claustrophobic streets within the city witnessed a glut of people striving to go about their business or proclaim their goods. Vendors of olive oil and fruit struggled through the crush, pushing crude wooden carts loaded with heavy clay vessels to whichever corner of the noisy town they considered to offer the best opportunity for sales. They rattled past cramped, dim little taverns that dispensed an assortment of pastries and rough wine. Shrieking children and yapping dogs scampered, careered here and there with playful agendas of their own.

Aegeus and his son had descended the stairs from the acropolis, passing by the small company of armed men placed on duty there to deter intruders. And though both carried swords they were dressed in the plainer manner of free citizens. Despite earlier misgivings, the king had no wish to disrupt the affairs of his people on this day by the presence of an armed escort. Yet while it was his wish to avoid attention, a number of people not unduly preoccupied did notice. Here and there tradesman hesitated in their haggling as the two approached. Some stepped aside out of respect, others from beyond the city were so presumptuous as to brandish their wares in front of the King and the Prince of Athens before backing away to let them pass.

Aegeus had stopped to examine bales of cotton laid out on the bench of two dark-skinned Egyptian traders when, from a narrow street some way over to their right, five men emerged dressed in the long, loose-fitting gowns of Libyan desert dwellers. The men's heads were swathed in white cloth, held in place by patterned headbands, from beneath which their narrow eyes peered. Theseus had fallen back several paces behind his father to peruse the wares of a fur trader but glanced up to observe the five elbow their way through the crowd. He wondered about their business since they appeared to carry no goods. And why did they approach so purposefully, pushing others roughly aside with not a hint of common courtesy?

Aegeus, too, became aware of their approach so turned to face them, hand dropping instinctively to the hilt of his sword. He observed the eyes of each were not the dark colour he would have expected with desert people but were paler, much as those of his own kind.

The five stopped a few paces from the king. Each pulled away his robe to reveal a bareheaded, stubble-faced, rough-set youth not of African but of Greek aspect. Each wore a short tunic of heavy linen with, sewn about the upper body, small bronze plates that glinted harsh sunlight. They closed upon Aegeus, eyes fixed hard upon him, jaws set firm with deadly intent. Their hands had fallen to their short swords, causing those close by to cry out for the guards whilst themselves scrambling to a safe distance. Aegeus, his back to a sturdy bench loaded with an array of small oil jars, drew his own sword and glared at the five in grim defiance, calling out, 'So, the farmer sends his goats to do his work does he!'

'Yer time's up, bastard so-called king!' yelled one as they pressed in, swords levelled, gleaming bright and ready for the kill.

'There's a better man ready to take the throne of Athens,' growled another, 'and it isn't that damned outcast you call yer son!'

Some in the ogling crowd spotted another glint of metal just steps away. Too late one of the attackers also saw it as Theseus bounded forward to swoop like a hawk, sword held high. Too late the man raised his own weapon but it was his last vision of this world. Theseus' blade flashed down, cleaving his opponent's head through from scalp to eyebrow so he fell quivering to the ground, his sword ringing on hard stone. Stunned momentarily, the attackers gaped at the exposed brains of their fallen companion. To a cry of astonishment from the crowd, Aegeus himself lunged at the second man as, distracted, the would-be assassin let slip his guard for a fatal moment. Aegeus' blade thrust with metallic screech between the plates, passing deep into the man's innards. As the blade withdrew, the would be assassin swung about as if to rush from the scene, collided with one of his gang then with a howling cry fell sprawling to the dirt.

People were shouting, dogs barking. In the ensuing commotion the other three assassins, seeing the peril of their situation, pressed their attack with yells of fierce defiance. Two of them forced Aegeus hard against the bench so that it part collapsed, causing its burden of jars to slide off and shatter across the cobbles. Deftly avoiding a swing from the third man, then grasping his sword arm, Theseus struck his adversary such a blow that his blade drove hard between metal plates through the other's middle to end his life with a shriek that soared above their heads. Another blade cleaved the air but missed its target as one of the assailants, turning upon Theseus, skidded in spilled oil, collided with Aegeus who was about to strike him then crashed down to stun himself against the wrecked bench. The remaining assailant, blinded by rage, confounded by fear, also spun about to face Theseus, his sword flailing the air as he leapt forward with a savage shout. Theseus avoided the blow then, to a whooping gasp from the crowd, administered his own, all but severing the man's head by a single thrust through the neck where the blade gleamed in bloody triumph at his rear before being wrenched out. The man reeled back, choking gore then fell sprawling with death-startled eyes lifted to the sky.

Silence fell as Theseus and his father surveyed their bloody work, a silence broken by the cries of excited children, by whimpering dogs, by the groans of the remaining man who lay oil-soaked and spattered by the blood of his companions amidst a shambles of broken jars. 'This man will tell us who they were,' said Theseus, stepping aside to wipe clean his blade on one of the robes thrown down by the assassins.

'It will come as no surprise,' replied the ashen-faced Aegeus, hand trembling as he likewise

76

cleaned his own blade. 'They are the sons of Pallas. If you were not convinced of his intentions before, then I wager you'll harbour no doubts after this. There will be others not far away of that I'm certain.'

Metion, captain of the palace guard and six armed men emerged from the crowd, helmet plumes swaying, swords drawn and eager for combat. Seeing the results of the encounter they sheathed their blades and, Metion exclaimed, 'My lords, I thank the gods you are safe! We received the summons only moments ago and hurried here quickly as we could. You should not have taken yourselves about the lower city without us.'

'Yes, it's the gods we have to thank,' agreed a man in the crowd, 'especially with the guards sittin'' on their arses!' Metion's cold glare caused the man to avert his gaze. Several began to cheer whilst others called out Theseus' name. Theseus reached down, grasped the surviving assailant by his long hair, hauling him roughly to his feet whilst two of the guards seized his arms. 'Where's the rest of your rabble?' demanded Theseus, his blade pricking the man's neck. 'Is Pallas out there with his men? Speak now or you'll not speak again!'

Dazed and feeling cold death at his throat, the unfortunate man stared at his slaughtered companions before replying. 'T-they – they wait outside the western gate. I beg you spare me! I beg you! I 'ave wife and children!'

'Slit the bugger's throat!' shouted someone from the crowd.

'How many are out there,' demanded Theseus, 'and how are they attired?'

'Th-thirty is all I know,' stammered the man, eyes starting bright with fear, his face glinting sweat. 'They're dressed as traders from Libya, as - as we were dressed. P-Pallas is with 'em, yes 'e is.'

'Cut 'is ears and nose off then send 'im back to 'em!' called someone else.

'Don't forget 'is balls if 'e's got any!' jeered another.

Two of Metion's guards had drawn their knives in anticipation but Theseus, sheathing his own blade, raised a hand to exclaim, 'No, let him return as he is, defiled by the blood of his kin! Let them see how merciful is King Aegeus in letting this man leave the city unharmed. But if Pallas' jackals are still at the gate by the time we have offered up the weapons of these dead at the shrine of Athena, then they should know that we will ride out against them to avenge their insult to our king, to myself and to Athens! Metion, take him outside the city wall. Send him off to re-join his fellows with our message. Watch what they do but report to us in good time if they're not soon gone.'

Two of the guards half dragged, half marched the dishevelled man, clutching his befouled robe, through a sneering throng who would have despatched him by whatever means pleased them had Metion and his men allowed it. Others dragged away the bodies of the slain whilst mongrel dogs howled, circled about then moved in to sniff at pooled blood.

As they left the scene of carnage, Theseus asked his father, 'Were those five men really sons of Pallas?'

'Yes, they were.'

'How many does the man have?'

'He boasts over fifty of fighting age if we can believe it,' came the reply. 'It's a part of my dear brother's image. He surrounds himself with slave girls the way a herdsman surrounds himself with goats. It's a wonder the whole of Attica to our south isn't heaving with his whelps if these tales are true.'

***

Early afternoon sun bathed the city when Theseus and his father, the latter still visibly shaken, emerged from the temple into harsh light. To the chanting of Athena's priests, the swords and armour of the fallen assassins had been ritually washed before their presentation at the shrine of the goddess. Soon they would find a temporary home on the walls of the megaron, then sometime later be consigned to the palace armoury. As they stood in conversation, Aegeus and his courtiers were approached by Metion and two of his guards. Accompanying them was a fourth man dressed in long white robe, a pale-bearded, stooping, willowy figure, dignified in manner as well as by the gilded staff of office he carried.

'Lord Aegeus,' announced Metion, 'Pallas still remains with some of his men outside the city wall. This man claims to be a herald from his camp. He wishes to speak with you if you care to hear him.'

Aegeus eyed the stranger who glanced nervously from him to Theseus, to the armed men of their company then over his shoulder as if in fear of being spied upon by others. Aegeus nodded to Metion.

'You may speak,' said Metion, turning to the herald.

'I will deliver my message to the lords in private if they will permit it,' replied the man. He eyed Metion with suspicion as if Aegeus' captain himself was a potential enemy.

Theseus turned to Aegeus. 'May I deal with this? Could be I need the experience.'

'As you wish,' replied Aegeus, 'though it seems to me you lack little in the way of experience. I will return to the company of Haemon and his lyre. You and I can discuss matters later.

Metion conducted the herald forward, saying, 'Sir, we've searched this man thoroughly. He carries no weapon.'

'Very well,' replied Theseus, looking the stranger up and down, 'let him follow me to the great hall. We will talk there. Metion – wait outside the door. I wish you to note our conversation whether he likes it or not.'

Neither Theseus nor the herald spoke until they stood facing one another by the empty hearth in the otherwise deserted, dimly lit cavern that the megaron presently was. 'Lord Theseus,' the herald began, 'my name is Leos. I bring news you will find to your advantage.'

'News?' smiled Theseus. 'I'd expect nothing less from a herald. But do go on.'

On seeing how ill at ease the man appeared Theseus regretted the levity of his manner as Leos continued. 'Pallas, sir – as your captain informed you, still has armed men gathered a short way beyond the city wall though his main camp is set up by the woodlands between here and the bay of Phaleron. I was sent to tell you that it is his intention to offer challenge. It is his belief that when given this information you will ride out to drive him and his men away. It is his belief also that because his numbers are small you in turn will not raise many men since this would cause him to flee rather than fight.'

'Not a bad guess,' replied Theseus. 'I take it you have no need to go back and tell him you delivered his message so there must be more to this than meets the eye.'

'Sir,' continued the herald, 'Pallas has more men than you know of – more than your scouts would have observed. They arrived unnoticed because of the many people thronging to the market. They wait now in concealment a short way to the north of your main route to the bay, between the pine trees and cultivated land. They will rise up in ambush when you have set out to confront Pallas. It is their intention to cut you off from the town so you will be trapped. I cannot be certain but I believe there are as many again as those you know of - all fully armed. If you do nothing they will turn their hand to rounding up your cattle and sheep. They will slaughter those they cannot take with them. They will burn or destroy anything they find of value, including your vineyards and orchards. There are also the traders outside the city wall. If they are threatened or harmed, it will not serve the name of Athens well in the future because she will be regarded as unsafe. All of this I overheard discussed by two of his men though I'm certain Pallas did not intend I should know of it.'

'I ought to be grateful for the information you offer me,' responded Theseus, 'but then I ask myself why you, a trusted herald of Pallas, should come here with the intention of assisting me, the son of your leader's sworn enemy. If any herald of mine acted so, he'd be condemned as a traitor and dealt with accordingly – if you see what I mean.'

The herald's expression remained fixed though he turned his head aside and his slender fingers gripped the staff ever tighter.

'On the other hand,' continued Theseus, 'you may be passing this information on because Pallas has ordered you to do it for reasons only he knows. Or perhaps you do know.' Theseus' manner hardened. He stepped back to regard the herald with a stern eye. 'So, my friend, what am I to make of you? Are you traitor or trickster? King Aegeus will not feel inclined to deal kindly with either and nor will I.'

'Lord Theseus, I am no trickster,' answered the herald, summoning up the courage to once again meet Theseus' gaze. 'As for being a traitor, you will make of me as you see fit but I tell you it is I who have suffered betrayal, therefore I consider I owe no allegiance to the betrayer. Until this last year I was loyal as any man. I served the house of Pallas well - as my position demanded I should. My two younger brothers also served; one as an attendant at his table and the other, Antiphos, as one of his palace guards. It was Antiphos who Pallas had condemned and executed by the sword for taking one of the palace courtesans to his bed – as though there were not enough of these women to go around. Knowing how she had openly encouraged my brother, I interceded with Pallas on his behalf. I begged him not to take Antiphos' life - to exile him instead but to spare him from so a cruel a death. He refused to consider any form of mercy. He rebuked then dismissed me, saying everyone knew the rules of the palace no matter what their circumstances. My remaining brother has since fled because he had transgressed in like manner and also feared discovery. Now I'm afraid for my own life because he begins to believe, or so I'm told, that I conspired with my brother to procure the women. It's as if our many years of loyal service to Pallas and his court meant nothing. He only uses me now because there is no other in his camp suited to act as herald and he did not expect to need one. I – I think it was, and still is, intended that I should not return alive to Thorikos.'

The herald laid aside his staff, dropped down on one knee and ended by saying, 'Lord Theseus, whatever your decision I will remain here subject to your mercy. I give my fate into your hands for I believe King Aegeus and yourself are more worthy and compassionate men than Pallas. He rules through his family who are more numerous than the wolves of the forest though he does so without the blessing of his subject peoples and their elders.'

'Well there's a sorry tale. But what you say comes as no surprise. I hear even his food taster employs a food taster.' Theseus continued to regard the herald then called to Metion who stood waiting by the entrance. 'Metion, did you take in what this man said?'

'I did, my lord. And as you say, it is a sorry tale. Do you believe him?'

'Let's put it to the test. Meanwhile, have our friend here conducted to suitable quarters. Ensure he is well supervised until we return.'

Two guards were summoned to escort Leos from the hall.

Theseus remained deep in thought for a time then turned to Metion. 'I'll drive away those men Pallas has sitting outside the gate then during this afternoon small armed parties will ride out toward the camp of these so-called Libyan traders but offer them no threat. Pallas may wonder why his herald has not returned but we'll not give him reason to think the man's told us what he has. Our forays will keep those hidden men of his under cover and out of mischief. Then I'll ride out with thirty of our men before sunset when the traders and merchants are starting to leave for their own camps outside the city wall. Some of these people will set themselves up for the evening close by but others will return to their villages. Only those few foreigners known personally to our elders will remain within the city so any spies thinking to pass themselves off as traders must also leave or risk being recognised. Your men must remain alert throughout.'

'I will be at your side, Lord Theseus,' declared Metion. 'But why only thirty of us when we're assured Pallas has as many again concealed for ambush?'

'Only thirty is what Pallas will think,' replied Theseus, slapping a hand to Metion's shoulder. 'Our small number will prove too great a temptation for them. Yes - if it leads Pallas to believe victory is within his grasp he'll be straining at the leash. My death or capture would enable him to secure control of Athens once and for all. But things will not be as they seem.'

84

'And your father the king?' asked Metion. 'Will he then be present?'

'He will shortly know what I intend to do. He'll lead our men out of the city but only I will be at his side. You, Metion, will have a different role in this – a role I'm sure you'll find much to your liking since it will give you ample opportunity to display your well-known spirit and valour.'

***

The city wall and western flank of the acropolis were bathed in golden light when the traders packed their wares and began to drift out from the city. Some employed cart or wagon, some carried a precious bundle as far as their tent beyond the gate where a son or slave might be tending their horse, mule or ox, or busy gathering firewood.

Two large covered wagons of rustic appearance, each drawn by a pair of snorting oxen, rattled out also through the narrow gate, one close behind the other with barely enough room at either side to scrape by. They rumbled laboriously on through vineyard and orchard to eventually reach the rock-strewn open land beyond, swaying, creaking, groaning as they negotiated uneven ground where an occasional large stone threatened to foul a wheel. Clear of cultivated ground, they headed a little to the south of the main route so as to avoid that area before the woodlands where Pallas' camp was established.

They were well within sight of the enemy camp when a shout arose from the driver of the first wagon. Watched with idle interest by a number of Pallas' men, long since divested of their desert dwellers' gowns, the wagon heeled then shuddered to a standstill. One of its front wheels appeared to have slipped into a rut. Its companion came to a halt close behind, evidently unable to get by. A commotion ensued as the driver of the second wagon, an individual of uncouth appearance, stood up in his seat to wave his stick in the air whilst haranguing the driver of the first. The first driver clambered down as did the second. Both men, arguing loudly with impassioned gestures, goaded the oxen in an effort to haul the leading wagon out of its unfortunate predicament.

Much to the amusement of the watchers, a group of whom had assembled to look on from nearby their cluster of chariots, the driver of the second wagon attempted to push the first wagon clear from behind whilst cursing its driver with lurid obscenities. At the same time the first driver hauled uselessly on the harness of the nearest ox, issuing a tirade of threats to which the creature remained stubbornly indifferent.

Stirred to laughter at the spectacle, Pallas' followers agreed that shifting the wagon was a challenge fit for at least a dozen men if there was to be any hope of success, though they themselves were not about to oblige. Their continuing interest in this farcical diversion was broken by a cry from one of their number who dashed out in front of them to gesture with his spear toward the city.

From the direction of Athens they observed the approach of a metal-glinting host - ten or more chariots, each one drawn by a pair of sinewy, tan-coloured horses. Each chariot carried a lightly armoured driver plus a helmeted man bearing a round or a more robust figure-of-eight shield of boiled ox-hide with metal fittings, his spear held in readiness with a second or third lance at hand. Theseus, Aegeus and members of their house wore more elaborately crafted arms with tall, prancing, helmet plumes that shimmered brightly. Light glared from polished spear blade, scale and corselet. A few soldiers boasted plumed helmets of burnished metal or boiled hide but most wore for protection interlocking rows of boars' tusks stitched to padded leather. Spear-wielding footmen marched amidst the chariots; each equipped as his station in life permitted.

Caught by surprise Pallas' men hurriedly prepared for combat, calling one another to arms, pulling on helmet, taking up sword, spear and shield.

From an ox hide tent behind the chariots a ruddy-faced man appeared, bearded and formidable in ornately scrolled helmet of gilded bronze with black horsehair plume swaying menacingly above it. His powerfully built form was attired in a tunic of drab, heavy linen replete with overlapping metal scales. In his hand was grasped a deadly spear, at his side, sheathed in tooled leather hung his sword with razor-keen edge, it and its owner impatient for blood.

'Lord Pallas,' called one of the men, dashing to his side, 'the Athenians have come out to do battle!'

'You don't say!' responded Pallas, thrusting the man roughly aside. 'Aye, they've got their king and his fancy son with 'em and all you damned fools do is stand about gawping at some peasants' side show!' Raising his spear high he called aloud, 'Ready yourselves! We move from here to meet them on open ground! We keep the sun at our backs!' Turning to one of his men who stood close by with a copper horn slung at his belt, he growled in lowered voice, 'And *you* know what to do once we close with them.'

'Aye, Lord, I do,' was the man's reply.

From the lead chariots, as yet well beyond the range of a spear cast, Theseus and Aegeus watched their enemy move away from their camp in preparation for combat. Aegeus, aware of the Athenians' disadvantage in facing the sun, ordered his men to turn aside then skirt about the enemy in a direction closer to the pair of stalled wagons. Seeing this, Pallas ordered a countermove but the Athenian chariots with their tough little horses snorting aloud, outmanoeuvred their adversary who was still part contained within the pinewoods. Neither side was now disadvantaged by glare and soon would be drawn close enough to join battle.

Aegeus gave the signal to halt whereupon the Athenians, some of their armed men stepping down from creaking chariots, began to ready their weapons for combat in the manner each thought best served his needs. Most tested the balance of their spears, others their swords, some hoisted their shields, large and small.

'Friend and foe may appear much the same in arms and numbers,' announced Theseus, raising for a moment the ornate bronze helmet whose red and white plume swayed threatening majesty, 'but Pallas and his men need a victory before darkness falls. The sun will soon descend behind those trees. The light of day will not oblige him for much longer.'

'They know it and are advancing to meet us,' Aegeus informed him. 'Soon enough men will meet their fate on both sides!'

'Father,' urged Theseus, 'you should not expose yourself except to cast your spear. They'll know you by the purple cloak you wear over that corselet. It was not a good idea to advertise your presence.'

'I hear what you say,' replied Aegeus, 'but I care less for myself than I care for you. The span of my life is all but accounted for. I beg *you* not to be reckless. You have the advantage of youth over Pallas but his experience on the battlefield is far greater.'

'We'll see,' smiled Theseus, grasping his father's arm as they stepped forward from the chariots. 'I intend to have the measure of him soon enough.'

Closer now, it was one of the enemy who stepped forward to hurl the first lance – his target Aegeus. His spear flashed through the air, whistled by its intended victim who had seen the missile cast, only to strike the helmet of a man behind him, piercing it through the crown so that the wearer, his face a bloody, contorted mask split asunder, was dead before he fell sprawling in the grass beneath his shield.

'Spread out, men!' ordered Theseus, striding ahead. Two Athenians cast next, one frustrated upon seeing his spear penetrate an enemy's banded shield but not entirely his leather cuirass, the other elated as his lance, passing between two of Pallas' footmen, impaled a third man through the thigh, ensuring death would have him marked down for possession. Close enough now to identify the enemy leader in spite of his tall shield, Theseus called out, 'Pallas, I stand in the way of all you desire! Let us settle this between ourselves before the day is ended!'

Pallas laughed aloud, passed his shield to a retainer and called out, 'Bastard son of a bastard king! This day will end for us all but for you it'll be the last day of your life!' Then stepping out before his men who jeered loudly whilst shouting with gestured obscenities at the Athenians, he raised his spear to hurl it with well-practised might at Theseus. No shield, both men knew, could have stopped the blow but in those brief moments as it hissed in lethal arc through the air, Theseus, resting his shield on the ground, lodged his own spear at an angle against the inner frame and bent low. Pallas' weapon rang loudly, crashing through boiled hide and wood to pass close over its intended victim's head before embedding itself in the ground where, denied the taste of blood, it quivered in anger. Convinced Theseus must be struck, a raucous cheer arose from the enemy who surged past their leader. So confident were they of victory that some laid aside their shields in order to reach the confounded foe ahead of their companions.

The rash expectations of Pallas' men were thwarted when to cheers from the Athenians, Theseus revealed himself unharmed and ready to return the shot. His intended target, Pallas, was obscured from view by the surge of men but Theseus nevertheless hurled his spear, catching one of his closer adversaries in the side as he attempted to avoid the lance. Cold bronze penetrated the man's innards, causing him to scream anguish at the skies before falling back with spear and helmet ringing together on the ground.

Exposing himself to danger for the moment, Aegeus, too, cast his lance, not with the strength of long vanished youth but with a judgement honed by time. It found a target as had that of his son, this time shearing through the soft flesh of its victim's neck below the helmet, causing lifeblood to shower copiously over his companions as the man spun wildly about, shaken by the hand of death. The spear continued on to penetrate the right arm of another as he raised his own spear, spinning him about in agony. The reappearance of Theseus as well as this last spectacle stemmed the enemy advance whilst the sight of the Athenian prince and his men bearing down with dust rising above them as a spectre of havoc caused Pallas' company to fall back in the direction of their chariots. At this point the horn sounded, braying loud and clear so that it was the turn of the Athenians to hesitate, knowing its call would not go unheeded, though hardly aware of by whom as the sound faded.

From defiles and ditches they emerged, from tall grass, from behind boulders where they had lain concealed. Pallas' hidden reserves, spear and sword at the ready, were approaching Theseus' right flank ready to assail the Athenians at their rear, ready to ensure there could be no retreat. A wave of dismay swept through the Athenians as, with the sun now vanished below the line of trees, the light of day was waning.

'We'll be sorely pressed unless help comes from the city,' said one man close to Theseus. 'We'll all die where we stand!'

'Damned to Hades before that happens,' remarked another, readying for his own use the bloody spear that had already accounted for one of his own companions. Even as they spoke, a spear flashed by to penetrate the shield of a soldier behind them, striking through the man's leather armour, passing deep into his chest. His cry was the cry of them all as he doubled up gasping against his shield, hands clutching the wooden shaft, his life ebbing as smoke in a breeze. Even so, the Athenians gathered about an undaunted Theseus, ready to give all in what they imagined must be their final encounter.

Another horn sounded – this time a different note, this time from amidst the Athenians, though to most it meant nothing other than perhaps a signal to press on.

No one had paid attention to the pair of beleaguered wagons since the clamour of battle had started. But hardly had the notes of the horn drifted by than heavy linen covers slid from wicker frames to expose the interiors - not filled with produce of the land, not with goods from the city, but crammed with armed men who were already scrambling out with sword, spear and round shield. For despairing moments many amongst the Athenians believed that Pallas had even more forces at hand whereas for Pallas and those about him, the chilling truth flooded large toward them.

It was happening quickly. Cries arose. A vortex of confusion circled about both sides until Theseus spun about with sword raised. 'The men from the wagons are ours! Metion is at their head! Athena Nike – Athena victorious marches with us! We go on to strike and rout the enemy!'

Ahead of Metion's company hurried six archers, heading directly for the enemy at Theseus' rear who in their enthusiasm for attack, in their certainty of winning, were largely unaware of this new threat. They now were exposed on open ground within easy range of the archers. The latter stood in line and as one. They drew their powerful composite bows of goat horn, wood and sinew to the full, took careful aim then unleashed a deadly, serpent-hissing flight. Two of Pallas' men fell at once, pierced through the body. A third, his spear arm transfixed, staggered away no longer able to fight whilst others swivelled their shields about in time to avoid death or injury.

Stepping forward, the archers prepared to release another volley but found Metion striding resolutely by, cuirass and greaves shining bright, golden plume dancing above his helmet. Close behind followed his grim-faced men vying in eagerness to accomplish deadly work, shields raised as an advancing wall, weapons at the ready.

The archers, striding forward, redirected their aim at Pallas' immediate company though these were further away. Here, seeing Theseus, Aegeus and the main body of their Athenians approach without hinder, Pallas, sword raised high, urged his men loudly to meet the onslaught with utmost vigour. Shouts arose on both sides, spears flew in deadly arc, some piercing flesh and bone, others thwarted by shield or by nimbleness of foot. But Pallas' men, most bearing their shields at the left, had their right sides exposed. Three were struck by blood-seeking arrows whist advancing to engage their foe, one stopping the point with his armour whilst another had it glance from his corselet to pierce his hand through. Less fortunate still was the third man when the shaft hit below his helmet to drive deep into the side of his head above the cheekbone. A third volley swept through the air and five of Pallas' men were struck - two stopping the missiles with shield or armour, three staggering back, hands clutching embedded shafts, one falling to the ground. Another flight, equally well aimed, swept in to inflict fear and death.

Metion and his men were close to the enemy's reinforcements, hurling their spears to good effect then moving in with each man selecting his opponent. With the Athenian rear-guard also turning on them, Pallas' second company could do little to recover the arms and armour of their fallen before themselves being struck down or forced to retreat. Those of the enemy standing aside from the melee, seeing how matters had developed, gathered up whatever arms they could and headed for Pallas' main group. Aegeus, Theseus and their grim faced company advanced more rapidly, bloodied weapons raised as Pallas' men fell back in disorder.

With his losses mounting, with the time of day against him, Pallas, cursing aloud, saw he and his immediate band risked defeat and worse. The situation, he realised, must be as bad for his men facing Theseus' captain and for all he knew there might be more of Aegeus' men riding out from the city. Slinging shields over their backs for protection, shouting above the clamour to one another, Pallas' company headed in disarray to their camp, again having no time to rescue their injured nor to strip arms and armour from the dead. Three more fell to the Athenians as spear and arrow found their mark but those of the enemy still able to run were soon by the trees and mounting their chariots with but one intent - to escape with their lives.

'They run as if the demons of hell are breathing down their necks,' Theseus laughed aloud.

'Let's chase after 'em – let's finish the job!' called one of the Athenians, starting forward with sword unsheathed. 'They'll move no faster than men on foot over this rough ground!' Others voiced equal enthusiasm.

But Pallas' much reduced company, swept by panic, were whipping their horses on, jostling, swerving, careering around boulders and stones, heading toward the two abandoned wagons which they would skirt in their flight to safety.

'Hold back!' cried Aegeus. 'Chasing them will gain us nothing. We'd never find them after sunset and I doubt Pallas will rest until he reaches Thorikos.' He looked across to where Metion and his men were dealing with those of the ambush party who still lived, adding, 'We have prisoners to question but first we must gather up the arms of the enemy then remove our own dead from the field while there's still enough light.'

'I also wanted to give chase,' said Theseus, stepping over to him, 'but you were right to call a halt. And I see the birds already circling above with an eye for their next meal.'

'Yes,' breathed Aegeus, 'our feathered friends benefit all too often from human folly.'

Several days had passed since the confrontation. Alone, apart from the slave boys who waited at a respectful distance, they sat by the parapet, a pitcher of spiced wine set down on the floor between them, each with an ornately wrought gold cup in his hand. A lowering sun cast long shadows whilst a gentle breeze offered some relief from the lingering heat of the day.

'Doubts over a ruler's succession always unsettle people,' declared Aegeus, 'But since you came to us, Athens' hopes are renewed. I feel her spirit has reawakened. We routed the enemy. Your planning and presence assured our victory.'

'I'm glad my training proved useful,' replied Theseus. 'I was encouraged, too, by the way our men fought; they have spirit and determination. I'm pleased also at the way the citizens have taken me to their hearts. But in spite of what you tell me, in spite of what has happened, I sense a deeper unease within Athens. I sense it even now – a malaise that casts a growing shadow as the days go by. It haunts the streets. It pervades the very walls that were built to defend us though its cause eludes me. It was not dispelled by the rout of our enemies. Father, I see it in the glances of those about me. I seem to hear not what is said but what is unsaid as if no one is willing to disclose its nature. There were rumours abroad in Troizen of a curse upon Athens but I took little notice at the time. It was after all none of my concern.'

'We are so often at war with others,' sighed Aegeus. 'It is the inevitability of yet more violence and bloodshed you perceive.' He drank deeply then muttered to himself, 'At least these diversions serve to waive other matters for a time.'

'No, it's more than that,' insisted Theseus. 'Like all cities in this land, Troizen had her share of conflict but during times of peace the town became a freer, happier place. Years ago you laid the plans that brought me here - now you have entrusted to me the succession of your house. You shouldn't find it so difficult to confide in me. Sooner or later I will have to know.'

Aegeus hesitated then sighed, 'Theseus, you look for a storm when there is only a passing breeze. There's nothing more I can tell you.' Aegeus looked him in the eye, adding, 'Really - nothing at all.'

He remained quiet for a while then continued, 'There is, however, a matter of some importance I had intended to discuss with you. What happened with Pallas has much bearing on it.' Aegeus drained his goblet then placed it on the parapet. 'From now on you must have our men of fighting age under your direct command – with leaders of your own choosing as well as horses, chariots and footmen. Even before the attempt on my life I had spoken with our best fighting men and I know they will vie with one-another to serve with you as their leader – especially Metion. Metion is the worthiest of men in times of conflict. He has stood solidly by me when others might have wavered. I advise you most strongly not to overlook him – no, rather you should favour him. Our young men will readily take up their arms whenever you call on them. You shine with a hero's light. No free man of our city will decline the opportunity to have his own image reflect a little of that.'

Aegeus turned away deep in thought. He stared toward the distant hills, above which a pale half-moon hung. 'Theseus,' he said at last, 'now danger has receded from Athens there is a task I must urge you to undertake. No, it is more than a task, it is a challenge that needs to be addressed. It is one that, should you succeed, will further raise your prestige as well as that of our city.'

'I imagine,' smiled Theseus, 'this is something you've long had on your mind.'

'I'll admit it's a subject I had intended to raise some time back,' replied Aegeus, 'until more pressing matters intervened. Tomorrow and in the days following you must -.' Here he hesitated and placed a hand on Theseus' shoulder. 'You must take yourself with a handful of armed men away from the city and pass north-east through the territories of our neighbours. I much doubt Pallas will see it as any kind of threat since Thorikos lies to our south. The real reason for this venture is to aid the people who farm the plain of Marathon to our north-east, between Mount Pentelicus and the sea. They've complained for many years of a great beast, a white bull that roams their land causing havoc. They say it was brought to Greece by Heracles as one of the twelve labours imposed upon him many years back by Eurystheus who was at the time King of Mycenae.'

'Oh, but I learned about the Bull of Marathon when I was still a child,' said Theseus. 'I was told it came originally from Crete, from the realms of King Minos, though I don't know much about him.

'Yes, Minos,' breathed Aegeus, turning his head aside for a while and again lost in thought.

I'm familiar with much of what Heracles did, as you know,' added Theseus, wondering at his father's pensive silence.

'Oh, er, yes,' responded Aegeus, 'I well recall your account of the great man's visit to Troizen. It was around that time he was said to have left the bull with Eurystheus who abandoned it to roam free, after which it found its way to Marathon. Since then we're told the thing has caused no end of problems. The people of Marathon see no reason why they should suffer through Eurystheus' or Heracles' negligence, hero or no. Whoever puts an end to the problem will outshine the great man himself – or at least he will in their eyes. If you were to - well what I'm saying is, if you were responsible for ridding them of this creature, its horns would grace our megaron. They would be seen by all hanging above the throne you are to inherit. I urge you, my boy, to accept this challenge.'

Theseus laughed. 'Father, perhaps you feel I'll have too much time on my hands here in Athens now Pallas has scampered off with his tail between his legs. If that's the case I'll go and tweak *his* nose. I'll bring it back to you in a box if you prefer – maybe with his head still attached! As for this famous Marathonian Bull – I'll go out alone and skewer it with my spear – then I'll skin the thing and stretch out its hide for my tent. But really, can this be a good time for me to go looking for a long vanished bull that may already be dead? Surely my presence here in Athens is far more important.

Theseus' light-hearted response was not shared by Aegeus, who regarded him gravely, saying, 'I fear youthful bravado causes you to underestimate our enemies as you seem to underestimate the bull. Pallas in turn underestimated you but I know he will try his hand again. Doubtless next time it will be with better planning and a more formidable company of men. And as for the bull – there'd be no greater prestige than its sacrifice here in Athens at the shrine of Apollo. But you must not go alone. You must not compromise the future by rash actions. Not now.'

'You mean actions like my confrontation with those assassins in the market and our skirmish outside the city?' responded Theseus. 'All the more reason why I should stay here.'

Aegeus closed his eyes. 'That I did not expect – at least not there – not then. I should have kept Metion and his men close by – there should have been more armed guards posted within the city and about the wall looking for suspicious activity. Theseus, your honour, your bravery can never be in doubt but you have the greatest responsibility a man of Athens ever had because in time you will succeed me.'

'Very well,' said Theseus, 'I'll take my pick of men tomorrow as you suggest then discuss what needs to be done, though I'll not deprive you of Metion. I imagine our citizens will give us a good send-off.'

'You are right,' said Aegeus in a low voice, as though he feared being overheard, 'Metion would be better employed here in the city – but we'll have no public gathering for your departure. You must leave before dawn. The fewer people who know you have departed Athens the better it will be, though rumour will soon get about as rumour always does. And the young women of the palace who seem to have taken to you so readily will be all the more eager with their affections when you return.'

Theseus considered his words before saying, 'Father I'm convinced there's more to this than you are willing to reveal though I'm certain it's not because you mistrust me.'

'No it is not!' responded Aegeus angrily. 'How could anyone doubt my trust in you? I have trusted and would again trust you with my life – with the very future of Athens. Yes, I'll admit there is much unsaid between us as you have evidently come to realise, but if you will do this then I promise upon your return I will explain matters fully. It is something that has not touched you so far and needs not affect our plans now but what I ask is for all our sakes. It is for the sake of Athens in years to come that you should do as I ask. Trust me, Theseus, as I trust you.'

Chapter 6
The SUMMONS from CRETE

There were few shrines in the city that Aegeus did not attend during the days that followed his son's departure. One thing only motivated his prayers and sacrifices – the safe return of Theseus to Athens. The elders attending and the priests of the temples heard him plead to the gods for this on each and every occasion. But one word was conspicuous because of its absence. That word was, "soon." Others heard him mutter often, 'Where is the vessel from Crete – where is she?'

Haemon the bard knew why Aegeus was so anxious for news of the Cretan ship. Others close to the king had already guessed.

The stream of days flowed by until they became a month. Armed men went from the city at sunrise each day to keep watch above the Bay of Phaleron. Each evening at sunset they returned with nothing to report. With the passing days Aegeus grew more pensive, more reluctant to appear at public ceremonies. He was seated one morning with some of his kinsmen, listening to the restful notes of Haemon's lyre, when Metion strode in to announce, 'Lord Aegeus, Prince Theseus and his men are approaching from the east. A man of theirs came ahead to announce it. He says they have with them the Bull of Marathon.'

Aegeus' response was for a time no response at all. At last he arose and said with a blandness of manner that surprised the captain of his guard, 'Then we must greet my son with an assembly of honour as he enters the city. We must have the people gather to witness the prize he has brought Athens.'

Astride their lean horses, Theseus and his companions entered the city, each bareheaded but otherwise clad in warrior's cuirass or hide armour with sword at his belt. Behind them drawn by a pair of snorting oxen, the big, course-hewn cart rumbled slowly on solid wooden wheels.

'Largest beast I ever saw,' remarked one man near the front of the burgeoning crowd, a burly bronze-worker glad of a break from ringing metal, relieved to emerge sweating from the suffocating heat of his workshop.

'It's a brute all right,' agreed another, whose clay-smeared leather apron identified him as one of Athens' complement of potters. 'Must 'ave taken some doing to bring down a creature that size.'

'So you say - but look at its ribs,' remarked a bushy-faced merchant from Mycenae whose allegiance to Athens was not so strong as to induce any degree of flattery over the deeds of its king's son. 'I reckon that beast 'as long since seen better days. If the poor bugger was human it'd need a walkin' stick to get about.'

There was no response from the first two but inwardly they could only agree. The opinions of a leather tanner, newly arrived from his workplace outside the eastern gate, one of few not hemmed in by the growing crowd, were left unheeded since nobody was of a mind to breathe the noisome vapours that advertised his presence.

Impressive in size it doubtless was though the longer people gazed at the creature the more evident

103

it became - the Bull of Marathon really had seen better days.

But what days they had been. Days of terrifying, bellowing glory, stamping proud, charging pristine white about his God-given kingdom, the Plain of Marathon. Days of rampant virility when it counted the cattle-herds tended by mere humans as its own gifted possessions, when it dealt with any impudent man who offered challenge in the way he ought to be dealt with – gored to death and trampled bloodily underfoot, unless he'd been wise enough to take to his heels with a good turn of speed. Now the infamous, all conquering bull peered, nose drooling, from the confines of the wagon with dull-eyed indifference. It wheezed, it spluttered, it passed wind loudly from its rear end and thought only of rest and sweet oblivion. Theseus hoped the creature's fearsome reputation would loom larger than did the Bull of Marathon in the flesh. He hoped that reputation would continue long after death clouded its eyes at the altar of Apollo's shrine.

The wagon creaked to a standstill in the open area where the markets were held, close to the spot where the attempt had been made on Aegeus' life. Children ran about, ogling the wondrous sight. Older boys, some waving sticks, dared one another to approach the wagon, to reach even a finger's breadth inside. One boy, venturing close enough with his stick to jab the bull in its flank, darted away as the creature turned its great head to let out a placid snort. Amidst growing clamour the young, bare-breasted, painted women of the palace appeared, their conspicuously rouged, red-lipped faces animated in nervous, giggle-punctuated chatter as they regarded the bull. Food and wine were not the only pleasures Theseus and his youthful followers could be certain of later that day.

Horns blared, drums rattled, echoes answered from the stone edifice below the acropolis as king Aegeus made his way down the steps amidst his entourage of guards and elders, a hand raised in greeting, the smile on his face contrived to make Athens' king appear happier by far than he inwardly was. Guards with spears formed a double line between the king and the stationary wagon with its wearily stamping occupant. Only briefly did Theseus wonder why Aegeus had not arrived to greet him before everyone else.

***

The sun was setting when, outside the shrine of Apollo, the sacrifice took place. The great, once all-conquering Bull of Marathon met its end meekly. Seeing the polished blade, razor-sharp, held below its throat, the beast seemed to know its allotted span was ended. It sank to its knees over the great bronze chalice with a final, burbling snort.

Night-time witnessed fires of celebration throughout the confines of the city whilst on the acropolis flames of sacrifice blazed high enough to touch the stars. The citizens had demanded to see Theseus and he had moved openly yet ever vigilant among them until the fires began to die. Afterwards he sought Aegeus but the girls had gathered some time since with a number already occupied in carnal sport with his followers - a sport for which Theseus had long hungered.

***

Early morning air bathed the city when Theseus stepped from the great hall to witness the sun peering over the horizon. There he observed his father, attired in his royal robes, ascending the steps to the guard tower above the gate that protected the acropolis at its southwest entrance. It was one of the few vantage points from where could be had a clear view over the pine trees to the approaches to the bay since men of earlier generations had constructed massive walls to encompass the whole area. He waited a while then followed to find Aegeus gazing out to the horizon. The king seemed unaware of his presence until Theseus spoke. 'You were absent for a greater part of the celebrations last night. I expected to see you presiding there.'

'I watched from where I would not be noticed,' Aegeus replied, continuing to look seaward. 'Too much wine unsettles me nowadays. In any case, the people wanted to see you and only you.' At last he turned to face his son. 'The bull was known throughout Greece, not just to the people of Marathon. Its reputation had spread well beyond our shores and everyone will know who defeated it. You are the idol of the people. I beg you never to desert them.'

'Desert them,' laughed Theseus, placing hands on the parapet. 'I don't understand. Athens is my home, you are my father; these people are my people just as they're yours. I find it odd you should raise the point after all that has passed. As for my capturing the bull – I hope the full truth of that doesn't get abroad too easily. Its fame of late seems to have rested on rumour rather than fact. The farmers and villagers of Marathon pressed me with

106

more tales of its exploits than I could count - of the terror the creature *had* been in the years following its abandonment in their lands by Heracles. When I tried to get it out of them where the bull was, no one could say for sure. Nor could anyone agree as to when they'd last seen it.'

Aegeus listened in pensive silence as his son continued, 'I was actually on the point of quitting when some goatherd came dashing up to say he'd spotted the thing. It turned out the boy was telling the truth; we found it grazing in the field of a disused farm. Oh, it raised its head then charged at us with a tremendous bellow, with a blaze of light in its eye that said it would trample us all to death given half a chance. But we managed to keep out of its way until after a few more attempts it grew tired and gave up trying. I now think – yes, I think the bull was waiting for us, though I find it strange hearing myself say that. Perhaps the gods had whispered news of our approach into its ear.'

'The bird of rumour alights in many places,' said Aegeus, a pale smile touching his lips. 'She has many eyes, many ears and many voices. She hides the truth beneath her feathers but perhaps in this case she will work for and not against you. Just as she kept the Bull of Marathon rampaging to the very end in most people's minds, so she will ensure the fame of its destroyer.' Under his breath he added, 'There is much irony in that.'

'Oh, well,' shrugged Theseus, 'I suppose I'll have to put up with fame and glory if they insist on it - but I won't encourage anyone. Now, back to other matters. You were troubled when we last spoke alone together and there's no disguising the fact that you still are. And, father, in spite of the celebrations, the unease I felt before I left Athens has not gone away. On the contrary I sense a poisonous growth spreading its roots unseen through the foundations of our city – a foul entity that will sooner or later burst forth to taint our lives by its presence. You promised to talk to me about this when I returned. You said you would help me to understand. I have a feeling that if you don't then no one else is going to because you have forbidden it. Well - here I am and waiting.'

Aegeus frowned, once more turning his face to the sea. Beneath the horizon a black speck wavered against the gleam of water - a sail that must belong to a large ship although little else could be made of it. 'Yes,' sighed the king, 'I had hoped that whilst you were absent from the city they would have arrived here and gone before -.'

'They?' queried Theseus, following his father's gaze. 'Who are *they*? Who are you talking about?'

There was a tense silence as both stood gazing out at the distant vessel. It was clear to Theseus that the ship was important to his father and that its approach did not bode well. Even far out at sea it seemed to cast a menacing shadow over Aegeus – a shadow Theseus realised must have fallen long before the day of his own arrival in the city.

It occurred to him then how grey his father looked. As though all the cares of the world had descended upon him since their present conversation had begun. He would have pressed his father about the ship but they were interrupted by voices from the stairs below. Two palace attendants appeared - one held back, the other stepped forward glancing uneasily at Theseus before stopping a short distance away to address the king. 'My lord, I must speak with you.' Glancing again at Theseus he seemed for the moment unwilling to express the message he had intended to deliver. Seeing Aegeus nod his approval he continued, 'My lord, there is a ship -.'

'I am quite aware of the ship,' replied the king, his anger not so well concealed that Theseus could fail to notice. 'We have to prepare as before for their arrival. I will follow you down in due course.'

With a sharp bow the attendant stepped respectfully back as Aegeus turned to Theseus. 'That vessel will enter our harbour well before morning is through. I expect those on board will be on their way to the city gate by the middle of the day.' He gazed back at the sunlit sea; his expression set firm. 'Theseus, there is something I must ask – no, not ask, but beg of you before I leave.'

'Beg of me?' breathed Theseus, glancing out at the vessel that ought to have been innocent by virtue of its distance but had even to him acquired a sinister aspect. 'Go on.'

'Stay here on the acropolis. Stay out of sight until that vessel has gone from our harbour – today, tomorrow, even the day after if that proves necessary.'

'Stay here! But why?'

'Why?' responded Aegeus, angrily. 'What a simple question that is! How it cries out for a simple answer – yes, if only I were able to offer one. Will you do as I ask? It is important to me but even more important is it to Athens. I will explain when the time is right but that time is not now!'

Theseus stared back at him, jaw set firm. 'If there is danger approaching with that vessel, and I'm convinced there is, then I intend to face it with you. Tell me what this is about. You promised you would before I set off to Marathon. I will not curl up and hide like a skulking mongrel!'

Aegeus turned abruptly with arms raised then strode toward the stairs, calling aloud, 'I feel in my bones we are all damned unless you do as I ask! Believe me I do!'

Theseus watched him vanish, followed by the attendants and two slaves, then he turned his attention back to the ship, still far out but growing imperceptibly larger as it headed for the Bay of Phaleron. To his father, perhaps to all Athens, it was an object of dire misfortune. He well realised how his father's desire for his absence was born of desperation yet, having been told nothing by him, Theseus had promised nothing in return. Nor could he make such a promise.

With a final glance out to sea he left the parapet, hurried through the portico then descended to the dimly lit corridor where, in one of the rooms off the great hall might be found the person he intended to speak with.

'Ah, Haemon, my friend – I see you are resting yet I have to disturb you.'

'Lord Theseus,' smiled the old man, rising from his couch, 'I was deep in thought but not asleep. I sleep less now than ever I did. Will you take wine with me? I would be honoured to have your company. I will play for you if that is your pleasure.'

110

'To hear you play is always as great a pleasure to me as it has been over these many years to my father but I'm of no mind to relax or to indulge myself at present. There's a matter I wish to discuss with you because I believe you must know of it at least as well as my father.' Seeing the old man frown, Theseus realised Haemon knew the question before it was put to him. 'Haemon, what is happening in Athens? The ship that right now is heading for our harbour – what is its purpose? What does it bring that causes my father so much anguish? Why does he insist upon my being absent when the people it carries arrive here in our city?'

Haemon dropped his gaze and was silent before replying softly, 'King Aegeus made me promise to say nothing about it. I – I do not wish to disobey him, even if your anger is to fall upon me.'

'No,' responded Theseus, seeing the wretched situation in which he had placed the old man, 'you are right to observe my father's wishes and - and I'll not question you again on the matter. I'll be there when the vessel enters our harbour whether it's today or tomorrow. That way I'll find out for myself everything there is to know.'

Theseus had reached the door to the megaron when he was halted by Haemon's call. 'Lord Theseus! Please hear me!' Theseus stepped back to face him and Haemon said, 'If I knowingly let you do what you say without first speaking, I fear I would be responsible for an even greater misdemeanour. If you will remain with me then I'll break my promise to your father so as to do him greater service than I would by keeping silent.'

111

'Very well, I will accept your offer of words and wine and I'll stay a while with you. I'm sure that's what my father would prefer. But I give you my word - there will be no recriminations against you because of what you reveal to me. Sit down, my friend and I'll sit by you.'

With Theseus seated reassuringly by him, Haemon summoned two slave boys to bring in flagons of water and wine, a copper ladle and a pair of blue-glazed ceramic goblets. Having dismissed them, he arose to draw the heavy woollen curtain across the doorway. Sunlight angled into the room and Theseus readied himself to listen, at the same time regretting how the window opened out to look across inland hills rather than toward the sea.

'The vessel you observed approaching our harbour carries men from Crete,' began Haemon, filling the goblets. 'They are a delegation from the palace of Knossos; they are sent by King Minos himself. But I must beg your patience and go back some years to describe the events that led to their coming here and why their presence is so despised.'

'Yes, tell me everything,' said Theseus, lifting his goblet.

With quivering hand the old man drank deeply from his own cup then continued. 'You will have heard about the misfortunes our city experienced whilst you were growing up in Troizen. Indeed Troizen herself suffered though nothing like as badly as Athens. It began when we were struck by earthquakes that had terrible consequences in both countryside and town. Our rivers dried up at a time when they ought to have been in full spate – something even the bards, even the oldest of our citizens said had never before happened. The earthquakes were followed by pestilence and famine on a scale I in my long years never experienced. And it did not happen by chance. These things never do – or so the oracles tell us. When we sought an answer from Apollo's shrine at Delphi the priestess declared that we must placate the ruler of the seas and shaker of the earth. With "ruler of the seas," we thought she meant Poseidon, naturally, so we debated amongst ourselves over what we could have done to bring his wrath upon our land. But our prayers, our sacrifices made no difference. Birds of prey continued to circle the city to pick what flesh remained on the dead bodies no one had got around to burying. After a time someone suggested that it wasn't Poseidon we ought to be addressing but Minos. I take it you know more than a little about Minos?'

'Yes, I learned about him in Troizen,' replied Theseus. 'His ancestors were our own kin. They long ago crossed the sea to establish themselves on Crete and from there they spread their power far and wide. They told me his vessels are to be seen in every harbour. They say he chopped down half the cypresses and cedars of Crete to build all those ships.'

'All this is true and more,' added Haemon. 'His merchants trade goods in every market from Troy and the Euxine Sea to our east to the great cities of Egypt where he has a colony of traders. His vessels even sail as far as the vast ocean to our west.'

'I've seldom noticed his boats in our own harbour,' said Theseus.

'That is so, my lord,' agreed Haemon, 'and I'll come to that in a moment if I may. Minos treats the sea as his own. They say he believes it *is* his own, just as it's put about he is descended from mighty Zeus, who is said to have been born on Crete. Well whatever anyone believes there's one thing certain; Minos' ships aren't just for trading – oh, no – in times of strife they carry armed men, Cretans and their allies as well as people who let themselves be bought off by Minos for one reason or another.'

'Hm, you make me think of Pallas,' muttered Theseus.

'As for the lack of Cretan ships in our port,' Haemon continued, 'your father will not allow them to trade their wares within Athens proper unless they bring something he particularly needs. Athens, like great Mycenae to our west, has always looked after her own interests when it comes to trade as well as much else. Throughout living memory we and others have clashed with the Cretans over trading rights and monopolies but they always had the upper hand.'

Haemon gazed up at the window for a time as if wondering how best to relate what had next to be said, then continued. 'The bull you brought back for sacrifice is the key to it all in a way. As we were often told, the creature that terrorised the plain of Marathon was taken there by Heracles. But did you know that he brought it all the way from Crete where it had previously run amok?'

'Ah, I know it well, Haemon. It was one of his twelve labours and I have noted them all. He was still undertaking these when he came to Troizen. I afterwards gathered all the traveller's tales I could get hold of about his exploits in the hope of learning from his example though some of those tales may be more imagined than real.'

'Well, sir, this one we do have certain knowledge of. Having completed the task with other matters pending, he was no longer concerned that the beast might get out of hand on someone else's territory – which it promptly did. The people of Marathon let their complaints be known to all and sundry so inevitably Minos got to hear of it. We had celebrated the Athenian games, in which the Cretans took part, with one of Minos' own sons, Androgeus, doing extremely well there. As soon as the games ended, Androgeus departed as did most of the participants but he did not return to Crete. He rode to the south of Attica where he met up at some deserted bay with twenty armed followers together with their chariots and horses. To justify their presence, to allay any suspicions we might have had, an envoy arrived in Athens claiming the Cretans had been sent by Minos to rid people of the Marathonian Bull. They said nothing of Androgeus' presence because he was disguised as an ordinary soldier. It was a trader from Thebes who recognised and reported his presence to us several days later.

On hearing this, your father suspected the envoy's account was a complete fabrication. King Aegeus sent out spies to have the Cretans watched so it was not long before reports reached us that whilst they wandered about the countryside supposedly looking for the bull, Androgeus himself had ridden off to Thorikos where he'd met up with Pallas. Naturally, your father considered another plot was afoot and so did our council of elders. The elders don't usually commit themselves to anything one way or another unless they're backed by an oracle whose pronouncement is almost certain to prove correct. Then there are many in Thorikos and thereabouts, as we know, who detest Pallas and his sons for their arrogance and brutality so it was not as difficult as it might have been to gain information from sources close to his court.

Pallas had done a deal with Androgeus, so it was reported, whereby the Cretans were to aid him in seizing the throne of Athens and Pallas in turn would keep our traders and those of our allies away from Minos' most important markets. One thing I must make clear, however; King Aegeus never revealed he knew Androgeus was still in Attica.'

'Then I regret my laxity a short while back in letting Pallas escape,' said Theseus. 'But I must not interrupt you, Haemon; please go on.'

'Once Androgeus was back with his companions wandering the Plain of Marathon, your father sent out a party of our soldiers under Metion to find him. They, like almost everyone else, were unaware of Androgeus' presence. Aegeus did not wish Minos to find out that his son had been recognised because that would make any attack upon him a far more serious affair.

Our men lay in wait one evening as the Cretans passed through a defile then sprung an ambush. Your father assured me the Cretans were expecting something of the sort because they evidently put up a good fight. They had been caught at a disadvantage, however, and were outnumbered. When our men returned with the Cretans' arms and armour they claimed to have killed every one of them and burned the bodies on a pyre with an offering of prayers, as was only proper.

Afterwards, your father put it about that some of the Cretans had been killed whilst trying to capture the bull and that the rest had been lost at sea on their way back to Knossos. I well recall there had been a convenient storm at the time but Minos was as sceptical as had been your father. Worse still it turned out not all of Androgeus' men were dead as had been reported. One of them, though wounded, managed to reach Thorikos then later made his way back to Crete where he informed Minos about what had happened to his son. Minos was convinced your father all along had known the identity of Androgeus and had slain rather than capture him, as would have been expected for one of his status.'

Haemon took another draught from his goblet then went on, 'I well recall what Minos did next. He landed his forces on the mainland to the west of Attica. He took the people of Megara by surprise, pillaged, destroyed much of their town then used it as a base to ravage our lands. The events in Megara at least gave your father sufficient warning of Minos' approach. When the Cretans arrived before our walls most of our livestock was safe and King Aegeus was ready to defend the city – which he did with complete success.

That enterprise cost Minos more in lives than he'd bargained for, so he was not willing to continue an outright land war with Athens on her own territory. Mainland fortifications, you see – the Cretans aren't really equipped or experienced to deal with that kind of thing. When Minos saw the strength of our walls he realised his power over us lay with his ships at sea rather than his soldiers on land. He relies more on Pallas nowadays to do his dirty work there - a marriage of convenience, you might say, since there's otherwise no love lost between them. Whatever else people may think of him and his ambitions, Minos is at least a cultivated man whereas Pallas is a tyrannical oaf.

Anyway, after Minos returned home events took a different direction. At every shrine in Crete as well as elsewhere throughout his empire he had the priests call upon mighty Zeus to avenge his son's death. Yes – that was when our troubles really began. That was when the earthquake stuck, then later the plague. On top of divine vengeance at home we found our ships harassed by the Cretans at sea and in foreign ports so that even trading whatever we had left for food proved difficult. We were spared the depredations of Pallas and his cronies; firstly because they didn't want the plague spreading to Thorikos and secondly because they hoped it would do their work for them.'

Haemon faltered a while in his narrative as if the memories were too much to bear.

'Our own priests,' he resumed, 'went to Delphi where they begged at the shrine of Apollo for guidance. They were advised to send a delegation to the court of Knossos to see what could be done. When our party arrived, Minos treated them well enough but sent them back with certain demands designed to reduce our status, and more - to demean Athens and her king throughout all of Greece.'

'Demands?' snapped Theseus. 'What demands did the great Minos make of us? And why was *I* never informed of it?'

Haemon closed his eyes as though he felt the words he was about to speak might bring the wrath of Theseus down on him. 'We expected he would have us relinquish some of our trading arrangements in the east but it was worse. Alas, it was much worse. Minos demanded a tribute from Athens each year of seven young men and women – the best of our youth. I'm told his damnable queen, Pasiphae, was at his side and that she was even more determined than Minos himself to bring about our humiliation.'

Theseus remained silent, his deepening anger contained as Haemon continued. 'Your father was furious but such was our situation, he was prevailed upon by the elders, the priesthood and a good many of the citizens in their despair to concur. He was loath to believe it really was Minos who had persuaded the gods to bring about such dreadful affliction. These things happen, he insisted. They always have - they always will, and I assure you Lord Theseus, I am old enough to know our king was right.

But soon after the first group of our young people was sent, the plague was lifted from our land then the rivers once more began to flow. King Aegeus still maintained it was nothing to do with Minos but he, our elders and our priests had sworn their oaths on Apollo's shrine before the Cretan emissaries. The Cretans had the whole sorry affair recorded on clay tablets, which they straight afterwards had baked hard as stone and sent back to Knossos with copies sent also to Delphi. In past years the Cretans have arrived within days of the autumn market ending – as we expected they would this year. Straight after your arrival in Athens your father ordered everyone not to discuss their annual visit on pain of death because he wanted to have you well away from the city when the Cretans showed up. The market was over but this time, when no one had appeared King Aegeus hoped the demands upon us had finished. But no - it was as if the Cretans had waited for your return, though they surely could not have known the details of your movements beforehand.'

'But why did my father want me out of the city? He could not hope to conceal this state of affairs from me much longer.'

'Because – because he felt you might not understand. That you might put a stop to it or to -.'

'A stop to what?' cut in Theseus, his anger clear as he rose to his feet. 'What becomes of this human tribute once it arrives at Knossos? Haemon - tell me all you know!'

'I - we do not know their fate, my lord. There is only rumour.'

'What rumour! Say it!'

'The rumour is,' replied Haemon, averting his eyes, 'that they are sacrificed to some dreadful creature that Minos keeps hidden from view beneath the great palace at Knossos. According to one account it is a monstrous being with the attributes of both man and bull. Some claim it is offspring of the Marathonian Bull. I cannot say but I feel the tale of that bull runs deeper than we imagine. It holds the key to far more than we know.'

'Has no one ever returned?' asked Theseus, sitting down again.

'No one has returned, my lord. It is believed they are all dead, or if this tale of the beast is untrue, then that the women are kept as palace slaves and the men sent to labour in the stone quarries as common criminals.'

'And what other tales are there of this beast that casts a shadow from so far away?'

'There are those who claim it exists not at all in this world,' replied Haemon. 'They maintain it is the beast that lives in the souls of us all. The beast that we imagine inhabits dark, forbidden places. They say it is the beast that stalks the realms of our night-time slumber but in the purifying light of day is banished to the hidden depths of our thoughts. But then we hear the gods do create such creatures. Is it not told how great Heracles himself encountered some of them during his twelve labours? The Nemean Lion they said no one could kill, the Hydra that arose from the swamps of Lerna and defied death by regenerating a new head each time one of its nine was struck off by his blade. He nevertheless did kill them before going on to further mighty deeds. This is all hearsay, of course. I confess I have never witnessed any of the things other people talk about as though they are an everyday occurrence - and neither, I suspect, have most of them. Accounts grow as they pass through time. They are embellished by the imagination of others who feel they must contribute some fancies of their own.'

'I have to agree,' sighed Theseus. 'The accounts of even Heracles' exploits vary in detail from one teller to another. Whichever of them turns out to be correct must mean the others are wrong.'

Haemon refilled the goblets. He watched Theseus lift his own then swirl the wine about whilst gazing pensively into his cup. Rays of sunlight, diminishing slowly as midday approached, slanted steeper now through the window to dapple the stone floor.

At last Theseus said, 'This whole affair has been kept from me by a conspiracy – a conspiracy involving not just my father's court but the whole of Athens. That is quite incredible. I dare say if I'd spent more time amongst the common people I would have found out soon enough since gossip is not easily contained. But it cannot go on. It is to the deepest shame of our city – a shame that will hang like a millstone about my neck when in time I sit upon my father's throne. I tell you, Haemon; since I was never a party to it, *I* will not accept its continuation!'

Haemon, deep in thought, watched him finish the wine but said nothing more. Theseus set aside the goblet, thanked the old man politely, then brushing aside the curtain, strode from the room with a hand gripping the hilt of the sword where it hung from his broad belt.

***

The two envoys had been conducted most of the way from Phaleron in gilded chairs carried by their men. Now close to the city they were let down to advance proudly in robes of gold-threaded crimson with blue, gem-studded headbands that glistened in the sun. Jewelled sandals cosseted pampered feet that rarely trod rough ground or had seldom known cool grass. Each carried a gilded staff topped by a small, double-headed axe of solid

122

gold – the symbol of Cretan power - the emblem of Knossos. A pair of boy slaves trotted close behind to lift trailing robes clear of the ground while the nobles laughed and talked together as if about to do no more than enter a place of feasting and entertainment. Their gestures were broad and expressive but to those citizens who had left their labours to watch the new arrivals progress through the western gate, both appeared dismissive and arrogant. Ahead and behind this small group, naked to the waist, strode the longhaired, clean-shaven Cretan guards, a little darker, a little leaner than most Athenians and most other peoples of the mainland. There were six at the front with six following up behind. Each bore a stout spear with gleaming blade, each displayed a short sword at his side in ornately tooled, copper-bound scabbard.

The citizens of Athens maintained a tense silence though dogs barked and circled about whilst some distance away a mop-haired goatherd waved his stick and berated his small herd of goats, his attention divided between his charge and the procession.

Murmuring broke out here and there. It spread through the crowd like the drone of bees. It promised to break out into torrents of abuse though Aegeus had issued orders that no one was to offer verbal insult let alone issue threats. No hint of violence must be noted by these unwelcome visitors. Metion with his armed guard stood by to ensure Aegeus' word was obeyed.

'Here they are yet again to steal away our lads and girls,' remarked one man, 'and our glorious king stands meekly by and lets 'em do it.'

'We all know why' responded another, 'so what's to be gained by grousing?'

'The point is it shouldn't go on,' added a woman shouldering a basket of olives. 'You'd think that fancy son of 'is would do something instead of buggering off at the very time 'e's needed.'

'Well 'e's with us now but 'is old man doesn't want 'im involved, does 'e,' put in the second man. 'Thinks the sun shines out of 'is arse if you ask me – though 'e gave a good enough account of himself in the market place a while back.'

'Who's it going to be this time?' queried the woman. 'One of 'em chooses the girls and the other the lads.'

'Whoever it is,' answered the first man, 'they'll already be assembling in the market place.'

'Poor souls,' added the woman. 'It's like seein' sheep off to the slaughter.'

King Aegeus, in plain, unadorned tunic of dark linen, hair tumbled about his shoulders, stood part way down the steps leading from the acropolis as the envoys entered the market place. But it was two of the elders of the city who stepped forward to address the Cretan dignitaries, not the ruler of Athens himself. The sullen, ever fickle crowd knew why. They knew his shame was too much to bear. They knew the reason he appeared at all was solely to avoid the accusation of turning his back on his people.

To one side of the market place others had assembled behind a palisade of spears held by stone-faced guards of the palace. Nervous, fidgeting, whispering furtively amongst themselves, milled the healthiest young people of the city – all between the ages of fifteen and twenty years, all as yet unmarried. They were attired in a simple manner, the males in plain white, short-sleeved belted tunics of linen, the females in long dresses of sparingly embroidered fine wool that covered them from neck to ankle. Aegeus' attendants already moved among them, ushering boys to the right, girls to the left.

Passing across the market place, the Cretan entourage halted at mid-point where both envoys turned to look up at Aegeus. They bowed slightly to ensure the execution if not the spirit of protocol and respect owing to a king in his own city. Aegeus acknowledged them with no more than a part-raised hand then one of the pair addressed him in Cretan accent. 'Lord Aegeus, we are come to carry out the task allotted to us by Lord Minos, ruler of Knossos, of Crete and of the wide seas, whose eminence is decreed by mighty Zeus. I request we be allowed to proceed without hindrance - at your royal pleasure, of course.'

The barely suppressed sarcasm in the man's request was lost on few as Aegeus gravely nodded his assent with a hardly audible, 'Yes, you may proceed.'

'Shame,' someone was heard to say as the two envoys strode toward members of the city guard behind whom were gathered the youngsters. Many pairs of eyes turned to Aegeus with expressions that asked unspoken questions but carried no respect. Aegeus, conscious of their thoughts, feeling their resentment, was physically bowed. He willed only that the onerous ceremony would soon be done with, that the Cretans would be gone from his sight until another year had passed.

His gaze turned to the youths and maidens who stood in quiet apprehension at the far side of the open space, then back to the simmering crowd. 'I am their king,' he breathed. 'And when this is over, when the people of Athens return to their daily business, they will once again have understood why this tragedy must be re-enacted. But for how much longer will they understand? Another year? Another two? Their anger will one day rise up to smother me.'

The city guard had parted ranks, allowing the envoys to pass through their line. There the two Cretan nobles moved apart, one stepping over to the young men, the other to the girls. Angry faces looked on as they scrutinised each male, each female, touching the left shoulder of first one and then another, then gesturing for the chosen amongst them to walk over to where the armed Cretans waited. Once more, murmurs of, 'Shame,' arose from the crowd, spreading as a breeze through swaying wheat but never rising higher than a restless whisper. The envoys ignored it and, having each directed his selected seven young people toward the waiting men, themselves proceeded back across the square a little quicker than they had come, tight-lipped and with their gaze directed firmly ahead.

Again the word, 'Shame.' This time it rippled across like a flock of dark birds about to rise in anger and wheel above their heads. In an atmosphere charged with sullen resentment, charged as the calm before an approaching storm, the Cretan party with their chosen fourteen moved in solemn procession back toward the west gate, their footsteps carrying on still air. Ashen faced, Aegeus remained watching from the acropolis steps, crushed beneath the burden of his own despair.

A touch on his arm. He glanced about to find Haemon at his side. 'Sir,' said the old man, 'you should retire with me now. If you do not, I fear the animosity of the people will be turned upon you.'

'Retire,' murmured Aegeus. 'You mean retreat – run away as I have done before, as I have done every year since our city was blighted by their visit? The people chant the word shame ever louder and they are right. No greater ignominy could befall us. Yes, I will follow you. Yes, I will hide my face until –.'

There was commotion below. Something had stirred the crowd. Something had halted the progress of the Cretan party in its tracks. Aegeus stared across then seized Haemon's arm. 'No! No – he must not do it!' With a hand fallen to his sword hilt, he hurried down the stairs where, reaching the bottom, he set out, pushing his way through the crowd with no thought for his own safety.

Barring the way of the Cretan nobles stood a fair-haired young man in white tunic, hands placed in defiance on his slim hips. The envoys looked about nervously, a number of the Cretan guards levelled their spears and were in the process of closing on the defiant newcomer when Aegeus burst out of the crowd. 'Theseus – stand aside! Let them pass! The honour of Athens demands we abide by our agreement!'

'Father, I will not! What you call honour is a brittle sword that will shatter in our hands. I will dismiss one of our own then I will go to Knossos in his place!' Turning to the envoys he asked loudly, 'Do you think the great and glorious Minos will accept a prince of Athens who is, of course, still unmarried?'

The envoys eyed Theseus, the guards, then each other, neither seeming able to make a decision until the intruder spoke again. 'Or do we need the archers I have placed about the city wall to be the arbiters? Their aim is most accurate!'

The envoys stared up to see men silhouetted against the sky, bows ready to fully draw, arrows fitted against cords of taut gut. The nearest of the nobles, looking ill at ease, peered about, cleared his throat then gestured for his guards to step back, saying, 'Our king will doubtless be pleased. He has yet to meet a prince of Athens.'

'No!' exclaimed Aegeus, stepping between nobles and guards to face his son, 'I forbid you to do this!'

'You may forbid it, father,' declared Theseus, raising his hand, 'but I *will* go with our people. I *will* get to the bottom of this.' Then turning to the envoys he smiled broadly, 'I have never been to Crete but I hear travel broadens the mind.'

'You may not carry arms on board our vessel,' put in one of the envoys, eyeing the sword at Theseus' waist. This was the sword of promise that Aegeus had all those years ago hidden beneath the rock outside Troizen.

'Then I'll go without,' replied Theseus, slipping off the belt then pushing the sheathed weapon at his father who, with unthinking reaction, caught hold of it.

'Let me talk to you alone for a moment,' pressed Aegeus.

'We have no time to waste,' put in the first envoy, eyeing the ominously silent crowd who in turn glared back at them.

Theseus smiled again, glanced up at the archers then turned to the envoys, saying, 'A little forbearance will help you safely out of our city – believe me.'

The citizens of Athens, pushing against determined guards to gain a better view, began to murmur.

'You make light of it but I say again you cannot do this,' insisted Aegeus, shaking his head. 'You are the promise of deliverance Athens needed. None of our people has ever returned from Knossos. None!'

'Promise of deliverance, you say! In that case, father, I cannot, I will not live with this humiliation knowing that one day I must inherit it as my own. I have faced much danger as well you know and I will not back away from it now. But if I return safely, which I have every intention of doing, the glory will be yours also because you sent your only son on this mission in the name of Athens. Should I not return then I will have been the sacrifice you made and the people will surely honour you for it.'

'This is madness!' exclaimed Aegeus, glancing upward as if to find a glimmer of hope emerging from some unseen dimension beyond the sky. 'Utter madness, I tell you!'

'The situation cannot remain as it is,' responded Theseus. 'That, too, would be madness.

You realise as well as I and all our people - a few more years of this will see Athens deprived of an entire generation!'

'Then there is one thing I must ask,' sighed his father. 'When you return - and the whole of Athens will pray each day that you do - your vessel must show a white sail. Not the black sail of death she carries now and has carried in the past. Promise me you'll do that. I will then know you are returning to us alive. And when you do, I'll make sure the whole city is ready to rejoice at your homecoming. Our banners will make Athens glow like a field of flowers. I'll set up wine casks at every corner of every street!'

'I will do as you ask,' replied Theseus, clasping his father's hand. With that he re-joined the Cretans where he stepped up to the youngest of the youths under their guard, ordering him away then turning to the nobles. 'Very well, we should go now.'

The crowd was becoming agitated. As the party moved toward the gate they began to chant - quietly at first, then ever louder, 'The-seus – The-seus – The-seus!'

Dogs yelped excitedly, children darted about, the people pressed forward and their chanting continued until the Cretans and their prisoners had passed beneath the gate to head out along the path leading back to Phaleron where the black-sailed ship waited.

Watching the party vanish from sight, Aegeus turned to Haemon with a tear in his eye. 'Did you see them, my old friend? Those stout sandals I left beneath the rock in Troizen for my son all those years ago – he wore them when he fought his way through so many dangers to reach Athens. He wears them again today. Yet now he is among our enemies without his sword.'

***

Two men stood together in the shadow of a side passage; two men who had not shared the feelings of Athens' people because they were citizens of another town. A town that harboured no sympathy for Theseus and none for Aegeus.

'This'll please old man Pallas no end,' muttered one. 'Aegeus' son is – was, the only thing keepin' this place together.'

'It could be Pallas' chance,' replied the other, 'though 'e'll not be so quick off the mark as 'e might 'ave been since 'is nose was bloodied.'

'Maybe, but time's a great 'ealer and I reckon time's what we're going to 'ave from now on. Aye – time an' plenty of it.'

***

Not Theseus nor any of the young men and women of Athens who accompanied him had been aboard such a vessel until this fateful day, though they had observed them out at sea and, on rare occasions, at the jetty of their own harbour.

She was a handsome ship, a large ship – larger than the boats of Athens, larger than those of most other mainland cities that traded the bays and inlets or fished the coastal waters. She was as spacious as the cargo ships from Mycenae, Argos and the great cities of the Peloponnese that sailed east, past Troy then on to the Euxine Sea. This ship did carry a cargo of her own, as Theseus could see from the rows of large terracotta jars standing packed in straw ahead of the mast, their surfaces patterned in

131

registers of swirling, sensuous geometry. The two envoys had conducted Theseus to stand by the high prow as she cast off then was pushed out by crewmen to drift clear of the jetty. The remainder of his party had been seated with the Cretan guard, beneath an open-sided canopy of timber and patterned linen that covered most of the boat's broad gangway from amidships to stern.

A throng of people had made their way down from the city to watch the ship depart in the heat of that afternoon. At the front of the crowd, swathed in black cloth of mourning, their heads covered, were assembled the parents, brothers and sisters of the youths and girls who they feared were to be lost forever. Some of the women wailed their grief aloud. Others shed tears of silent anguish. From further back came shouts of anger, though more called the name of Theseus. Some voices rang with hope. 'Bring our children back!' they cried. 'Lord Theseus, bring them home safely to us!'

Aegeus had declined to join them. He had no wish to see his son carried away on a sea of despair after so short a time at his side. He instead watched from the acropolis in the company of Haemon, the only man who was able to share his grief.

***

In contrast to the melancholy theatre on the jetty, sea-spray danced sun-jewelled brilliance as oar blades struck the water. Theseus counted fifteen oarsmen at each side. He wondered if they were slaves though their condition did not speak of deprivation or ill treatment. To exhortations from the pot-bellied, grizzle-faced captain who stood by the two steering oarsmen at the stern of the ship, the rowers manoeuvred their vessel into open water. Only then was the great spar raised to a clatter of ropes. Only then did the black canvas sail ascend, rumbling and flapping up the tall mast, hauled by the youths of the crew, lean, crinkle-haired and naked save for their linen kilts. In white and gold upon the black sail was emblazoned the double-headed axe that proclaimed the power of Minos.

Their ship rolled gently as the sail bellied and, once under way with the wide blue sea opening before her, the oars were raised clear, drawn in and stowed aboard. To the smaller boats crossing the bay, this vessel would be a fine sight as she rode out beneath a sunlit sky, steering west-southwest with the prevailing breeze filling her sail. Perhaps some would know the sinister purpose of her journey. Perhaps they would be aware of the anger, of the distress she left in her wake.

'I take it, Prince of Athens,' remarked the closer of the two envoys, 'that until now you have never had the pleasure of sailing on a vessel such as this.'

Theseus did not care for the hint of condescension in the man's voice. He reflected upon how easy it would be to seize him bodily then hurl him overboard like a sack of figs. But even had it not been for the Cretan spearmen and crew, his determination to face whatever dangers lay at the end of the journey caused him to retain the manners that ought to be expected from one noble when addressing another. 'You are right,' he responded, 'she appears a fine and, yes, a most seaworthy ship. It makes me wonder all the more why she arrived at the bay of Phaleron so much later than expected –

though had she been on time I, of course, would not be on board to raise the point.'

'That is no fault of our vessel or of our men,' retorted the envoy with thinly disguised contempt. 'As it happens – as *most* people are aware – the prevailing winds are not in our favour when sailing north to the mainland. During our journey out, they prevailed rather more strongly than usual for this time of the year and so confined us to harbour in the Cyclades Islands for many days longer than expected.'

'Ah,' smiled Theseus, 'so the gods no more favour the mighty than they do the rest of us wretched mortals. Perhaps I should take comfort from that.'

'As you please,' sniffed the envoy. 'But the winds are with us now and though the voyage will take under three days, we will pass by many islands with the opportunity to take on whatever goods and provisions are required. I fear you and your companions will not be able to go ashore, however. You would do well in warning them also that to jump ship will gain them nothing. All islands where we make harbour are loyal to our king. That means there is nowhere for a fugitive to hide.'

'My friend,' responded Theseus, eyeing him with harsh stare, 'Athenians are no cowards as Minos found out when he invaded Attica. It is by decree of the gods that we sail with you and not through the force of Cretan arms. You'll do well to remember that.'

The man averted his gaze, smiled weakly then swung his way along the guide ropes to join his fellow noble.

To a lively thump of waves against the hull, to the creak of timbers, they were running clear of the headland and would soon steer due south. Theseus regarded his companions where they sat grouped in the stern of the ship, holding hands, talking among themselves, now and again singing together. They appeared undaunted in spite of the situation, the youths effecting a brave face whilst the girls sometimes laughed as they might when setting out on their way to nothing more sinister than the market. How well, he thought, did they endeavour to contain their real feelings.

With that he turned his attention to the wide expanse of sea that lay ahead.

Chapter 7
The PALACE of MINOS

The day was drawing to a close as the mainland coast fell away. Theseus, still at the bow of the vessel, was aware they would see little of the islands until the following morning. Intending to question one of the envoys further about their journey, he turned to find the man he had spoken to earlier standing by the mast in conversation with one of the crew.

'As we are to sail through the night,' Theseus said, stepping over to him, 'how far from land will we be by sunrise tomorrow?'

'Far enough,' replied the envoy. 'You will see the island of Serifos to our east but it will be late morning when we reach Melos. There we will enter the great bay but remain in port only long enough to deliver goods and take on a cargo of obsidian to be worked by the artisans of Knossos. After Melos we do not sail close to any land until reaching Crete. At Melos we will be greeted by men from the Cretan garrison.' A faint smile crossed his face as he added, sarcastically. 'It might be of some benefit for you to know this.'

'Oh, a welcoming committee,' replied Theseus with a yet broader smile. 'Then I'll make certain none of my people attempt to leave your boat.' Then leaning close to the envoy he added, 'Though I might wring your miserable neck and throw you into the sea before we arrive. If I do it quietly, tonight, no one will know what happened.'

'Think as you please,' breathed the wide-eyed noble, stepping quickly away.

***

The island of Crete loomed out of a pale morning haze. It had been in sight for some time before Theseus was able to make out any detail of the port to which they were headed.

Visibly wary of him, the two envoys had declined his company for much of the time since departing Melos. When land was close, Theseus made his way past the envoys to the stern of the boat where, sitting amidst his young Athenians, he assured them as he had the previous evening that whatever was to happen, he would meet any challenge, that he would strive to his very limit in order to ensure their safety. The girls remained cheerful despite the uncertainty of their fate, whilst the youths expressed their determination to stand by Theseus come what may, most rising to their feet to emphasise the point in spite of the boat pitching in rougher water.

To a thump of waves against her timbers, to a swish and clamour of rope against fabric and timber, the black sail was lowered. The boat rolled to the swell of the sea as her oarsmen prepared to manoeuvre her into the harbour of Amnissos. Theseus remained with his companions aft of the mast, watching as they entered calmer waters where boulder breakwaters reached out to embrace their vessel. A gladdening sight to the Cretans on board, this was not so to the young captives of Athens.

But all thought of the perils ahead left Theseus for a time as he watched the people who, as soon as the ship was spotted out at sea, had converged to gather about the harbour and quayside under a seamless blue sky. There were men, women and children, many waving, most bearing cheerful smiles as the vessel drifted closer, as the oars were shipped for the last time. Many were colourfully, some gaudily attired as though attending some great outdoor ceremony. If antagonism toward the captives occupied the thoughts of anyone on Crete, there was no hint of it in the chatter of those who gathered to welcome the boat.

Behind the crowds stood the harbour buildings of Amnissos, their façades ranged with either pale-plastered, rectangular pillars of stone or russet coloured, downward tapering wooden columns topped by thick cushion-capitals that in turn supported painted timber lintels. The closest buildings, of two storeys, Theseus judged must be warehouses. The russet columns were familiar to him from his own as well as other mainland towns where they were used mainly for internal support. Here they had proliferated to colourful serried ranks where at home would have been grim walls of cyclopean masonry. Atop the structures ran another familiar sight; the stylised bull's horns in pale stucco that were a common architectural feature on so many mainland buildings including those of the acropolis at Athens. Here at Amnissos all these features were employed with a degree of exuberance unseen on the mainland.

Behind the colonnaded warehouses were other structures even more impressive. Some rose to three storeys, their balconies arrayed with coloured fabrics and livened with flowers that glowed bright in the sun. Such brilliance, such a sense of open space amazed those whose eyes were used only to the dour stone wall that enclosed their hometown. Reaching up the hill beyond was a paved road the like of which the Athenians had never witnessed.

With the ship drawn close to the quay, lean, white-kilted boys fell like a shower upon the ropes then scampered about laughing with their on-board companions to perform those numerous tasks needed to complete her docking. The vessel was quickly secured alongside broad stone steps. The two nobles strode ashore ahead of the Cretan guards who ushered their human charge from the ship to assemble on the quayside beneath wheeling gulls. Remaining for a short time on the quay, the envoys held brief conversation with two of the guards, now and again glancing at Theseus, whilst the rest of the Cretans, joined by other armed men from a guardhouse close by, contained the Athenians in a tight group. As they were ushered away from the ship, one of the nobles walked over to Theseus, saying, 'You must keep with us now in good order.'

'Your buildings are unfortified,' remarked Theseus, moving forward with him. 'I take it your enemies have never set foot here.'

'Our enemies?' replied the man with thinly disguised contempt, more confident now on his home ground with substantial protection at hand. 'Our lookouts would spot them far out at sea. Our ships would set off against them long before they landed. If we were informed well beforehand then we would meet them even further out. They might arrive here eventually - washed up ashore as bloated corpses. *We* are not burdened with the fear of enemies here at Knossos.'

'But possibly with too much pride,' responded Theseus with an expression that said he was not in the least impressed by the other's claims.

'I note the words of a condemned man,' retorted the envoy, leaving his side.

Ahead waited a pair of lithe white horses in gilded harness with an ornate, two-wheeled chariot into which the envoys climbed. Close by it stood a wicker cart before which a dusty ox was tethered. As Theseus' party approached, it became clear that this latter was to be their transportation to wherever they were to be held. Once cooped inside with his companions, Theseus saw the grim irony of the situation. It was by similar means he and his men had transported the Bull of Marathon to its doom.

They set off to the plodding gait of the ox, the creak of timbers and rumble of wheels. Marching at each side were the Cretan guards who would ensure no prisoner jumped from the cart to escape. Theseus, knowing Crete to be a large island, wondered how easily it might be to find refuge should flight from Knossos prove possible. Though from what he had seen, from what he had heard, the control Minos exercised was absolute.

The small procession turned west to continue on along a road that outside Athens would have been no more than a worn track but here consisted of large, well-fitted stones ascending a gentle rise. Once clear of the port they found themselves passing through olive groves and vineyards but further out they could see fields of wheat and barley ripening in the sun. Scattered here and there were the modest houses of land workers and the larger cubic conglomerations of estate owners. Amidst the fields and houses moved people on foot or on horseback; all going about their business in what appeared an amiable kingdom. To the young captives from Athens staring out from their wheeled containment, this also presented a peaceful, bountiful land; a land that had never trembled beneath armies of marching men bent upon violent destruction and bloody slaughter.

They continued to climb, crossing a number of streams spanned by superbly constructed stone bridges and now the chariot drew alongside the wagon so that the nobles were again able to communicate with Theseus. 'Soon,' called one of them, 'we will reach the palace of Knossos. Once there you and your people will be taken before our king.'

'I dare say he'll be wanting to gloat over his conquests,' retorted Theseus. 'We must endeavour to look our best.'

'The gods have decreed what is to pass,' replied the noble.

'Yes,' responded Theseus, fixing him with an eagle stare that caused the noble to step smartly back, 'and those same gods gave us free will. Never forget that!'

The sun was high overhead when they at last drew close to their destination. The road on which they travelled led directly upward to the north entrance of the great palace and now they were able to see further along this. Continuing inland to the south, they observed the road supported by a series of nine, corbelled stone arches carrying it through two shifts in direction high over a valley through which gushed a wide stream. Turning from the road they approached a sight that Theseus and his companions had heard about but never visualised in its true splendour.

'We arrive now at Knossos!' proclaimed one of the envoys with a gesture of pride.

They were confronted directly ahead by a vast assemblage of flat-roofed buildings of assorted sizes, each geometrically ordered in itself but clustered together in terraces on rising land with a multitude of others to form a great, harmonious but seemingly unplanned unity – a single, rambling structure that must have accumulated over considerable time. Some buildings were of one storey whilst others rose to an incredible four, even five floors in height. Supporting most of the buildings were those same square piers or the more familiar downward tapering columns in white and black as well as red – advancing, receding and crossing by as marching men. To Theseus and his companions, Knossos was more than a palace – it was a city of light, a city of colour. They were consumed by a sense of wonder tainted by an uncertainty underlain by fear. How could such a wondrous place harbour evil? Prisoners they may have been but the young Athenians gazed in awe.

'Even here they have no defensive walls,' commented one of the youths. 'I see no fortified gate, no citadel, no place of refuge in time of siege.'

The road had become busy. Their attention was drawn to people who walked to and fro under the hot sun, talking and laughing. Landsmen passed by leading their donkeys, some whose panniers sagged with fruit or olives, others bearing a wealth of farm produce – bounty of the Cretan soil. Some hesitated

142

when their attention was drawn to the prisoners crowded within the wagon. Artisans and slaves stopped to peer up as did those citizens of wealth who bore about their hair and limbs, male as well as female, the luxuries that must be common in Knossos but were less often encountered on the mainland, even in Mycenae. Mycenae was said to be rich in gold though, as in Athens, the common citizen saw little or nothing of it except on occasions of ceremony.

There were fewer women than men to be seen but as in most mainland towns those fussily coiffured ladies of higher status were bare-breasted though their ankle-length flounced skirts appeared more delicate, more intricately patterned. Their skins were fair and they or their attendants shielded them from the sun beneath brightly coloured linen parasols. By contrast the Cretan men of the palace were simply, even sparingly clad, though a significant few were as vainly ornamented with precious bands and trinkets as were the women. The Athenians noted, too, that unlike older men of the mainland, most here were clean-shaven. Those with facial hair were also proclaimed by their dress as foreign traders rather than citizens of Knossos.

'You'd never dare wander around with such valuables outside the towns in Attica or Argos,' remarked another young Athenian. 'The bandits would be closing in like jackals.'

'Yes - and that would be the end of you,' agreed another. 'Yet some of these people flit about like gaudy butterflies with hardly a sword or a dagger between them!'

'Their island appears a bastion against the ills of the mainland,' said Theseus. 'Trade secures their wealth. Their navy protects it. We should learn whatever we can from them and return to Athens the better for it.'

'Return to Athens!' responded the first youth. 'We'd love to share your optimism, Lord Theseus.'

The Athenian girls continued to stare about, grouped tightly together but not speaking.

Close to an ascending flight of stone steps the wagon was brought to a halt and the side unfastened. Before the Athenians climbed out, other guards appeared, stepping smartly down the staircase from the palace entrance. These men, twelve in number, were more elaborately dressed – the headbands that kept their long hair in place were, like their sandals, of finely-tooled, gilt-ornamented leather. Their kilts were gold-embroidered and from the belt each had about his slim waist hung an elaborately fashioned sword scabbard with gilded hilt. One of their number carried a decorated staff surmounted by the now familiar golden, double–headed axe. This man exchanged a few words with the envoys before dismissing the attendant guards. Recognising Theseus as leader of the captives he stepped over to address him. 'You and your people will follow me into the presence of our king. There you must show respect. You must speak only if and when you are spoken to. Do you understand?'

'I'd prefer it if we were honoured with food and refreshment before meeting the great man,' responded Theseus. 'We've only just set foot on dry land.'

'In due course, perhaps,' replied the officer, coldly. 'Our king may not be kept waiting.'

Closer and the buildings grew ever more imposing, ever more lavishly decorated than those ranged about the harbour. People peered down from upper floor balconies, dogs yapped, though there were not nearly as many as might be seen around Athens nor in evidence was the sight and stench of their excrement. In the shadows monkeys scampered, squealing, peering furtively at the newcomers before vanishing from sight. Amidst the cacophony that reached their ears as they walked on were sounds familiar to the Athenians. The hammering of bronze, the rattle of treadle lathes, the clatter of looms, the scraping murmur of pottery wheels. Workshops that in Athens were scattered throughout the city, often outside the wall, were here located within this great assemblage of buildings. Earthenware jars, tall as a man, stood here and there, their exteriors replete with meandering abstract designs, whilst some bore moulded images of sea creatures so realistic as to appear swarming busily over their surfaces.

'To our right is the customs house,' said the envoy closest to Theseus, indicating a wide gallery with substantial square pillars. 'Trade from the mainland and the islands to our north has to pass this way.'

As they carried on upwards the passage narrowed, drawing level with, on each side, a russet-colonnaded gallery. That to their right bore upon its inner wall the partly sunlit fresco of a great, russet-coloured bull ready to charge forward. The party continued up the stone staircase flanked by more columns, behind which could be seen yet more openings. All about were bright frescos; not portraying merciless warriors on their way to do the gruesome business so readily displayed in mainland towns, but of spirited dancers, gaudy processions, young people engaged in a sport of one kind or another – the flesh of the men depicted in a muted red, that of the girls rendered white.

One fresco in particular caught Theseus' attention in passing, though it was visible only for a moment. It depicted young men and women involved in a strange acrobatic event. One man gripped the horns of a charging bull, the girl was shown poised in mid-flight as she somersaulted over the back of the beast, while the second male waited with arms outstretched to catch then steady the audacious leaper when she landed. The bull image, thought Theseus; how significant it seemed here – more so than in Athens. All about, he glimpsed its symbols - repeating images in the upper parts of galleries, some cast as bronze statues in shadowed recesses. In one niche they observed the statuette of a bare-breasted priestess holding a sacred serpent out in each hand, with what appeared to be a cat seated bizarrely upon her head. There, too, were the ubiquitous double-headed axes running as subsidiary motifs along walls and corridors.

Now came the sound of running water, surprising because it issued from the oddest of places. Along passages, through galleries it flowed, contained by square stone channels, gathering here and there in shallow, rectangular pools before continuing on its skilfully directed way to gurgle down stairway conduits, cooling, reassuring. With restless gaze, the Athenians marvelled at the wonders surrounding them. Everything was so well ordered, everything so contrived to ensure comfort and to maintain gracious living.

'What harm could befall anyone in this place?' asked one of the Athenian youths.

'I wonder,' responded a girl, 'if our predecessors chose not to return home because they preferred to stay among the luxuries of Knossos.'

'I dare say we'll find out soon enough,' added Theseus, 'but I'm certain there's more to this than meets the eye.'

They eventually found themselves ushered along a series of well-lit, frescoed galleries, turning right, left then right again until they were no longer certain from which direction they had come. Sunlight fell through numerous stairwells; cool air flowed from window grilles but the place had, to these bewildered strangers from a harsher land, become an unfathomable maze. Open sky greeted them as they entered a great ceremonial courtyard across which they were led diagonally to their right. Half way across, the two nobles ordered the party to hesitate so that the Athenians could take in the splendour of their surroundings. The Athenians saw how the fresh water channels opened out to form larger, stone-lined shallow pools spacious enough for people to bathe themselves and so gain relief from the heat of day. One of the nobles announced with an air of conceit, 'See – all about us rises the glory of Knossos!'

'And what rises must one day fall,' smiled Theseus.

'But not in your lifetime,' muttered the envoy as they moved on.

Concealed behind a slatted window, breathing air that carried subtle aromas of iris and precious saffron oil, two perfumed, bejewelled females adorned the brightly cushioned seats of ornately carved cedar and ivory couches. Honey-sweet notes tingled their delicate ears, played at discreet distance by a musician concealed behind drapes of patterned linen. Though less gaudily attired than many others of their kind, the girls' intricately fashioned earrings, their ornate bracelets, were of the finest gold inlaid with silver. Their full, sensual lips were tinted red as were the nipples of firm, fully revealed breasts but their hair was fairer, less elaborately contrived than was the Cretan palace fashion. It reflected more the plainer styles of the mainland and was more in keeping with the traditions of their ruling family. Her wide green eyes peering out across the courtyard from beneath long lashes, one of the girls watched the small procession emerge into sunlight then halt close to the centre.

The younger of the two – neither had yet reached her twentieth year - held a mirror before her face. It was a precious mirror brought from Egypt, its handle formed by the standing figure of a goddess, her arms upraised to hold the disk of highly polished bronze. In the mirror she gazed upon the face of the young male slave who slowly, oh, so sensually, ran the gold inlaid ivory comb through her lustrous hair. Reflected eyes fixed upon each other's for infinite moments; moments that spoke of past intimacies, of simmering desire, of voluptuous promises yet to be fulfilled. Her reverie was complete.

'Phaedra, dear' intruded the voice of her older sister, 'the Athenians have arrived.'

Lowering her mirror with a sigh, the girl reached up to take the comb from him as the slave moved to her side. Red-nailed fingers paused momentarily to squeeze his hand whilst she whispered, 'Thank you, Hylas. You may continue later. I will call when I'm ready.'

As her sister leaned forward to obtain a better view from the window, the slave glanced up to ascertain Phaedra and he were not observed. He brushed his lips across her long neck, causing her to draw breath and to close her eyes. Having placed the mirror at the side of the chair, her hand hovered at his thigh. Long nails prickled his flesh just above the edge of his short linen kilt. He tensed involuntarily but knowing he must show no further response the young man bowed slightly, backed away then stepped quietly from the room. Phaedra glanced up, lips parted as if about to call him back whilst her sister remained preoccupied with the scene beyond the window.

At last Phaedra arose. 'Ariadne, darling, do move over so I can get a proper look.'

Both pairs of eyes followed the Athenians as they resumed their progress across the great courtyard toward the west wing.

'Look at the one leading them,' breathed Phaedra, 'they can bring him to worship at my shrine any day. Oh and he's so fair. Many of the mainland men are, aren't they. I like that.'

'Eyes off you little bitch!' countered Ariadne. 'I spotted them first. I noticed *him* before the rest. And just look at those mousy little tarts trailing behind. I wonder if he's fucked any of them on the way over.'

'I hardly think so,' remarked Phaedra, 'there can't be much privacy on boats. Not even large ones.'

'Really, and what d'you know about boats?' responded her elder sister, her eyes remaining fixed on the prisoners as they reached the far side of the courtyard. 'And since when did *you* worry about privacy? I've seen the way Hylas as well as some of the others look at you - and you at them, and I know what goes on in your rooms – don't I just.'

The Athenians had halted again, still in full view at the far side of the courtyard, whilst the two nobles moved to the front, allowing the palace guards to arrange the party for their royal presentation.

'Know?' gasped Phaedra. 'What are you trying to insinuate? Exactly *what* do you know – or think you know?'

'You continue to ignore the fact,' replied Ariadne, turning to her 'that I usually don't sleep until the sky begins to lighten - and you know perfectly well why. So I've seen – well, I've seen what I've seen. You and him – that vain oaf Hylas and his pals - three men at once, indeed! It's a wonder you can walk or talk properly afterwards. You're as bad as our dear mother. Then there are the female slaves you've taken to your bed. Mind you, at least they better understand what other women want. Don't I know that as well, if you care to ask.'

'You spying bitch!' exclaimed Phaedra. 'You and your wandering about at night because of stupid nightmares! And what about Tauros? If father found out what you and his top general, not to mention some of his pals, were up to in *your* bed as well as theirs he'd have their balls cut off. Yes, and the lot of them would end up in the quarries. Even worse if he found out our mother was also fucking him as well as several of -.'

'At least Tauros is a soldier and not a damned slave!' cut in Ariadne, eyes afire. 'And please don't pretend he hasn't sheathed his weapon in your scabbard because – wait –! Oh, look, sister dear, they're moving off. They're going to be paraded in front of father before being confined.'

'Such a waste,' mused Phaedra. 'All those fresh young men – don't you think?'

Ariadne turned to her with an expression of disquiet, 'I - I dread to think of it. Each year I pray father will not do what he intends. I've begged him to stop but he dismisses what I ask then goes about as if nothing mattered – as if no one had said anything.'

'The gods have willed it,' responded Phaedra. 'At least that's what we're told, though I do sympathise. I dread the merest thought of being condemned to wander about down there, will of the gods or no.'

'Will of the gods is what *he* tells us,' responded Ariadne. 'Just as much the will of our mother if you ask me. He has to make some concessions to keep her off his and other people's backs. But sending them down to that, that –. Oh, it's too dreadful to contemplate! Whatever the reason, I think father's gone much too far with this tribute nonsense. It's become an unhealthy obsession.'

'You shouldn't let it play on your mind, Ariadne, dear. That isn't healthy either.'

'Healthy? Phaedra, *dear*, you didn't witness what I did all those years ago when I – oh, never mind. And father expects us to think he's being considerate when he says if any of them survive then he'll let matters be and only make demands for tribute in silver from Athens. *That* is quite laughable!'

'Look,' suggested Phaedra, 'why don't we follow the Athenians inside? We can listen out of sight to what goes on as we have before. No one will dare question our being there even if they do see us.'

'Very well, we'll stand and listen for all the good it will do.'

They stepped from the room clutching their skirts, pitter-pattered in gilded, flat-soled leather slippers along columned, frescoed corridors then out into the glare of the sun-splashed central court. After crossing this they re-entered the building and continued on, silent as stalking cats, until finding themselves in a narrow, dark passage that would have led directly into the throne room had it not been for a barred door of cedar wood with slatted upper section. It was easy enough to crouch low and peer through this without opening the door, easy enough to huddle close, easy enough to listen in the shadows without being observed.

152

The Athenians entered a pillared ante-room where they were brought to a halt. First to go before the king were the two envoys. A pair of guards remained, their spears crossed to prevent Theseus and his companions from entering the room beyond until the nobles, who remained visible to those outside, had bowed and announced, 'Sire, we bring before you the seven youths and seven maidens of Athens as decreed by the will of Apollo.'

'Have them enter,' came the deep, commanding voice of one still hidden from view.

With the guards deploying themselves about the door Theseus went first, followed by his people. The stone-flagged room looked at first glance to be divided along its centre by three columns but it became clear as they entered that to the left of these was the well of a descending staircase. It was to the right of the columns that the Athenians were ushered. The room was not what Theseus had expected for a man wielding such power as the fabled Minos, a man who dominated the seas and could demand tributes in human flesh from the ruler of another land. No, the king's megaron must lie elsewhere with this room serving as an informal reception area. Here were none of the great figure-of-eight shields like those mounted on display within Aegeus' great hall, but all around the russet walls above the cushioned, low stone benches occupied by officials and priests, were painted crouching griffins and swirling plant motifs. Hardly, thought Theseus, the stuff of warfare.

The Athenians were ordered to stand with their backs to the columns opposite to where the king sat upon a richly cushioned throne flanked by two armed guards. Set on the floor between king and prisoners was an alabaster basin that Theseus assumed must serve some ceremonial purpose. The king's throne, of carved alabaster with tall scalloped back was, to his surprise, little different to that used by his father. If there was shared ancestry between the rulers of Knossos and other mainland kings, here was added proof of it along with the largely common language.

Dismissing the two nobles, King Minos turned a bushy eye upon the Athenians. He was a stocky, round-faced, red-haired man with frowning expression but unlike the majority of his fellow Cretans, wore a full though meticulously trimmed beard. Across his cheek, running diagonally beneath his right eye, was an ugly scar. He appeared to be chewing food though no plate lay within sight. He evidently had considered the occasion worthy of regal presentation as his attire included a shallow, upwardly flared copper crown set with precious stones of various colours and topped with an exotic plume. A necklace of equally rare stones hung over his naked chest whilst his heavily belted kilt of pale linen was richly embroidered about the lower edges. In one, gold ring embellished hand he held a jewel encrusted golden goblet whilst close by waited a white-gowned, dark-skinned slave boy in whose lean arms was clutched a blue-glazed wine pitcher. Athens, like Mycenae, was not short of precious materials within the palace environment but even in this modest chamber was a refinement, an opulence of light and colour to rival anything Theseus or his father's court had witnessed.

154

'Bow to our king,' hissed one of the guards close behind Theseus.

The Athenians did as they were ordered, except for Theseus who stood resolutely still with arms folded. In the charged silence that followed, the guard, a wiry man of lesser build, placed a hand roughly on Theseus' neck in an attempt to force his head down. Theseus spun about, dashed the spear from the man's hand with a ringing clash of bronze against stone and would have hurled him protesting against the nearby column had not other guards intervened to seize his arms. Above this commotion the voice of Minos boomed out, 'All of you stop! Let the Athenian be!'

Releasing his grip on the startled guard, Theseus thrust the man away then turning to face Minos, declared, 'I am a prince of Athens. I bow to no man. I have made this voyage with my people of my own free will. I have come here to discover what fate befell those who were sent before us. My father, you should know, disapproved strongly of my journey.'

'Is that so,' responded Minos, gruffly, leaning back on his plushly appointed seat whilst drinking deeply from the goblet. 'I take it then you're the son of old man Aegeus – the one he kept secret from the world all these years then brought out of hiding to keep the hounds of Thorikos at bay.'

'That is indeed who I am,' replied Theseus, hands on hips, eyes fixed firmly on those of Minos.

For tense moments the two stared at one another with the king's expression growing dark as a thundercloud. Then Minos, shaking his head from side to side, laughed aloud as if on the verge of revealing the whole affair as some form of charade – no more than a trick intended to slight Aegeus for the amusement of an idle Cretan court.

'Spirit,' he spluttered, 'That's what I like. Spirit! And entertainment! Yes – and that!'

Suddenly his expression changed. 'The son of Aegeus!' he growled. 'Then the great King Aegeus must consider his offspring of little worth by allowing him to come so willingly into my domain!'

For tense moments it looked as though Minos might rise up, take hold of a spear and go for Theseus who yet remained calm and alert. Then as his voice moderated he leaned forward to peer more closely at the silent Athenians. One of the young women began to cry. Minos feigned sympathy, nodding his head to the amusement of courtiers and guards, whilst raising a hand to his own cheek so as to wipe away a mock tear. 'Be that as it may,' he continued, now effecting an impression of near indifference, 'flesh and blood are flesh and blood. You'll be taken from here to your quarters at the northern end of the courtyard and there remain for a number of days. You will not be locked away like criminals but will have freedom to use the open space of the courtyard as well as the area of your designated rooms. You will find Knossos somewhat cleaner, mercifully lacking the foul odours and the street filth of Athens. However,' Minos' expression once more hardened to one of carved stone, 'my guards are ever present so should any of you go beyond those set limits,' he paused effecting a broad, humourless grin, 'the penalty will be swift and it will be final.'

This was evidently to be the sum of their audience and as the Athenians were led away one of the youths asked Theseus, 'What will they do with us?'

'I don't know. I have heard only rumours in Athens and rumours are best kept under wraps until I am able to find out more.'

'But how *will* you find out?' asked another. 'They intend to watch us constantly.'

'I cannot say just yet but sooner or later I'll find a way of knowing their intentions. Meanwhile we should avoid provoking them to anger.'

***

Their quarters were light, airy, and compared with those enjoyed by most citizens of Athens, spacious. Food, which at Knossos seemed abundant, was brought to them by slaves. The food was set out on pottery dishes, exquisitely decorated with those ubiquitous marine motifs. On hand during the days that followed was a choice of bread, fish, mutton, pork, olives and figs, not so different from the home choice of mainland nobles but not the common fare of Theseus' young companions and their like. Honey seemed more a favourite here than on the mainland but above all there was the produce of the sea. The water they drank was untainted, the wine more delicate and satisfying than any they had known.

The rooms allocated to them each contained four wooden benches covered with a straw mattress and woollen blanket to serve after dark as their beds. The youths and girls had not been separated but were allowed to do as they pleased day or night. No one seemed to care that the sexes mixed freely

157

in a manner that would have been frowned upon by ordinary people in any mainland city. They had been informed by one of the guards that these rooms were used as prison cells but neither during the day nor at night was any door locked. Theseus, however, had noted armed men positioned at the ends of passages as well as in rooms close by. Discreet, yes, but always close at hand.

Late on the third day following their arrival two of the Athenian youths approached him in the courtyard. 'Lord Theseus,' said one, 'we're treated well and lack nothing except what is most important - our freedom. Most of the time the Cretans ignore us as if we have no reason to be here. We have little to keep ourselves occupied though there is always food and wine on hand. So much wine that we're tempted to drink more than we ought and when we do we forget we are prisoners.' The youth hesitated, glancing at his companion.

'Well, go on,' Theseus said.

'Why do we remain here,' the young man continued, 'when we could leave quietly at night then make our way to the harbour? You must have seen how lax the guards have become. At night they drink wine, they entertain slave girls in their quarters and seem quite unconcerned about us.'

'We may not be seafarers,' added his companion, 'but some of us have helped our parents with their boats when out fishing and we watched how they managed the ship that brought us here. We've sufficient confidence to handle a smaller vessel at sea and that's all we'd need. We're becoming restless. We want to see Athens, our families and our friends again.'

'Doing what you suggest is most likely what they expect of us,' responded Theseus. 'It could be the excuse they're waiting for, though eventually none may be needed. The laxity they have shown toward us is no act of kind consideration by Minos. The fact that they let us eat, drink and sleep together is a sign that whatever we do no longer matters since it is sooner or later to end. Yes they prefer to keep us fit and healthy but I feel Minos is playing a deadly game – no, I'm quite sure he is.'

'You're saying we really are to die?' asked the first youth. 'How?'

'I believe that's their intention. How, I cannot say, in spite of certain rumours, but if it were not so then our purpose in Minos' palace would have been made clear by now.'

'Then,' insisted the second youth, 'we've nothing to lose in trying to escape. Why should we wait around until they decide to kill us? We all agree - we should find a way out of the palace and head down to the harbour as soon as we can. We could do it tonight.'

'I urge you *not* to attempt anything yet,' insisted Theseus. 'Listen to me; I will stay up tonight or the next night and make my way past the guards. I planned to do it from the beginning but it would have been foolish to act too soon. I intend to find out all I can so if there *is* a way of our getting out unnoticed then I intend to discover it.'

The pair seemed unconvinced so Theseus continued, 'Look - we have to know what we're up against before we try anything. The palace is large and you don't know your way about any more than I do. Its passages and stairways are so complicated

159

we'd wander aimlessly until they caught up with us. Worse still, we have no weapons to defend ourselves and the girls. D'you understand what I'm saying?'

'We understand,' replied the second youth. 'But Lord Theseus, the air of Knossos may be sweet but in it we taste approaching danger. It's as if the Cretans are fattening us up for sacrifice. We'll pass your words on, nevertheless - but the others grow more restless by the day.'

'Hold back a while and trust me,' smiled Theseus. 'I didn't come here for the food and wine, either.'

Chapter 8
The CHARMS of ARIADNE

The Athenian had dominated her thoughts from the moment he and his party entered the courtyard. If Apollo himself, the ideal of manly beauty had appeared before her, the god could not have presented a more desirable image. Ariadne peered into the night. She waited in shadowed silence, savouring the cool air as a fine wine, listening to the call of insects, to the playful flow of water with as much pleasure as she might her favourite harpist. The light of this new masculine image dispelled for a time the shadows that all too often haunted her during those long hours of darkness. Even her nocturnal diversions with the redoubtable Tauros had hardly managed that. How could this beautiful man, this prince of Athens, be condemned to breathe the same air as that abomination nurtured by her parents?

From the obscurity of the colonnade where oil lamps on elaborate stands eased back the darkness a little she stepped into the open space, gazed up at the moon and stars, looked about the deserted courtyard and caressed her naked breasts, imagining her hands to be those of the Athenian. 'Perhaps he will take the air tonight,' she whispered, 'though he did not last night or the night before. I have prayed at our shrines. Perhaps if I will it to happen – perhaps if I call into the darkness.' Ariadne gazed to the northern end of the courtyard. Within its obscurity stood the door from which she yearned for him to appear.

A sound. Footsteps. Not from the direction she faced but from her right - from the east wing of the palace. Ariadne feared to retreat back the way she had come because in so doing she would attract the attention of whoever was moving unseen in the darkness.

Then a voice. 'Lady Ariadne - are you alone?'

With a sigh that failed to stifle pangs of disappointment, she replied, 'Oh, Daedalus, it's you. I thought perhaps – oh, never mind.'

'Yes, it's me, and I see you are indeed alone. But perhaps I'm intruding on your privacy. If so I will continue on my way.'

His voice was reassuring though it was not the voice she had wanted to hear.

'No,' she answered as the gowned figure stepped into the moonlight, 'you are not intruding. I couldn't sleep as usual. I find the air indoors so oppressive at times.'

'Then I must apologise for any deficiencies in my method of channelling fresh air,' he smiled. 'I know you often walk alone after dark. I myself do so on the odd occasion. Now and again I see you but I go on my way because I know you prefer to remain alone with your thoughts. I on the other hand have many plans. Yes, my inspiration is at its best when the sun has gone from the sky. I'm planning a more efficient kind of loom - one that will enable us to –. Oh, do forgive me, princess – I shouldn't bore others with my schemes until they are ready and demonstrable for all to see.'

Ariadne smiled. She had been familiar with his wise face since her earliest childhood. Daedalus had with his own hands made the toys she, her sisters and her brothers had played with. They were clever, beautifully crafted toys that only his fertile mind could have conceived. Cunningly jointed dolls – so life-like. She recalled her brothers playing with those little wheeled chariots that carried tiny figures painted in exquisite detail.

But more than the manufacture of mere toys, Daedalus had added significantly to the comforts of the palace. He had improved the supply of water with his clever system of pumps, pipes, conduits and channels. To grey-haired, bearded Daedalus, craft and ingenuity were all, no matter what their purpose. And Ariadne knew his deepest secrets just as he knew hers. She knew of his fleeing Athens all those years ago after the murder of an apprentice whose body was found below the acropolis. She knew of his devious work for Minos, of that unmentionable, of that bizarre contrivance fashioned for the king's wife - a tale she was soon to reveal.

'Yes, I have trouble sleeping,' she breathed. 'And you know why.'

'Yes,' he said in a low voice, 'I know to what you refer and I am in the end to blame. But what I did was not undertaken with thoughts of malice to anyone – no, it was a challenge to my imagination, to my craft. But it was in any case done by the order of Queen Pasiphae, your exalted mother. Sometimes she and your father give me contradictory orders, which means I must appear to obey them both. Dear me - things can be rather trying on occasion, especially at my time of life.'

'I don't blame you, Daedalus. Others might if they knew, and there are those who think they have guessed the truth. Still, my father will always protect you unless -.'

'There's no need to say it, Lady Ariadne. We see the king's moods swing in one direction and then the other. There are times when he is at odds with himself. Everyone close to him is conscious of that.'

Ariadne looked beyond him to the darkness of the colonnade. 'How soon must the people from Athens be -?'

'I cannot say for sure,' replied Daedalus. 'Much depends upon your father's disposition - if I may put it that way. But I doubt it will be long before he is prompted to act. Your mother above all would not allow for undue delay. On the other hand I doubt anything will happen before the bull leapers' ceremony - and that is almost upon us.'

'Yes,' she sighed, 'their blood will taint the stones of Knossos even before that of the Athenians. The pleasure of witnessing our bull leapers is one of the few vices I do not share with the same enthusiasm as other members of my family.'

'It is a tradition going back many generations,' said Daedalus. 'It was old even before the Greeks, your father's ancestors, came here. Tradition tells us it has always been an honour to take part in the ceremony. And dangerous or no, there has never been a lack of volunteers, men or women, high or low – even criminals. The rewards are great for those who succeed.'

'And often a pitiable end for those who do not,' responded Ariadne.

'Yes indeed, pitiable,' muttered Daedalus, turning his gaze from her.

'But at least they have a choice,' she continued. 'At least they enter the ordeal willingly – unlike those people I saw paraded across this courtyard only days ago. The young man who led them is a prince of Athens - or so I hear. Should not he at least - should not all of them have some hope of reprieve? I ask the question even though you'll tell me they have no hope whatsoever.'

'Your parents would never hear of it,' replied Daedalus. 'It's not just that they are content to bow to the gods in this case. A few sacrifices, a few oracular consultations might throw a different light on things if they themselves cared to look upon the matter with greater leniency. Though your mother seldom speaks of it she is consumed inwardly with thoughts of little else as the time for its implementation approaches. And consider your father. His desire to avenge himself upon Athens is boundless. They defied him, you see – they drove his army from the walls of the city, they humiliated him greatly when our noble king is used to getting his own way. Above all there was his son, Androgeus, who was killed - murdered as your father insists, by the Athenians.'

'Yes,' breathed Ariadne, 'but my father becomes more impetuous as time goes by. Only last month he banished his own daughter - *our* sister, Acalle, to our trading colony in Libya. He said it was because she'd become pregnant by a man he didn't approve of. At least that was the excuse he came up with. We're not supposed to discuss it but you can't keep that sort of thing secret for long. She was too independent for his liking – *that* was the real reason. It made things worse when the silly girl claimed she'd been visited in the night by Apollo. That was her excuse to try and get away with it.'

'I agree, very sad,' nodded Daedalus. 'And her a royal princess as are you and Lady Phaedra.'

'That's the irony of the affair. Since being daughters of a king we have fewer rights by far than most high born Cretan women. *They* can marry whoever they wish – a servant, even a slave if it takes their fancy, as well as doing as they please with their own property. We're subject to the rules of father's court. As for our brothers, Glaucus and Catreus, he barely tolerates them of late but instead gloats over Deucalion, whose mother could be almost any of the palace women but certainly isn't *our* own mother. Just look at his eyes – at his nose. Mother tries to pretend he doesn't exist. Give her half a chance and I doubt if he would exist for much longer.' Ariadne wrung her hands together. 'Then there's that loathsome creature they -. Oh, it's all too much! I almost envy Acalle being in Libya. At least she's out of – of all of it.'

'And your sister Phaedra,' asked Daedalus, 'how does she feel? She seldom passes time in conversation with me. She regards me as some kind of relic to be dusted off and brought out whenever there's an odd job to be done. Her mind always seems elsewhere.'

'You're right - she cares about one thing and one thing only much of the time, though I'd better not go into that.' Ariadne squeezed his bony arm, adding, 'Look, I shouldn't be speaking like this. I hope you'll forget everything I've said. You know I trust you.'

'Oh, consider it forgotten, dear lady,' answered Daedalus with a dismissive wave of his hand. 'But I must go now. Icarus, my own son, and I have another little project we need to discuss over a cup or two of wine. I have this other new idea, you see. It's a device that could improve the – er, no, I won't bore you with that right now either; so if you will excuse me, Lady Ariadne.'

'Of course, but one more favour you could grant me, Daedalus, dear. One that would put me ever deeper into your debt.'

'Anything in my power,' he smiled, 'but never must you consider yourself under obligation to me.'

'Then,' she continued, 'it – it would please me to speak with this Athenian prince. I wish to know more about him; more about his people – without, that is – without my father or anyone else at all knowing, including Phaedra.' Ariadne folded her arms and turned aside. 'No, perhaps I'm making it appear too important. It really isn't. But - but if the opportunity happened to arise - that's all.'

Daedalus, his head lowered deep in thought for some moments replied, 'It wouldn't surprise me if he were to take the air here in the courtyard tomorrow evening at about this time - perhaps a little earlier. No, not at all it wouldn't. And as you are so often about when others sleep you er, yes, you might encounter him. If you do, I hear his name is Theseus - yes, that was it, Theseus.'

Daedalus left her alone under the stars and Ariadne smiled.

***

'I am given to understand you are a prince of Athens, sir, and that your name is Theseus.'

167

Theseus turned away from the balcony overlooking a courtyard that still lay in morning shadow. The sun was yet to appear above the palace buildings. Gazing upon the man who stood there in long gown of finely woven white wool he was reminded of Haemon, whose lyre so sweetened the air of his father's too often cheerless court. This man, however, was not as venerable and might have appeared a little younger had he cut back or shaved away his abundant facial hair. He had no stoop and at first appeared to have retained all of his teeth, though another glance told Theseus this was not quite as it seemed.

'Several of them are crafted from ivory, sir, if that is what you were wondering,' smiled Daedalus on noting his interest. 'I make them for others hereabouts just as I made these for myself. Better than using teeth from the dead even if mine don't last as long.'

'I didn't mean to be rude,' said Theseus, suppressing a grin. 'They're quite remarkable.'

'No man, indeed no woman in Knossos needs fear the embarrassment of a toothless mouth, a hairless head, the shame of an empty eye socket or the inconvenience of a missing hand or foot if they have but modest funds to part with. Except, that is, when I, Daedalus, am too busy dealing with such mundane matters as our water supply or the palace drains.'

'Ah, so you are the Daedalus whose reputation has spread to every city on the mainland. They still speak of the day in Athens when you pushed your – well, never mind that. I regret to say neither I nor any of my companions are likely to need your services unless the nature of our intended punishment is such that one day soon we will. An artificial hand or foot, perhaps?'

'I think it most unlikely, sir, even though you jest. But before we talk further I would be happier if we moved back into the shadows so that we may remain out of sight. The king would be none too pleased if someone reported me as having bribed the guards to obtain private conversation with you.'

Both men stepped back between two of the great columns of the balcony.

'Oh, you bribed the guards,' smiled Theseus. 'With gold? With silver? With new teeth? D'you do this often?'

'There are occasions, young sir, when I feel I am obliged to do it. Sometimes it's with a promise of keeping quiet over what I know they have been up to when they're supposed to be on duty.'

Theseus peered at him in anticipation of hearing the message a man of such importance might be about to impart.

'I came here to discuss your situation,' continued Daedalus. 'It interests me.'

'Oh, does it!' responded Theseus. 'It interests me as well, *and* the rest of my people so I hope you're going to throw some light on it – starting with Minos' intentions and an account of what happened to those brought here from Athens in past years. My companions are understandably restless. They talk of attempting to escape. I have so far dissuaded them.'

'Quite right, sir,' agreed Daedalus. 'You'd never find your way out before the guards were onto you – and I ought to know. Whichever route you took there would probably be a short cut somewhere or other for them to head you off. Either that or they'd ride you down well before you gained the harbour.'

'Then what's the purpose of your visit? Is it to determine our state of mind so you can report back to Minos?

'If that were the case, dear boy, I'd hardly trouble to conceal myself. No, it is for your possible benefit - if I read things correctly. At least that's what I'm hoping.'

'Then as you're concerned about our wellbeing,' said Theseus, eyeing him closely, 'perhaps you'd care to tell me what Minos has planned. And what is the truth, if any, about this hidden beast I heard tales of back in Athens? There are rumours our people have been sacrificed to the thing?'

Daedalus had until then presented an image of good-natured calm. His expression changed to one of unease. He gazed aside before replying, 'I – I cannot tell you anything of that at present.'

'You mean you *will* not!'

'Please,' responded Daedalus, raising his hands, 'I have little say in what Minos does under these circumstances and - and my past service would count for precious little if my tongue became too loose. In fact he might have it removed altogether. Hardly anyone is safe nowadays if he turns his anger upon them, except perhaps -.'

'Except perhaps who?' demanded Theseus.

'Young man,' answered Daedalus, 'I recommend you enjoy the cool air of the courtyard

170

after dark this evening, as your quarters are close by.'

'Enjoy the air! You risked being seen just to tell me that?'

'You should do as I suggest,' he replied, gravely, turning to leave, 'it could be most beneficial to you, sir – yes, most beneficial. And I have a feeling you may learn somewhat more than I have felt able to divulge. And as far as the guards are concerned – well, I doubt you will experience any difficulties. As a bonus for their dedication to duty I'll see to it they receive an additional flagon of my strongest wine to augment their evening rations.'

Before Theseus could question him further, he was gone, making his way back along the corridor from which he had shortly before emerged. Thinking over Daedalus' words, Theseus returned his attention to the courtyard only to see the old man himself appear below, hurrying across the open space with his gown billowing like a sail.

***

Amidst the sea of stars a three quarter moon hung poised above the rooftops, gleaming through the silhouetted line of stylised stone bulls' horns that topped the upper storeys. Somewhere in the night the distant yapping of a dog broke an otherwise charged silence.

Theseus, in belted linen kilt and sandals, savoured the cool air of the courtyard. Watching from amidst the deeper shadows of a recess he began now to wonder if this could be a ploy to lure him away from his people so that Minos' men could seize him. If that happened his companions and those back in Athens might never know his fate. There was nothing he desired more than to have his sword at his side so that should they come for him, their task would be no easy affair. Some at least would choke on their own gore and never again taste the sweet air of morning. His hand passed instinctively down to where the sword should have been. Backing into deeper shadows he listened hard for approaching footsteps, for the sound of voices, for the death-hiss of blades sliding from scabbards.

Something moved. A shadow amidst the darkness of the colonnade opposite to where he waited. A figure. Theseus watched in silence. The figure, that of a woman, passed into the vague pool of light cast by a hanging lamp before moving into the courtyard where she hesitated to look around. Theseus watched for guarded moments before stepping out from the columns. He moved quietly, pausing only when she sensed his approach.

'Stay where you are,' called the girl, though she did not sound afraid. 'Who are you?'

'I am one of your king's recently acquired Athenians,' he answered. 'And you?'

'I am Ariadne, a daughter of the king. Tell me why you are here.'

'Why? Well - I came out to take the night air. I, er – I thought it was a good idea. Please don't go - I intend you no harm.'

'No, I'm sure you don't,' she replied. 'You may come closer if you care to speak with me. But, no, I will join you where it's darkest; it would be better if I did. We ought not to raise our voices. You never know who might overhear.'

'Are you alone?' he asked as she stopped an arm's length before him.

'For the time being,' she answered. 'And I trust you are also alone. You are lucky; you didn't have far to walk. You need a slave with firebrand to find your way about after dark unless you're as familiar as I am with the palace. Anyway, father doesn't like people wandering about at night – not nowadays. It's easy for us, my sister and I, that is – though our rooms are quite some way from this courtyard.'

'Lucky? Well that depends on your point of view.' With eyes by now accustomed to the night, to the soft illumination of the stars and the moon, he was able to make out her features. She was captivating; the kind of woman who stalked the mind of every red-blooded male long before his gaze falls upon her. Her hair was laced with beads strung on fine gold chains. Where free it cascaded about her shoulders, about her full, firm, breasts. Naked breasts held as a perfumed offering by the stiffened bodice of her gown.

'So,' breathed Theseus, glancing cautiously by her to confirm she really was alone, 'a daughter of the king. Whatever next? Then permit me to say, Princess Ariadne, that you are very beautiful and surely fit to entice the gods themselves.'

'You are very kind, Prince Theseus,' she replied with a red-lipped smile.

'Oh, so you know who I am,' he grinned. 'Then I regret I'm unable to offer you any of the gifts a prince ought to offer a princess. But as I'm sure you are aware, I and my companions are here as prisoners of your father and we still don't know what delights he has in store for us. Maybe you do

173

and maybe you'd care to enlighten me; we hear strange tales.'

Ariadne lowered her gaze then looked back into his eyes. 'Then let this princess offer a little comfort to the prince. Father would fly into a perfect rage if he saw us together but you will be safe enough taking wine with me. The slaves are dismissed and those guards not stupefied by drink occupy themselves at the gaming board or with the slave girls. I'm not supposed to know about that but what they get up to seems to harm no one.'

Theseus followed her slim, swaying figure along the east-side of the courtyard, through a folding door that led into a long corridor dimly lit by oil lamps glowing on slender stands. Immediately to their right ascended a stone staircase. About to climb this, Ariadne hesitated. 'Before we take wine you might care to see the king's megaron. There should be enough light.'

Theseus once more suspected a trap but replied, calmly, 'If that is your wish then, yes, I'd certainly like to see it.' Should it be a trap with Ariadne as voluptuous bait, he thought, then she might in turn serve as his hostage. How far would Minos risk the wellbeing of his own daughter – if this alluring girl really was his daughter.

At the top of the stairs they entered another corridor where, beneath a repeating motif of double-headed axes, the richly frescoed walls were adorned with processions of young people carrying all manner of rich offerings. Admirable as he knew they must be, Theseus had little inclination to study them in detail.

Some way along they turned right. Ariadne pushed open a folding door and was followed by Theseus into a spacious hall. Over twice the size of Minos' throne room, this was lit by small braziers placed at intervals close to the walls as well as from flames that burned in a circular bronze hearth placed on three squat legs in the middle of the area. Here the theme of the double axes was expressed in the round. A number of them hung in gilded splendour along walls painted in wave-flowing russet and pale yellow. The axes alternated with large, figure of eight shields more ornate than those on display in his father's great hall. This was the first warlike display he had witnessed at Knossos though he considered these must be ceremonial.

One wall was given over to painted ships, great fleets of vessels – some in full sail with coasts, harbours and cities depicted in the background. Other vessels were shown under oars, many in battle, having archers and swordsmen on their decks as well as men with firebrands at the ready to torch their enemies' sails and timbers. Now unavoidably fascinated yet instinctively alert, Theseus followed her from this hall into an adjacent room of similar size and style of decoration, divided from the former by a row of square piers fitted with cedar wood dividing doors that presently stood open. In here stood a royal throne similar to that occupied by Minos on the occasion of their first encounter.

'So this really is the great king's megaron,' remarked Theseus, gazing at reclining griffin frescoes depicted either side of the throne. 'I'm suitably impressed.'

'This is where father entertains the lords and ambassadors from other lands,' said Ariadne, facing back the way they had come. 'Beyond here are the rooms where they are housed. But we must return now. Father would burst a blood vessel if he knew I'd brought you here. He'd show you little mercy and I'd be locked away for days. I'd probably end up in one of our colonies as my sister did.'

'Then why *did* you bring me?'

'I – I wanted you to see the wonders of Knossos and the way we live because -.' She hesitated, gazed into his eyes then whispered, 'Please, we should stay here no longer. Someone may see us even though most of the palace sleeps.'

Ariadne started back not to the stone staircase but along another passage, this open to the sky along one colonnaded side. Theseus glanced down to see below the courtyard where they had met only a short while before. He trod close behind, ever attentive yet lured onward in the wake of her perfume and by the alluring sway of her body. She turned sharply but within the next passage stopped, glancing about to ensure they remained unobserved. Confronting them were more screens, yet another, narrower corridor, as confusing to Theseus as those on the floor below. Some way along she pushed open yet another folding door and stepped through, gesturing for him to follow before closing it.

Almost opposite the room they had entered, another door stood slightly ajar. From the darkness within, eyes watched Ariadne's door swing shut, the jealous eyes of a hungry soul, the eyes of one whose carnal desires were great as those of Ariadne. One who had not yet learned to harness those desires to serve beyond the realms of her bed. 'So, sister dear,' came her sigh, 'Tauros and his men aren't enough for you. Now you have the Athenian. Well, you know what we were taught as children - share and share alike. Make the best of him while you can.'

Ariadne possessed a smouldering charm Theseus was finding irresistible. There was to be no pursuit of conquest here, no pleasure of the chase. Pleasure was an incoming tide from which he had no urge to flee. Her naked breasts were warm and full in his caress as they kissed in the dimly lit, luxuriously furnished haven of a painted chamber where across frescoed walls leaped blue dolphins and other denizens of the sea. Each bathed in the aura of other's arousal yet for Theseus, thoughts of trickery and danger that might be the motive behind this liaison persisted despite the glowing heat of passion.

His lips tingled her ear. 'Lady Ariadne, you are quite as intoxicating as the wine of your country.'

'Something we're never short of my darling,' she whispered, running hot-feather fingers down to the base of his spine.

'And beautiful as the sun is bright,' he breathed, lips brushing her long neck, fingers and tongue teasing inflamed nipples. 'I'd challenge any mortal – no the gods themselves, to deny it.'

'Better not do that, Prince Theseus,' she sighed. 'You never know what might happen if the gods were listening.'

Ariadne offered no resistance as he unfastened the small hooks at the rear of her long dress but encouraged him instead by the ardour of her kisses and the intimate play of her hand that caused him to groan softly. Soon they were naked, abandoned to an ardour so intense as to banish from both all thoughts of the world beyond, writhing together on her bed as serpents locked in mortal combat. Three times Ariadne's cries swept like cooing birds about the darkened corners of the room whilst Theseus, consumed in a turmoil of lust no longer cared that he might have been lured into mortal peril by her wiles. If she was bait to bring about his demise then for the time being life seemed not too great a forfeit.

Only afterwards, only when both were sated by the fruits of pleasure, did they relax side by side to take the wine Ariadne kept in a painted flagon by her curtained window. 'You're an adorable man,' she smiled, as Theseus filled the goblets.

'Lady Ariadne,' he replied, raising the goblet, 'how could such good fortune fall upon me, a mere hostage to your father's vengeance?'

'Good fortune may not always announce itself in advance,' she smiled. 'It has fallen upon me also now you're here.'

As she spoke the deep chime of a gong drifted in from somewhere beyond the walls. Theseus, putting aside the goblet, half rose from the bed. 'What was that? It sounded like a warning. If it's to call people out then I'd better leave you for both our sakes – except I don't have the slightest idea how to find my way back.'

'It's not a warning,' she replied. 'The priest whose job it is to measure passing time strikes it to announce the middle of the night. I'm told people usually don't hear it if they're asleep. During the day it's used to proclaim the beginning of a festival or important event. There's no need for you to go yet. Morning is a long way off.'

'Those who came with me from Athens will be concerned over my absence. They look to me for reassurance even if I presently can offer them little.'

'I, too, need reassurance,' she said, placing a hand on his shoulder, and I promise you, no harm will befall your people tonight. I know it will not.'

'Then you must know what Minos has planned; you must know what happened to those who preceded us. Ariadne, what does Minos intend to do with us? What truth is there in those tales we hear in Athens of a beast they keep here?'

Ariadne rose to her feet, her eyes searching into his, her voice tinged with misgiving. 'Yes, you – you must have heard about -.'

'Tell me the truth,' insisted Theseus, rising to grasp her arms, making her face him as she attempted to look away. 'Tell me and I'll gladly stay with you until dawn if that's what you want – but I have to know!'

For several heartbeats Ariadne remained silent, unable to give voice to her thoughts. When at last she spoke it was in a calm but grave tone. 'Yes, Theseus, you must have the truth. What I'm about to tell you is known in full only to a small number of people here at Knossos, though I dare say others even beyond Crete have made much of hearsay. The walls of this palace seep rumour about all sorts of things – far too many of them truths about which we dare not speak. But when I'm finished I will ask something of you.'

'Then ask me now. I can't think of a better time.'

'No - not yet. First hear what I have to say - then I'll ask. But first refill our goblets. More wine will certainly help me keep calm.'

Muttering, 'Probably me as well,' Theseus poured a generous measure for both then returned to sit on the bed. Ariadne joined him, drank deeply then began. 'You saw Knossos when you came up from the harbour with your companions. You saw our people going about their business though you have seen little more since you were brought within the palace walls. Still, I'm sure you had the impression every visitor has of a happy, a powerful and prosperous kingdom. That is true enough as most outsiders measure things. But - but beneath the light, the life and colour of the palace, beneath these wonderful buildings and the beautiful people you see flitting about the corridors, there is a hidden world. Theseus - it is a world of darkness where something so terrible awaits that those who truly know of it are forbidden by our father on pain of death to utter its name. And if they were not forbidden, they would still be loath to speak it. Even that far greater number within the palace having no involvement dare not be heard relating any tales they might have heard for the same reason.'

Ariadne's hand trembled as she again lifted the goblet to her lips. 'Queen Pasiphae, our mother, began it all when we were small children, though I've heard say the cause runs deep within our family. You may in the end make of that what you will. What I'm saying is that she was – is, quite insatiable. Her lovers have been more in number than even she can remember. When father bothers to take notice, which he does if she gets too brazen about it, he has them exiled or worse – but that's mainly to keep up appearances.

When we were children, father would tell us of the time he acquired his kingdom and his power over other men, including his own brothers. He claimed it was through his frequent prayers and sacrifices to Poseidon that Knossos became his. He later boasted how he would sacrifice anything to the god of the sea in order to show his gratitude. Poseidon evidently took him at his word by calling up a storm so fierce that no ship could ride it. From those breaking waves emerged a great white bull. It scared the wits out of those who first saw it but when word got about that it wasn't too dangerous, it was brought here to the palace. Father later received instructions in his time of prayer to glorify Poseidon not only in Knossos but throughout all Crete by public sacrifice of the bull in the open ceremonial area west of the palace. Father never intended to defy the god for longer than necessary but saw the creature as good breeding stock. Our mother persuaded him to keep putting the sacrifice off but the priests insisted he get it over with so as to avoid angering Poseidon. Oh, he acted all right but not the way he was supposed to, though he wasn't entirely happy about it.'

'It seems the good lady has quite some influence over him,' Theseus remarked.

'She certainly has when it suits him, yes. He sacrificed a different bull – a substitute coloured with paste made out of fish glue and white chalk in the hope that it would fool everyone.'

'Fish glue and white chalk!' laughed Theseus.

181

'Our mother prevailed on him to do that with the help of Daedalus,' she continued, 'the cleverest and the greatest craftsman this land ever saw. Of course it didn't fool quite everyone - imagine the smell if you were standing close by – though as most people were not that close, he thought he'd got away with it. Yes, we all thought he had for a time.'

Ariadne drained her goblet then resumed her narrative. 'That piece of trickery soon became common knowledge within our household but much of what I'll reveal next was not learned so freely. Unknown to father she approached Daedalus again. How she persuaded him to do what he did may not be difficult to guess at but he did it anyway. There was gossip about in those days that he'd shared her bed – he's not that much older than her after all, even though he looks it. Nowadays it's the last thing either of them would admit to, even under torture.'

Theseus drained his goblet and gestured for her to continue.

Ariadne paused, sighed aloud then resumed, 'Well whatever the truth, she had him construct a life-sized model cow – much more than just a model. It was clad in cowhide; it even had false eyes that stared out at you and he somehow got it to smell right. It was so realistic, so convincing, that the bull sent by Poseidon needed no goading to mount the thing, which it did on several occasions. Only the two men who took the bull to the cow saw it do that, or so it was intended. They must have been much amused and must have asked themselves why it was being done. Mother had sworn the pair to secrecy on pain of death and both men have since disappeared without anyone daring to ask how or why. What those men didn't know – at least what only she and Daedalus were supposed to know - and I swear by the gods this is true - was that when the bull coupled with the model, mother was contained inside it to receive the creature in her desire for lustful satisfaction. That, she insisted afterwards when Phaedra and I told her that we also knew about it, was Poseidon's punishment for *her* part in persuading father to pervert the god's wishes. A neat excuse if ever I heard one. The only reason she didn't have us punished or sent away from Crete is because she knew we'd tell everyone what we'd seen.'

'My, what an interesting family you have,' grinned Theseus, slipping an arm about her slim waist while refilling their goblets. 'But how did you and your sister discover this so closely guarded secret?'

'We did what children often do if they're as curious as we were. We and our brothers used to creep about the corridors at night, daring one another to go where we were not supposed to go. It was innocent enough. All we wanted to do was play hide and seek. We wandered into parts of the palace where we risked getting lost, and sometimes we did. You've seen for yourself what a rambling maze of a place Knossos is.'

'You can say that again,' breathed Theseus.

'Phaedra and I crept out after mother one evening when she wasn't aware of it - this time without our brothers who were playing in the courtyard, or Acalle who was feeling unwell. We followed mother to an unused part of the palace below ground level then hid behind some old storage jars. To us it was no more than a harmless game. Even when we saw her open up one side of the model cow then climb into it quite naked we thought in our childish innocence she was playing some kind of grown-up's hide and seek. We were on the verge of running up and banging on the side to frighten her - then we heard voices and snorting, and thought better of it. When the bull was brought in to mount the model cow, we understood even at that tender age we were witnessing something we were never meant to see. Yes, we knew we'd better keep quiet about it no matter what.

Anyway, her secret ritual came to an end when the bull realised what it had been missing. It broke out of its compound one night then ran amok in the countryside, destroying fences, doing what bulls usually do with cows and terrorising the farmers. It had learned a thing or two about humans by then so it was too crafty as well as too powerful for anyone to catch. When the situation got bad enough the country people threatened to march on Knossos with firebrands. Tauros, father's general, wanted to ride out with his archers and shoot it dead but father forbade that. He wouldn't dare see such a holy offering killed on Cretan soil. You can imagine how relieved everyone was when Heracles appeared on the scene with orders to capture it single-handed and take it off to the mainland as one of his twelve labours.'

'I can indeed,' breathed Theseus. 'That was when we met and very busy he was at the time.'

'Well, by then,' she continued, 'father must have heard gossip concerning the false cow but since our family has always been awash with scandal he chose to ignore it for a while. When the rumours refused to die down he suspected something outlandish had been going on and started asking questions. Fortunately for her, mother had seen the model cow burned to ashes before father or anyone of importance had a chance to set eyes on it. What he'd have done to her, even to Daedalus if he'd discovered the whole truth at the time doesn't bare thinking about.

Since then she and that crafty old man imagines each has a hold over the other. Mother has tried all manner of plots in the past to get rid of Daedalus, including poison, but he's too quick-witted. I'll swear he knows her better than she knows herself. In any case there are people in the palace who keep him informed of whatever she's up to. She's put it about lately that Daedalus has taken to sorcery; that he spends his time conjuring up all kinds of horrors, but father takes little notice. It's because I'm often about at night that I hear what they and others intend no one else should hear. What I know scares me so I pass much of it on to Phaedra and to Deucalion in case my dear parents find out.'

'And now you're telling it to me, a stranger condemned by your own father. Why?'

'Because of what I intend to ask when I'm finished. And anyway, Theseus darling, you're hardly a stranger any more, are you.' Ariadne kissed him on the cheek, adding, 'And what if you did tell anyone? Who would believe it except mother and once she got to know, you'd be feeding the crows – or something very much worse.'

Theseus raised his goblet. 'Well here's to a happy family.'

'You'd better keep the wine on hand if you want to know the rest,' breathed Ariadne, raising hers. 'I know we're both going to need it.'

Ariadne turned aside, a hand pressed against her cheek, her eyes wide. Their shadows, cast by the two small lamps, swayed eerily across the walls. She peered into her wine as though in the amber liquid was mirrored those darker memories she was now to recall. 'A few months after the false cow was destroyed we noticed mother was pregnant again. This was to be her eighth if you include my sisters and brothers. Everyone except father, who seemed to no longer care, wondered who it would look like - himself, his general or one of the palace guards – even one of the slaves. She'd visited several oracles in secret to ask about the child's future but always came back tight-lipped so we never found out what their response was.'

Gripping her goblet in both hands, Ariadne stared hard into Theseus' eyes. 'I was there when the child was born. Yes, at the time it was a child to all who saw it - frail and vulnerable as any human baby. They had already decided it was to be a son because of the way it kicked and moved inside her so they dropped all thought of a female name well before the birth. They determined on the one name – Asterion. At least mother did – she claimed it had been given to her in a dream by some unseen god.

Father sent our priests out, this time officially as would be expected, to consult the major oracles but they were for once reluctant to speak other than in terms vague even for them. Except – except at Delphi where the priestess announced the child would one day be master in his own kingdom.

Father took it to mean he would conquer someone else's once he grew up rather than rule here at Knossos. That suited him since he's always had his eye on Deucalion for the succession.

There was something wrong with the child from the beginning - we could all see there was. But at first no one dared say what they thought in case Pasiphae flew into one of her rages. Even our father kept his mouth shut though I often saw him look at little Asterion then walk away shaking his head. We children could tell they were as disturbed by the sight of Asterion, especially when mother refused to have him at her breast. He was squat and ugly, his head too broad, his little piggy eyes too wide apart. We all found him quite frightening after a month had gone by. And when it – when he, cried it wasn't the cry of a normal child – no, it was more a snarl.

To keep up appearances, mother insisted Asterion was no more than an unhealthy child who would grow up to be normal if properly cared for. Except,' Ariadne shivered, closing her eyes as if trying to come to terms with her memories, 'except that when he stared at us with those cold eyes, it was as if he knew we detested him. Yes, as if he had known it even before he was born. His gaze was hard and menacing as though he regarded us as we regarded him - loathsome. I became so fearful I dared not stay alone in the room with him in spite of his small size, though he was growing quickly. Nor did my sisters. Nor did the housemaids. My brothers were fortunate in not being around to see him at all. Eventually, only the slaves would tend him – but that was because they were ordered to and dared not disobey. Just the sound of him, pitter-patter, pitter-patter, pitter-pattering over the tiled floors left me cold and fearful.

As time went by he started becoming aggressive and – and worse. They would catch him in the palace kitchens devouring raw meat on the floor the way a dog does with scraps. He'd snarl and bare his teeth at anyone who tried to stop him then one day he actually went for the throat of one of the female slaves, killed and was caught trying to eat her. Father was appalled, especially as the girl had several times shared his bed. He ordered Asterion confined to a secluded area of the palace in case word got about that he and Pasiphae had brought a monstrosity into the world. Father now came to accept this as Poseidon's vengeance upon *him* over the affair of the white bull but was convinced that to kill the thing – the child, would call yet more of the god's anger down on us. He consulted the oracles for guidance but would not reveal their response, which meant it could not have been good.

Armed men from the palace guard were appointed by drawing lots each day to keep Asterion out of sight and feed him the way he seemed to prefer but they abstained from that duty whenever they thought they could get away with it. Word got out as it had to sooner or later so father told everyone that Asterion was deformed but was to be kept alive because the gods spoke through him. Which gods he referred to, I really can't imagine.

Mother avoided him entirely, as did the rest of us. Those who had been ordered to tend him called Asterion the 'Minotaur' – the Minos-Bull. The name soon got around. People whispered it though at the time I had no idea why. Months passed before I saw Asterion again and I thank Father Zeus it was the last time though I - I will never forget that day. No, never.' Once more Ariadne closed her eyes, raising a hand to her face and drinking more wine before she was able to continue her account. 'Theseus, I had a small white dog - a present given me on my seventh birthday. He had the run of the palace. He used to play games of hide and seek with us. One day he ran off into a wing of the palace where we children had been ordered never to go but that didn't seem to matter to us at the time. I expected I would find my dog or that he'd come running to me if I called him. But he didn't appear when I called, so - so I went on looking.

I found myself searching in empty rooms, around deserted corridors with only the echo of my own voice for company. I heard him barking somewhere close ahead then - then squealing in terror. I pushed open the door to a darkened room and - and as the light flooded in I saw Asterion crouching in the far corner. Since I had last seen him he'd grown much larger than I could have believed. Dark hair had appeared in curls all over his body and that - that terrible face – that head. Theseus, it was a horned head. Almost a - a bull's head. Yet the mouth was full of sharp teeth more like a big cat than a human being! There was a stench of corruption about the place – quite unspeakable, with chewed bones laying everywhere. He stared at me and there was blood smeared about his jaws. Then I saw what he held in his hands. Oh, it was the remains my little dog! It was torn apart with its head laying at his feet and its eyes staring at me. I ran screaming from that dreadful place, certain Asterion was close behind – reaching out to seize me. But I was lost. I had no idea which way to go. I – I just ran in blind terror.

It was fortunate my brothers, Catreus and Androgeus had come looking for me or I swear that insane abomination they once called my baby brother would have killed and devoured me as he had my dog. Oh, Theseus, I was sick with fear. I hid in my room for days afterwards and refused to talk about what I'd witnessed. It was plain to me, to those who had attended him, how Asterion had become a thing of utter evil. I wished again and again father had ordered him killed at birth – it's not uncommon with defective children, even here at Knossos. And now –.'

Theseus took her hand, breathing, 'You're right, we need more wine.'

The flame of the lamps danced bright in Ariadne's eyes, a flame that cast their forms grotesquely about the frescoed walls where painted images seemed to tremble with the fear that possessed Ariadne as she continued, 'Father had Daedalus seal off an older area of the palace laying below ground level. It's the remains of a much earlier palace upon which this one was built, smaller but just as much a maze, so I'm told. Part of it was once used for storage as well as living quarters for the slaves but was too dark, too unhealthy to be of any real use. I know the creature is fed raw meat through a grille at ground level in one of our smaller private courtyards. They say all entrances except one have been walled up to stop it getting out. I've overheard those few who claim to have glimpsed

Asterion and lived to speak of it, the ones who take him his food, claim he has grown much bigger and yet more abominable. They say the human side of him is utterly lost - that he desires only the flesh of beast and man. They are ordered never to discuss it even among themselves but how could they not do so at night when they think there is no one listening?

Often, when most of the palace sleeps, I hear him in the darkness beneath the palace. His bellowing sounds like distant thunder. I cannot keep it out of my mind. I hear it even with my head buried under a blanket. I feel it shiver the very walls of my room. It's as though – as though he knows when I'm alone. I believe he can hear what people above are saying. He waits seething in darkness amidst a stench of death. The rumour that condemned prisoners are sent into that labyrinth is widespread but I know it's much more than a rumour. I believe that's what eventually happened to the men who knew about the false cow. If it were not for father's protection of someone he finds so useful, I'm sure our dear mother would have had Daedalus and his son follow them.'

Ariadne gazed up at Theseus with dread in her eyes. 'I believe Asterion craves human flesh above all else and - and if it is not given to him I fear he will one night break out of the labyrinth below us. He will rage through the corridors, tearing apart those who cannot escape. Knossos would become a charnel house with that insane and bloody creature reigning as its master! When moonlight shines into my room I see shadows move. I imagine I hear him breathing. I imagine he's found his way up here and has come to take me. Every shadow, every sigh of the breeze has become for me a prowling beast. So terrified am I that I want to scream and throw myself from the window. That's why sleep eludes me until the sky lightens. That's why I so often walk out late at night and hear spoken what I was never intended to hear.'

'Hmm, hardly surprising your one-time little brother has no friends, only victims,' said Theseus. 'So it is to this - this Minotaur my people have been given in sacrifice and it's into the lair of this creature your father intends I and my companions should also be delivered.'

'Yes,' she sighed, 'that *is* what he intends. And, yes, he too fears the Minotaur. He believes he must maintain it in part because it is the offspring of Poseidon who extends his power beneath our land when he shakes the earth to remind us of his presence. I once overheard him claim Asterion is an emissary of the god himself. Our priests have to support father because he is their head. Mother's interest in the beast has grown since it was confined below the palace but I tell you it's a very different interest to father's.'

'But the Minotaur is not immortal like the gods,' said Theseus, stroking her hair. 'The great bull that was the cause of his birth was not immortal. I with a handful of men rounded him up and brought him back from Marathon to Athens for sacrifice.'

'Asterion is as much flesh and blood as the rest of us,' replied Ariadne. 'He needs to eat to stay alive and – oh - do you hear?'

Ariadne grasped his arm. Theseus listened hard.

'It sounded no more than a distant rumble,' he replied at last. 'It could have been a mild quake. Such things happen from time to time throughout all of Greece.'

Ariadne spattered wine over the table as she thumped down the goblet, gripped his arm tighter and breathed, 'No, it's *not* the same. We are all familiar with earthquakes. It is Asterion I tell you. He bellows! He beats at the walls to find a way out! He senses your people are close by and he craves their flesh!'

Theseus loosened her grip, pulled her arm away then sprang to his feet. 'Whatever the sound was, that damnable creature you speak of will have none of my people! I swear by the gods I will destroy it! Lady Ariadne, if you wish to be rid of Asterion then help me obtain arms for myself and my men so we can do what has to be done. We have nothing to lose.' Ariadne stared up at him as Theseus continued, eyes shining defiance. 'I have defeated many enemies in my time – man and beast. I've no intention of being led like a lamb to the slaughter!'

'I'll do all I can to help,' she replied. 'It's the only chance you will have to get out of Knossos alive. But before that you must promise to grant the favour I said I would ask in return.'

'Yes – if I can grant it then I surely will.'

Ariadne arose to face him. 'I know you find me desirable, Theseus, dear, but there must be many other women ready to serve you at your own court. Do you have a woman in Athens – one who is special to your heart?'

'I have no particular woman in Athens other than the girls of the court. And as for you – why, you are the most desirable, the most beautiful woman I ever met.'

'That's, good, oh yes,' she purred softly, passing fingers sensually down his chest and stomach, her fears seemingly on the wane. 'Then – then if you do succeed I want you to take me with you? I want you take me away from the memories that so torment me - away from the confines of this palace – away altogether from Crete. If father and mother agree on anything it's that Phaedra and I ought not to spend time outside Knossos in case our skin is darkened by the sun as it is with the labourers of field and orchard. We are prisoners in what others see as paradise. We are butterflies snared in a net.'

'Very well,' he replied, 'I'll take you back to Athens. What man would not have a woman such as you as consort on the day he took his throne? And once your father came to terms with it he'd maybe stop supporting Pallas against Athens and instead become our ally.'

'Then,' she said, kissing him, 'there are those here within Knossos who will help us. There's one in particular whose ear I have because of what I know he has done.'

'Oh, is there now,' responded Theseus with a broad smile, his hand caressing her cheek. 'Someone I've already met, I presume.'

'That's right,' she replied, kissing him again, this time more earnestly as his arms slipped about her naked body. 'He knows the palace and the maze of galleries lying beneath as no one else could. He is familiar with secret places where others dare not go. His keys unlock all doors. I'll speak to him when the time is right - before the bull-leapers' ceremony.' A smile crossed her lips as she whispered in his ear, 'So for now let's finish the wine then return to our bed.'

'What, again?' he grinned. 'And you say your mother's insatiable.'

Chapter 9
The BULL LEAPERS

Theirs was a mood of quiet apprehension as Theseus and his people gathered in one of the sparsely furnished rooms occupying that area of the palace to which they were confined. A most important event was to take place. The guards, the staff, the slaves of the palace scurried purposefully about their business. There was great tension in the early morning air.

'Are they going to kill us?' asked a tearful Athenian girl.

The young men were restive again. One stepped over with a determined look in his eye. 'Lord Theseus, we say this has gone on long enough. The Cretan woman one of us saw you talking with at first light this morning – you spent the night with her did you not. You were enjoying yourself in her bed while we languish here awaiting our deaths! There's to be some kind of ritual. We've seen them putting up wooden barriers around the courtyard where it's to take place. We do not intend to be a part of whatever they have planned.'

'And what is it you propose to do?' Theseus asked, placing a hand firmly on the youth's shoulder.

The young man glanced at his companions, all of whom had turned their eyes upon Theseus, some questioning, others mistrustful. 'If this is anything like the festivals we have at home,' the youth said, 'then the wine will flow like water and they won't be too concerned about us. We've all agreed we should do it when the ceremony gets started. We should get out of here as soon as we can - whilst there's light enough to find our way through this maze of a palace.'

'I doubt this will be the drunken debacle you're all hoping for,' replied stern-voiced Theseus. 'The guards appear lax because they're confident they will prevent our escape. If you try anything you'll be caught before you reach the harbour, if not while you're still inside the palace. The Cretans are quite aware of this. I suggest you don't attempt anything. I say you wait, as must I. We have some freedom of movement at present – don't give them an excuse to take that away. And yes, I did spend time with the woman and she may well be the key to our freedom.'

'Lord Theseus,' added another, 'until now we've placed our trust in you but it seems you have no plan. How long are we expected to wait?'

'Until I find out what I need to find out and that should be soon. Yes there's to be a ceremony but it will not involve us - that I do know. And I swear by Zeus I'll not let you down. Believe me, I value my life as much as you value yours.'

Theseus' companions did not appear convinced.

Further discussion was forestalled by the arrival of a Cretan noble – one of the pair who had accompanied the Athenians on their sea journey. The man pushed through the door where the Athenians waited. A number of armed guards were visible in the corridor outside.

'Our king,' he announced with detached air, 'has granted you and your companions the opportunity to witness our ceremony from an excellent vantage point. You will accompany the guards to the floor above where there is sufficient room on the balcony.'

Theseus glanced at his companions; the girls now anxious, the young men expressing thinly disguised anger. None showed inclination to refuse the offer.

'As the great man wishes,' responded Theseus, 'we'll watch your ceremony since we have little else to occupy our time today.'

Visibly displeased with the manner of Theseus' reply, the noble responded with an icy smile, 'You are privileged people for now; you should make the most of it.'

'Last indulgence of the condemned,' remarked one of the Athenian youths.

The noble backed through the door gesturing them to follow.

A confusion of corridors, more stairs, more turns to left and right brought them to an open-sided gallery overlooking the courtyard. But it was not the space below that first demanded their attention. Peace and order appeared to have taken leave of Knossos that morning. Citizens had gathered at almost every point about the courtyard. Shutters were swung wide to reveal windows crammed with eager faces. Balconies, galleries, colonnades bubbled over with a clamour of people whilst not a space on any rooftop was left unoccupied by bobbing heads. It seemed as if all the inhabitants of Knossos were out there and more – traders, artisans and field labourers who had laid aside their tools for the grand occasion.

Stout wooden hurdles had been fixed to heavy posts, which in turn were set into sockets in the surrounding stone floor. Many of those pressing in to observe the events at ground level were obliged to stand in order to see over the barrier. Theseus noted that in areas reserved for the nobility and officials, the sexes appeared to be segregated. The bejewelled, bare-breasted, painted ladies of the court sat in their colourful, flounced dresses, enjoying pride of place amidst the audience with painted parasols wagging above chattering heads. Morning light emphasised how pale these pampered aristocratic women of Knossos looked compared with their counterparts in Athens and other mainland towns. It appeared none of them ventured into the sun but rather spent their days within the luxurious confines of the palace; confirming what Ariadne had earlier told him she and her sister were obliged to do.

Diagonally opposite the Athenians, halfway along the west side of the courtyard, stood a small, square-sided shrine having a single, russet column with bull's horns set where its base rested on the plinth. On the floor above this, on a shaded balcony protected from the heat of the day sat Minos, bedecked in regal glory, together with his immediate family.

Theseus studied them from across the open space. One, a sharp-eyed, red-lipped woman, was lavishly adorned in a gown of precious purple embroidered with spiral designs in gold and silver wire. Her exposed nipples were brightly rouged; her elaborately piled and coiffured hair fell in ringlets from a jewelled band fitted about her head. This was his first glimpse of Pasiphae, the queen. Theseus appraised her with narrowed eyes. While her youth had been compromised by the passage of time plus a surfeit of indulgences covering all manner of gratification, she appeared to him as desirable still as many a younger woman. With Ariadne's bizarre tale in mind it took little effort for him to imagine how physically demanding she must be; little effort to appreciate why Minos must long since have turned a blind eye to so many of her carnal digressions.

Almost as richly attired as the queen were Ariadne and another girl who Theseus reasoned must be her younger sister, Phaedra. His gaze remained fixed for a while upon the latter because he had thought that, since meeting Ariadne, he was unlikely to encounter another woman of such physical, such sensual appeal. Now there was Phaedra. Phaedra turned to look at him. Phaedra smiled. Nor was it a guarded smile. It was a smile that said, 'I'm waiting.'

Ariadne noted the direction in which her sister's gaze had fallen. She prodded Phaedra hard in the ribs with her elbow whilst Theseus, one hand resting on the parapet, raised the other in greeting to them both.

'All these people,' remarked Theseus to the noble, 'how do they find their way through your maze of passages?'

'Some already work within the palace,' he answered with a wry smile, suspecting Theseus might be angling for clues to escape, 'though except for servants of the king and queen, most have access only to their areas of employment. The majority

200

first have to gather in groups at the east side. There each party has a leader with an emblem for them to follow – a sea creature, a bird or an animal that is also displayed on a cloth pennant at every turn on the route they must take through Knossos. Our chief of works, Daedalus, reproduces the images as many times as he wishes with his carved wooden blocks and dyes. The pennants are, of course, removed as soon as the crowds are gone from the palace.'

'Of course,' smiled Theseus. 'We'd expect nothing less.' He would have questioned the man further but something was happening below. Two drummers had appeared from the south-east entrance and as they began to beat in unison, the babble of the crowd lessened. The drummers strode to the centre of the open space to position themselves before the royal party whilst continuing with their beat. From the same direction stepped a group of sun-bronzed youths and girls in brightly decorated loincloths, each carrying a musical instrument, pipes or systrum. Joining the drummers they began to play as a small band. More people stepped into the courtyard - again young men and women, similarly dressed but carrying pitchers, bowls and baskets.

Theseus, standing with arms folded at the front of the balcony asked the noble, 'What are we seeing here?'

'They symbolise the harvest of land and sea,' he replied. 'It is to demonstrate before our king the riches that flow through Knossos by trade and by the labour of his subjects.'

Watching them, Theseus was reminded of the wall paintings they had passed by on their arrival at

Knossos. Here the frescoes of parading youth had come to life before his eyes, as though stepping down from dry plaster only to transform themselves into flesh and blood. They continued in ceremony about the great courtyard to the rising sound of the music, each small group hesitating briefly in its progress to face Minos and his family, who peered down at them from above to see each lift up his or her burden for royal scrutiny.

'Now is the time,' hissed a voice at Theseus' ear. 'They are preoccupied,' said the youth who had spoken to him of escape only a short time before. 'Once we get down from here we could mingle unnoticed with the crowds. We could follow the same signs all of them used to find their way through until we reached the outside.'

'Look behind and think seriously about that,' answered Theseus, casually. 'And ask yourself why they've placed us up here on full view.'

The youth turned. Blocking the exit were two, hard-looking fellows with daggers and short swords ready to hand at their belts. In the corridor behind there would doubtless be more. The youth's male companions muttered amongst themselves but there was no further talk of escape. The girls stood, hands clasped before them, faces turning as they whispered in furtive tones to one another.

With the displays of abundance ended, the musicians stepped back. Young boys, each naked except for a coloured sash at his waist and leather glove on his right hand, dashed into the open. The boys, numbering six in three pairs, began to spar with one another, punching, circling about in an energetic game to the sound of drums and pipes, to cheering from the crowds. This was an entertainment performed to rules the Athenians could only guess at. Others joined them, stick fighters, acrobats, then female dancers whose skills appeared to be in weaving a complex pattern about their companions without making any form of contact in what was otherwise close to becoming a mêlée. As they retired, swirling away beneath the shadows of the colonnade, on came more young men and girls, slim and naked except for loose, deep-belted kilts. They displayed further, intricate skills with dancing and acrobatics but Theseus' attention was held now by the ruler of Knossos who, goblet in hand, perched amidst his family group. They talked, laughed and gestured to one another. They must have seen all of this before – they must regard it as little more than harmless entertainment, so Theseus imagined. But things were soon to change.

The performers, followed by the musicians, made their exit from the courtyard in good order - then silence fell. A silence of almost tangible intensity. A silence that presaged something of altogether greater import. From beyond the Athenians' sight, the drumming resumed, this time to a slow, portentous beat.

With the sun risen higher, the main area of the courtyard was largely clear of shadows when the next players in the ritual, accompanied by two royal officials in red robes, entered from the obscurity of the northern colonnade. They were twelve in number, including four young women, and they moved in solemn procession to the far end of the open area. All wore gold-edged loincloths and short, pointed boots though in appearance, in style of hair, colour of skin and body adornment, some were evidently not of Cretan or even Greek origin. The officials lined them up before the king's vantage point then departed via the south colonnade. At a raised-hand gesture from Minos the rhythm of the drums increased and the twelve spun around, spread out then proceeded with leaps and cartwheels to the southern end of the courtyard where they stood in a loose crescent with arms folded.

Theseus, having observed spearmen place themselves at intervals at the shadowed rear of the courtyard, concluded armed men had surrounded the entire area. The drumming slowed to its former ominous beat. A cry of, 'Aah!' arose from spectators at that side with a view toward the north colonnade, a cry repeated through much of the audience. This was followed by reverberant snorting, by an echo of hooves staccato-cracking on stone flags. An incoherent babble welled as people strained to see the spectacle that was about to emerge from the shadows.

The bull, mottled brown and white, was a heavy, barrel-bodied, low-slung animal with short neck and squat legs. Inelegant it may have looked but it obviously possessed considerable strength as the two Cretan youths, aided by ropes fixed about its horns, half dragged, half cajoled the beast with grunts and shouts into the centre of the courtyard.

'You must have heard about our bull-leapers ceremony,' remarked the noble, turning to Theseus, 'though I imagine you have nothing like that on the mainland.'

'No, we're too busy ridding ourselves of invaders - but yes, we have heard something about it.'

'It is an ancient rite dedicated to Poseidon the earth-shaker,' boasted the noble, 'to whom the bull will afterwards be sacrificed. The ceremony was old before our own ancestors came here to establish the line of our present king.'

'Then if it's worth it,' smiled Theseus, 'we'll take an account of what we see back to Athens.'

The noble stared at him for uncomfortable moments then abruptly turned away.

In the open space below, the bull had been released and its captors were retiring in haste from the square, dragging the ropes behind them. The drumming stopped. The bull began to stamp, to snort, to rock its heavy head up and down, tasting the air, trying to make sense of the novel situation in which it found itself. The twelve, obviously acrobats of considerable skill, resumed their display by leaping about until they formed a wide circle around the bull. The bull swivelled its head about, eyeing them with dubious intent.

One of their number, a dark-skinned youth, strode forward as if to confront the beast then stood before it, hands raised. The young man swayed from side to side. The bull shuffled, snorted, waited. A drum-roll began then from one side dashed another of the youths, heading straight for the bull. On reaching it he had gathered enough momentum to affect a sideways vault that took him clear over its back to land firmly on his feet before spinning about then stepping back with arms raised. Vexed at this blatant liberty, the creature stamped around and might have set off in pursuit had not the next performer, one of the young women, repeated the act with equal skill and audacity from the opposite direction. A ripple of clapping spread amongst the onlookers while others shouted for the next performer. The bull, meanwhile, was in no mood to tolerate further indignity. Jerking its great horns up and down it regarded those nearest to it with a view to imminent revenge. Not the quickest witted of creatures, it nevertheless became aware of a third player sprinting toward it – but too late. Letting out a sharp cry, the youth sprang, succeeding in his attempt though with less time to spare and with not so sure a landing as his predecessors. Letting out a raucous bellow, the bull lowered its horns, intent on starting after him. Even so, to yet louder exhortations from the onlookers, another intrepid acrobat made his play, rushing forward to perform the leap, clearing the bull with deceptive ease.

Maddened and confused, the bull stamped hard, threw back its head, drum-roll snorted then began to circle about with eyes glinting malice. The tension heightened, the spearmen readied their weapons in case the beast decided to charge. Undeterred, its tormentors danced about, further confounding the animal with rapid changes in direction - approaching, receding, always moving.

A gasp flew from the crowd when two sturdy male figures dashed inwards from behind the bull whilst it prepared to lunge at a youth who had approached too closely. The two seized its horns then whilst hanging on with teeth-gritting determination, managed to stay the animal in spite of its vigorous efforts to shake them off. Again the drums, even more urgent in their beat as a dark-haired girl of no more than twenty stepped forward. The onlookers quietened as she stood on her toes to face the bull directly, arms raised, ready to sprint. Now silence, except for the drums, as the girl bent slightly then began her dash. The drums ceased. The girl, darting at full pelt, reached the bull and as the two holding it released their grip she seized the horns then leapt high, propelled in part by the momentum of her dash, in part by the creature throwing up its head in an attempt to catch her on its deadly horns. Over she went in a somersault, balancing momentarily on the broad back before leaping away to land on her feet behind the creature where she was steadied by a male companion who had strode forward during her tumble through the air. Her startling act prompted wild cheers from the onlookers. Others of her team attempted to control the bull as they had before, the two men maintaining their hold upon its horns with considerable difficulty.

Theseus noted his companions, the youths especially who, seeming to have waived all thought of escape, were as engrossed with the scene below as were the Cretans themselves. Glancing across the square he observed Minos sitting upright in his richly draped chair. But it was Pasiphae who appeared most excited, leaning forward, clutching at the edge of the balcony whilst her two daughters sat attentive and the king's sons, leaning with arms folded against the wall directly behind, watched with less consuming involvement.

The act that had so enthralled the onlookers was repeated twice over to the roll of drums, to renewed cheering, this time by young men who exhibited no less skill than had been demonstrated by the girl.

'Who are these people who so willingly risk their lives?' asked Theseus.

Reluctant to switch his attention from what was happening below, the noble replied, 'Some are performers who do it to gain gold or other benefits from the king or members of his family. When they are rewarded many say it will be their last appearance but as soon as their new-found wealth is squandered most return to face the bull. A few are of noble blood, including the women. They perform in such holy ceremonies because it gains prestige for their families. Others are criminals or slaves who train with the rest to earn their freedom. If the king or queen consider they have given a good enough account of themselves then they are released.'

'Or when they're gored to death,' put in one of the Athenian girls who had overheard the conversation in spite of the general clamour.

'What you witness here is held for the glory of Poseidon and our king!' snapped the official. 'Whatever the outcome.'

Then as if giving foresight to the girl's words, the fourth attempt to vault the bull fared with less fortune. The leaper, a lighter-complexioned youth of mainland appearance, performed his somersault well enough but the bull jerked angrily as he landed on its back, causing him to lose his balance. The man tumbled aside with a cry, hit the flagstones then with hands clasped to his head, rolled away with difficulty to avoid stamping hooves. Gasps and cries arose all about and whilst his companions strove to divert the attention of the bull, the man struggled to his feet with the help of the girl who had been positioned behind the animal to catch him. He was obviously hurt, limping badly, bright blood streaking his thigh and elbow. But the performance would continue, that much was certain – now with deadly challenge whilst the surrounding watchers quietened once more to a whispering hush.

The air simmered with tense expectation. The two holding the bull's horns had not resumed their position so the much enraged creature was again free to stamp about. This it did, snorting sporadically with an eye to gaining at least one victim from amongst those who so blatantly ill-used it. With clattering hooves, with a defiant bellow that seemed to elicit an echo from hidden depths as well as from the surrounding walls, the bull lowered its head then lunged at a male and female performer. The two sprang aside, easily avoiding the charge, though the bull pursued the girl a short distance until shuddering to a standstill, distracted by the shouts and waving arms of her companions.

Tension increased further. The noble turned to declare, 'Now we will witness that which the people anticipate above all.'

The performers, including the injured youth whose arm was wrapped in a bloodied white cloth, stepped well back – except for one. She, a dark-skinned girl with hair wound into a tight cone above her head, pranced about with the intention of drawing the creature's baleful gaze. The drums rolled. The bull fixed upon her, lowering its head as she raised her arms in readiness to begin her sprint.

Even those witnessing this act for the first time must realise the girl's timing had to be perfect and they all knew what would happen if it were otherwise. There was no longer a steadying grip on the horns to restrain the creature. The drumming ceased, the bull started forward but she was ready and at full speed, lunged on to seize the horns before leaping upward. The bull swung his head high, adding to her momentum so that the girl somersaulted over to gasps of awe from the onlookers, landing squarely on its back then leaping off to be caught and steadied as she landed firmly on her feet by a male companion who had darted into position.

Wild cheering ensued during which Theseus glanced over at the royal party. Minos was clapping slowly as were the king's sons. Her mouth agape, Pasiphae gripped the edge of the balcony as if transfixed. Their daughters, chattering in wild animation, lurched up and down in their seats. The performers regrouped, bodies glistening sweat now the day was hotter. The bull was primed for the kill. Eyes wildly agitated it stamped about, shaking its head violently up and down. The surrounding galleries and rooftops were alive as a bees nest. People jostled with one another for a better view.

'Will they all attempt to do that?' asked one of the Athenian youths.

'Perhaps – perhaps not,' replied the noble. 'For some it will be the chance they have waited for though the anger of the bull may deter them until another day. For others it will be sheer bravado; perhaps a chance to win greater favour from the king and queen – like the next man we are to see take his chance. He has succeeded many times but it is pride rather than gain in kind that drives him.'

As he spoke the man in question stepped forward. He was a bald, sun-bronzed muscular figure, older by some years than the others but intent on proving that he could render as good an account of himself as any – especially a mere woman. The bull obligingly turned to meet him upon which he began his dash. The horns lowered, the beast charged. The man reached it and with a cry, with a mighty bound, was over before his helper could reach the spot behind the creature where he landed. A great cheer arose from the crowd whilst the victor of this last encounter raised his arms, ran in a wide circle about the mouth-foaming bull, gesturing playfully, shaking clasped hands above his head before the royal watchers then swaggering back to re-join his companions.

'That fellow,' explained the noble, 'was a condemned criminal; a pirate captured by one of our ships. It would seem his expertise in clambering about the rigging in stormy seas helped develop his skills. He is much favoured by the queen so will be rewarded by her.'

'In her bed I imagine,' remarked Theseus.

'Presume whatever you wish,' retorted the man, acidly.

'The fellow who was hurt,' asked one of the Athenian youths, 'where is he from?'

'From the so-called Great Mycenae. Yet another criminal sailing with the pirates. He was also taken in conflict at sea. He needed only one more successful leap to reach his goal. Now he will need to wait until -.'

211

His words were cut short when, to gasps of amazement from all about, the subject of their conversation stepped toward the bull and limping still, took up his stance. His female companion, the one who had earlier helped him from the ground appeared to beg him not to attempt what he was so obviously intent on doing.

'Oh - he'll be killed!' exclaimed one of the Athenian girls, pressing hands to her face. 'Will no one stop him?'

'The man is desperate to gain his freedom,' replied the noble as the crowd fell silent and the drumming resumed. 'For him as for others, death may be worth the risk, though should he succeed I have no doubt he will return to his old ways.'

Theseus studied the man with pity then looked up to observe gleeful anticipation on the face of Pasiphae. Lust shone bright in her eyes. A lust for blood and more. The man she anticipated would heighten her entertainment with his death might equally have been one of Theseus' own companions. Pasiphae's daughters also pressed to the edge of the balcony in their enthusiasm not to miss any detail of the spectacle. Bloodied and bedraggled, the man swept back his long hair, flexed his arms, pushed out his chest then as the bull turned snorting to meet him, started off with arms extended. His dash began with a falter when the injured leg seemed unable to give much needed support but grim determination drove him on. The bull charged. The Mycenaen lunged at it, grasped the horns then bounded hard as Pasiphae shrieked, springing from her seat with hands raised high. Her daughters half arose to peer by her, open-mouthed and straining for a better view. Wild cries erupted from the audience as the Mycenaean arced over the rearing head, hung for eternal moments then landed on the creature's back. As he continued on under the momentum of the leap his female companion and a male were hurrying to the rear of the bull. Not a moment too soon were they in position for the injury caused him to fall aside where he would doubtless have ended up under the merciless hooves had they not caught and steadied him. Others flew forward to distract the beast as this last performer was assisted on the point of collapse to safety. The surrounding crowd had erupted into a cacophony of shouts and cheers, and whilst Minos and his sons clapped in appreciation of the man's bravery, Pasiphae fell back into her seat, gazing skyward in despair at the denial of witnessing his anticipated end. Ariadne and her sister shrank away from the balcony in close conversation.

'Will Minos now release the Mycenaen?' asked Theseus.

'I believe he will,' answered the noble. 'Our king was never one to break his word in such matters. If the rewards were not perceived to be real I doubt the likes of that man would care to take part.'

The ceremony continued when, to excited chatter from the onlookers, out stepped a young woman of aristocratic Cretan appearance, hair adorned with gold wire and precious stones, gold-bangled arms raised high. Lithe and agile in the extreme, she did not hesitate before taking her dash at the stamping, head-heaving bull. She grasped the horns, leaping high to land squarely on its quivering back before completing her vault as though the effort was hardly more than a routine event. The arc of her flight ended with a faultless landing that prompted an outburst of wild cheering even before her male assistant had reached his designated spot. The bull clattered around in maddened perplexity as the girl backed smiling through the barrier.

'Ah, yes!' exclaimed the noble, showing for the first time an uninhibited enthusiasm. 'That's the way it ought to be done.' Turning to Theseus he added, 'She is a niece and a favourite of our king. There are few able to match her skill - certainly none to ever exceed it. She will not begin her move unless others have gone before. She claims it makes the leap easier when the creature is enraged.'

'I admire her devotion,' muttered Theseus, his eye fixed upon the slim figure of the girl who now stood smiling up at the royal enclosure from where beamed an appreciative Minos and from where gazed an attentive Pasiphae. Theseus was about to speak again when a spontaneous, 'Ooh!' arose from the watchers. Another man paced forward to confront the bull. A tonsure-headed, muscular, well-proportioned individual of North African aspect.

'He is a Nubian,' offered the noble. 'A condemned slave. He murdered one of his master's sons here at Knossos. He would have been put to death had he not begged to take part in our ceremony. Our king has allowed him ample opportunity to practise.'

'Then he's nothing to lose,' remarked Theseus.

'No, nothing whatsoever,' breathed the noble.

There was no time for further dialogue. The bull had spotted the Nubian and with sharp-eyed determination was intent upon dealing with this latest affront in the only manner it knew. The creature snorted, stamped, lowered its head as the man raised his arms to begin the dash. But his timing was ill-considered. He had started too soon. As he gripped the horns the bull did not throw up its head but lurched back causing him to plunge down - not to the flagstones but upon one of the deadly horns that pierced his shoulder through. The man screamed aloud in blood-spraying agony as the beast hurled him upward only to impale him once again as he fell, ripping open his belly then hurling him aside like a torn and ruined doll. There he sprawled in the harsh light, spilled entrails shining ghastly red, jaws agape, limbs quivering as the bull stamped about. Groans mingled with shouts from the audience but from across the courtyard echoed a sharp cry. Theseus looked there to see Pasiphae, hands clutching her breasts, lips parted, eyes closed as if about to swoon. Her expression was not one of horror at the gruesome death she had just witnessed but more that of a woman seized by the passions of the bedroom. Minos and his sons displayed little emotion but their daughters, eyes averted from the grisly scene, chatted closely to one another as if the violent end of the slave had been little more than a diverting interlude. The Athenian girls had turned aside, stricken with horror and the young men were rendered silent.

But this was not an interlude. The ceremony for that day was concluded.

Armed guards emerged to keep the bull at bay whilst the remaining performers in what had ended as a dance of death were ushered from sight. Those who had not attempted the bull leap on this occasion would no longer care to continue.

Slaves hurried from shadowed doorways – some with poles and ropes with which to ensnare the gore-streaked bull, others carrying sailcloth in which they would wrap and carry off the flaccid corpse of the man whose death had punctuated the contest with grim finality. The last to appear bore heavy linen bags containing sand to spread over the blood. The onlookers continued to chatter amongst themselves but were gradually withdrawing.

'That man's death makes the bull a yet greater sacrifice,' remarked the noble. 'Its worth will be enhanced when offered at Poseidon's altar.'

'In Athens,' responded Theseus, 'we pit men against men for sport – not against dumb animals, skilled as your athletes are.' Yet he admired those skills far more than he would care to admit, just as he was beginning to grasp the significance of the ceremony.

The noble eyed him coldly then left his side.

Theseus glanced once more across the square to see Minos and his family in the process of quitting their vantage point. Slaves busied themselves in moving seats, in lifting robes to assist the regal wearers on their way. A face turned to Theseus, a face of one whose gaze lingered for only brief moments. Ariadne. An impatient Pasiphae ushered her away but another turned to stare at him also. Phaedra. Her stare lasted somewhat longer.

'Show's over - it's time to go!' came a gruff voice as the flat blade of a sword touched cold against Theseus' arm. This man was one of the armed group that had been positioned close to the gallery. Already the other Athenians were being herded through the door. The guard squinted up at Theseus in expectation of instant obedience. Theseus regarded him with a calm gaze, knowing he could seize the man, take his sword then hurl him bodily into his comrades. It would be a good fight, it would be one that he, in the confined area of the gallery, might win.

As if reading his thoughts, the guard raised his sword defensively then backed away to the safety of his companions. Theseus stared at them with disdain before pushing by to re-join his companions. Ushered back along corridors and stairs, Theseus expected he and his young Athenians would return to the relative freedom they had enjoyed earlier. It was not so. The women were diverted along a side passage whilst the men were conducted on through an unfamiliar gallery until reaching a series of smaller rooms. Here they were to be confined in twos and threes. One of the Athenian youths thought to resist as the heavy, bronze-banded door opened before him, but the two sword points held at his ribs were arbiters of his decision.

'And what awaits us now?' asked Theseus as three of the guards gathered close, weapons poised to ensure he entered the cell. Theseus saw he was to be imprisoned alone.

'You'll be allowed food, wine and fresh air as before,' replied one, 'but in between times you will remain here until orders arrive from our king.'

Theseus eyed the three blades glinting before him, smiled, 'How am I to manage without your company,' then backed into the room. The door grated shut, followed by the course rasp of bolt and lock.

The small window was fitted with two stout, square section bronze bars set into stone sockets at sill and lintel. He grasped each in turn, determined to test their strength, only to confirm there could be no means of escape via that route. The window let out onto a modest courtyard beyond which lay a jumble of white, cubic buildings and colonnades rising up the hillside in terraces amidst the cypress trees. Everywhere proclaimed the joy of colour - in vivid splashes of flowers, in patterned fabrics hanging out to dry beneath the sun. People called from balcony to balcony whilst from below arose the high-spirited cries of children at play. Further out spread the well-tended orchards and olive groves of Knossos with the sea beyond glinting the bright light of freedom.

To the visitor, to the envoy from other lands, this must appear a land of peace and plenty. Were they ever aware of the discord that loomed over the table and shared the bed of its ruling family? And what of Ariadne and the pact they had made? Would she prove no more than a straw to a drowning man? In his confined silence there seemed little enough to hope for. Theseus felt now it might have been better to let his companions have their way and attempt an escape. At least he would not have suffered the shame of an empty promise.

His thoughts turned to Ariadne's younger sister, Phaedra. He recalled her expression as she watched him from across the courtyard and wondered if she desired him as did Ariadne. Was it Phaedra's desire also to be free of Knossos, this ripely succulent fruit that harboured at its core a pit of darkness?

He remained deep in thought for some time, a time during which the shadows beyond his window lengthened to flow twilight through narrow alleyways. The sound of grating metal caused him to rise. The door opened to reveal the official who had accompanied them earlier, backed by three armed men. 'The king requires you to attend his presence,' he announced. 'I trust you are ready and willing.'

'Well I'm not too busy as it happens,' responded Theseus. 'Do I, er, have a choice?'

'You do indeed have a choice,' shrugged the noble. 'You can come before the king or you can stay here like the rest until -.'

'Until what?'

'You would do well to oblige him,' responded the other, visibly angered. 'He seldom makes any kind of offer to one in your position. In fact I don't recall he ever has.'

'Oh, then in that case I will oblige him – provided these men of yours keep their swords out of my way.'

The official nodded to the guards who, eyeing Theseus warily, sheathed their blades. Of his companions there was no sign as Theseus, the noble walking ahead, the three armed men behind, weaved through anonymous, frescoed corridors, then down steps before entering the courtyard. The posts and hurdles were gone and Theseus noted as they crossed how little evidence remained of the spectacle they had earlier witnessed, other than a thin spread of sand beneath the innocent light of a calm and cloudless late afternoon.

In the small audience room where the Athenians had first set eyes on Minos, the king sat enthroned, dressed now in plainer, gilt-edged tunic more in keeping with the less pretentious styles of the mainland. On the cushioned bench at his right sat Queen Pasiphae, bedecked more or less as she had been during the bull leapers' ceremony, her lips red, her hair cascading in gold-braided ringlets, the nipples of her naked breasts rouged to prominence. She regarded Theseus with dark, unblinking eyes, drinking in his image as she might a fine wine until it became intoxicating, staring at him until he could no longer fail to be aware of her thoughts.

Others, too, sat about – personal attendants of Minos and his queen as well as numerous male and female courtiers. Theseus did not bow, nor was he asked to do so as he stood waiting for Minos to speak. The king, preoccupied in whispered conversation with a noble, looked up suddenly as if his visitor's presence had come as a surprise.

'Ah, so here is the Athenian who chooses to show us no respect. What are we to do with you?'

'I thought that was already decided,' answered Theseus whilst the queen continued to regard him with unabated interest.

'Oh, did you now!' responded Minos, his head tilted quizzically aside. 'And what tales have you been hearing – and from whom?'

'The usual,' answered Theseus. 'Occasional rumours - even in Athens. I'm sure you know what I mean.'

'Occasional rumours,' repeated Minos, a smile crossing his face as he continued, 'Well we need not concern ourselves with rumours – no, not yet. There is something you may wish to consider – something of greater importance than mere rumour. You are a man of considerable spirit and that pleases us. And though we risk the displeasure of the gods we see an alternative to your present situation. We offer you a chance to serve here within the palace, to train with others of your age and fitness, to leap in honour of Poseidon like a breaking wave over the back of the bull. You will have all the comforts you desire under the circumstances together with, er, most of the pleasures Knossos has to offer.' Pasiphae mouthed her approval as Minos continued, 'Perhaps in time you will serve directly under me. What d'you say, Athenian?'

Theseus had already determined his response, at the same time noting the nods of agreement from Pasiphae who smiled knowingly as she added, 'You should heed the king's words and do as we suggest.'

That she had spoken at all seemed to annoy Minos who glanced aside at her with a frown that said, simply, 'Shut up!'

'I will remain to do as you wish,' replied Theseus, 'if you will release my people - if you will send them home safely to Athens.'

Until that moment Minos' manner had been agreeable enough to keep everyone feeling at ease. Now his face darkened. As he half rose from the throne his courtiers, officials and guards promptly stood then stiffened to attention. Pasiphae looked in anger first at Theseus then at her husband as the latter declared loudly, 'You do not offer *me* conditions! It is I who offer *you* life or death!' His voice cascaded about the walls with menacing echo.

'Offer me whatever you like!' responded Theseus, folding his arms in defiance as the guards moved closer. 'But if you intend my people to suffer then I will *not* desert them!'

Minos rolled his eyes, collapsed back onto his cushions, laughed aloud, raised his hands then spluttered, 'Oh, the gods will welcome you with open arms – such glory you'll have in the afterlife! Elevated to the ranks of the heroes, d'you think? No - more likely swept into the rubbish heap of fools!'

Pasiphae stared blankly ahead whilst the king's staff and armed men in turn aped his humour on their own faces. Then he spoke with calm authority to the noble. 'Take our illustrious Prince of Athens back to where you found him then return here.'

A gesture from the noble prompted the three guards to close upon Theseus, hands gripping their sword hilts. Other armed men in the room watched keenly in case their companions should require assistance. As Theseus was escorted to the door, Minos called, 'Wait!' The guards turned to hear him declare in a matter of fact way, 'The Prince of Athens is to go below first. Inform me when it happens.' Then eyeing his queen with a grim smile he declared, 'Defy me would he. Hah - might as well throw sticks at a lion!'

No one was aware of the figure concealed in semi-darkness behind the slatted door. Even after the guards had escorted Theseus away she remained listening a while longer. Then lifting the hem of her long dress, Ariadne stepped quietly about to hurry back along the deserted corridor.

***

The courtyard below his window was pooled in shadow, yet the higher buildings of the palace still glowed in the mellow warmth of a lowering sun set upon a blue fabric sky laced with placid flames. But Theseus was unable see bright Helios settling over the mountains to the west. He wondered now if he should have accepted Minos' offer. Might it have gained possible extra time and opportunity he no longer possessed for the escape of his young Athenians?

He recalled his days of labour on the farm at Troizen, his rigorous training for combat at the hands of Pittheus' stern captains and, at the time, those demanding, time-consuming lessons in writing and court behaviour. Such a distant world it now seemed. Had it ever been quite as he now remembered?

His thoughts were interrupted by the scrape of the bolt. He stepped over to the door, drawing a deep breath, intending to strike down the first man who entered then seize his sword. He would fight for his freedom even though the chances of winning through could never be in his favour. His jaw was set firm, his fist raised to administer the blow, but when the door swung in he was confronted instead by a wide-eyed young woman holding a polished copper tray. The tray bore ornate pottery dishes of lamb and vegetables and a pair of golden goblets. A blue-robed Cretan courtier stood directly behind her with two of the palace guards hovering close by. Theseus stepped back in surprise as the girl entered. The courtier reached into the room to place a pitcher of red wine down inside the door.

That the girl was slim and curvaceous he could not help but observe, nor that she was seductively beautiful, with obsidian dark hair cascading about her shoulders from beneath a patterned headband. He also noticed more guards. There were now at least five crammed together in the corridor in readiness for the reckless escape attempt they anticipated Theseus might make.

'The woman is to remain with you,' said the courtier. 'She is a gift of our king who cares greatly for the comfort of princes – even Athenians.'

'How very thoughtful of him,' smiled Theseus, breathing in the girl's exotic perfume, 'I'm touched by the great man's concern for my well-being.'

'And so you ought to be,' sniffed the courtier. 'Her name is Kasmut. She and her sisters were sent as a gift to Knossos by the great King of Egypt. They dance for our king and queen at banquets and at festivals. It is also their duty to entertain high-ranking guests in whatever manner most pleases. This is an honour for which you should be grateful.'

'Wouldn't any of us be,' smirked the nearest guard with blunt innuendo.

Theseus regarded the girl's limpid brown eyes. She in turn offered a coy, full-lipped smile as he took the tray from her and placed it on a nearby bench. He appraised her barely concealed breasts, firm beneath a plain, long dress of diaphanous white Egyptian cotton belted at her waist. Ornate copper and bronze serpent-bangles graced her naked arms. In his mind arose ominous thoughts. 'She is beautiful. She will spend an evening of wine and pleasure with me. She'll occupy my time in full – that I do not doubt. Then what? While I sleep contented with those pleasures she offers and with my wits dulled by Cretan wine, these same men will return in the night to take me.'

The girl stepped further into the room, the guard was about to pull the door shut when Theseus grasped the edge, saying, 'Thank your king for his generosity. Tell him I appreciate his concern over my welfare. Tell him also that I'll deny myself this lady's company, perhaps until another evening.'

'Another evening?' queried the courtier, eyebrows raised. 'What other evening did you have in mind, Athenian.'

'Men have killed for the pleasures I have to give,' pouted the girl, moving close to Theseus where she lifted a red-nailed a hand to tingle his cheek. Her every well-practised nuance implied a smouldering, carnal desire. Theseus felt her heat sensually beguiling as she gazed up at him with crimson lips slightly parted in anticipation of his kiss. But he resisted the fires that already stirred within his loins whilst his hand, poised to slip about her waist, fell to his side. 'Well,' he breathed, 'if one of your men will lend me a sword I'll see what I can do.'

'Have it your way,' said the courtier, gesturing the girl to leave with an impatient stab of his thumb. 'At least you'll have the wine to console yourself.'

The girl stepped away without a second look. The door slammed with ringing finality. Bolt and lock were secured. Theseus stood facing the door then breathed, 'How easily I might have taken the bait. She would have undermined all thoughts of resistance. As for the wine they've left, I'd be a fool to touch it even were it not drugged. No, I'll not accept that either, nor will I go meekly to the slaughter to satisfy that blustering oaf they call their king. I'll take one, two, maybe three of them with me and fall in honourable combat.' With that he took up the pitcher, raised it to the bars then tipped its contents out of the window. 'At least they've left me plenty of fresh water,' he mused. 'That'll do for now.'

Theseus turned his attention again to the visible frame of sky that was his meagre view of the world beyond the cell. He moved closer to peer through the bars. Where before the sky had been almost empty, clouds now towered high beyond Knossos, flamed by a sun otherwise gone from the land. As he stared up at the clouds they shifted against the darkening heavens, forming, reforming into ramparts, bastions, rearing horses, elusive faces. Was it his imagination or were they gathering to take on the semblance of a human figure? 'What's happening?' he breathed, hands grasping the bars. 'What are those clouds becoming that I find so oddly familiar? Ah, there is an upraised arm holding a spear. Yes, a spear, that's what it is. And there a face gazing down at me, a face bearing a warrior's helmet. I know that figure. Oh, I know her! Lady Athena!'

Towering in glory, the figure appeared to radiate golden light, to raise up the spear, to thrust it high in a gesture of defiance. Theseus stared in awe as the image grew, as it slowly, majestically turned in the sky. A breeze sprang up through the bars, cool and refreshing to ruffle his hair. Within the breeze a message unfurled as a wraith of sound. A distant voice that touched his ear. A voice that made his heart quicken. 'Be of good courage, Theseus of Athens. Be of good courage and keep my image always in your thoughts.'

Theseus watched the figure soften, break apart, then as quickly as it had formed to become once again a drifting, amorphous vapour fragmenting against a placid sky. 'How could that have been?' he asked himself, now assailed by doubt as the sky began to clear. 'Is the water they left me to drink tainted with some drug to weaken my mind?' For a time he remained where he was, looking out at the sky. 'Yet did she not come to the aid of Heracles in his time of need?' Only when the first stars had appeared did Theseus lay down beneath a light woollen blanket in the hope of finding sleep. But such was the turmoil of his thoughts, sleep would have no easy admission.

Moonlight cast window-bar shadows across his prison when, sometime later, he lay with only the vague sounds of night beyond his prison for company. Waking from a fitful slumber, the cloud image shimmered large in his imagination. There were sounds from beyond the room. Someone, approached along the corridor then stopped close outside his door. Silence. Then barely audible came a man's voice. 'My friend – are you awake?' The voice was oddly familiar.

'Yes, I'm awake,' replied Theseus, rising from the narrow bed. 'Who's there?'

No reply came but the lock creaked and the bolt drew slowly back. Slowly as though the person doing it had no wish to attract the attention of others. Whoever might be out there Theseus had already concluded was not a guard and was probably alone. The door swung inward with a squeak of bronze tenon in stone socket that in the night-time silence sounded fit to alert the entire palace. Theseus recognised the face as his visitor eased silently into the room. 'Daedalus!'

'For heaven's sake keep your voice down,' responded the man, placing a finger to his lips whilst pushing the door shut.

'What are you doing here?' hissed Theseus. 'Where are my people?'

'Patience, patience, patience,' muttered Daedalus peering about the shadowed room. 'Let me rest a while then we can discuss things properly.' Both men sat on the low bench to face each other as Daedalus resumed. 'Your people are quite safe at present. They are locked away on the floor above this one. Now then, in case you are wondering how I arrived here unnoticed – I have to tell you I didn't. As I may have mentioned, I occasionally present the guards with a generous pitcher of wine – when it suits my purpose, that is. Tonight that was so and I trust such generosity on my behalf will be of further use to you and your companions. The guards were discussing amongst themselves how you kept your wine but rejected the girl, who they feel should now be entertaining them instead. A wise move on your behalf, may I say, since her presence here could have made things difficult. Pour me a drop of wine and I'll tell you what's going on – I don't expect you'll have drunk it all yet - at least I hope not.'

'No I, er – I poured it through there,' replied Theseus, gesturing to the window. 'I didn't want to risk drinking the stuff.'

Daedalus stared hard at him in the gloom. 'You threw away good Cretan wine?' he croaked in disbelief. 'But that was wine from the royal cellar. Young man, you have fallen sadly in my estimation. Oh, well, I shall go on nevertheless.' He adjusted his position on the bench then continued, 'You need help, of course. Fit and strong as you are you will never leave Knossos alive without help. Even if the guards were absent, even if I managed to undo all the doors where your people are imprisoned, even if I managed to lead you safely through the palace, your chances of reaching the ships would be slim indeed. Then even if you did, Minos would soon be after you by sea. He'd not rest until he'd punished Athens and I imagine the demands for tribute would be even greater than they are at present.'

'You mean human tribute for that creature of his? Am I correct?'

'Yes, Asterion is perpetually hungry for blood. He must have his sacrifice and Minos believes the gods favour his kingship because of it. He is convinced beyond all reason that as the beast thrives it channels energy up through the earth to fuel his power. More than that, the creature has become his oracle. Seldom nowadays does he consult Apollo's shrine on important matters but often instead has the priests, of whom he is head, keep watch by the grille at night to interpret the grumblings and bellowings of Asterion.'

'But what can any of *that* mean?' asked Theseus. 'Surely it's no more than noises made by a crazed beast.'

'You might as well ask what most oracular pronouncements mean. It's all too often a matter of what people care to make of them. Personally, I don't give a fig. It's all nonsense to me though I have to be careful what I say since people are always asking my opinion over matters I care little about. Anyhow, I know you have spoken with Ariadne and I'm aware of most of what she's told you. What she may or may not appreciate is that I, too, could be in some danger. Pasiphae, that bitch of a queen, is now trying to have *me* poison Deucalion in case Minos finds out he's not the young man's true father, though I'm sure Minos suspects it anyway. She's not past doing her own dirty work but dares not in this instance in case she's found out. Naturally, I've avoided getting involved. Poisons and incantations are her style - certainly not mine, though it's what she's been accusing me of until recently.'

'What a caring mother they have,' remarked Theseus, wondering when his nocturnal visitor would explain his reason for being there.

'Quite so,' continued Daedalus, 'Someone, probably one of her lackeys, has been spreading malicious rumours about Deucalion but he does have support in high places – not least from Tauros, the king's general. In any case, Deucalion is the best of the bunch by far and most of us know it. His only real fault is his naive loyalty to her as well as to Minos so I have it in mind to tip him off before things go too far – anonymously, of course. Hmm – that could be tricky. Anyway, because I continue to defy her, she's threatening to confirm the rumour that I was instrumental in her giving birth to that loathsome creature they keep down below - that I tricked her with my alleged spells and potions into doing it. You wouldn't believe at the time how that insatiable woman begged me to – no, I won't go into the sordid details though I expect you've been informed of the basics. Minos might or might not believe a word of it – there's no telling - but she *is* the queen so I need to tread carefully. And all this when my only son, Icarus, has of late discovered an appreciation for women other than mere sexual gratification. Dear me, he's already talked of marrying one of the palace girls.'

'But you have no need to stay in Knossos,' put in Theseus, wishing he would end the narrative and get to the real point of his visit. 'You came originally from Athens so why don't you go back there?'

'Well, dear boy,' replied the Daedalus, 'apart from my being accused of murdering my assistant all those years ago, who happened also to be my nephew, there is the quality of life to consider. In Knossos there is light, sweet-smelling air, clean water and better wine by far. And there's ample opportunity to develop my ideas further. The much improved fresh water system – now that I *am* proud of.'

'You mean you were responsible for that aqueduct - that great stone structure we saw the other day reaching toward the hills beyond Knossos?'

'Oh, of course I wasn't,' Daedalus puffed indignantly. 'The aqueduct is much older than I am – anyone can see that. No, I greatly enlarged the distribution system so most of the palace has access to clean water as well as the proper disposal of unpleasant waste.'

'Ah, the drains,' groaned Theseus. 'I hope you're not thinking to get us out of the palace that way.'

Ignoring the remark, Daedalus continued, 'I did, however, invent the kind of lock they employ here as well as for the palace valuables. I first witnessed the use of locks in Egypt, you know. Clever they are, yes, but *not* as good as mine. That's how I got in here to see you, obviously. I have keys to everything – oh, yes, which brings me to the point of my visit. Now the ceremony is ended, Minos will have you thrown into the labyrinth, possibly tonight – if not, then most certainly tomorrow.'

'Yes,' breathed Theseus, 'I gathered that at our last meeting. Right now, though, I wouldn't mind hearing what you have in mind. If there is time enough.'

'Ah, yes, time enough - we need to act rather soon. What I mean by soon, dear boy, is before too much of the night has passed. After you arrived word got about as to who you are so there were some who regarded you as a kind of rescue party – a number of them slaves from beyond this island who want to go home. Two of them you watched in the bull-leaping ceremony earlier today - though one was killed. Many of the rest Minos captured at sea as pirates so they are skilled sailors and know the use of arms as well as boats. Now then - Ariadne assures me you'd like to see the beast dead – and wouldn't a lot of people. It's mainly in the daytime Asterion sleeps - which is rather unfortunate as tomorrow would have been the most advantageous time for you to enter the labyrinth. But tomorrow, as we know, could be too late to save you from being thrown in there without a weapon. They guard the grille at such times so there could be no chance of anyone slipping a sword or spear down there after you. And, obviously, you aren't going to do any good with your bare hands.'

'Probably not,' muttered Theseus, rising up to pace back and forth.

'Yes, night-time is when Asterion wanders those dark galleries. That is when he cries in mindless anger from below the palace. Should you succeed in killing him and the king is informed of it there will be alarm and confusion throughout Knossos – the very situation we require in order to assist in your escape. More, Minos may well see it as a kind of retribution. He may consider his power on earth to be undermined - but in any case, there would be no point in his demanding further tributes. On the other hand, if you do not kill Asterion – well, I fear nothing is likely to change. Athens will be damned with more unhappy years of attrition from among its young people.'

'Give me the right weapon and I'll do it or perish trying!' declared Theseus, swinging about to stare down at Daedalus.

'I will furnish you with a weapon, sir - one of the very best if not your own, I assure you, but we have precious little time to get ourselves organised. My son, Icarus waits nearby. He knows the palace and its secret passages almost as well as I do. When I give him the word he will inform your companions over what we intend to do and he will alert those who would help us in manning the boats at Amnissos. We must not release any of your people yet, however, because if you fail Minos will punish all those involved – maybe even myself and my son. There are others who are free, however, some who will be ready to play their part at the harbour once given the signal. I have in fact invented a kind of lamp that allows one person to communicate with another by -.'

'Look,' cut in Theseus, 'I've no doubt this lamp of yours is brilliant in every sense of the word. But if as you say we have so little time, maybe we could get down to the essentials.'

'Ah, yes, the essentials, you're right – we really ought to make haste. I will go shortly but you must remain awake and alert. When you hear them strike the midnight gong, this is what you must do -.'

Chapter 10
BEAST of the LABYRINTH

Daedalus had not long since departed but time quickly became a burden as Theseus paced the floor of his cell. Often he hesitated, turning his face to the window then to the door - listening. He tried the door to confirm Daedalus had left it unlocked. With bated breath he pulled it open far enough to look outside. The brazier-lit corridor beyond was deserted.

Was that the midnight gong? Was it time to go and follow the route he had so carefully memorised? What if he missed it? What if he was too late? He stepped back to the window, straining to look through the bars over a Knossos that lay in pallid glow beneath the moon and stars. An owl's hoot drifted on cool night air. Somewhere in the distance a dog barked.

Then another sound. At first, as when he was in the company of Ariadne, he took it to be a minor earthquake. But as before, there was no vibration, no movement. It came again, an ominous, muffled roar from the depths of the palace. A voice that seemed to speak his name as if it knew he was listening. Theseus experienced the cold touch of primordial fear.

He returned to his bed and there lay in troubled silence. His thoughts now were of Athens, of his father, Aegeus, of Haemon and his soothing lyre. In his mind was the old man's tuneful strumming as they sat by the hearth in the golden light of good cheer with goblets brimming. The songs, the recitations came back to him. Songs of heroes, gallant deeds, of heroic death. Once more he recalled how Athena's image had towered golden in the sky. Once more there was hope.

The gong sounded with a clarity that shocked but it brought him scrambling to his feet.

It was at last midnight.

Stepping across the room, he hesitated before opening the door to just a hand's breadth. There were men's voices, the laughter and shrieks of women, all of them rendered carefree and careless, he hoped, by a surfeit of Daedalus' potent wine.

Theseus waited only long enough to ensure no guard loafed about the corridor then stepping out and pulling the door shut behind him, he set off in haste. Helped sometimes by the light of braziers but more often in darkness, he made his way through passages and down steps, eventually reaching a point where, at the far end of the corridor the moonlit courtyard was visible. Silhouetted dimly at the exit, each armed with sword and spear, three guards leaned against the wall, their chatter punctuated by wine-induced laughter. Theseus watched, concealed in the shadow of a side passage. 'Move away from there,' he breathed, 'it isn't every day I get a chance like this.'

Theseus decided - if they didn't move soon he would stroll openly up to them as though on normal business, knock one of them down, seize his sword then despatch the other two in the hope they would not have sufficient time or wits to summon help. He was about to step from the passage when the three started toward him, swaying from side to side, one man relying upon his two companions for support as they talked loudly between themselves. They had imbibed liberally and were heading off somewhere to lay their addled heads. He backed into the shadows as they reeled by, oblivious to his presence but close enough for him to smell the wine on their breath.

A short, silent dash and he was breathing the fresh night air of the courtyard. Hurrying through the colonnade to the south side, he stopped, waited and listened. What if the plan had been thwarted? What if nobody came? He was free yet there could be little chance of his finding a way out of the palace before dawn and no chance of saving his companions.

'Theseus.'

The voice, a woman's voice, sounded close by. A small lamp flickered as she appeared from behind a pillar.

'Ariadne,' he answered.

'Yes, and Daedalus is with me.'

Another figure emerged from the deeper shadows.

'We're safe for the present,' said Daedalus. 'Those guards will have no inclination to come back here but will lose themselves in sleep until the morning. Young sir, you should take the lamp then both of you follow me - but remain as quiet as you can.'

Theseus wondered what it was Daedalus carried inside the wrappings of a heavy linen bundle he clutched in both arms as they stepped through a low opening to descend a narrow flight of stairs. At the base of the stairs they turned abruptly right then moved on stooping in near darkness through a small passage with Ariadne gripping Theseus' arm from behind. He sensed she was truly afraid. For a dozen or so tentative strides they followed the passage until it opened out to reveal a stout, bronze-banded door.

'Until I came down earlier this evening,' informed Daedalus, placing his bundle on the floor then inserting his metal key into the lock, 'this door had not been opened in many years. In fact without my key, nobody could – but then, nobody would wish to try.'

The door shuddered inward on stone sockets to a protesting groan, not to reveal further gloom but a cheerless vaulted chamber where the yellow glow from a pair of oil lamps situated on a plain wooden table at the far end wavered in the draught of their entering. There were no frescoes in this dank place, no illustrations of colour or of life to enrich the walls but only plain, course-hewn stone that in places glistened wet.

'I thought it a good idea to bring the lamps down in advance,' said Daedalus placing the linen bundle down close to these. He turned to Theseus, took and extinguished his own small lamp then gesturing up at the wall, said, 'Hand me that torch, sir, if you please.'

Theseus grasped the wooden shaft of the heavy, unlit brand, lifting it down, smelling of pitch and oil, from its metal bracket.

'I devised its composition some years ago,' continued Daedalus, peering at the brand. 'Some ingredients are not to be found in Crete but come from far to the east. It will burn considerably brighter and for longer than one might expect – oh, and it hardly splutters at all.'

'Hardly splutters - oh good,' breathed Theseus, feeling Ariadne's hand tremble as she rested it on his shoulder, 'I'm sure it's all worthwhile but I take it our Minotaur isn't afraid of fire – or is he?'

'I don't recall anyone ever dared put it to the test,' replied Daedalus, stooping to unwrap the linen bundle as their shadows swayed grotesquely on the rough walls of the chamber. Turning to Theseus he added, 'I, er – I take it you are still willing to -.'

'Willing?' responded Theseus with an ironic smile. 'Well thank you for asking but it seems my choices are somewhat limited. If I'm to confront the thing down here it's better I go on your terms rather than someone else's otherwise I'll not leave Knossos alive and nor will the thirteen others who came with me. But where is my -?'

'Ah, of course,' cut in Daedalus, 'you will also have this. It has no need of testing.'

The dim light revealed a finely tooled leather scabbard with attached belt. The details incised on its surface as well as on the metal fittings were not easy to make out but Theseus saw they were of other than Greek origin. From the scabbard Daedalus withdrew a short sword, which he laid close to the lamps, causing them to sway fitfully in the disturbed air. The dull sheen of the blade told Theseus it was not forged from bronze, however, but a grey metal the like of which was not so familiar to him.

Daedalus answered his unspoken question. 'This weapon came from Minos' personal armoury and it's the king's favourite. It was brought from

Egypt where the metal of its blade is valued more highly than gold but I'm assured it originated in Hittite lands where such weapons are well tempered and are superior to bronze.'

'I hope – I mean I'm sure you're right,' said Theseus with a wry smile, taking the sword from him, 'but if the thing breaks you may not have time to fetch me a new one.' The levity of his remark hardly disguised a growing impatience.

Ariadne clutched his shoulder ever harder. 'I took the sword from father's locked and guarded private chest,' she breathed, 'and yes, he does value it above all others. He claims it has ended the lives of many men.'

Theseus wondered by what means of persuasion she had obtained access to a chest containing items of such value only the king himself would be allowed to approach.

'It is forged from a metal we know of,' continued Daedalus in his matter-of-fact way, 'but armourers even here at Knossos cannot yet work it to this degree of perfection, I have begun to study it in order to find out how we can forge the stuff because I find it far stronger than bronze if prepared correctly. Let me assure you, sir, this will pierce the toughest boiled hide. Nor will bronze armour stand up to it – this I have ascertained in my workshop. The blade I have tested and it's as keen as a razor. With *this* sword I believe you will have a better chance by far of killing Asterion.'

'Now you're talking,' responded Theseus whilst Ariadne moaned, 'For heaven's sake – I can't stand much more of this. It's so cold down here.

Will the gods not pity us? Will the fates not decree our salvation?'

'Piffle,' muttered Daedalus. 'The fates haven't a clue.'

'The fates or no!' exclaimed Theseus, slapping the blade flat against the palm of his hand. 'This will be the arbiter of our salvation. Nothing else - and that *I* decree!'

He returned the weapon to Daedalus while Ariadne squeezed shut her eyes and pressed hands to her cheeks.

'Oh, do forgive me for chattering so,' muttered Daedalus, noting her distress. He slipped the sword back into its scabbard then returned it to Theseus, adding, 'but I'm afraid we have to go a little further.'

'F-further?' murmured Ariadne as Theseus buckled the sword about his waist. 'No, I don't think I care to. This place is simply awful.'

Even as she spoke the deep, guttural cry reverberated, all but tangible, from regions below their feet. It arose to course about the grim walls, seeming to close in upon them with the breath of annihilation. A cold tide of fear swept over Ariadne who, letting out a choked cry, appeared on the verge of collapse. Daedalus remained unperturbed as he took up one of the lamps before shuffling toward a smaller, bronze-barred door at one side of the chamber, set two steps down beneath a massive stone lintel.

'I won't go any further,' Ariadne whimpered, her fingernails all but piercing Theseus' flesh. 'I won't. Really, I can't.'

'Then stay where you are,' said Daedalus. 'I doubt I'll be gone for long.'

'I will not stay here alone,' she insisted. 'That dreadful thing is close by. It might climb out of there!'

'Pah - women,' Daedalus muttered. The flame of his lamp shone bright in her fearful eyes. 'There's no point in fussing,' he declared, handing the unlit torch to Theseus. 'If I thought it could reach us here I would never consider -.'

'We're wasting time in idle chatter!' cut in Theseus. 'Show me the way through. Let's get this over with!'

Turning his key with no little effort, the old man had to release not one but two locks before dragging aside the metal bars. The door grated inward, allowing Daedalus to push through with his oil lamp outstretched. Ahead of him, a second flight of stairs descended into forbidding blackness. As the two men prepared to go on, Ariadne reached into a pocket of her gown, whispering, 'Theseus, you must not go without this.'

In her cold hand rested an ivory spindle, about one end of which had been wound a large white ball of heavy linen thread.

'Dear me, I'd quite forgotten about that,' said Daedalus in a low voice. 'Yes indeed, it is vitally important. You must trap one end in the last door and then pay out the thread as you go. It will serve as your guide when you return through the labyrinth.'

'I doubt I'll have far to go,' breathed Theseus. 'He seems well aware of our presence.'

'Oh, yes, he senses we're close by all right - that is why he now becomes silent, but I believe he will not be so quick to show himself. Asterion has no need to rush things since once people are down in the labyrinth they're there for good. From what the guards who listen at the grille tell me, I gather he is wont to stalk his prey as they grope around in the darkness trying to find a way out. I hear he does it for many hours. I believe for him it is a kind of cat and mouse game.'

'Hm, most reassuring,' commented Theseus. 'And you say this is the only entrance apart from that grille where they drop in his food or wait at night after the victims have been forced inside?'

'Since we walled up the few remaining exits, that is so,' answered Daedalus.

Still trembling, Ariadne kissed Theseus' cheek, whispering, 'May mighty Zeus protect you from harm. May he bring you safely back to us – back to me.' Her cheek glistening wet with tears, she remained by the door, a single lamp illuminating her pale features, causing her face to shimmer disembodied against the darkness. Theseus, accompanied by the old man, trod carefully downward into a dank, echoing well of oblivion.

'Hold your torch level,' hissed Daedalus as they reached the bottom of the steps where a short, vaulted passage led to yet another bronze-barred door less than the height of a man. 'I'll light the kindling at the top. By the way, you may be interested to know, this leads to the oldest part of Knossos. It was built long before the Greeks came – yes, long before the original palace was destroyed.'

'Was it really,' muttered Theseus, shaking his head in disbelief that Daedalus should choose this of all times to impart his knowledge of palace history. 'It'll make my visit all the more interesting, I'm sure.'

Daedalus lit the brand held by Theseus from his own lamp. The cramped passage shivered with a pallid light that cast swaying demon shadows about ancient stones that wept tears of black water.

'How can we be sure Asterion won't be waiting to make his escape through here?' asked Theseus. His words, though spoken softly, rolled about the confining walls in mockery.

'Very simple, sir,' came the none-too encouraging reply. 'Even should the beast crawl on his hands and knees, he has grown too large by far to push through this modest opening, although it was through here he was forced by armed men before he attained full size – even then with much difficulty. I always intended to have this passage blocked with stones but I never got around to it. Now if you please, young master, do try and keep that torch steady.'

Theseus watched him crouch to fumble with his key in the confined space by the door. The metal grinding of the lock sounded much too loud, ringing as it did about the passage walls. At first resisting his efforts, the door grated inward but only a short way. Even cool and logical Daedalus was wary of a blackness that breathed out such a dire odour of corruption. This, an odour unlike anything Theseus had known, writhed from within to assail their senses with cold evil, with maggot-crawling touch about their flesh. Daedalus turned to Theseus, saying, 'Ah, yes, I should have mentioned; this area is not served by the drains.' Theseus stared hard at him as he continued, 'I will close the door so as to trap the thread but of course I will not reset the locks.'

'That's most considerate of you,' breathed Theseus, easing by him. Holding the torch, which burned with a reassuringly bright flame, he stooped low and with his foot pushed the door further in to pile up the years of black dirt that had accumulated behind it. He bent low, thrust the torch ahead, peered into blackness then stumbled forward into what he imagined must resemble the pit of Tartarus. Able once more to stand, Theseus, gasping on fetid air, turned to see Daedalus peer in after him. He shook loose the end of the thread and offered it to Daedalus who reached up to take it, whispering, 'My son will ready your Athenian friends while I wait above with Ariadne. Should you, I mean, when you return they'll be all set to make a dash for the harbour. If you do not return then I fear your people are as good as dead, and probably myself also. I will pray for Athena to extend her guidance and strength.'

'Maybe I ought to join you in doing that,' Theseus replied.

The thread tightened. The door drew back into place with a dull thud that shivered the darkness ahead of him.

Theseus had known fear like many a man. He had faced danger. He had faced death. But as he eased up to his full height and lifted the torch high, as he swayed it from side to side, as he gazed into a grim unknown, those past dangers seemed as nothing. Men of flesh and blood he would challenge but here was an unseen peril, one heightened by every bounding shadow, by every thumping beat of his heart. This was a realm where no man ought to tread - a nightmare domain reeking of excrement, of death and of putrefaction, a realm fit to crush the very memory of light and life. The darkness threatened to engulf, to swallow him body and soul.

'Athena be my guide and strength,' he muttered, 'though I doubt she'd wish to enter this place whatever the cause. Still, I have the great king's finest sword, I have Daedalus' bespoke firebrand and I wear the stout sandals that protected my feet on the perilous road from Troizen to Athens. What more could a man want - except for ten or more well-armed soldiers?'

Unwilling for a while to move on, his thoughts turned to the man who would forever remain his hero. 'Heracles,' he thought, 'what would you have done? For your twelfth and final labour you descended unarmed into the realms of Hades to destroy Cerberus, the gruesome hound that devoured the souls of the living and the dead' He listened to his own breathing, to the beating of his heart then murmured, 'Perhaps you'd care to join me now.'

He became aware of noises. Scratching, scurrying, sounds that lay beyond his pool of light. Then the thought occurred – what if they had tricked him? What if this was some bizarre game contrived for the amusement of the court? Could it be that in his zeal to nourish Asterion, Minos, together with Pasiphae, driven by her blood lust, waited at the grille even now in gleeful anticipation of his death cries. Would the queen's carnality be sated by the roar of triumph from the creature she had spawned. If that were the case then the door behind him would already be locked. The temptation to return and try it he found difficult to resist, but resist it Theseus did.

The darkness had receded a short way now his eyes were adjusted but this offered little comfort because everything appeared blackened. 'Soot, that's what it is,' he mused. 'I heard it said that the older palace had been burned. Yes, it's soot.'

Close by, where anything might lie in wait, stood massive square piers supporting a low, beamed ceiling. Moving further inside he was able make out passages leading from the large chamber in which he found himself. If the floor had once consisted of stone flags these were no longer visible because a soil-like covering and other detritus spread as far as he could see. It was not smooth but heaped about and pockmarked so that it was impossible to say whether or not any were footprints.

Peering from side to side, torch held high in his right hand, Theseus paid his thread out until reaching the first of the square pillars. Beyond it lay impenetrable blackness, so thinking there was little point in proceeding that way he moved cautiously on to the second pillar. At first there was only more blackness but then something caught his eye. A short distance ahead and to his right lay a pale object that demanded he take a closer look. Moving forward, paying out the thread, his light illuminated what he saw was a human skull, sitting on heaped up dirt as if placed there to mock anyone unfortunate enough to pass that way.

'Did you come from Athens?' he breathed. 'Were you one of our young people given for sacrifice? As he looked on, the open mouth seemed to gape wider. It seemed to leer at him in silent laughter. Swirling beyond his meagre island of light he imagined disembodied voices. 'How nice to have you join us. How nice. How nice. How nice!'

On his flesh a sensation of crawling insects as something moved within the skull. Something glistened. Was an eye peering at him from within the socket? The rim of the socket grew aside – a lobe of emptiness. Lowering the torch closer, Theseus held his breath. A black beetle emerged to stagger blindly down the cheek on a cryptic journey from oblivion to oblivion.

Again something scampered in the darkness. It would be so easy to return the way he had come provided the door could still be opened. But to what would he return? To nothing more than shame - to a captivity with no means of escape. Then unless he died in resisting them he would be brought back to this dreadful place with neither light nor sword - with no more meaning to his life than the beetle that had so distracted him.

'Asterion, show yourself!' he cried aloud though his voice rattled about to echo, to scorn him in hollow vortices that diminished until wavering above the foul earth in unseen corners. 'Hear me! I am Theseus the Athenian! I come here to end your life! Asterion, show yourself!'

He continued on past the skull where bones lay strewn or protruded stark white from the ground. He hesitated on seeing what appeared to be small red spots moving to and fro and the scampering sounds were closer. Stepping forward, torch thrust out, he came upon a wall where his light revealed a cluster of bloated grey rats that scurried away to vanish from sight. On the wall were blackened and crumbling frescoes – scenes from ancient times, now hardly recognisable. But it was the object at the base of the wall that held his attention. Amidst an overpowering stench of decay were heaped the dismembered remains of more human beings – two, perhaps three. There was an arm with fingers outstretched, ribs together with other vestiges he did not care to try and identify. It, or they, were not as old as the skull he had passed by because rotted flesh still hung from the bones. And now the rats had retreated, unspeakable crawling vermin emerged to stake their claim to what remained.

Paying out the thread he continued on, moving the firebrand from side to side, now and again glancing back to see his own monstrous shadow waver from pillar to pillar. To his left loomed another passage and though he could see in it no obvious sign of human remains, there hung in the air a foulness that threatened to penetrate his very blood and bones. About to enter this passage Theseus stopped to regard the ball of thread. 'What if those rats make a meal of my lifeline?' he breathed. 'What if they destroy the only means I possess of finding my way out? Even now I could not say for certain which way I came. Yet I will go on. Yes – oh, yes, I will find that damnable creature even if I remain here afterwards to rot.'

He glanced anxiously at the flame of his torch but it continued to burn steadily. Nevertheless, it must expire sooner or later and when it did, shrouds of darkness would close over him more profound than any night. Without the torch he would be nothing. Nor without the thread, which he continued to pay out through a series of confusing, disorientating twists and turns, through pillared galleries, through chambers where lay pallid bones and sometimes, beyond the meagre spread of his light, horrors he had no desire to look upon. There were narrow passages altogether free of human remains but the significance of that would not become clear for some time.

At one point the thought entered his mind; what if he was re-crossing the route he had taken? Several times, Theseus hesitated at a junction to see if this had happened but he saw no thread.

He became aware on glancing at the spindle, that over half the thread was used. Was the beast watching from some hidden place as he wandered without direction through its noisome domain? Would Asterion wait unseen until the flame of his torch wavered, until it finally died, then spring upon him from the darkness? 'Oh, Heracles,' he breathed, 'I would exchange my future throne for your company now. Yet surely Athena is with me. Surely she would not have mocked me with her image in the clouds.'

The gallery he next entered went on a short distance before turning abruptly right. 'Should I go that way? And what is to be gained if I stay here? Nothing. I will go on until the thread runs out, until I must retrace my steps - until -.'

Around the next corner, a short way ahead, something else lay on the ground. A vague form, though he hardly needed to guess what it must be as the rats retreated. Yes, it was a body, partly eaten, headless, but not entirely succumbed to the ravages of decay. A few cautious steps past it found him gazing upon the head. If fear and loathing had been his companions since entering the labyrinth, they were to press yet closer upon him now. In spite of pallid worms that writhed glistening within the eye-sockets, within a gaping mouth that screamed in silence to all eternity, in spite of the blood-caked hair, he realised this had been a woman. The pitted, once frescoed plaster close by was spattered almost to the ceiling with dried blood and he knew it was here she had died after having groped her way in blind despair through this black hell. Had she been young or old? He could not be certain though he suspected her life had not blossomed to the full before she perished. Had she been brought from Athens? Was she one of his own people from the previous tribute, held prisoner until her time of condemnation? Had she prayed aloud to the gods or wept in silence? Perhaps she had entered the labyrinth with a flame of hope still burning in her heart then later, feeling that flame extinguished, begged for death to come quickly. The very walls must hold memory of her screams. He imagined that should he remain too long, the stones would release their burden of sound to torment him.

He trod carefully by, not wishing to look again at a sight that, should he survive, would forever haunt him. Further along he entered another pillared chamber with passages leading from it. Within his pool of light lay more bones, old, fragmented as though something had walked over to crush them in disdain for what they once were.

Theseus had determined to take the closest and widest of the three galleries leading from the chamber when he halted, torch held high, to listen. There was no furtive scurrying, yet there were sounds. It took him little time to realise that what he heard was not the sigh of a breeze nor the draught of a door opening. It was a sound of breathing. A deep, a monstrous breathing.

'So you are there!' he cried aloud. But his voice returned as a rattling confusion of empty echoes from the darkness. 'Show yourself!' he called. 'Come and face me! I am Theseus, Prince of Athens - a man of flesh and blood like the others you have slaughtered! Come now! Show yourself!' The hollow cacophony died away yet still he listened and still there was the sound of breathing. But from where? It seemed to coil from all about, from behind every pillar, from the black depths of every gallery.

He would continue along the passage but if the sound lessened he would retrace his steps then try the next. 'Lady Athena, grant me courage to go on.' The voice, though his own, gave a morsel of reassurance as he moved forward. 'If you are true to me I will magnify your name throughout Greece. In your name I will conquer all who stand against me. I will lay the spoils of war at your shrine and at no other!'

Some way along the passage to his right, there emerged a high doorway topped with massive stone lintel. He had not yet become accustomed to the stench of corruption when the air took on an even more ominous taint - the fresher, blood-choked fetor of the charnel house. Theseus approached slowly, hesitated at the portal, then entered.

He had experienced the battlefield. He had witnessed scenes of butchery and carnage that he thought could never be surpassed but nothing could have prepared him for the nightmare spectacle within as he held up the firebrand. The ceiling of what once must have been a modest hall was higher than other chambers through which he had passed with almost soot-free walls pale-plastered above areas once adorned with frescoes. This allowed his torch to illuminate the scene to greater effect.

At first the room appeared full of movement. Rats, clambering about disordered human remains, scurrying away before his light, though even as he watched, some of the dead continued to heave with the vermin that had invaded their innards. Above the bloodied lower walls protruded bronze bars that once might have been fitted with torches. Impaled on three of these, limp and dripping gore, were the partly dismembered bodies of men not long dead, hung there to keep them clear of the rats until meat and muscle had been stripped away. The faces of two, still intact, bore stark expressions of horror preserved at the moment of their deaths. The face of the third was much distorted by his final agony yet Theseus, staring at his disembowelled form, recognised the man who had died on the horns of the bull during Minos' ritual. He, too, had been cast down to feed the beast.

Such a foul theatre of despair could exist nowhere in the real world, of that Theseus was convinced. Had he been hurled into the depths of madness? Was he consumed by wild, macabre imaginings from which there could be no return to the light of reason? Should horror possess a sense of humour then he would surely be overwhelmed by torrents of shrieking laughter. A question crossed his mind: could this world be in some way more complete, more meaningful to the one that prowled its depths than was the world above to humankind?

Despite the scene confronting him he moved further inside - further because he had observed at the far end a stone lined chute that disappeared upward into obscurity. Was this chute topped by the bronze grille? If so it must be here that the condemned were precipitated living into the lurid hell he had so freely entered. Did enough light filter through in daytime to enable the beast to savour with its own eyes the stage of death over which it presided? Perhaps this was why there were so many bodies strewn about. Some must have remained close by the chute in vain hope of climbing back out. The cries, the screams of those dead men and women - those of his own people who had been sent here over the years, raged within his head. The screams grew louder. Echoing. Deafening. The very fabric of the hall shivered reeling in witness.

Then silence.

Or so it seemed for those numbing moments that followed. But it was no silence. Still there was the breathing. Now closer and something scraped against stone. Theseus spun about, his torch raised high. Peering at him through the doorway by which he had entered was the monstrous face of Asterion.

'So, you've shown yourself at last,' breathed Theseus.

Taking a step back toward the doorway he could see more of the beast – enough to determine its shape and form. Wide-spaced eyes, red jewels of death, glared upon him with a grim intent no man, even in the clamour of mortal combat, had ever encountered. Dark, thick-curled hair, blood-matted about the face, covered those parts of his body that were visible - a body that, although fuller and squatter, parodied that of a man so much in torso and limb that Theseus saw Asterion almost as one of his own gender. As he let go the spindle of thread the beast gave out a snort - not of rage but of malignant satisfaction. This foolish, this fragile little man had entered his lair; an intruder whose bleeding innards would be spread about to feed the rats once Asterion had gulped fresh blood and dined upon prime flesh.

One hand holding the torch aloft, Theseus grasped the sword hilt at his side then swished the weapon from its scabbard. Fired with a grim determination beyond any even he had known, he stepped forward. 'One of us now must die,' he called aloud, 'but by the gods if it is to be me then your blood will mingle freely with mine – that I do promise!'

The beast let out a thunderous bellow, thrust a hand into the room to grasp the doorframe with yellow-nailed fingers. The Minotaur snarled, drawing back thick lips. Pointed teeth gleamed pale against a blood-red maw. The sounds he made, the guttural hisses, the clicking from his throat – came as if he tried to speak. But if he did speak, what message other than a promise of death might he deliver? Theseus moved nearer still, sizing up the beast, oddly reassured by the knowledge that he could at last see what he faced. No longer did he fear what the shadows might conceal. On observing Asterion's eyes quiver half closed, he called, 'Ah, so you are troubled by the light of my torch.'

Asterion tilted his head, at last revealing the horns in full, pallid sheened beneath streaks of clotted gore. Growling from deep within, crouching lower still, he began to ease through the doorway with an awkward jerking motion of his great head. Theseus saw why the head was tilted. Asterion could not pass through otherwise because the width of his horns would not allow it so that was why the narrow corridors were freer of human remains. He saw it would take some moments for the creature to push through with horns scraping against the columns. But once inside the room, once able to stand, Asterion would tower head and shoulders above his intended victim.

Now! Now was the time to strike!

As a second arm reached beneath the lintel Theseus lunged forward with a cry of, 'Athena, guide my blade!' Brandishing the torch before Asterion's face and thrusting with all his strength, he drove his blade deep into the beast's thick neck. Wrenching it free, he stumbled back as the Minotaur swung an arm wildly at him, almost dashing the precious torch from his grasp. But with instincts honed in combat he brought down his sword with a mighty swing, cleaving through flesh and bone behind the wrist so the hand, larger by far than a man's, was severed through to spin aside in a spray of blood. The roar of anger that burst from the beast did not deter him from a third strike as, darting closer, his torch held before its eyes, Theseus plunged his blade into the gaping mouth where soft flesh offered no resistance until the metal struck bone. He dragged the blade back as Asterion's jaws slammed shut to screech fang-like teeth against smooth metal.

Theseus stepped back to see the beast struggling free of the doorway, his blood-drizzling head jerking from side to side. He was beginning to rise when Theseus stepped forward to deal a fourth blow. Thrusting the firebrand into the Minotaur's face he drove his blade beneath the chin before springing back to what he hoped would be a safe distance. Asterion fought to stand though blood issued freely from his wounds. Foaming red at the jaws, eyes blazing insane hatred he faced Theseus, roared aloud then lunged with startling agility, his head lowered and ready to strike with his deadly horns. On he pounded as Theseus, human bones cracking beneath his feet, leapt aside, knowing he must once more confront the beast whilst a voice within called, 'By the gods will he not die? Will he not die?'

Asterion halted then swung about to face Theseus. There he rose up, a black demon with at his rear the impaled corpses poised as his morbid trinity of dissolution. Lowering his head to charge once more, he staggered forward, faltered, thrust the mutilated arm at Theseus then snarling blood, spun about and fell backward to the floor with a bestial cry amidst the decaying wreckage of his victims. In choking agony he twice attempted to rise then, horns grinding against the stone floor, the great head settled with eyes frozen in upward stare.

Theseus looked on for a time then, 'Ah, at last you're done for!' he cried, raising high torch and sword. 'Yes – oh yes! At last you are done for!' Stepping cautiously over to the prostrate beast with sword at the ready, he recoiled at the fetid exhalation from Asterion's mouth as the shades of his life departed. He looked up to face the chute and called aloud, 'If you are listening, know this! Asterion is dead! And know that I, Theseus the Athenian slew him!'

As the echoes of his voice receded only the scamper of rats broke an ensuing silence but in that silence Theseus regretted having raised his voice. Should anyone have heard him they, and Minos in turn, would be alerted. They would without doubt ensure his triumph was short lived. He turned his attention to the thread that would lead him back to freedom and his gaze followed the meandering line back to the door through which he and the Minotaur had entered. But there was one task remaining - a task he regarded with a vengeful determination sufficient to overcome his loathing. Stepping over to the body of Asterion he propped the torch upright within the rib cage of a nearby corpse long since stripped clean of flesh, then began the grisly work with his sword.

In his mind Theseus watched himself from close by in numb, disembodied silence. He watched his sword cleave through flesh as if another wielded it. Watched his blade rise and fall in blood-spattering rhythm as it hacked through flesh and bone to sever head from body. The grinning dead who lay all about seemed to luxuriate in the spreading blood of their slayer - blood that pooled outward as though it would flood the whole chamber with a tide of gore.

It was done. The illusion dispelled. Theseus wiped his sword on the black-furred corpse before sheathing it, took up the firebrand, grasped one of the horns then wrenched the weeping head clear of its body. With the weight and size of the thing it would be no easy task to find his way out of the labyrinth but the torch, much to his relief, appeared to be burning as vigorously as before.

A final glance from the portal by which he had entered was met by the light of his flame reflected in furtive eyes. Grey rats skulked in the encroaching darkness to await their next feast – the headless body of the beast. Asterion's kingdom now belonged to them. His corpse would be their greatest, their final banquet.

Provided his light remained strong, the thread should not be difficult to follow but there would be much turning, twisting here and there between chamber and passage. The head of Asterion was a burden even for one of his strength, its other horn snagging frequently on one obstacle or another. But it was a burden he would not have relinquished even had it meant groping blindly by the feel of the thread. Then he spotted, snaking from a smaller gallery across his route, another length of his own thread. He must have crossed that way earlier but in which direction? Peering down he noted how the black earth in the narrower corridor was less disturbed, that one set of footprints, his own, was just visible. Heaving, dragging the head behind, he proceeded in the opposite direction to that of the prints, following with studied care as the precious trail led this way and that. At last the passage opened out into the hall with great square pillars that was familiar. A little further and Theseus came upon the grinning skull he had encountered not long after entering. This time it lay to his left and that meant the door was not far ahead.

***

'Did you hear that?' exclaimed Daedalus as he sat by Ariadne in the upper chamber.

'Hear what?' she cried, sitting bolt upright to seize his arm.

'The door,' he answered, disengaging her hand, reaching for a lamp then stepping over to the descending stairs. 'I believe I heard the door opening!'

'Daedalus!' she cried. 'Don't leave me alone!'

Daedalus ignored her and continued down to disappear from sight around the corner. He arrived within the short passage in time to see the door at its far end grate fully inward, the brightly burning torch appeared, followed by the blood-spattered face of a crouching Theseus who peered out at him. 'Sorry to keep you waiting,' he announced. 'Take hold of this, will you.'

Daedalus leaned forward to grasp the torch then backed away from the door to allow Theseus through, saying, 'Well, I take it you managed to kill the thing as you're back here in one piece.' He turned his attention to the torch then continued, 'Hm, I'm glad to see this is still burning properly but it is smoking more than it ought. Perhaps the mixture was not quite right. I'll take another look at it and – Oh! Oh, my goodness you've brought back Asterion's head! How utterly revolting!'

'Couldn't agree more,' gasped Theseus, clambering upright. 'But I assure you it's far better off him than on!'

Though still jammed in the doorway, the severed head of the Minotaur was fully visible to the old man as Theseus grasped one of the great horns in an attempt to manoeuvre it through the restricted opening. 'Better if you -,' he gasped, wrenching the head clear with much difficulty, 'better if you close this door. Once the rats find there's no more fresh food to be had down there they'll be looking for an easy way out.'

Theseus hauled his prize part way along the narrow passage then paused to watch as Daedalus, holding his breath, pulled shut and locked the door. Daedalus pushed by then clambered backward with lamp and torch to illuminate the way, unable to take his gaze from the gory trophy. He emerged into the upper chamber gazing back down the stairs then turned to find Ariadne standing in the middle of the room, hands clasped knuckle-white beneath her bare breasts.

'Wh – what has happened?' she asked, weakly, backing toward the exit.

Her voice trailed to nothing when Daedalus, torch and lamp held high, moved aside to reveal a blood and sweat-streaked Theseus struggling to the top of the steps to a scrape of horn against stone. A grunt, a final heave brought the head of Asterion swivelling into view where the grim trophy was released to glare up wide-eyed from the stone flags.

261

'Oh, my goodness!' cried Daedalus as Ariadne let forth a sharp cry and slid to the floor.

Theseus strode across to the prostrate Ariadne thinking to render help but hesitated to stare down at his befouled hands.

'You need a good clean-up, young sir,' offered Daedalus, nostrils twitching. 'You're covered with – with whatever was down there; you carry the odour of death and heaven knows what else about you. She'll not be too pleased with that when we bring her back to her senses.'

'The odour of death,' breathed Theseus. 'I carry more than odours. I carry memories enough to stalk the hours of sleep for the rest of my life. After what I witnessed down there, combat amongst men will seem an altogether lighter affair. But you're right – my flesh is crawling, I'm spattered all over with his blood and as you put it, heaven knows what else.'

'Take yourself up to the courtyard, young sir,' suggested Daedalus, placing his torch back into the wall bracket. 'Wash in one of the pools while I help the good lady out of here. The fresh air will doubtless revive her, yes, and I wouldn't mind a little of it myself.'

A plaintive moan caused them to glance down at Ariadne who, with a hand pressed over her eyes to avoid further sight of the Minotaur's head, was attempting to rise.

'Oh, and by the way,' continued Daedalus, 'what are you planning to do with that abominable thing? I doubt this poor girl will relish seeing it a second time and nor will I.'

'That,' replied Theseus, 'is going out of here with us. From what you told me the other day it could assist in our escape.' So saying, he seized one of the horns then dragged the gruesome object across the room to the higher flight of steps, streaking the flagstones with blood as he heaved it upward, muttering, 'Maybe I should do this more often.'

Daedalus waited until both had disappeared before placing the lamp aside so as to assist trembling Ariadne to her dainty feet. 'Rest a short while, dear lady,' he consoled, 'then we'll go outside.'

'Rest!' she responded. 'Not down here - no! Get me out now!'

Stars were still visible though the sky was brightening above a courtyard cool and quiet except for the bubbling of water in stone channels. Steadied by Daedalus, Ariadne emerged from beneath the colonnade, breathing deeply, thankful for the taste of fresh air. 'Are you feeling better, now?' he asked her as she rested with eyes closed against a square column. For a time Ariadne said nothing. Daedalus, gazing across the courtyard, observed another figure approach from the shadows opposite.

Ariadne looked up as Theseus approached to halt before them dripping wet, cleansed of Asterion's blood and of the foulness of the labyrinth that already was becoming for him an unreal, a distant world. 'It's done,' he announced calmly. 'I'm ready.'

As he spoke, three figures approached from another direction. On observing them, Theseus reached to draw his sword.

'No,' hissed Daedalus, staying his arm. 'It's my son, Icarus. He's been waiting with others in case you got out alive.'

'Nice to know they shared your confidence,' mused Theseus.

A fair-haired, bright-eyed, honest-faced young man in colourfully patterned kilt stood smiling before them. He was similar in age to Theseus but of slighter build and more delicate features. Theseus straight away took a liking to him. Close by, dressed in coarse tunics of ochre and green hovered a pair of burly, bearded men whose demeanour suggested they relied on brawn rather than intellect to negotiate their way through life. Both were armed with short swords and daggers.

'These men serve here as slaves,' explained Daedalus. 'They were captured as pirates off the mainland. They have no desire to remain in Knossos though I suspect their lives were never quite so comfortable. They are more than willing to assist in sailing the boat that carries you to Athens if you will give them men's work and allow them to serve under arms.'

'That I promise provided they serve us well on the journey,' replied Theseus.

'We'll do that, good sir,' answered one of the men. The other nodded his agreement.

'Very well,' said Theseus, glancing up at the sky, which had further brightened to the east since they had emerged from below. Turning to Icarus he said, 'What we need is some confusion to get things moving now daylight is almost on us. What's the situation with the guards who were left to keep a watch on me and the others? Are they still asleep?'

'No,' replied Icarus, 'one got up to relive himself but finding you had escaped he roused his fellows. They were so in fear of telling Minos they talked of fleeing into the country to save their skins – especially when I reminded them how our king deals with serious lapses of duty. I suspect they're already gone.'

'And what about my people?'

'They're with one of our men. He will take them through the palace at our signal. They will collect the arms that have been placed for them in readiness then they'll make their way down to the harbour at Amnissos. We've more men waiting there to help work the boat. They will begin their part as soon as they know we're on our way.'

'Then we'll stir things up here,' said Theseus. 'Where are the palace guards who come on duty during the day?'

'I imagine they'll be sound asleep next to their women after all the wine I had sent around to them last night,' replied Daedalus. 'They'll have no idea what's been going on.'

'Good – then wake them up. Tell them there is something in the middle of the courtyard the king needs to be informed about.'

'Lamos,' said Icarus, addressing one of the slaves. 'You do it – you know where their quarters are. They won't suspect you of anything.'

'I will, sir,' he answered, loosening the stout belt that held his scabbard, 'but they'll not expect to see the likes of me wearin' this so I'll leave it with you until I'm back.'

Crossing the courtyard he disappeared into obscurity. Theseus turned to Daedalus. 'And you, my friend – I imagine you'll no longer be safe in Knossos. You and your son will surely be sailing with us.'

'No,' replied Daedalus. 'As I said once before, I am too settled here, though I will not hold it against Icarus should he wish to leave with you and head for Athens - which I strongly recommend he does.'

'My father will see your hand in what has happened,' insisted Ariadne. 'He needs someone to punish even when he's not feeling especially vindictive - but vindictive in the extreme he will be over this.'

'I dare say he'll bluster somewhat,' answered Daedalus, 'but we've seen it all before.'

'Please,' begged Icarus, 'this is no small matter. It won't be dismissed by Minos in a day or two - you know that as well as anyone. You should take your chance with Prince Theseus and his people. I'll go as well but I won't leave Knossos without you.'

'I'm staying,' shrugged the old man. 'Minos can do as he likes. He'll soon come to his senses when the fountains stop working and the drains get blocked.'

'But Pasiphae won't look at it that way even if he does,' insisted Icarus.

Ariadne was about to speak again when the sound of agitated voices reached them. From the north colonnade emerged Lamos accompanied by two of the palace guards. With a gesture of his hand the slave directed them to the centre of the great open space where in the half-light some large dark object could be seen laying on the stone flags.

Ariadne clapped a hand to her mouth. 'Father will never forgive us!'

'And I'll not forgive him!' responded Theseus, gazing hard at her.

Lamos returned to reclaim his sword whilst the rest watched the two guards approach the object, rubbing their tired eyes before stopping in their tracks. Agitated words passed between them as they circled warily about it. Silence, then both, taking no more than a glance at Theseus and his party, hurried back in animated conversation the way they had come.

'Let's be off now!' exclaimed Theseus.

***

The mighty ruler of Knossos was ill pleased to be woken as the pale light of morning seeped about the edges of the leather blinds covering the windows of his suite. It was the king's custom to remain at rest until the sun was high enough to dapple his frescoed walls with light, until his as well as the queen's earthenware bath were prepared, until the palace was fully alive with staff and slaves hurrying about their business. Apart from that, the two slave girls he had summoned to his bed had not taken their leave until some considerable time after the midnight gong had sounded.

The attendant who with some misgiving had roused him from slumber, now stooped at a respectful distance from the royal bed with white-knuckled hands clasped tightly at his waist. One of the several guards whose responsibility it was to stand sentinel at the end of the outside corridor hovered by the door, issuing orders to his comrades. A woollen wrap pulled loosely about herself, hair awry, Pasiphae peered out from the curtained doorway of an adjacent room, glanced along the corridor to a nearby light well, blinked in disbelief then complained aloud, 'Why are people shouting and running about? It's hardly daybreak!'

'Yes, what *is* the meaning of this?' demanded Minos, sitting upright.

'M-my Lord,' stuttered the man, 'the guards and many other people – they are gathered in the courtyard because of what has been found there.'

Seeing she was not to be the subject of attention, fearing also she did not at that moment present to the world her best image, Pasiphae let the curtain fall back then returned to her bed. Her companion of the night, a young, athletic man of Nubian aspect, now reappeared from within the anteroom where he had taken refuge in fear of discovery.

The babble of raised voices from the courtyard below filtered ever louder into Minos' room until it was evident that what had been described as a gathering had by then become more a sizeable commotion. Heaving his bulk from the bed, Minos dragged a leather kilt about his waist, gave the attendant an angry glance then stepped over to the window where he rolled up the blind. He stared for some time before turning about, his expression clouded with anger. 'What is the meaning of this?' he growled at the quaking attendant.

'Sire, I - I cannot say. I was not present.'

'Just *what* is going on?' shrieked Pasiphae from her chamber.

'What's going on, you ask!' bellowed Minos in crimson-faced rage. 'If you can drag yourself from your damned bed you'll see what's going on!'

Pasiphae, pulled on an embroidered robe, shook then pushed back her hair, reappeared through the curtain, looked about then hurried across to the king's room.

'Look out there!' barked Minos, gesturing to the window.

Seeing what lay in the courtyard below, Pasiphae drew back, exclaiming, 'No, it cannot be! It's a trick. That scheming old fool Daedalus is behind it – mark my words.'

'Use your eyes, woman!' growled Minos. 'Can't you see his blood streaked across the flagstones from where it was dragged? Down there lies the head of Asterion!'

'But who,' she gasped, 'who could have done it if it wasn't him?'

Minos ignored her and thrusting the attendant aside, bawled at the guard, 'Get Tauros up here - now!' Glaring at Pasiphae he continued loudly, 'I'll have the entire guard out. I'll find out who's behind this and when I do they will pay most dearly. They will suffer! Yes, they will suffer until they beg me to let them die!'

Another guard, out of breath through hurrying, pushed by the one at the door and blurted, 'My Lord, the Athenians have escaped! They were seen fleeing the palace and some claim Lady Ariadne was with them. There are slaves of ours said to be among them and those men left on watch during the night are also gone.'

269

The king appeared momentarily speechless while his wife, hands placed firmly on hips confronted him to declare, 'The hand of Daedalus *is* in this, I tell you!'

With a deep-throated cry of, 'Shut up, woman and get out of here!' Minos strode across the room, pulled on his tunic, delved into the pine chest to extract belt and sword which he buckled hurriedly about his stout waist. He was in the act of fastening on leather boots when another figure entered the room. The newcomer, in metal-scaled leather tunic with plumed bronze helmet clasped beneath his arm, scabbard buckled at his side, was strongly built, stern-faced and short-bearded. Stepping before the king, he affected a slight bow. 'Sire, I received your summons but was warned of the escape on my way here. I have ordered my men to arm and assemble at the north entrance. They'll soon be there in sufficient numbers to give chase.'

'Good!' responded Minos, 'the Athenians will be making their way to the harbour since there's nowhere else for them to go. We'll head there as soon as your men are ready!'

As Minos strode to the door his general hesitated to glance back at Pasiphae who had retreated to one side of the room. In that frozen moment, as their eyes met, his thoughts were hers and her thoughts his. Thoughts that expanded into memories of dark passion that each hoped would soon again be theirs. The persistent rumour that one of her daughters was also involved with this man, Pasiphae had dismissed as no more than malicious gossip. What more could any woman do for a man than she had. And when it came to her looks, when it came to her figure, everyone agreed the gods had been most considerate.

The attendant, waiting at a discreet distance in case the king should find his presence a further irritation, had observed what passed between the queen and the general. He would doubtless add nourishment to the fertile shoots of well-established rumour.

Returning to the window, Pasiphae gazed across to the palace buildings opposite. In the courtyard below, guards had cleared people away, leaving the severed head of the Minotaur to stand in gruesome solitude. That the object laying down there might have been anything to do with her, Pasiphae could no longer accept. Her Asterion had died long ago as a small child. This Asterion, this loathsome creature, had been sent to take his place by the gods to bring retribution upon her husband as well as death to the enemies of Knossos, including those at present in flight to the harbour.

Her thoughts were broken by the arrival of Phaedra who entered in a state of bewilderment. 'Mother,' she blurted, 'there are people dashing about everywhere! Father almost knocked me flying in the corridor! What *is* going on? And where's Ariadne - her bed has not been slept in.'

'Not slept in!' snapped Pasiphae. 'What d'you mean, not slept in?'

'I mean she hasn't been there, mother! You know – not slept in her bed. What else am I supposed to mean? And that – that foul thing in the courtyard I saw from the balcony and -.'

'Yes,' declared Pasiphae, 'someone has killed Asterion and what's more the Athenians have been

271

set loose. Your dear father has cleared off with Tauros to chase after them.'

'So the thing is dead,' muttered Phaedra. 'I thank the gods for it.'

Pasiphae turned her face to the window, muttering under her breath, 'Well that damnable creature is no more though he's had his uses over the years. No - Ariadne wasn't the only one having bad dreams about him. I had a few myself though I thank the gods there were sufficient consolations to help me pass the night.' Then much louder she added, 'Your father will have to find other ways of dealing with undesirables, won't he, dear! Still, a few people will rest easier in their beds - don't you think?'

There was no reply. When she looked about, Phaedra was gone.

Minos and his general, Tauros, each in light chariot pulled by a grey mare, rode side by side before a cohort of spearmen and archers. They were clear of the palace, heading north along the paved road when they saw smoke billow ominously into the early morning air above Amnissos.

'Damn them!' exclaimed Minos. 'They have fired some of the ships!'

'I'll ride on ahead!' responded Tauros, one of only a handful of similarly mounted men. 'I beg you, sire, hold back and do not place yourself in danger. The Athenians may be armed – the slaves also. They'll be desperate men!'

'Not as desperate as they're going to be,' growled the king, 'so you'd better get moving! Yes, and watch out in case my daughter is with 'em!'

Those about their business in the harbour town were also aware of the disturbances. They had already tasted the odour of burning timber and hemp as it spread invisible tendrils through alleyway and home. Stepping outside, those newly awake were greeted by the sight of drifting smoke while others at a higher vantage point observed a number of vessels belching smoke and flame. Men dashed back and forth on the harbour quay in what looked like general confusion whilst gulls circled noisily overhead. On seeing others sprawled motionless on the quay, the watchers knew this was no minor incident.

Close to the ships, a fair young man of slim but rugged stature, was conspicuous by his determined stance. Together with four younger companions he stood half way along the quay, sword and circular shield of boiled hide ready to drive off or strike down anyone who attempted to approach in pursuit of his people. Seeing no immediate danger, Theseus glanced over his shoulder to observe the freed slaves, Lamos among them, hauling ropes, raising the mast, readying for departure a large boat, the very same boat that had brought them to Crete. That vessel was last in line and was moored where the quay turned abruptly left to extend seaward as a boulder breakwater.

'If we're not quick,' declared one of Theseus' companions, 'the flames will reach our vessel then we'll have no means of getting away!'

'We'll manage,' he replied. 'They'll not hoist sail until we row clear of the flames.'

'Look out!' called another. 'There are men in chariots heading our way and they're all armed!'

The clatter of hooves grew louder as Theseus looked about but thick, acrid smoke rolled across the quay, obscuring those who approached. When it lifted the Cretan chariots were much closer.

'There are five of them!' called one of Theseus' men. 'They'll try to ride us down!'

'And there are five of us!' he exclaimed though he did not stand waiting for the onrush. Letting drop his shield then sheathing the blade that had served him so well in the labyrinth, Theseus dashed to the nearest boat. This was well alight with angry flames raging and cracking skyward from her midst. There were loose timbers strewn about her deck – many of them ablaze – some within easy reach from the quayside. Seizing one of these to brandish as a flaming torch, Theseus prepared to meet the pursuers who by now were almost on them. Two of his companions followed his example and shouting loudly, darted forward to thrust flaming brands directly at the oncoming horses. Confronted by the danger, aware the quay did not allow enough room for them to get to the rear of the Athenians, the Cretans reined back their terrified mounts, pulled their chariots around then retreated a short distance to more open space nearer the town end of the quay. The Athenian youths, emboldened by this transient success would have dashed forward but Theseus called, 'Stay where you are or they'll cut you down! Stay!'

His companions obeyed but the Cretans were already stepping from their chariots and drawing their swords. They approached resolutely with the formidable, plume-swaying Tauros striding in their midst. Once more the breeze shifted. Dense smoke

274

charged with dancing red embers swept between the two parties while burning timbers cracked. The smoke obscured one party from the other causing men on both sides to reel back choking but it enabled the besieged Athenians to retreat further along the way they intended to go.

'Be ready!' ordered Theseus. The smoke swirled about then began to ebb. As it did so, their adversaries appeared as spectral images about to emerge from the shifting vapours, some with hands over their faces, others coughing through the effects of the smoke. Theseus did not wait to identify the closest man but sprang forward with brand and sword, taking the Cretan off guard, thrusting his flame into the man's face then striking with his blade through bronze armour and deep into his ribs. The soldier's cry was short, his death quick though Theseus had not the time to relish victory.

Unlike the Cretans who faced him, unlike those of Minos' men who were soon to catch up with them, Theseus' companions were too young to have acquired the skills of hardened warriors in battle. And like Theseus they wore neither helmet nor armour but only a tunic or kilt of linen. He must somehow distract the enemy if his comrades were to stand a chance of survival. But as sword clashed against sword there was one of their adversary's number who singled Theseus out for combat, one bigger, one more formidable in appearance than the rest. This man faced him squarely with horsehair plume of menacing aspect swaying above a bronze-clad head. Theseus guessed the man was Minos' general but a cry from one of the Athenians distracted him. In that moment a blade flashed, cleaving the flaming timber from his grasp, causing him to leap aside. The Cretan thrust hard at him with a cry of, 'This is the end of your journey, Athenian!'

Theseus men would have to fend for themselves but he hoped their extra number would tell. Confusion grew as the two circled one another. There was shouting from along the quay as well as from the people of Amnissos gathering above to witness the combat.

Calamitous flames had spread to take hold of other boats, bright embers spat upward to scamper on the breeze whilst smoke continued to sting eyes and throats of the combatants. As the smoke once more swirled to envelop them, Theseus, expecting Tauros to lunge at him, leapt aside. So doing he encountered one of his own men with gashed and bleeding head, struggling bravely with a Cretan. Each grappled the sword arm of the other in desperate attempt to prevent him using his blade but the Cretan was well protected and about to better his adversary. Theseus struck the man in the side of the jaw with his sword hilt to send him sprawling then jumped aside as Tauros emerged from the smoke with sword levelled. The smoke was shifting yet again as the two faced one another, eyes bright with deadly intent. Men were running along the quay toward them from the burning ships, shouting, waving their arms as the two men lunged to seize the sword arm of the other. The pair of Cretans still fighting disengaged, retreating to a safe distance as two more Athenians and two slaves approached with swords drawn. Theseus took advantage of

Tauros' distraction to strike the sword from his grasp, sending it ringing to the ground.

'The boat is ready!' yelled one of the slaves, circling, levelling his sword to strike Tauros from behind.

'No!' cried Theseus, thrusting his enemy aside to avoid the blow. 'He is not to be stabbed in the back! He will fall in honour or he will prevail against me!' But over his adversary's shoulder Theseus saw them. Tauros' armed footmen, having descended from amongst the harbour buildings, were hastening onto the quay. There were spearmen and worse, the much-feared Cretan archers with at their head the stout, red-bearded man Theseus knew well. Minos himself. The danger was now acute as, striking his adversary with his sword hilt, sending him reeling back he called to his men, 'Leave us and flee!'

The slaves backed away then held their ground when seeing the Athenians would not leave until the contest was resolved. Time was Theseus' enemy whilst Tauros, scrambling to pick up his sword, saw how rapidly the flames were spreading toward the ship his adversaries sorely needed. Theseus leapt at him, intending to force the matter before it was too late, his blade hissing through the air as Tauros sprang aside to avoid the blow. The two lunged, thrust, circled and parried. The smoke thickened, flames gushed onto the quay yet neither man was able to gain advantage over the other. Another cry from the boats and seeing Tauros glance aside, Theseus struck his adversary's sword, shattering the bronze blade with the tougher metal of his own weapon.

'Kill him!' yelled the Athenian youth with the gashed head.

Theseus eyed Tauros who stood his ground calmly though death was surely a heartbeat away. 'No,' Theseus responded, 'I'll not kill a defenceless man who has met me in fair combat. Let us go – quickly!'

The disarmed Tauros made no attempt to impede, no attempt to follow as Theseus and his comrades sprinted along the quay. Past smouldering bales of cloth they ran, past clustered piles of smoke-blackened jars waiting to be loaded onto ships that issued stinging vapours or roared bright tongues of fire above their heads.

The requisitioned boat, already cast off, was endangered by burning fragments that leapt back and forth to the caprice of the breeze, some scattering over her broad gangway where men and girls ladled them over the side. The vessel next to their own smouldered heavily, its timbers cracking from stem to stern. It must soon erupt violently into flames. Theseus and his men leapt down onto the deck of their ship while those on board, including some of the girls, thrust determinedly with oars against the stone quay in their efforts to drive the vessel far enough away for her oars to be deployed. Even with the help of the less skilled Athenians, the ship was undermanned though she rode higher in the water and proved more responsive because little cargo had been loaded.

Amid the turmoil of smoke, archers were seen hurrying along the quay with Tauros at their head. Very soon they would be in position to loose their arrows at those in the boat, most of whom were exposed and defenceless. The gaudily attired Ariadne who, clutching a large patterned bag containing a number of her prized possessions, had been moved forward for safety where she crouched terrified in the bow, partly concealed by the gangway, together with four of the Athenian girls.

Some of the men uttered prayers to Zeus, some to Poseidon, some to Athena, others to deities of foreign lands as teeth-gritting oarsmen strained hard to drive the ship clear. Theseus remained in the stern, watching events about the harbour, shield at the ready to try and stop any arrow that might fly their way.

Some would later argue over which among the gods had answered their pleas but, as the boat ploughed on with maddening slowness a series of dull reports sounded from the quay. Lurid incandescence belched high into the air above a billowing chaos of smoke. Someone behind Theseus called out, 'It's the oil jars! The heat's burst 'em! Oil is fuelling the flames!'

A large section of the quay was engulfed in rolling black clouds as hot oil flooded into blazing timbers and bales of fabric to further heighten the conflagration. Amidst blinding confusion, men ran back and forth, some attempting to cut away burning vessels whilst others, clothes afire, hurled themselves into the water. So many boats had become blazing lamps that, had it been night, they would have lit the skies above Knossos in ghastly majesty.

A small number of archers had nevertheless reached a point where they could draw their bows and take aim. Theseus' oarsmen strove ever harder to distance the vessel from peril as other men struggled to raise the sail. Arrows hissed by. One embedded itself in the mast, one glanced harmlessly from the timbers close to an oarsman, another took root in planking next to one of the women in the bow while a fourth planted itself in Theseus' raised shield. Storm-cloud smoke swept along the quay to obscure the archers, spoiling their next aim. By the time it subsided, the ship was clearing the breakwater, soon riding the waves in a northerly breeze, her hull creaking, her sail well filled and straining at the cords. With a shift in the smoke, Theseus could make out two of those watching from the town end of the quay - Minos and Tauros. Vengeance would surely be striding large amid their thoughts.

From a warehouse balcony above the harbour another gazed: one whose journey from the palace had been made in unplanned haste. Phaedra had watched the spreading flames as her father rode out, listened to sounds of clamour and confusion when the vessel at the end of the quay was altogether hidden by smoke. She had waited in anguish until the boat reappeared. She had watched the sail fill and had seen the golden image of the double axe catch morning sunlight, then gasp aloud as oil from the jars fuelled the flames into greater intensity. She had watched the boat draw clear of the harbour then cried out in anger because she was far too late to join her sister who she knew was on board. Phaedra continued to watch as the vessel headed into open water. It was some time before her attention returned to the commotion by the quay. There her father, surrounded by armed men, looked across as those few of his ships still undamaged weaved out into the harbour while the rest were devoured by hungry flames. Phaedra stepped back for fear of being observed and once more turned her attention to the diminishing vessel, knowing her well clear of harm with her course set on breezes of freedom.

'Ariadne, you bitch,' she murmured. 'You knew what was going to happen. I bet you even helped plan it with old Daedalus. You and your lover boy from Athens, yes - and with never a thought, never a word to me, your own sister. And now I'm left here with the screaming, the shouting, the recriminations. I know what I'm in for, don't I just –, "Whose side are *you* on - mine or your father's? What did *she* tell you before she left? Who was behind it all?" Well, sister dear, you won't shake me off that easily. There will be ships coming in soon enough and ships going out. Knowing you, you'll not dote too long over the Athenian once you find your home comforts out of reach. And I've a feeling once you and him are far enough away from here he won't bother too much about you either. Well I'll keep out of the way of things here. I'll bide my time - then we'll see what happens.'

She had never spoken to Theseus, she had never stood in his presence yet Phaedra had conceived a desire for him surpassing all reason. A desire so strong that she told herself the gods had to be responsible and must have a purpose beyond her understanding for inciting within her the same unquenchable lusts that possessed her mother and sister. In Theseus she, too, had envisaged salvation. She perceived him as a light to guide her from the vicissitudes, from the ongoing turmoil of family life in Knossos. Now he was gone - fled from Crete with Ariadne. For the time being nothing would change. Apart from her brothers with whom she shared little in the way of interests, Phaedra's days would be spent mainly in the company of her attendants and her slaves. Often, too, her nights.

***

'You must execute them!' Pasiphae shrieked. They sat opposite one another in the otherwise deserted megaron, Minos with his face buried in his hands. 'He,' she continued vehemently, 'that man you have wandering about the place messing with the drains and playing with his stupid contraptions – *he's* behind it all – him and that pasty looking son of his. The Athenians could never have escaped otherwise. There are already rumours here in Knossos - rumours that you've grown weak in the head so, yes you need to act the way people expect. Death is the only answer to my mind! Death for the pair of them!'

Lowering his hands to grasp the edge of the seat, Minos glared at her. 'Yes, woman – and as we're on the subject of Daedalus, there's that other rumour, the one that's been around for years. Yes, the one about how Asterion was conceived! I've ignored it until now because it suited all concerned. If it's true then I dare say the old man's in part responsible for that as well. But the way *I* look at it,' he growled, rising from his seat to stare down at her with fists clenched, 'the main culprit is *you*, my own damned wife! And talking of drains - what a splendid reputation from the depths of iniquity *you've* earned for yourself!'

282

'How dare you!' she cried, leaping to her feet then striding about in circles. 'It was *you* who regarded Asterion as a gift from the gods! I never did. And let's not forget whose idea it was to keep that damnable creature under the palace to scare the wits out of everyone. *Your* idea – not mine! That's why Ariadne, *our* daughter, has fled! Yes, fled with those Athenians to escape the very memory of the thing!'

'The gods decreed we kept Asterion no matter how he came about,' Minos snarled, stepping over to bring his face close to hers. 'And whenever you had the opportunity we knew where *you'd* be found after the tributes took place, didn't we. Oh, yes – hovering by that damned grille waiting to hear their screams – waiting to satisfy your own perverted needs! If you'd found some means of doing it you'd have witnessed at close hand every bloody moment of what took place down there! Hah – then maybe you'd have died from a surfeit of orgasms!' Minos stepped away from her then turned to declare, 'I should have confined *you* in the labyrinth to keep company with the thing you gave birth to! As for Daedalus and *his* son – they at least would be of use to me even if I kept them locked away until they forgot what the rest of the world looked like. In fact, woman, they already *are* locked away since I'm not quite as addle-headed as you like to think.'

'Locked away!' she responded, striding up to him. 'Locked away where?'

'In the highest part of the palace as it happens - in the top room of the north-west tower where there isn't anywhere for them to go except through the window. That will teach them to defy me. Yes - might as well throw sticks at a lion.'

'Might as well -!' she mocked. 'Lion? Hah! You let the Athenian defy you and look where it's got us – most of the ships at Amnissos burned to a cinder and all their cargoes lost. Your precious Daedalus will find a way out. He'll cause more mischief yet. Mark my words!'

'Mischief!' he blurted, shaking a finger before her face. 'You'd know all about mischief wouldn't you. But don't work yourself up over them escaping – they'll need to sprout wings to do that! And you can keep your damned nose out of my affairs from now on or – or else I'll have you thrown down there to take Asterion's place! Yes, and that would put an end to the most persistent rumours of all – those that say how and with whom you keep yourself occupied when my back is turned!'

'Oh, and just what d'you mean by that? I suppose you've been listening to the little tarts I've seen sneaking about at night near your -.'

Her tirade was cut short by a deliberate cough from one who stood by the main entrance to the chamber. 'You sent for me,' said Phaedra, stepping cautiously inside and looking from one to the other.

'Did I, now,' growled Minos. Pasiphae kept a sullen silence as he turned to his daughter. 'Yes, I did, didn't I. What were you doing near the harbour this morning when all that was going on? And don't bother to deny it – you were seen by several of my men staring out to sea from the warehouse then running back here. You were hoping to follow your sister if I'm not mistaken. Did you know what she was up to? Did you know she was going to run off with those damned Athenians?'

'No I didn't,' responded an indignant Phaedra. 'If I had, I assure you both I'd have set off to Amnissos a damned sight earlier to catch the same boat!'

'But you must have known something was going on,' pressed Minos, his outward manner growing somewhat calmer in spite of Phaedra's comments.

'No I didn't,' she insisted. 'Not until I saw you chasing off after them with the soldiers.'

'Don't believe her!' interjected Pasiphae. 'The two of them were always whispering behind our backs. They were *always* conniving together.'

'I don't care whether you believe me of not,' responded Phaedra, her voice rising higher by the moment. 'I don't give a fuck if you banish me the way you did Acalle! At least in Libya I'd be away from this madhouse!'

'You ungrateful little bitch!' exclaimed Pasiphae, lunging over to strike the girl hard across the mouth with the palm of her hand. 'After all I've sacrificed for you and the others when you were children. Why *ever* did I bother!'

'Sacrificed for us!' yelled Phaedra, thrusting her away. 'You wouldn't sacrifice a fucking hairpin! Not for us - not for anybody! We were all brought up by household servants – yes, and by slaves - and everyone knows it! That's how much *you* sacrificed! From what I've heard *you* were too busy fucking the palace guards to bring anyone up! What surprises me mother, is that you never set up house by the harbour. You could have serviced father's entire navy - unless you already have!'

Hands clutching her face, mouth agape as Phaedra dashed from the room, Pasiphae shrieked, 'Oh, you venomous, evil little slut!'

Raucous laughter from behind did nothing to placate Pasiphae's mortified expression. She swung around to see Minos clutching his belly, swaying from side to side on the seat as though in the midst of a drinking bout. 'Women!' he spluttered. 'Women - what *would* we do without 'em?' He was still laughing when Pasiphae gathered up her skirt and fled from his presence. Eyes ablaze, jaw set hard in dire anger, she almost collided with another figure who she might or might not have acknowledged but on this occasion ignored altogether in her dash along the corridor. Deucalion paused to watch as with her long skirt billowing, she vanished around the corner.

***

Phaedra stood by a column, her cheeks wet with tears. She gazed up at the sky, imagining herself in another land. Earlier that day she would have been too afraid to enter the great courtyard but during that afternoon the severed head of Asterion had been removed by those slaves unfortunate enough to have been conveniently at hand. Later, the priests had congregated to chant aloud whilst the grisly object, covered in sailcloth to hide its features, was burned to ashes at the shrine of Poseidon. Minos himself had lit the flames. Minos had spoken the dedication. Minos had led the chanting. It was after that Phaedra had become embroiled in their quarrelling.

She was lost in contemplation when footsteps approached. At first she thought it must be Daedalus then she recalled overhearing her father confirm he and his son's incarceration. She looked aside to discern in the moonlight another figure, tall and well-groomed in richly patterned tunic.

'Deucalion,' she breathed, 'it's you.'

'Yes,' I heard mother and father sounding off at each other and at you a short while back. She almost ran into me straight afterwards. I only found out what had been going on around here when I returned from the hunt this afternoon. I saw the results down at the harbour so it must have been quite a show. I take it you're all right.'

'Yes, it was quite a show and yes I'm all right, thank you. I suppose you heard me dare father to banish me. Perhaps now he will. It was a foolish thing to say. Libya doesn't appeal to me one bit.'

'He won't banish you,' said her brother, placing an arm about her shoulder. 'I won't let him do that.'

'Hmm,' she smiled, 'he might decide to banish you as well, though the way things are going, the way father and mother are behaving, you're the only one fit to take over affairs in Knossos.'

'No, he won't banish me either. He needs someone in charge when he's away from Crete. Neither Glaucus nor Catreus would be suited to stepping into his shoes even if he felt inclined to allow it - and someone needs to keep an eye on mother for reasons we already know. Apart from that, I'm not sorry to see the end of that damnable thing we kept below nor an end to those pointless sacrifices. As you know, I wanted nothing to do with any of it. Our situation will change now the

Athenian has slain Asterion, for it was surely he who did it. That and the fact they so readily escaped will undermine father's confidence. A firmer hand will one day be needed here.'

At his mention of the Athenians her thoughts turned once more to Theseus. Had her father ordered his pursuit at sea? Probably not. It would take time to send out messengers, time to gather enough ships from other ports to replace those destroyed at the harbour - and now was not a good time for him to leave the palace.

'Would you really have sailed with Ariadne to Athens?' asked her brother.

'Yes,' she replied. 'I saw Theseus, their prince. I - I wanted him more than any man I ever knew, though I knew him not at all. He gave me hope. Ariadne imagines she's using him, I'm sure of that. I think before long she'll regret it.'

'Who but the gods can know what is to happen,' said Deucalion. 'Perhaps one day -.'

'Yes, perhaps one day,' breathed Phaedra.

Deucalion squeezed her arm, saying, 'Enjoy the night air,' then continued on his way. She had not cared to ask what he was about that evening. Phaedra was aware of her brother's assignations with various women of the palace but the dapper Deucalion conducted such affairs with more discretion than others of their family. He was calm, self-assured, and Phaedra had always admired the way he refused to become involved in family conflicts.

When darkness fell she waited, savouring the pleasant air of the night and listening for footsteps. The now silent courtyard should have held no more anxiety for Phaedra than ever it had, yet having witnessed that day the face of Asterion, the shadow of the beast now lingered. She peered into the darkness and listened. It was not so unusual for Tauros to pass this way in the evening. Should he not do so, there were always the girls who attended her chamber. They well understood her needs.

Chapter 11
The ISLAND of NAXOS

Crete lay well astern in an early afternoon haze, a vague mass dominating the horizon. For the first time in her life Ariadne had found herself in open water, far from land, though they were not entirely beyond the realms of human contact. Other vessels passed by, most plying southward on their way to Crete, occasionally within hailing distance. The journey was not to her liking. She had not expected to fear the sea but fear it she did even though conditions were fair and the breeze warm. The constant buffeting together with the sway, rise and fall of the boat she found unnerving. The hard wooden seat, the planking against which she was obliged to prop herself imparted an aching soreness she experienced now for the first time in her life. She regretted not having brought a gown though they had given her a rough linen sheet with which she had wrapped herself to keep the salt spray and harsh sun from her delicate skin. The breeze had disarrayed her hair to the point where she imagined herself looking like a tavern whore and she was fearful of the damage that might be caused to the nails of her fingers and toes whilst scrambling about the boat.

Until obtaining the sheet her breasts had been naked whilst those of the Athenian girls were covered by their pale gowns. The crew manning the boat, some rough slaves, some even rougher pirates with scars, sores, missing and discoloured teeth, one minus his ears, had ogled her. They had passed remarks, had grinned lewdly when they knew Theseus was not looking. The expressions on their faces Ariadne saw as ripples upon a well of unspeakable thoughts.

Amidst the luxuries of the palace where almost everyone, especially the slaves, had good manners, it pleased her to be regarded with desire by others. Like her mother and her sister Phaedra, Ariadne all but demanded it. The sensual pleasures of the palace could never be found amongst these people. In their relations with women she imagined they behaved much as mongrel dogs in the street and so she regarded them in the same light. In the harshness of this wider world and in spite of everything that had passed, Ariadne already felt stirrings of regret over having abandoned Knossos.

As the hot afternoon wore on the breeze stiffened. Cold spray now and again hissed by to sting her face and for a while she felt very sick. Several times she was obliged to hang over the side of the boat though the sickness was not to last. Nor did she welcome offers of consolation from the fussing Athenian girls. She feared it might place her under an obligation. To her consternation she heard someone remark that even should the winds remain favourable, it would be well into the following day before they reached the southernmost of the Cyclades Islands. The following day! Such a long time. Such an unbearably long time. She had never thought to question Theseus about the length of the journey.

She had expected his full attention throughout the voyage so had later moved to sit behind the mast, away from the chattering Athenian girls. She regarded their small talk as banal. But Theseus, sword at his side, had spent the greater part of the time so far in dialogue with the crew as well as with his own people. Now and again he would step along to offer Ariadne a little conversation and a cup of rough wine. The wine she had refused until thirst overcame a dislike of something she would otherwise have tipped disdainfully over the side.

'I hope you're feeling better,' he at one point remarked.

'I'd feel better if you spent more with me instead of those brutes,' she replied.

His response was, 'Forgive me but I must keep an eye on them – especially where the young women are concerned. You, I doubt they would not dare molest.'

'I'd drown myself rather than face that,' she declared.

'I don't think you would,' he grinned, 'it would spoil your complexion.' Moving closer so as not to be overheard, he added. 'These men were wholly with us when it came to escaping Crete - but one or more might consider reverting to his old ways now we're clear of danger. Some may have realised by now that we need them more than they need us. Believe me, I'll cut down the first of them and any man who shows signs of disorder – crewman or no.'

'I'll try not to look at them,' she said. 'I'll go back to where I was and keep myself to myself. But when will you sleep?'

'I'll sleep after dark with our Athenian lads in the bow. Two at least of them will remain awake until the sky lightens in case anything happens. Don't forget, the crew will need sleep as well.'

But even as he spoke he sensed his feelings toward her were changing. Once a pampered bird flitting about realms of opulence, she had now been divested of her plumage and swept into the uncompromising world beyond Knossos. Though still a woman of great beauty, the sea spray had washed away her charisma. Two boxes of dried figs were the only food the men had been able to bring into the vessel in their hurry to escape but she had no wish to eat until landfall in case her sickness returned. Ariadne did not belong here. The voyage for her had become an ordeal.

To the relief of most aboard, however, several of the crew proved adept at fishing. With hooks and lines already to hand in the boat they secured as reasonable a catch as would be needed, including squid. Glad of the diversion Ariadne watched as two of the crew, with the aid of flints, tinder, scrap wood and charcoal stored in pottery vessels near the stern, contrived to light a fire beneath a small brazier with which to fry their catch. Still she would not, could not, be tempted to eat.

The boat thudded, pitched and swayed. Rigging creaked as the great spar was swung about to best gather a blustering wind into the black sail. The sun vanished in flaming glory to the west, the sky began to darken and Ariadne suppressed a desire to call aloud words that so dominated her thoughts. 'Take me back to Knossos. Please - I want to go home!'

**

Later the following day land was sighted. Rising steeply from the sea ahead, the island of Thera basked in afternoon sun. Apart from the small, barren island of Dia that lay off the Cretan coast north of Amnissos, it was the first land they had encountered since leaving. Ariadne, of course, had never been to Thera but so many people including her father had described it, she found the sight almost familiar. Theseus stood regarding the island from the high prow of the boat, which plied the waters more gently as they drew closer. A hand touched Ariadne's shoulder. 'If you'll excuse me, lady,' came his voice, 'I'd be pleased to tell you something of Thera.'

He was one of the crew, an escaped slave in a plain tunic of care-worn linen. And though in appearance he was sun-darkened, though as rough-featured as some of them, his manner as he spoke suggested one who in the past must have enjoyed better fortune. She wished he had approached her earlier in the voyage but realised that his duties and, perhaps more so the presence of Theseus, had been a deterrent.

'Yes, I would be pleased to hear about it,' she replied, brushing hair from her eyes.

'My name is Antheos,' he began. 'I once sailed vessels of my own. I know these islands as well as any man. I know the stories people tell about them.' Sitting down beside her, though not too close, he went on with his tale. 'It is believed that before the line of Minos was established on Crete, Thera was a large, high island with a city whose countless people had grown wealthy through trade and seafaring. They say it was blessed by the gods, that there were great halls adorned with gold, more lavish even than those of Knossos, if anyone can believe that. I saw much of Knossos when I visited

Crete as a free man so I doubt it could ever have been equalled, let alone surpassed.'

Glad of this diversion, Ariadne was contented to give him her attention.

'Then, many generations ago,' Antheos continued, 'the gods deserted Thera because the people no longer made due sacrifice. In spite of warnings, in spite of quakes and rumblings, they had grown arrogant in their wealth and comfort. Mighty Zeus in his anger, raised his thunderbolt against its people so that catastrophe befell them. The island together with all those living on it was utterly destroyed by fire and thunder. Some even now talk of a darkness that closed over the world for many days, of stones that fell from the sky and seas that raged against all the islands – yes, as far as Crete and beyond. Today only fragments of Thera remain. What you see ahead is the largest of them. Behind it, where much of the island once stood, you would find only open water and a few small islands rising steeply from the sea.'

'I've heard our bards relate a similar account,' remarked Ariadne, 'though I imagine it will be quite safe when we land there, as I hope we soon will.'

'Land at Thera? I doubt your Lord Theseus will wish to do that. No, lady, we will sail through the night amidst the islands until morning when we reach the port of Naxos.'

'Not land at Thera - but why?' she asked, unable to quell the anguish that tinged her voice. 'We are so close. Please, I beg you – give him a reason to land there while we can. There must be other vessels - vessels that will take me back to Crete?'

295

'Back to Crete? But I thought you -.'

'Please,' she interrupted, seeing Theseus approach, 'don't repeat what I just said about Crete. Really - I didn't mean it.'

The man smiled and as the shadow of Theseus fell across them, stood up, nodded, then made his way to the stern of the boat.

'You seem none too happy,' observed Theseus. 'I regret I've needed to leave you alone for as long as I have. What was that man saying?'

'I was asking him about Thera,' she replied with what she hoped would be a convincing smile. 'We've been so long at sea every bone in my body aches. That man told me we are not to go ashore at Thera but will sail by it and continue on to Naxos. Why all the way to Naxos? Why can't we get out of this wretched boat and rest for the night on Thera?'

'With good reason - Thera is peopled by Cretans so is under the control of your father, as was Melos where his envoys took us on the outward journey. If Minos sends a vessel in pursuit of us it will call at Thera first. If they discover us there we'll find ourselves in a difficult situation. On the other hand,' he continued, sitting by her side, 'it is the Carians who rule Naxos. Teuthras, their king has kinsmen on the mainland far to our east. He visited my father in Athens only a month after my own arrival there and I got to know him then. He's never been a formal ally of Crete though Minos regards him as his subject and many Carians man your father's ships.'

Seeing her expression of doubt, he assured Ariadne with a smile, 'We'll be safe in his company and old Teuthras values his comforts above all else

– in particular his stomach. He has a reputation for good wine and food and I've heard my father as well as others comment on the luxuries of his palace. I'm sure it will be better than anything we'd be offered on Thera, though I doubt we'll find there another Knossos. Then within a day of leaving Naxos, provided the winds don't turn against us, we'll reach the shores of Attica and soon afterwards be in Athens.'

'On Naxos,' she informed him, 'I will require decent attendants and a hot bath. I feel quite unwholesome – fit to present myself at a goatherd's hovel rather than a king's court. Look at my hair, my hands, my feet. Really, Theseus, I could scream!'

'Don't scream just yet,' he grinned, 'you might frighten the crew. If what I'm told about Teuthras proves correct then you should have all you need and more. Trust me - I'll make sure you do.'

'I'll speak with his wife,' remarked Ariadne. 'Perhaps she will advise me on dress and court procedure.'

Ah, don't expect to meet any queens in Naxos,' said Theseus. I hear Teuthras did have a consort half his age but she ran off one day with a Mycenaean sea captain and that was that. He's not turned against women altogether, no – just queens.'

Ariadne forced a smile as he left her side, though it was a smile moulded in cold clay.

She watched Theseus, fair and sun-bronzed, standing tall at the prow of the vessel.

Always he had been considerate but did his eyes any longer hold the light of desire that had shone so brightly at Knossos? She asked herself whether it was a bride he wanted now or rather living evidence of his triumph over her father. And might he have planned for her to serve as hostage if her father invaded Attica and laid siege to Athens as he had several years before? But then would the ruler of Knossos go to that much trouble given the circumstances of her departure? That was a moot point.

Theseus had fired her lusts within the opulent confines of her father's palace but those fires had been quelled by the stinging spray of the sea, by the discomforts of the boat, by the stresses of a voyage that had taken her far from a home she had despised yet craved now to see once more. Her other cause for misgiving, once greatest of all her fears, the abomination that had haunted her since childhood, was gone forever. Ariadne no longer cared what her father might say about her having deserted Knossos or about the part she had played in the Athenians' escape.

***

Sunlight sparkled on calmer waters when Ariadne awoke. She was startled and confused by the swaying motion of the boat, by the chatter and bustle of the crew, yet surprised she had slept at all on the folded linen laid for her comfort against the planking. The night-time breeze had been cool, her limbs were stiff and she shivered despite the welcome warmth of the sun. Raising awkwardly, pressing fingers to her eyes, she gave no thought to the young Athenians still huddled at the bow end of the vessel. They who had enjoyed less comfort by far than she.

By mid-morning they were sailing by the mountainous south of Naxos, running ever closer to the island's western coast. So close now that Ariadne could make out how fertile and green the island was, how numerous the clusters of farmsteads. To their left had appeared another large island she heard one of the men refer to as Paros. Earlier steeped in discontentment she was enlivened by the prospect of her once pampered feet treading solid ground. Where other than Teuthras' palace that solid ground might lead she cared not to think, provided it included the harbour where her hopes were firmly rooted. She recalled from the comments of visitors to Knossos that relations with Naxos had not been as cordial as they might be. Ariadne remembered her father on more than one occasion state his intention of bringing Naxos directly under Cretan control. They nonetheless continued to trade with one another, which meant there would be vessels in the harbour destined eventually for Crete.

Once they had sailed around the westernmost promontory of Naxos the port and town came into view. As they drew closer Ariadne noted with unease how Naxos town in no way reflected the extensive structures, the light or the welcoming colours of Knossos. It grew instead out of the rocks above the bay, a grim and forbidding assemblage of towers and walls consisting in the main of raw, grey stonework.

Again at her side, Theseus said, 'Those are strong walls but not as great as you'll see at Athens nor as mighty as they have built about Mycenae. Here they were needed to keep out pirates rather than armies but pirates are fewer in number nowadays so I'm told.'

'Cleared away by my father,' she remarked, coolly. 'It's a well-known fact.'

'In which case I'll admit we have at least something to thank him for.'

The prospect of the town had done nothing to arouse her enthusiasm but Ariadne's spirits were stirred by the sight of many boats in the harbour below. Several smaller vessels were drawn up on shore close to where nets lay stretched out to dry in the sun. A number of larger vessels, merchant ships with deeper keels like those of Crete, were tied up at the long timber jetty. Men were already gathering at the jetty to receive the incoming vessel and whilst sail and spar were lowered to the shouts of the crew, oars bristled in readiness to enter the harbour.

When the wind calmed in the shelter of the bay, Ariadne pinned up her disarrayed hair as best she was able. Without the luxury of a bronze mirror she had to rely on the touch of her fingers, and reluctantly, on the opinion of the Athenian girls, most of whom regarded her fussiness with open amusement. About her neck and arms she still wore the precious, bejewelled ornaments that were taken for granted by those women of her status at Knossos. She was as self-conscious of them now as she had earlier been about the nakedness of her upper body. To the captain of a boat, any one of her bangles would be a treasure worth enough to ensure her passage home provided he and his crew could be trusted. The matter of trust was something she cared not to consider as she removed those valuables for concealment inside her bag. But how long did Theseus really intend to remain on Naxos? How soon would the opportunity arise for her to board a vessel back to Crete?

***

They ascended the steps from the harbour in the company of three nervous officials, clad in formal robes, who had been despatched in haste to meet them. Theseus' party was greeted in person at the entrance to the great hall of his palace by the conspicuously rotund, bald-headed, bushy-faced Teuthras, petty king of the island. Greeted as best a prince of Athens and a princess of Knossos could be without advance notice of their arrival.

'I welcome Prince Theseus, and his good lady as my honoured guests,' he announced. 'Follow me, please, and let me assure you of a fine welcome.'

Theseus and the young Athenians were escorted in the rolling-vessel wake of Teuthras' ample figure. 'No one advised me of your coming,' he continued in a voice that reminded Ariadne of a squeaking bronze gate, 'though my men spotted the insignia on your sail when you were out at sea. We thought it might be trickery of some kind. Those damnable pirates have tried it in the past. But tell me the reason for your journey and let me again assure you of our hospitality.'

At his signal the youths and girls, whispering amongst themselves, were escorted away by two attendants. The court of Teuthras was never strong on protocol.

'Your young people,' he added, 'will be placed somewhere comfortable and my staff will see to their immediate needs whilst you advise me over what has been happening.'

Ariadne fancied that whilst Theseus and the King of Naxos had met before, trust between them was not absolute when Theseus replied, 'I have concluded a long standing dispute with Knossos on behalf of King Aegeus and now we are returning to Athens. This lady is Ariadne, a daughter of King Minos. She returns with me to endorse the agreement with my father.'

'Oh, do I now,' breathed Ariadne, glancing about the gloomy megaron, wondering what would be the outcome if Teuthras was made aware of the facts as he eventually must be when news arrived from Knossos. She gave little thought to the abundance of arms that festooned his walls to proclaim the King of Naxos a greater man by far than any deed of his could possibly justify.

'My father,' continued Theseus, 'will repay your generosity in offering us sanctuary for the night - that I promise.'

'No, no, no,' responded Teuthras, 'it is I who must repay the generosity King Aegeus showed me when I was last in Athens.'

The king's mastery of their Greek dialect was good whilst that of his immediate courtiers was to prove at best adequate. And though Teuthras would doubtless feature modestly if it came to an assessment of his domains, in girth he far surpassed Minos, squeezed as he was into an ornately carved and gilded but sturdily constructed timber throne that could otherwise have accommodated in comfort two well-built men.

'I can't wait to hear details of your visit to Knossos,' wheezed Teuthras whilst his small, pale blue eyes fixed upon Ariadne's bared breasts with

302

more than casual interest. To her relief she observed that the women of his court, young and old, also dressed in Cretan fashion.

'I never go there myself,' he continued. 'I worry that Minos has designs on my kingdom, but there we are. And this lady, you say is a daughter of the king, and returning with you to Athens! Then Athens' power and prestige must be in the ascendancy. Her relations with Minos have hardly been amicable over the years and you will be familiar by now with the onerous demands he imposed upon your people long before you arrived. When I was there your father charged me not to mention it. So, what has altered the situation? I take it those boys and girls you brought with you are an important element.'

'If you'll forgive me, My Lord,' replied Theseus as he and Ariadne sat before him, 'what has been agreed between us must first be imparted to my father – that is only right. But let me assure you, the problem we had is laid to rest, permanently, and will result in no disadvantage to your own situation.'

'Then I'll press you with no more questions,' responded Teuthras with a wheezy laugh. 'I'll have rooms prepared for you both and see to it your young people are afforded proper comforts. Your crew, of course, will stay with their ship though I will have food and wine sent to them.'

With the assistance of two slave boys and considerable effort on his own behalf, Teuthras heaved himself up from the throne to a series of loud grunts then hesitated to adjust an extravagantly embroidered, over-tight gown that appeared ready to burst apart at the seams. 'I will have our forthcoming dinner suitably enhanced in your honour,' he said. 'But whilst we wait I will show you both around the lower floor of my humble palace.' He exchanged words with an attendant who stood waiting close by. The man hurried away to ensure his master's promises were realised.

'If there's any truth in the saying that fat people are more contented than the rest of us,' whispered Theseus to Ariadne as the king issued further orders to various of his retainers, 'then this fellow must be the happiest man in the world. And from what I recall of seeing him in Athens it looks as if he's grown even happier.'

Ariadne raised her eyebrows and forced a smile.

Teuthras conducted them about the main rooms, his conversation punctuated by an occasional wheezing gasp. They entered a large chamber with frescoed walls displaying scenes reminiscent of the marine life compositions at Knossos though of less accomplished artistry. Here a long wooden table was being set out for a considerable repast whilst from the nearby kitchens drifted tantalising odour of cooking meat and vegetables. Servants hurried to and fro, their attention to duty fuelled by their king's magnificently corpulent presence.

'I imagine you'll both welcome a chance to wash away the sea salt before sampling a hearty meal,' declared Teuthras as he waddled ahead of them past a stone staircase down which two flustered servants were hurrying.

'Hot water - food,' muttered Ariadne, savouring the smell of food that lingered in her nostrils. 'I'm desperate for both, and a couple of girls to tidy up my hair.'

'Hot water will soon be made available,' confirmed Teuthras, 'oh, and the girls. And when our main meal of the day is prepared, you will find set before you the best this island and the seas about have to offer.'

Theseus twitched his nose and agreed. 'Yes – it already smells wonderful.'

'This place isn't as big or as fancy as Knossos,' their host continued jovially, waving his arms about, 'but it'll do for the time being. Main part was built generations back by the Thracians, you know – though they ought to have made the doors larger. Hmm, look how narrow that one is. They must have been emaciated!'

Ariadne was in silent agreement with his first comment. Here was not to be seen the opulence of Knossos. In different circumstances she would have found the king's gasping, gesticulating mass a source of entertainment but instead was relieved when an aged male servant strode up to announce that accommodation for herself and for Theseus had been made ready. Teuthras turned to Ariadne, saying, 'If my lady would care to retire to her room, I'll have her notified as soon as the food is prepared. And, oh yes, she must inform my servants at once should she feel anything is lacking. And please, she must take her time.'

To Theseus' guarded amusement though much to Ariadne's discomfort, the king once more scrutinised her breasts to the point where she feared he might salivate over them. She was glad to be clear of his attentions when the boy conducted her up narrow, dismal steps to an upper floor passage where they halted at an open doorway. Outside the door waited two slim, attractive, bright-eyed young women in plain white tunics, their dark hair pinned back in the Carian manner. Were they slaves? Ariadne concluded they probably were not. The two were delicately perfumed, each wore about her arms ornamental bangles of exquisite workmanship and each boasted intricate gold earrings – all this adornment of a quality denied those in servitude, except on occasion at Knossos. There a favoured slave of the palace might appear better off by far than a free man of the country.

'Are you sent to assist me?' she asked them as the boy scurried away. The two smiled but appeared to not entirely understand her words. Ariadne assumed they may have been instructed to perform some domestic task or check on her comforts before leaving her alone.

They entered what proved to be a modest but comfortably furnished chamber richly adorned with flower and bird-frescoed walls. Afternoon sunlight blazed through the stone-arched window to illuminate a small table below the window directly ahead. There Ariadne was reassured by the sight of a comb and a cluster of miniature jars of a familiar type that doubtless contained cosmetics. Welcome, too, was the highly polished bronze mirror with carved ivory handle. But the main feature to hearten Ariadne was a brightly painted earthenware bath positioned by the wall to her right, already charged with steaming water that could only have been added a short time before her arrival. On a ledge next to the bath were arrayed additional gilded pots containing perfumes and oils. Her bath, at home a routine event, was, after her ordeal at sea, a vision of paradise. Occupying one corner close to the bath was another feature not uncommon at Knossos – a flushable device for the disposal of bodily waste. Against the wall opposite the bath stood a low wooden bed covered with sheepskin blankets and next to this a pine chest.

'You may go now,' Ariadne said, but the two girls again smiled, firstly at her then knowingly at each other. 'What are you waiting for?' she asked as one of them reached back to close the door. By this act and by their manner and their gestures, Ariadne decided the girls had been allocated to serve as her personal attendants – a situation she was accustomed to each day at Knossos - though not as here, with complete strangers.

One of the girls stepped behind and began to undo Ariadne's dress while the other kissed her naked breasts. 'How dare you -!' she exclaimed as the girl behind brushed her lips with burning moth kisses about her neck and ear. 'Stop at once!'

Both ignored her protests and Ariadne asked herself, 'Is this Theseus' doing? Have they contrived to occupy me while he indulges himself with the palace girls?' About to push away the girl standing before her, Ariadne drew breath, once more on the verge of protest – a protest muted only in part by the effects of the wine. And as the dress slipped away she sighed, 'Ahh – then do as you please.'

The two eased her, now naked, into the confined space of the bath where she sat with her knees drawn up, her back against one end and her feet pressed against the other. The fact that this bath was of lesser dimension than was her own at Knossos mattered hardly at all.

Having removed their own clothes the two girls bathed Ariadne with an intimacy she had until then allowed only from those personally selected attendants at her father's palace. It was an intimacy of delicate hands - an intimacy that under the circumstances might have shocked her - but did not. Ever smiling, they rekindled within her an ardour that had waned with her departure from Knossos, a hunger she had imagined would remain but a memory until her return there.

'What can it matter,' she sighed, stepping from the bath where they gently dried her with towels of fine Egyptian cotton, 'soon I'll be gone from here.' Ariadne savoured in full the tingling pleasures these two young women so enthusiastically bestowed. They were pleasures she prayed would continue as they dribbled perfumed amber oil coolly over her shoulders, about her breasts then down her stomach and spine as a prelude to massaging her from neck to toe. In the comforting warmth of the room, in the blissful caress of their hands, with the heat imbued by the oil, Ariadne trembled. The dark-eyed pair gazed into her eyes, pressed voluptuous kisses to her face and over her body. They bit gently about her neck and breasts as their fingers descended to explore her in the most intimate possible manner. Ariadne, her heart fluttering, her breath shortening, responded to their attentions with gasps and abbreviated cries. The two ushered her unresisting across the room and thrust her down onto the bed. There she returned with full enthusiasm their wanton caresses in what had become a tableau of mutual ecstasy staged upon an altar of lustful abandon. Wails of passion soared as crying birds within the small chamber. In orgasmic reverie, Ariadne imagined herself already returned to the voluptuous pleasures of her bed at Knossos.

Afterwards, as they sat close together on the bed, she wondered if the two girls intended to stay with her for the rest of the day and perhaps through the evening. The prospect appealed strongly but would compromise her burgeoning plans. She stepped across to ease aside the linen blind. A glimpse at the harbour, basking in late afternoon sun beyond her window, was enough to banish further temptation. The girls, after further kisses and smiles, were dismissed.

At last alone, she lay back and drew up the sheepskin cover to rest a while. Before the summons to return downstairs, she might have time to consider the possibilities ahead. She was startled when, deep in thought, someone tapped on the door and a voice called, 'If My Lady is ready, our king and Lord Theseus await her company.'

Ariadne could not deny how liberally Teuthras entertained them in his dining hall. Before her was spread a fare she considered almost worthy of her palace home on Crete. Cooking pots, supported upon great metal tripods, spluttered above smoking, stone-enclosed fires by one wall. Servants of mainly tender age, perhaps most were slaves, bustled about the hall with ladles and dishes. Older male attendants stood by with brightly painted flagons, ready to recharge gilded goblets with wines she was about to discover would surpass even those of Crete. Here amidst the bustle and chatter was an abundance of fish, squid and mutton as well as vegetables, the latter fit to be eaten raw or cooked. If tables could groan beneath the weight of food and drink, thought Ariadne, then the one at which she found herself seated, close by Theseus and the verbose Teuthras, would surely have cried out in agony.

The bare-breasted girls of the court chattered, flitted and fluttered like gaudy birds though as Theseus observed, none surpassed Ariadne in beauty. It was to her the eyes of the male courtiers often turned though she exchanged words with them only when obliged. By contrast the group of minstrels who played and sang in raucous disharmony a short way from the increasingly garrulous diners would have been hard put to find work at Knossos other than as menials.

Mongrel dogs darted about, snapping, yapping, appearing, disappearing under the tables, each intent on seizing any scrap of food offered by the diners. Ariadne frowned. Dogs were not allowed at the royal tables of Knossos. Only now did she discover how strong was her aversion to the canine clan.

'The rest of the day is ours!' declared Teuthras, his mouth bulging with food. Let us make your visit a memorable one!'

Raising his goblet, a refreshed, newly attired and cleanly shaven Theseus turned to Ariadne. 'I'm sure it will be,' he smiled.

The enthusiasm with which Teuthras engulfed his food made her grimace. The King of Naxos also proved foremost in setting an example as to how the famed wines of his vine-clad island ought to be consumed – in liberal and unending quantity. His occasional loud belch prompted a round of obligatory laughter from his seated courtiers. In spite of a previous hunger, Ariadne ate and drank less than she otherwise might. It was Teuthras who voiced objection when, complaining of weariness brought on by the voyage, she requested the opportunity to take her rest but to be woken before dusk.

'Dear me, no,' he insisted, almost choking on a pastry, 'mmm – er, stay a while longer. Let us refill your cup. Let us drink once more to your enchanting presence before you retire!'

'Yes, we should do that,' agreed Theseus, whose conversation throughout had been sparing.

When the boy appeared at her side, flagon raised and ready to pour, Ariadne conceded, Ariadne drank, staying until it seemed no longer so impolite to depart. She left the hall then made her way unsteadily along the semi-darkened corridor, glad to leave behind the incessant cacophony, wondering why she was not escorted as before yet glad to be alone.

***

The sun was close to setting when the two young women returned. They entered her room unannounced carrying a bundle of clothes; plainer garments obviously intended to replace her care-worn court dress. These they placed next to hers on top of the pine chest with the manner of their smiles hinting at what had happened earlier. Both made clear in broken Greek their willingness to stay but Ariadne insisted as best she could her wish to remain alone. She ushered them to the door while they chattered in their own tongue, running fingers about her shoulders, pouting mock kisses so as to have her change her mind. Realising they were not to have their way the two hurried off along the passage without a backward glance.

Alone once more, Ariadne wondered if Theseus intended to join her after dark but hoped he would not because his presence would negate her plans. She stepped over to the window and peered again across the harbour and the bay. Lamps and braziers glowed where the boats were moored. Smoke drifted where people busied themselves cooking over wood fires. Fishing boats prepared to set off for the evening with stern lights swaying. She would dress in the clothes left for her. She would make her way to the harbour and the jetty where the larger boats were moored. She would find out which was to leave first for Crete. It had to be soon but would any sail in darkness even if the sky was clear and the moon bright?

In the diminishing light of her room she sat before the bronze mirror, straightening her hair with an ivory comb then pinning it up with bronze clips as best she could. She wanted it set now in the manner of a Carian woman, plainer than it had been when she left Knossos. She regretted just then not having one of the girls to assist her.

Among the garments they had brought was a woollen gown in the Carian style as well as soft leather ankle boots. The gown, heavily embroidered at the neck, had short sleeves and a patterned sash. It would cover her down to the ankles. It would be warmer than her palace dress for the voyage home and being more modest ought to attract less attention from the crew. Her more valuable body adornments she would not wear for the voyage and those items she intended would serve as currency to pay for her return, Ariadne transferred to a deep leather pouch at her belt. The conspicuously fancy bag she had carried on the outward journey would be left empty and concealed beneath the bed with her Cretan clothes.

Oil lamps fixed upon tall stands provided light enough for her to find her way through the deserted passage, to the stairs, then down to the corridor leading to the portico. Teuthras' palace might be unfamiliar but was no labyrinthine maze. At the bottom of the stairs she hesitated. Sounds drifted from the dining hall. Someone was beating a frantic rhythm on small drums whilst another blew hard on the pipes with an enthusiasm that by considerable measure exceeded his skill. Louder yet was the raucous laughter of the men and the squeals of the women. Ariadne crept along the passage until, hidden in shadow behind a stone pillar, she could peer into the hall.

The heavy wooden table about which Theseus, Teuthras and his noble companions sat had been cleared of food but now supported a generous complement of goblets and wine flagons. The King of Naxos nodded in alcoholic stupor at its head whilst Theseus maintained his position as honoured guest close by with a jewelled goblet swaying in his hand. Plied with wine by idolising females, he was attempting with questionable success in the face of such distractions to recount the bull leapers' ceremony witnessed at Knossos. It appeared the king only avoided sliding into drunken oblivion by hanging onto Theseus' words.

Ariadne held back, fearful of discovery, listening longer than she intended. She wondered if Theseus, his tongue loosened by wine, would refer to Asterion or to the epic departure from Crete that had followed his exploits in the labyrinth. After some thought she was certain that, no matter how addled by drink, he would say nothing to alert the King of Naxos or those about him with the truth or with the grim details of what had occurred in the labyrinth beneath Knossos.

Meanwhile, the young female courtesans of this modest estate had drunk as freely as the men and appeared close to shedding what precarious hold remained on their inhibitions. Nowhere in sight were the pair with whom Ariadne herself had experienced such consuming pleasures. She heard raised voices of the Athenian youths from a nearby chamber and wondered in what manner they, too, were being entertained. As for their seven female companions, perhaps the sleep denied them on the boat was all they cared for.

'Yes, *that's* how much you think of me,' she murmured, seeing Theseus relish the attention of two young women who were intent upon overwhelming him with their charms. Other courtiers were likewise occupied whilst Teuthras had slumped aside in his chair.

Ariadne hurried away, encountered no one when leaving the palace, but close by the gate leading out to the harbour two guards with spears stood engaged in conversation. She hesitated, took a deep breath then walked on half expecting to be challenged. Neither acknowledged her as she passed by so she continued at an unhurried pace, suppressing a desire to run while anticipating any moment a summons from behind. There was no summons.

Her twilight route was not difficult to follow but on reaching the wide path that curved down to the harbour, Ariadne paused. There were men gathered about a brazier near the boat that had brought her – doubtless members of the crew left to their own devices. They would sleep within or close to the vessel - but for how long would they remain awake before she could hide herself on board, if hide she could? They must not know she had left the palace nor must they see her at the harbour in case others came searching. 'I must wait in hiding through the night away from the harbour and the taverns,' she whispered to herself. 'Yes, into the following day until Theseus and his Athenians have sailed. Then there will be another boat leaving for Crete. Yes - then at last I'll be on my way home.'

Ariadne glanced nervously about with no idea as to where she might head for comfort and concealment in this strange and unfamiliar land. Night had already claimed the hills with the sea taking on a glitter of molten gold in the light of a full moon. 'Ah,' she breathed, 'I recall seeing the ground rise steeply at the far side of the bay where it's thickly wooded. I'll make my way over there and maybe find somewhere to shelter. At least the night is warm.'

Now and then in moonlight, more often in deep shadow, she made her way past the silent hovel of peasant and fisherman until coming upon a rough path that wound upward from the town into the pine trees. The path became steeper, rockier, more overgrown so that several times she needed to halt a while before going on. Eventually, when whatever remained of the path was lost to darkness, she found herself encroached upon by moon-obscuring trees until there was no longer a view of the sea. Stumbling further along, Ariadne realised that until daylight returned she might have little chance of finding her way back.

'Oh, where am I,' she breathed, 'what have I done? I should have stayed close to the harbour.'

Totally lost, she stopped where moonlight fell through the trees. A gentle breeze whispered amongst the branches and close by a stream played about the rocks. A hooting owl gave voice to the nectared breath of night. Somewhere below in the distance, people shouted and dogs barked. Were there wolves on this island? Were there bears? She had no idea what lived or did not live on Naxos.

'I should have waited until morning,' she sighed, gazing into obscurity, 'I should have stayed with Theseus all the way to Athens and boarded a Cretan vessel there. Now I – I must find somewhere to rest.' With the shroud of darkness closed about her she dared not attempt to retrace her steps. Ariadne was afraid. She was beset by profound loneliness – a loneliness unlike any she had ever known. And not since that dreadful childhood encounter with Asterion had she felt so vulnerable. A sighing breeze, vague noises in the undergrowth suggested unseen menace. She imagined someone, something, might be watching and might emerge suddenly from the darkness of the woods to leap out at her. The forest had become a realm of nightmares with the Minotaur reborn to stalk the night. Ariadne came suddenly upon a level rock where she sat, pressed hands to her face and wept.

There were other sounds. Sounds that she had been unaware of until that moment. She looked about. Somewhere, not so far away, a flute was playing. She arose cautiously and gazing through the trees observed a light. Had the light been there last time she had looked about? She was certain it had not. But it was there now and growing brighter – now so bright that she thought someone must have lit a beacon though there was no sign of smoke or flame.

'They could be outcasts,' she told herself. 'They could have been banished from the town to live their lives here in the forest; it's the kind of thing father does. I must be careful. I must make no sound in case they hear me.'

The music was becoming clearer. Notes swirled on the night air, wistful, melodic, compelling. Sweet, reassuring sounds. Yet still she was afraid.

'Hello,' came a girl's voice from behind. Ariadne spun about with a cry of alarm.

'Hello,' the voice repeated. A figure stepped naked into the moonlight. She was almost as tall as Ariadne and just as fair. Her long golden hair was entwined with roses, her feline eyes aglow.

'Wh – who are you?' stammered Ariadne. 'What are you doing here?'

'Who am I?' smiled the girl. 'Well I'm whoever and whenever I am but ever so sorry if I scared you. As for what I'm doing here; our Lord said I must invite you into our gathering. We have them now and again here on Naxos, it's the perfect spot.'

'A lord - a gathering, I – I don't understand. What gathering – who?'

'Please come along, you really must,' insisted the girl. 'There's good wine to be had and he is waiting to meet you. I'm sure you'll take to him at once. Most people do, you know.' Her manner was warm and reassuring.

'Meet me! Me?' queried Ariadne. Perplexed but less afraid, she peered by the girl to see the light grown so vivid that it could not possibly be a fire. It almost rivalled the brightness of day - as if a miniature sun glowed amidst the trees. Cymbals and drums could now be heard accompanying the flute. There were voices. There was laughter. Girls were singing.

'But I -,' she objected, then the girl took her hand, saying, 'I wouldn't keep him waiting if I were you. He might lose interest, then where would you be. All alone and miserable again I dare say.'

'Where would I be?' muttered Ariadne. 'You might well ask since I hardly know where I am now.' She walked hand in hand with the girl, thoughts of the boat to Crete, of Knossos and of Theseus ebbing from her mind.

There was, of course, no sun. The air itself seemed to glow, to illuminate everything inside the small grove with misted light while the music, especially that of the flute, emanated from all around to soothe her ear, to enchant her soul. There were many people gathered there, youths and girls as naked as the one who had brought her. Beyond the misted light others moved, danced, cavorted - odd, spectral figures that appeared not altogether human. Ceasing their chatter, those nearest Ariadne, circled about, smiling as if they knew her, as if they had always known her. The cymbals and drums stopped playing, though the flute continued wistfully on.

'Why – who -?' she started to ask as she was guided to the centre of the clearing where, in the midst of the light, she perceived the focus of their gathering. The figure reclined in upholstered comfort upon an ornate couch of polished ebony supported by carved lion's legs, the whole encircled by gilded vines with bunches of golden grapes festooned about its heavy frame. A high-handled goblet sparked rainbow colours in his hand. The occupant - Ariadne perceived him to be a youth of fair complexion - laid the goblet aside, smiled at her with golden eyes that matched the hue of his curly hair, then slipped with athletic grace from the couch with a hand raised to greet her. He was slim, sun-bronzed, of well-proportioned aspect - not unlike the Theseus she fleetingly recalled, though his smooth-skinned features were such as to border on the effeminate. At first thinking him totally naked apart from the wreath of vine leaves set about his brow, she noticed the gilded leaf of a fig tree positioned to conceal his manhood. He smiled at Ariadne who stood in awe as he moved closer, saying, 'Follow me. Talk with me. Share my company and my wine for as long as it pleases you.'

'Er, yes,' murmured Ariadne, gazing about in wonder. 'Yes I could do with another drink.'

One of the girls handed him a golden goblet banded with flashing rubies which, with eyes fixed upon hers, he lifted to Ariadne's parted lips, saying in deep and gentle voice of reassuring tone, 'It's our new vintage. I think it's rather good myself.'

'One of our very best, actually' agreed the girl, 'and I should know.'

Ariadne stayed his arm, at first reluctant to taste the unknown contents, then took a cautious sip of honeyed wine. It ignited within her a gentle flame. Ariadne took a longer sip. Then another, and the flame grew.

'Who are you?' she asked in barely audible tone, taking the goblet from him. 'This place is so strange. Are you one of the gods? Am I dreaming? Yes, that's what it is – I'm dreaming but I don't care in the least.'

Light grew brighter in his eyes as he answered with a broad smile, 'Not quite a god. Not full time anyway. Not just yet - but I'm working on it. And as for dreaming – well, who can say when we are dreaming or when we are not? But it really doesn't matter. Not in the least. Not now.'

'Did you know I would come here?' she asked, gulping more wine, feeling herself drawn closer to him by invisible hands. 'You did know, didn't you? I – I can tell you did.'

The girls and youths in full light had spread to form a circle about them and holding hands, began to dance around, chanting, 'Di-on-y-sos! Di-on-y-sos! Di-on-y-sos!'

Raising a hand to her cheek, a hand whose touch infused her with burning ecstasy, he gazed deeper into her eyes, searched into her very soul, his voice now a whisper inside her head. 'Sweet Ariadne, I watched you enter Naxos from the sea with your companions. I watched as you slept a dreamless sleep. I watched a short time ago as you sat alone, so afraid, so tearful. Such rare beauty do you possess for a mortal. Such rare beauty. Yet such a burden of anguish do you carry. Such fearful memories.'

'Yes, I -,' she began, clutching the goblet. 'But why – but please tell me what you're doing here.'

'What am I doing here?' he smiled. 'Often I stay over on Naxos. The people are rather fond of me as it happens. They worship me with every draught of wine and it's me they thank at their altars for the good harvest of their vines. Just as well they do, I suppose.'

'Quite so,' smiled the girl, 'it was never a good idea to upset him.'

In the presence of these curious people, in their microcosm of warmth and light, before the gaze of this strangely beguiling figure, the ardour that had been fired earlier that day by the two girls had returned with compelling urgency. Ariadne quivered at his touch. For the first time since leaving Knossos she felt elated by the presence of a man, but more - so very much more. Flames of passion licked through her belly and limbs as she murmured, 'I – I don't understand. The light – they will see it from the town. They will come searching. They will find me – find us.'

'They will see and hear nothing,' he answered. 'I am here for no one but you if you will stay.'

'Stay,' she breathed. 'Where else now could I wish to go?' Ariadne somehow understood; the guards at the gate had not seen her leave at all. The sound of the pipes grew louder. The trees, the branches, the very roots beneath the ground stirred with life. The stars above blazed as gemstones. The dancing figures circled ever quicker. Becoming a blur - a rushing vapour slowly diffusing into the living night. Again his touch and Ariadne drifted within a bubble of pleasure. Hardly did she care as he slipped the dress from her shoulders, as his kisses drifted, burning feathers, over her naked body. 'Oh - oh yes - I'll stay,' she breathed. They embraced as writhing serpents in a sweep of orgasmic fire whilst Ariadne cried aloud, 'Oh, yes – forever! Oh, yes – oh, yes!

***

'Disappeared,' quizzed Theseus as he and his companions gathered about the palace entrance. 'How could she disappear? What about the two who were sent to keep her company through the night?'

'I'm assured the Cretan lady wished to remain alone and so dismissed them both,' replied the captain of the palace guard. 'The clothes she brought with her were still in her room but those and an empty bag were all we could find there.'

'Would someone not have noticed had she tried to leave the palace?' Theseus was curious rather than angry.

'No one did, sir. I have questioned the men who were on duty at our gates yesterday and during the night. They swear they never saw lady Ariadne.

They have no reason to lie as they had no orders to prevent anyone leaving. Since daylight my men have searched the palace, the town and every boat in the harbour. They have scoured the woodlands hereabouts but have found nothing. It's as if she walked into the sea or - or was spirited away.'

'You have informed your king, I trust.'

'Our king is, er, indisposed,' replied the captain, averting his eyes. 'But the lady is nowhere about his chambers.'

'Indisposed,' whispered one of the Athenian youths to his nearest comrade, recalling their own excesses of the previous evening and conscious of a pulsing soreness that lumbered as heavy boots inside his head. 'I looked into the hall earlier. He was sprawled out drunk and laying in his own vomit. It'll take a pair of oxen to get the fat old sod upright.'

Muttering, 'Yes, I don't feel quite my best this morning,' Theseus shaded his eyes against the late morning sun, glanced across to the harbour where their boat waited ready to sail, then said to his companions, 'I'm loath to abandon her, a daughter of Minos and a woman of such rare beauty. Her presence would have been of great value to us but time is now the enemy so we must be away from here soon. We're a day's journey from home provided the winds remain fair and I'm impatient to be in Athens again. I fear danger may have come upon the city during our absence. The Minotaur was a beast of flesh and blood but there is another beast we must sooner or later confront. One not so well confined. One with many followers who will devour our city as Asterion would have devoured each of us. I'll remain a while longer at the quay in case someone discovers what has happened to Ariadne. But if she has chosen not to sail with us and if she cannot be found, then so be it. When Helios begins his descent toward the west, we cast off and we sail for Athens.'

***

When the day brightened there was no ragged goatherd to witness the curious procession that, having made its way up from the harbour of Phaleron, emerged from amidst the pine trees. The beaten gold cup that had been the boy's reward stood in the centre of a rough wooden bench, subject to jealous attention by members of his family, more than had ever jostled together at any one time within the confined space of his parents' stone and timber hovel.

They debated noisily over what advantages they might gain by virtue of its possession, for what goods it might be traded and where. The boy, dismissed from this boorish conclave, stood sulking outside the door in profound regret at not having kept quiet - at not having buried the precious cup, *his* reward, in the ground so as to recover it later. Perhaps much later. He ambled forlorn along the pathway having decided the only thing left for him would be to round up the goats and drive them to higher pastures. His remaining hope was that wolves or lions, now and then seen hereabouts, had not done their grisly work. By the time he reached the turning where the bay came into view, the people from the black-sailed ship had already passed by and were out of sight. The vessel was moored there, however – the very one he had reported approaching late that previous day.

***

Six armed guards observed their approach from the tower at the city's western gate while the citizens and farmers of Athens, passing to and fro about their business, stopped to watch the strangers draw near. Having no idea who they might be, four of the guards careered down narrow stone steps then into the open air intending to question the new arrivals before they could pass into the city. A fifth hurried away to summon their captain.

The guards counted twenty-six in the party. Eight were stocky, rough-weathered seamen wearing kilts of course linen. Four were a mixture of characters that might have been seen about the streets of any town. Seven were young women of fairer complexion, still wrapped in garments of wool to keep them warm from the sea breezes of the previous night. Seven were young men of noble bearing but unkempt and dressed in crumpled linen tunics. All the men, regardless of attire, carried sword or dagger at his belt.

A small crowd had already gathered when the party arrived at the gate. The guards pushed through with spears raised to confront the new arrivals. One of the newcomers stepped forward, tall, well built with dishevelled golden hair and a broad smile on his lightly stubbled face. Speculation over his identity buzzed in the air. Some already knew. Then others. An awed silence fell. The voice that broke that silence came not from the crowd but from beneath the dank shadows of the gate as a tall, dark-bearded, well-armed, bronze-scaled figure with red

325

plume quivering above his helmet pushed by followed by six men likewise attired.

'Lord Theseus!' exclaimed the first man, handing his spear to the one closest to him and affecting a short bow. 'By the gods you have returned to us!'

'Is this to be our greeting, Metion?' responded Theseus. 'We have returned from Crete. Did no one bring news of our coming? We saw someone on the headland as we entered the bay yesterday of that I'm certain. There were boats at the harbour but the sight of our Cretan sail seemed to deter anyone from approaching.'

The crowd pressed closer. People began to murmur his name. Some fell to one knee whilst others reached out to touch the young man's tunic.

'My Lord,' responded the captain of the palace guard, 'I beg that you follow me - we must speak at once and in private. Our young men and women should go straight away to their homes and their families where they will be greeted with joy at their deliverance. My men will conduct your crew to the city elders who will see to their comfort.'

Theseus was puzzled by the gravity of Metion's expression, by the urgency underlying his request. He eased his way through an ever growing crowd who, realising that their prince had returned, assailed him with cheers and calls of, 'Tell us, Lord Theseus! Tell us about your journey!'

'Later - later!' he exclaimed. 'I must go straight to my father. It seems he may not know of our return.' Theseus followed Metion through the busy market place where heads turned, where people called their prince's name, abandoned their business to mill about in speculation over one they thought would never return alive to Athens. Reaching the stairway leading up to the acropolis, they were met by a bearded, longhaired figure in blue gown who raised his arms in astonishment though his expression was not one of pleasure as he cried, 'Oh! Lord Theseus - it is you! Oh, I thank mighty Zeus! You have come back to us!'

'Indeed I have, Haemon. I take it my father will also be surprised since it appears no one in the city was forewarned.'

The old man eyed Metion uncertainly. Metion glanced back at Haemon as if neither felt able to respond to Theseus' comments. Then Haemon said to the captain, 'Sir, if you will permit me, I alone will conduct our young lord to the palace.'

'As you wish,' replied Metion, watching Theseus with marked unease as he stepped aside to let them pass. Haemon went ahead. The two ascended, their climb dictated by the old man's laboured tread. In the market place below the crowds continued to gather and gossip amongst themselves as the welcome news spread.

They entered the megaron to find a number of slaves clearing ashes from the central hearth while others carried in armfuls of dried logs and kindling. Theseus had sensed Haemon's deep unease from the beginning, as he had that of Metion, and well before they entered, well before they reached the far end of the great hall, he was prepared for news of ill fortune having visited Athens during his absence.

By the entrance to the king's chambers, Haemon turned to face him. 'Your ship was seen, my lord, but - but she carried a black sail. A shepherd boy reported this to King Aegeus as you sailed into the bay of Phaleron late yesterday. Everyone, including your father, thought you and those with you would never again return to Athens - that you were confined at Knossos or indeed were dead. No one set out to meet the ship because we assumed it would carry Cretans bearing news we would not wish to hear, if not their unwelcome traders.'

Theseus closed his eyes. 'By Zeus! Yes – the sail. My father had asked me to show a white sail if we were returning safe on board the ship and I forgot my promise. Haemon, it's as though the gods themselves had driven all thought of it from my mind. Where is he now? He must be distraught. Take me to him.'

Falling awkwardly to one knee, the old man clasped trembling hands together as he replied, 'Forgive me but King Aegeus, your dear father, has departed this world. When news of the ship was brought to us he was stricken by despair - a despair so great that he took his own life. I was the last with whom he spoke though I did not know he had determined to do it.'

'Dead,' breathed Theseus, anger clouding his face. 'How? How did he die?'

'He left the palace in the middle of the night when there was no one to see him,' replied Haemon, lowering his head.

Theseus grasped the old man's arm, saying, 'To your feet, man. You've no business in grovelling before me. The blame for this cannot be yours. Now go on.'

'Very well, my lord,' replied Haemon, rising with some difficulty. 'Your father, our king, threw himself from the acropolis into the valley below. That is the truth.'

'Or was pushed,' muttered Theseus. 'And by who, I wonder.'

'No, my lord – I say to you with the greatest respect, he was not pushed. Metion would allow no strangers about the acropolis. No, none. Pallas, is elsewhere in Attica conniving with our enemies as always. As for your father - unless matters dictated otherwise, he would at each daybreak leave the city with two of his men. He would ride to Phaleron. He would gaze out to sea through much of the morning. Often as not he would leave a slave or servant on watch until dusk. In the days leading up to your return he had stopped making the journey because of his declining health but watched instead from the acropolis until the sun's glare in the west prevented it. He was of late persuaded in his own mind you were lost to us and the black sail was confirmation of those fears. It was the final blow that pierced him through. He never confessed as much to me but I had the ear of his physicians, so those of us close to him knew how sick he was in body as well as in his heart. He was discovered by palace staff at first light lying in the ravine and he now rests awaiting burial. He – he had put on his finest robes, his stoutest corselet with bronze plates and wore a sword at his side as if ready to do battle. It was the fine sword he gave to you.'

Theseus eased himself down to a stone bench, lowered his face into his hands then sighed, 'Ah, I was so flushed with pride over our victory at

Knossos; such were my distractions that I allowed this most important matter to lapse in forgetfulness. It should have been foremost in my mind the day we sailed from Crete even though we left amidst chaos. Yes, the sail could so easily have been changed at Naxos. What have I done? Have I returned to Athens only to destroy my own father?'

'Lord Theseus,' whispered Haemon, leaning closer, 'even had he known of your return, even had he set out to greet you, his remaining days would have been few. Our physicians assured me that was so.'

'But at least he would have known!' responded Theseus, angrily.

'Yes, he would have known, but I doubt even the gods could alter what has passed. Word will by now have spread through much of Athens that you are with us again. At the same time they already know that Pallas is gathering his forces against our city. They will see you as their saviour. Such you were before and I truly believe will be again. Tomorrow the elders must arrange your father's funeral, the city criers must announce your succession as our king. If you will forgive my seeming haste, my lord, I will send for your steward and have him attend for your instructions whenever you are ready.'

'Haemon,' he replied, rising to his feet, 'you may carry the burden of years but as always, as with my father, you are strong enough to offer me your support and the wisdom of your advice whenever they're needed. We will arrange my father's funeral. But the news of Pallas you spoke of – tell me now about that.'

'Lord Theseus, it seems Pallas found out you had gone not long after you set out from Athens with the Cretans.'

'Inevitable, I suppose. He'll have had his spies here. But do go on.'

'Metion knows more than I because it was he who conferred with your father when the reports came to us three days ago. We are told Pallas boasts about preparing a large force of men for war and it's rumoured he has sent his envoys to Crete. We may sooner or later expect news of his raiding parties entering our territory.'

'Then,' said Theseus, 'Athens must prepare herself to deal with them. But other matters have to be attended first.'

***

Close by Aegeus' body had been laid the bowls and ornaments of silver, gold and bronze that were to remain with him in death. Draped over his corpse in royal splendour was the precious cloak of rich purple Aegeus had worn on occasions of state. Beneath this the priests had arranged his shattered limbs as best they could. Placed about him, too, were the weapons that as a younger man he had often taken up in the defence of the city and her lands. There lay the serpent-hilted blade he had left for the yet to be born Theseus at Troizen. Part-concealing his battered head was a bronze ceremonial helmet, decorated with fine scrollwork and inlaid with gold and silver, with close by, the stout leather helmet circled by rows of boars' tusks and topped with a magnificent plume of white horsehair that designated him a true warrior. On his chest had been laid a gold chalice, its sides

331

embellished with a repoussé of swirling, many-tentacled marine creatures.

Inside the entrance to the soaring tholos tomb, one built long before Aegeus' death by architects brought from Mycenae, a fire cracked, belching orange-sparked smoke as perishable offerings of timber and fabric were hurled onto it. A ring of oil lamps, set on the clay floor, followed the curve of the stone wall where they helped lighten an inner gloom. Beneath the sombre shadows of the beehive roof, a short distance from the body, a small group of mourners had gathered with at their head Theseus in plain belted tunic and cloak. As they watched, a weeping Haemon stooped to place his lyre, the one and only offering of real value he possessed, at the dead king's side before stepping slowly back, hands clasped in reverence as were those of his new master. Even in this time of grief, Haemon wondered what his role could possibly be in his remaining years without that cherished lyre.

All those present were aware that in times past, when a king died, he was accompanied to the afterlife by a man and a dog, both of which were sacrificed by knife or sword at their dead master's side. Against the wishes of some city elders and against the vocal demands of a conservative priesthood, of whom there seemed far too many with advice to offer, Theseus had broken this long tradition. He had decreed that no man should forfeit his life. Aegeus, he said, would not have wished it and neither did he. That man, after all, might have been faithful Haemon, as some of the more zealous members of the priesthood had insisted it ought properly to be.

Outside the dromos, the long, stone-lined entrance passage cut at an ascending slope through the hill into which the tomb was built, the common people milled. Though open to the sky, the entrance was by now out of the sun but oil lamps placed along its length helped keep the shadows at bay.

The people were anxious for a glimpse of the ceremony taking place within the tholos but stern-faced guards would allow no one into the passage, let alone to approach the bronze-banded oak doors that stood over twice a man's height beneath a massive stone lintel. For the citizens, the occasion was heightened by a chorus of female slaves gathered about the passage entrance, wailing aloud to the gods on Aegeus' behalf in their role of mourners.

Children ran back and forth from the city gate with food, wine and beer in pottery vessels while from time to time a priest would appear to recite in sonorous verse the deeds of Aegeus, assuring the people of his rewards in the afterlife. The crowds remained until the setting sun brought the ceremony to an end, though lamps were left to burn before the newly sealed doors. Guards would remain on duty throughout the coming night but at daybreak the workmen would arrive with their oxen and carts ready to begin the task of filling the passage in with earth, sealing its entrance with stone blocks then finishing off the hillside with turf.

***

The light of a full moon bathed the acropolis when Theseus approached the palace entrance. By it waited Haemon and both men, rather than entering, greeted each other before moving to sit down on a stone bench in the darker shadows of an adjoining wall.

'You, Haemon,' said Theseus, laying a hand on the old man's frail shoulder, 'have related the deeds of our ancestors and our heroes to my father and his court over many years. In your mind they live on. I was aware before going away that you had been relating all you know to others who learn well so they might succeed you in the art of recitation. I trust that through your skills my own tale, everything I did and learned while on Crete, will be passed on to later generations - if, as I hope, you have the inclination and patience to hear it. If so, you will memorise my tale so that in the many fruitful years you have still to come you will take up your lyre and recite it in verse as only you are able. It can never be as well delivered on mere tablets of clay. It's a strange, bizarre tale but one that I hope will sound as a rolling drum down the ages.'

'Lord Theseus,' he replied, 'It would be the greatest honour for me to hear it from your own lips. I will remain by your side for as long as needs be. Over the days, through the months ahead I will recite it back to you in verse though it will no longer be accompanied by my lyre because that is now at rest with your dear departed father.'

'Ah, but it *will* be accompanied by your lyre,' smiled Theseus. 'When I saw you lay your instrument by my father's side I determined it would be replaced. The bard must have his lyre and you, dear friend, will have the very best. Gathering dust in our treasury is as fine and as precious an instrument I ever saw. It's inlaid with gold, lapis-lazuli and precious stones. I'm assured it was a gift to my father from the King of Egypt himself. I promise it will be yours tomorrow. You must have it tuned to your own tastes and I'll listen when you play. But for now I think you and I should go inside for greater comfort and a little wine, then I'll begin my account on the day I boarded the vessel with the black sail.'

Chapter 12
The PERILS of ATHENS

'So, there you have my account as I'm best able to tell it,' said Theseus, raising the goblet to his lips as they sat by a hearth of smoking embers in the otherwise deserted megaron. 'To you and only you have I related in full my vision of Athena and what happened when I entered the labyrinth. I've no wish to describe to others that succession of horrors though I can't imagine a day will pass when I don't relive at least a part of it in my thoughts. No, nor the stench of death that still haunts me though I was much pleased with what I'd done at the time and the world seemed by far a better place. You, Haemon, will doubtless relate what happened in a manner I could not. Lit by the glow of the hearth you will make my tedious account sing in the ears of those who gather to listen. What afterwards transpired at Knossos will doubtless be known to us in time. As for Ariadne – perhaps she really has found her way back to the joys of family life at Knossos or maybe the gods took her. If so, they have my sympathy.'

'Oh, but what a picture you have painted for me,' nodded Haemon, lifting his own cup. 'You have destroyed the evil beast that drew the fairest, the most innocent of our young people across the sea to their deaths. You have shown that tyrant Minos he can no longer punish Athens with impunity. How your father would have basked in the light of your triumph. How the cloak of pride would have warmed his twilight days.'

'Well old friend, perhaps he watches us now. Perhaps he knows what has passed. If that is so then his soul will surely be contented. As for the preservation of his memory – once other matters are settled everyone will know by my edict that the waters reaching out from our land eastward to the coast of Asia are to be called the Aegean Sea in his honour. You will I'm sure wish to question me further unless more pressing matters demand my attention. I must have Metion see to the arms of our fighting men. I must ensure Athens is prepared to meet the threat gathering to our south. I will leave by sea in a day or so for Troizen to find out how things fare with Pittheus. He cannot yet know of my return so he'll have much to tell me. And – and I must see my mother and visit those honest people who cared for me through childhood.'

'Troizen is the staunchest ally we ever had,' said Haemon. 'Pittheus and his people would rise and fall with us no matter what.'

'Yes, so as well as renewing our treaty with Troizen I have it in mind to dedicate a temple there to Artemis. I will also make generous offerings at the shrine of Athena in thanks for my killing of the Minotaur and safe return from Crete with our young people. We talked about treaties while my father was alive but the time never seemed right until now. It's a great advantage that both our peoples look to Athena as their protectress in peace and war. Pittheus and his people will deny Pallas any support he might have expected in the area. The people of Megara will also resist Pallas since he has as an ally those very Cretans who sacked their city and made their lives a misery.'

337

'If those rumours are true about Pallas appealing to Knossos for military help,' said Haemon, 'which they surely are, then they'll have advantage over us. Minos will be more than willing to assist him after what you did though he may not wish to have fully revealed the true nature of Asterion. If his daughter does not return home he will assume in the absence of contrary news that you hold her prisoner or have been responsible for her death. That for him would be the perfect excuse. It would justify his actions regardless of your having slain Asterion. And if she has returned then there is doubtless the burning of his ships to fall back on as good enough reason. It must be the greatest affront by far Minos ever suffered.'

'Oh, well,' mused Theseus, 'we can't go through life without upsetting someone, can we. And while it's a pity about Ariadne, I doubt she'd have proved the most level-headed of consorts. Even so, the presence of a Cretan princess at our court would have added much to the prestige of Athens. It would surely have stemmed Minos' enthusiasm in his support for our enemies. But I agree with what you say - Minos will doubtless support Pallas. That will be first amongst the points I intend to discuss with Pittheus. I anticipate, too, Pittheus will be ready to send us aid, though if the Cretan ships arrive first, Phaleron will be denied to any vessel from Troizen.'

'True,' replied Haemon, 'but though it is a greater distance from Athens than our harbour, there is good landing at the smaller bay of Piraeus to the north-west of Phaleron. I myself have not been there in many years but I recall it well enough. I hear it is used at present only by fishermen.'

'Aye, and a landing there would most likely pass unseen by our enemies if our timing was right.'

'Pallas' agents will surely have reported your return,' said Haemon. 'They will be alerted if you leave Athens again. Will that not prompt him into action all the sooner if he thinks help from Troizen is to be called upon?'

'You're right, my friend. I'll go disguised as a merchant, under cover of night with only two men. You, Metion and my trusted staff must tell everyone including our elders, some of whom may not be quite the loyal citizens they ought to be, that I am spending time alone in private. Tell them I continue mourning over the death of my father through my own guilt in the matter. It will wear thin as a pauper's blanket after a while because I'll be gone several days but it should keep our enemies guessing. And by the time it reaches Pallas, by the time he begins to doubt the tale, I intend to be back here in the city. Early tomorrow I'll go through this in detail with Metion. For now let's refill our goblets before we retire to our beds. It must be well past midnight.'

***

The winds seemed to carry rumour quicker than the voices of those who witnessed its source. Men on horseback were seen, sometimes alone, sometimes in twos or threes. They watched Athens from a distance whilst others of ill intent skulked unnoticed about the narrow streets, the market stalls and in particular the taverns of the city to glean whatever information they could from the wine-loosened tongues of its citizens. What they did not observe was Theseus' departure via a little used passage below the city wall. Nor, six days later, were they aware of his return.

***

The fire at the centre of the great hall cracked and coughed glowing embers. Smoke curled about soot-laden beams above as the new King of Athens spoke.

'We have increasing reports of scouts and spies,' said a plainly attired Theseus, addressing the pale-gowned city elders seated about the great hall. 'From what I and others have gathered, it seems Pallas and his Cretan allies intend to move against us soon.'

Though seated on the throne that was once his father's, Theseus had abjured those attributes of kingship he deemed unnecessary. No longer seen were the shallow-rimmed beaten gold crown with gem encrusted dome and lavishly embroidered robe fastened with gold pins worn on formal occasions by Aegeus. Absent, too, were the richly attired retainers who once stood by to issue commands on the king's behalf so as to garnish his authority. Theseus had passed his early years unused to the trappings of affluence and had no wish to adopt them now. Close by him stood the hardy Metion and a handful of his chosen warriors. All were equally plainly dressed though each boasted a sword and dagger at his belt.

'Then should we not move against Pallas first?' put in one of the elders. 'Even before your fortunate return from Crete our own spies reported them gathering arms and testing their skills in sport as do

340

we. They are said to be preparing horses and chariots to carry their men to the field of battle - the field of battle being *our* territory. There's talk of Cretan ships being sent to invest our harbour at Phaleron. A failure though it was, the attempt on your late father's life as well as the ambush that followed later must be seen as no more than a prelude to what they next have planned.'

'Then let them head our way. I will not send men out to meet our enemy because Pallas will learn about it and will spread his men across southern Attica. They'll be difficult to find until they reassemble somewhere closer to Athens. Also, the city will be left poorly defended should any Cretan vessels arrive.'

Metion nodded in agreement as Theseus continued, 'As we know, there are too few mainland towns in any position to join us. King Atreus of Mycenae might have sent men and arms but has too many troubles of his own and finds it necessary to remain on peaceful terms with Knossos.'

'Plus the fact that they share a common ancestry,' declared one of the elders.

'So they do for what it's worth,' responded Theseus. 'Anyhow, we rely mainly on Troizen and a just a few dozen men from Megara, otherwise we stand alone. Let Pallas drag his men and arms here over rough country. Let them leave themselves exposed on open ground beyond our walls. Pallas has a great many men, his allies in the south of Attica are sufficient to back his ambitions there but he has no support in these parts. Nor has he any power at sea other than those ships Minos lends him for transport. As for his chariots – they'll be of little use for combat away from level ground and they know it as well as we do. Pallas, however, will most likely be planning on a siege rather than a quick victory provided he is kept supplied by sea and that is an advantage I intend to deny him.'

'And how is it to be achieved?' asked one of the elders. 'The sea is where Minos takes on his enemies and wins his battles whereas we do not have enough ships available. And even if we had, where are the sailors with sufficient experience in manning them for combat at sea against the Cretans?'

'That I'm not prepared to discuss,' responded Theseus, 'but the men of Athens will be ready with their arms and when victory is ours I will put an end to Pallas' ambitions once and for all. Aye, and this time I'll not be inclined to let him slip back to Thorikos!'

'Lord Theseus,' said another of the elders, 'as I set out to join you here I was stopped by one of our merchants newly arrived in the city. He and his companions reported seeing Cretans come ashore several days ago close to Thorikos. They claim there were many vessels – some carrying a cargo, others full of armed men. If this is true then they will certainly re-embark those men and bring their ships up to Phaleron. Our man questioned the local people who told him the majority of the Cretans they had seen were archers. It is rumoured there are more of them housed out of sight around the countryside.'

'Then we must ready ourselves for battle,' replied Theseus. 'Aid from Crete or no, Pallas will not wish to keep his fighting men idle and living off his supplies. Nor will the Cretans care to suffer delay in the harsher conditions of Attica when they could be sailing open seas. In the meantime, our herdsmen and sufficient of their livestock must be brought within the city wall and their families sent north for safety.'

With the meeting ended, Theseus called back his captain of the guard. 'Metion, have a number of your men posted as lookouts above the harbour then you and I will discuss further what needs to be done.'

'Very good, sir,' replied Metion, 'and I look forward to riding by your side when we meet the enemy.'

***

For the past three days he had trod the city wall, sometimes with Haemon, more often with Metion or a group of his guards, sometimes as now, in the early morning air, alone.

Theseus looked out, thinking today there might be a storm because clouds were welling above the eastern horizon, dark and ominous to blot out the sun. Yet the air was not still and oppressive as it so often was when a storm was due. He recalled watching the clouds rise up, form and reform from the window of his prison at Knossos. The clouds now approaching drifted slowly, rising higher until they towered as a range of dark battlements above Athens. As they billowed, as they changed shape Theseus imagined he discerned a figure and wondered if once again the image of Athena would materialise to raise his spirits in this time of approaching danger.

'What do I see?' he breathed as the shifting forms became vaguely recognisable. 'It is a figure but - but it is not her. Now I see what it is and by the gods I no longer wish to see. There are the horns. There are those baleful eyes. It is the beast! Yes, the beast, and its shadow spreads over me as the gathering powers of darkness! What can this mean?'

Theseus grew cold though the air was warm. He could not avert his eyes from the monstrosity that dominated the sky above the city. Then the image began to fragment with shafts of sunlight braking through in several places. One fell upon Theseus to bathe him in warmth as the clouds drifted apart. The clouds were dissipating, Helios was repossessing his realm when the voice fractured his thoughts.

'Lord Theseus,' said Metion, 'our scouts report men and chariots gathering to the south less than a day's march away. Unless they are deceived by their own eyes they tell me the enemy number fewer than Athens can muster but are too numerous and well equipped for a raiding party. Our men saw no supply wagons.'

'Pallas would never dare confront us with equal, let alone inadequate forces,' replied Theseus, turning his gaze from the sky.

'That is so,' agreed Metion. 'It means others of his men may be taking a separate route. And there are those who will come by sea with the Cretans and the bulk of his supplies.'

'Yes, it would appear Minos has been generous with his vessels and crews. Pallas no doubt intends to bring them ashore once his men are positioned between ourselves and the harbour. Is all going as we planned?'

'It is, sir - as we planned. They'll find no food hereabouts and there'll be precious little water as the streams will not flow again until winter. Our own wells will suffice.'

'Good, and I have seen how well equipped are our men and how well stocked is the city. But Athens cannot contain so many people indefinitely, not with all those farm animals. Pallas may have no need to wait long if disease proves a greater enemy to us.'

'The oracles,' asked Metion, 'what do they say? I'm told our party returned after dark yesterday from Delphi'

'So they did,' replied Theseus, 'and if I now relate the priestess' message I wonder what sense you'll see in it. "One ruler will triumph. Two shall die. Two shall gain their father's throne." D'you make anything of it, Metion? I don't – nor does Haemon.'

Metion thought for a while then answered, 'No, I find no sense in it, either. There seem to be too many rulers – and who might gain his father's throne apart from one of Pallas' sons? But then there are sharper wits than a soldier's when it comes to these matters.'

'Sharper than mine also,' smiled Theseus, 'and I have already put it to the so-called experts amongst our priesthood, for what that's worth. None of them could make any more of the message than you or I so we needn't feel ashamed over it.'

'Nor, Lord Theseus, will there be any shame in the account we give of ourselves when Pallas gathers his forces to confront us.'

His captain was on the point of leaving when Theseus said, 'Oh - and Metion, did you notice the clouds passing over from our east a short time ago?'

'The clouds, Lord Theseus?' Metion hesitated, puzzled. 'Yes, I noticed the clouds. It looked as if a storm was on the way but then I saw them broken apart by the rays of the sun. Broken the way we will break the enemy. Why d'you ask me?'

'Oh, it was nothing of importance,' shrugged Theseus. 'Just clouds as you say, and broken apart by the sun. The sky is clearing now.'

Metion left and Theseus, once more alone, laid hands on the parapet and gazed up at the sky, saying, 'Yes, broken the way we will break the enemy. Yet I wonder what message the Delphic oracle gave to them.'

***

Later that day rumour of a different kind spread consternation throughout Athens. Three merchants of Troizen had arrived with a string of mules to set up their wares within the city wall. They were carrying goods from Cyprus; mainly copper ingots and alum - the latter highly valued for its use in dyeing fabrics. They gossiped freely with the townsmen as traders will, so that before long the tale they brought with them was common currency in every tavern and street.

Their intended destination had been their home town but a half day before reaching port they had encountered another vessel bearing terrible news: The gods had brought plague down with devastating suddenness upon Troizen. Pittheus their king was among the dead. Order had broken down. The population had fallen into a state of panic, some fleeing with whatever goods they could carry, some looting deserted homes, others simply dying in their beds or falling down in the market place. On hearing this, the merchants had changed course for Athens because, like those of Troizen, her markets were more open, less strictly regulated than those of Mycenae and other mainland towns.

Before long their account had spread beyond the city wall, into the countryside about Athens, then further still, carried by traders and by certain others with reason to regard the news as welcome. To the people of the city, to anyone hearing it no matter where, it meant only one thing. Athens had to stand alone against the forces of Pallas, his allies and the fighting men sent by Knossos.

***

Several days had passed when hidden eyes watched the boats begin to swarm around the headland. On they came, growing in size, ominous and dark in the calm silence of an awakening day. As they drew closer, as the sky lightened, the young goatherd knew they were not vessels of Athens because two of the larger, broad-beamed ships bore on their sails the double-headed axe, the symbol his people feared – the symbol he had reported to the now dead Aegeus on that fateful day not so long ago. Remaining where he was as the high prowed ships lowered their sails, he watched the first of them guided by oarsmen toward the harbour of Phaleron. He suspected these intruders must be in collusion with the invading forces led by Pallas, the

347

evil man who intended to overwhelm Athens. So he had been told many times of late by his parents.

A day earlier, at the great western gate, he had seen the older cattle, pigs and sheep slaughtered outside the wall, after which their carcasses were dismembered before being boiled down in copper vats. There he had scrounged sufficient food to ward off real hunger. There he had watched them drain the fat into pottery vessels of many shapes and sizes. Several times someone had approached to ask, 'What are you doing here? Why are you not with your parents?' Each time he had answered, 'They're waiting for me inside the city.'

His family, including his father, had been ordered to depart as had most other country dwellers, taking with them any livestock that had not been impounded or slaughtered. They would have forced him to go with them had he not ran away before sunrise on the day they departed, had he not stayed hidden from sight while they searched for him in vain, calling his name here and there to no avail. The gold cup given him by King Aegeus was seldom far from his thoughts. His parents had not considered it wise to carry such a precious object with them for fear of encountering bandits. The reward that had been his – that was still his by right - lay where he had watched unseen as they buried it for safekeeping. He intended to unearth his treasure before they returned - whatever their fate or that of Athens and at least now there were no goats to demand his attention. These had been rounded up the previous day. Roughly half of them his parents had retained whilst the rest had been herded into the city together with, as far as he could tell, a portion of the livestock belonging to several of the farms within Athens' domain.

Several Athenian vessels, mainly fishing boats, were drawn up on the deserted beach. There was nothing odd about the way they were spaced out along the narrow shore. Some of the new arrivals drew close alongside them but the larger, deep-keeled Cretan ships, each boasting over forty oarsmen to manoeuvre her close enough to the harbour, would have to remain in deeper water.

What the boy did consider strange, because under a cloudless sky he was able to observe the scene clearly from his higher vantage point amidst the thickets, were the objects left within the boats. There were pottery jars protected from damage by straw, all resting on bundled brushwood. More brushwood and jars, covered by fishing nets, had been abandoned partway along one side of the jetty. These it seemed to him could serve no purpose in having been left where they were. The reason, he concluded, was that their owners had intended to flee up the coast by boat with the jars containing those commodities they deemed to be of value. They would now be prevented from doing so by the arrival of the Cretan vessels.

As for his own situation that day: he had left his abandoned hovel then set out in darkness for the city. Arriving there he had intended as on the previous day to search out scraps of food where traders had been busy at their stalls late into the previous afternoon - anything that had survived scavenging dogs, cats and rats. When sooner than expected the big gates swung wide, he had crouched low to observe whoever would emerge.

There had been many more of them than he could have counted on the fingers of both hands. All armed men - most of them archers in plain, dark kilts. He had followed them discreetly as they made their way in silence along seldom-used paths that avoided entirely the area between Athens and the much-frequented route to Phaleron. It was a longer detour by far; one that had brought them out some way to the north of the harbour. From that point they had made their way back south along the shadowed slope overlooking the bay, always in silence, always keeping low, until they were positioned above the narrow beach where twilight still lingered. He had watched them conceal themselves behind rocks and bushes on the slope, rendering themselves as invisible to him as he guessed they would be to anyone on the beach below. They were still hidden there when the Cretan ships arrived.

The boy was afraid. He knew he ought to be elsewhere. He told himself that whatever was going to happen need be no concern of his. He would scramble away, keeping low until reaching the larger bushes on level ground, then hurry back to his empty home in the warmth of a rising sun.

He was startled by sounds from behind, from the direction of the forested ground backing onto the slope where he hid. There were voices, snorting horses and the clicking sounds made by men equipped with arms and armour. The boy sensed looming danger. He would keep low until the men went away.

Still he watched. Some of the first ships, having reached their destination, would serve as moorings for those that followed. The boats would be grouped closely so their crews could clamber from one to the other. The two large Cretan vessels were tying up at the jetty where the water was deeper. Others would need to stand off and wait their turn. Accompanied by much shouting, a number of men with spears were leaping over the sides into shallow water or clambering onto the jetty. One group of four, equipped with body armour of bronze or boiled hide, walked along the beach, weapons at the ready. These men checked inside the cluster of stone buildings, looking here and there for signs of opposition, while others continued hauling on ropes to secure their vessels. One of the armed men looked up in the boy's direction, raising his spear high in what seemed a signal. The boy crouched lower, wishing there was a hole into which he could wriggle. He assumed the people whose voices he had heard a short time before must be waiting close by to acknowledge the man below but he dared not glance behind. Again the sound of voices and horses - now retreating. When he summoned enough courage to peer over his shoulder, there was no one to be seen.

But what if they were still close by and saw him when he stepped into the open? They were after all enemies of Athens and so would probably try to kill or capture him. No - he would stay where he was and witness whatever was going to happen.

A small number of the men below seemed diverted by curiosity over the pottery jars stored in the Athenian boats but frantic activity was in progress generally on the beach when a horn sounded some distance away. The boy saw those below who heard it looking about to ascertain from where the sound had come. The rest of those on shore, in securing their position whilst loudly encouraging each other to greater effort, appeared too busy to notice.

There were many men on board the ships as well as those now ashore. Perhaps not as many as the boy had seen when all the able-bodied citizens of Athens set out to do battle but still very many, and it would take considerable time for them all to disembark. They had hardly begun to unload wicker baskets containing their supplies when glinting metal caught the boy's attention. A group of some twenty well-armed men had appeared from among the trees where the northern end of the bay curved out of shadow into direct sunlight. They marched with resolute stride toward the ships, warriors' plumes swaying above their helmets. The boy saw at once these were Athenians. More shouting arose from around the boats.

Abandoning their tasks, the men by those vessels already made fast, took up whatever weapon was to hand then prepared to meet these intruders who, though fewer in number, were advancing ready for combat with spear and sword, round shield and gleaming cuirass. The two groups drew closer. Spears flashed through the air from both sides. Cries of defiance arose. Men fell to the ground stricken and bleeding. Only one Athenian had fallen when a spear penetrated his shield; the rest were those of the boat people because, apart from their own armed party returning to join them, they had not sufficient time to gather up shield or armour. Even so, sheer numbers must soon count as others disembarked in haste. Again the horn sounded but it could hardly have been heard on the shore above the clash of battle or the commotion of voices as more of Pallas' men, intent on driving away or destroying the outnumbered Athenians, seized what arms they could from their vessels before advancing against these rash intruders.

In his excitement at witnessing the spectacle on the beach, the boy had all but forgotten about the archers concealed a short distance above the ships. Those unseen men arose now as if from beneath the ground, a company of apparitions amidst swirling wraiths of pale smoke. Wide-eyed, he watched them fit arrows to their bows – long arrows that burned at their tips with lively flame. The men stood, as yet unnoticed from the shore, drawing back powerful bows in unison to loose their shafts as a burning flock that arced downward toward the ships. No longer concerned about his cover, the boy clambered to his feet to stare fascinated as more arrows sped through the air trailing smoke. A small number had fallen wide of their target to hiss in the water but most found their mark. The Athenians' own boats and the jetty itself.

More arrows were being readied but the Athenians on the beach were giving ground, retreating northwards, a circumstance that, because of their modest number, the boy well understood. This had caused the invader to spread out along the shore regardless of their not being fully armed, it had spurred them to move away from their boats in expectation of an easy victory. In the general disarray, frantic calls for help from the men at the ships went largely unheeded as a third volley of shafts was released to swoop down in flaming deadly swarm.

A few of the enemy, having cast their spears, looked about for other weapons and were alerted to the peril as thick smoke, swirling on the breeze from the Athenian boats, showered glowing motes across their own vessels. Some hurried back to assist those already clambering aboard to quell rapidly spreading flames only to have the brushwood, loosely laid and already afire in places, give way beneath their feet. Their vision hampered by smoke, Cretan archers on board those vessels in no immediate danger loosed their arrows to little effect before pausing to consider their own situation. Those of their comrades engaged more closely with the Athenians realised what was happening at their backs but in the turmoil of confusion these men fell into disarray. The four fully armed enemy pressed to continue a fight they supposed they were soon to win but soon were felled whilst most others were drawn back by the prospect of their supplies being destroyed in what threatened to become a conflagration.

Dark, acrid smoke shrouded one end of the line of vessels from the other, flames danced with growing intensity. Another burning volley fell upon the ships and jetty whilst Pallas' men, in hurrying back to preserve their vessels found themselves fighting a rear-guard action against the newly advancing Athenians with a red-plumed, bronze-clad Metion striding in grim resolution at their fore, his sword already bloodied to the hilt.

Amidst the tumult, many of Pallas' men were still scrambling to retrieve weapon and shield. Some attempted to douse the flames with seawater but had too few containers. Others struggled to push smaller boats clear of the flames in desperate hope of regaining the safety of the sea, only to find the way blocked by other vessels attempting also to escape. To their consternation they found themselves exposed to the well-aimed missiles of the archers who, moving down the slope, were able to execute their deadly work with unassailable ease.

Pots of olive oil and melted animal fat in the burning Athenian boats were splitting asunder, causing fires to gush with alarming vigour, creating an inferno no one could hope to quell. Flames erupted to embrace those enemy vessels close by, belching incandescent fragments that rained a deadly shower to ignite the timbers of two boats the Cretan sailors had almost succeeded in pushing clear. The jetty, too, was ablaze while, strewn from stem to stern with burning material ejected from it, the two large Cretan vessels moored there smouldered heavily. The crews of those vessels further out or not yet secured were frantically rowing clear while amidst a chaos of flames, blinding smoke and cracking timbers, desperate men on the beach took to the water in hope of reaching them, only to find the very sea alight with molten fat and oil. Above all arose dense smoke, swirling, writhing like a dark beast.

Seeing his vessels lost or putting back to sea together with the bulk of his arms and supplies, their leader harangued his men to abandon their struggle at the ships and with whatever weapons they retained, to confront the Athenians who they still outnumbered. But the formidable Metion called his men on. Better armed and with the archers advancing closer still to continue their deadly work, the Athenians were no longer about to retreat. After more of their number had fallen, Pallas' men and their marooned Cretan allies saw they had to dash for safety or die. Grim faced Metion and his battle-hardened warriors were determined few if any would escape.

***

Smoke rose lazily into a clear sky above Phaleron, drifting out to sea but easily visible from the city wall where Theseus stood together with a number of his guards, three elders and two priests of Athena's temple.

To Pallas and his men preparing their camp with much noise before the dense spread of trees screening the bay, the smoke would not be visible. This was the ground where Pallas had gathered his warriors on that earlier attempt to gain victory over Athens by slaying Aegeus, her then king. Now his numbers were greater by far though he did not expect to take the city with ease even when, as had been planned, his men with their supplies made their way up from the harbour.

***

'It would appear Metion and our archers have done what they set out to do,' said Theseus, turning to his companions. 'And once again fire has proved an effective ally. Our scouts estimate the enemy setting up camp out there still exceed our number by two to one but now is the time to offer Pallas battle. Now, when he has it in his mind he's going to win the day.'

'Those are great odds against us,' put in one of the elders. 'As we can expect no help from Troizen would we not be better served by relying on our fortifications?'

'Surely he's right,' added another elder. 'If their supplies are done for they'll not be able to remain outside our walls for as long as they intended. They cannot live off the land whereas we have ample food in storage and water from our wells to sustain us.'

'If we wait until they discover the truth about the harbour, which they soon must, they may fight as desperate men from the start,' replied Theseus. 'Let them think it's we who are desperate.'

'I thought we *were* desperate,' muttered the first elder.

'We'll see about that,' responded Theseus, patting the hilt of his sword. 'We go out fighting for our own city on our own land. Some of Pallas' allies and those Cretans still with him may not be so charged with enthusiasm, especially when Metion and our other men show up.'

'We'll be on 'em like lions,' added one of the guards. 'We'll beat 'em or die!'

'I assure you,' responded Theseus with a broad smile, 'dying was never a part of my plan. At least not today.'

Another guard arrived to announce, 'Our men are waiting for you to lead us, Lord Theseus.'

'Aye and now I will,' responded Theseus. 'I'll have no man step out from the city gate before me. My arms and my armour are ready and waiting!'

***

Smoke from cooking fires drifted about the encampment when the scout dashed up, halted his snorting mount, drew his sword and clashed it repeatedly against his small shield. As the ringing stopped, Pallas, not yet equipped with arms or armour, emerged from his tent wearing kilt and chewing food.

'The Athenians are coming out in force!' called the horseman, gesturing in the direction of the town.

'So they're on their way to challenge us are they!' Pallas responded, shading his eyes from the morning sun.

'That they are, sire!' came the reply. 'I watched them assemble.'

'I hoped we'd have a day or so's foraging before they dared show their faces,' he grinned to those about him. 'No matter, it'll save us hanging about the city wall.'

'We've again scoured the area between here and the city,' confirmed the horseman. 'There are no wagons stuffed with armed men and archers – not this time around.'

'Well that's good to hear,' responded Pallas. 'So if they attempt a retreat we've enough men to circle about and cut 'em off from the town. There'll be no help from outside now the plague's struck Troizen and that old fool Pittheus is out of the way. Hah - see if they don't shit 'emselves and run like rabbits!'

'And our ships,' asked one of his sons, 'is all well at the harbour?'

'A few of our lads watched 'em sail in,' replied Pallas. 'The beach was deserted, they said; not even a fisherman down there. All they noticed was some brat skulking in the bushes. They'd have skewered the little sod if they'd had more time but I'd told 'em not to hang about when there's work to be done. And now there *is* work to be done!'

'So it's all or nothing for Athens,' remarked one of Pallas' companions as word spread rapidly through his eager host. 'They'll face us in fewer numbers now and soon our men and supplies will be up from the harbour.'

Pallas armed himself for battle but determined his head would remain bared a while so all could witness the expression of contempt smeared across his face at the forthcoming sight of his adversaries. Soon enough he and his substantial company were massing in readiness, spread broadly before the trees with each man keen to draw first blood. Sunlight glinted on Pallas' bronze scales. A stout spear rested impatient in his grasp, eager to claim its first victim. 'The buggers'll not be so lucky this time!' he declared to his sons, a group of who had gathered around him. 'After we've done with the Athenians I'll send a bunch of their own slaves to burn what's left of Troizen. Looks as if the gods have done a good bit of our work for us.'

The Athenian forces had come fully into sight, crossing rough open ground beyond vineyard and orchard, a small number only in chariots with Theseus, in heavy bronze cuirass over thick linen in the lead, his driver more lightly armed. Theseus' head was also uncovered so men of both sides had no doubt as to who was chief amongst Pallas' adversaries and no doubt as to who would be prime target for Pallas' spear.

Several of Theseus' men had questioned the absence of Metion and his men but Theseus had told them only that, 'Metion will join us soon.' The Athenians now halted to stare across in silence at the enemy.

'We outnumber 'em mightily even now,' boasted one of Pallas' company, raising his spear. 'If those idlers at the harbour don't get a move on they'll miss the best of it.'

One of his sons glanced about, muttering, 'Aye, they seem to be taking their time.'

'They're still cooking their damned food if you ask me,' remarked another. 'Don't I smell wood smoke drifting from somewhere?'

'Two of you get over there now and see what they're –,' began Pallas.

He was interrupted by a cry, of 'Lord Pallas!' Two men in blood-spattered tunics, dishevelled and smoke-stained emerged staggering from amidst the trees behind Pallas' tent. One, his eyes wild with fear, supported the other who, head bowed and coughing blood, clutched at a gash in his chest from which protruded the broken shaft of an arrow. This man appeared close to death.

Pallas stared hard at them to demand, 'What's this about?'

No one would move to help the two men unless Pallas allowed it.

'Lord Pallas,' gasped the man, lowering his wounded charge to the ground, 'they - they came at us! Burning arrows – many armed men! Th–the ships are on fire or gone back out to sea! M-most of them are lost!'

'On fire – lost!' growled Pallas, thrusting his spear into the hand of a startled companion. 'The rest of my men - where are they? And where are those Cretan archers?'

'Most are - are dead,' stammered the other, propping himself against a tree trunk. 'Dead or driven into the water. Lord Pallas, this man is my brother! Have mercy! Help us!'

'Better shut the bugger's mouth before this gets about,' hissed one of Pallas' men.

Pallas shook his head from side to side in grim anger, drew his sword and declared, 'Help you? By Zeus I'll help you down to Hades!' He plunged his blade deep into the man's ribs, withdrawing it as his victim fell choking. He next finished off the already stricken man with a blow through the neck that all but severed his head. 'Get these two out of sight!' he growled at his nearest men, wiping his sword on the tunic of the still twitching man who had addressed him. 'Throw 'em into the bushes. Let's get this over and done with –Cretan fucking archers or no!'

The two bleeding corpses were dragged away and Pallas turned his gaze back to the Athenians, who were halted some way beyond effective arrow shot. 'Fetch my chariot!' he called, snatching back his spear. We'll need no supplies now the buggers have come out to meet us. Men can go down one for one on each side and we'll still be left holding the field. Before the day's out Athens, its riches and its women will be ours!'

'Its women!' exclaimed one of his sons. 'Now you're talking!'

361

There were cheers from others of his men. They moved aside as his chariot, drawn by two snorting, black-plumed grey mares, was brought over. Pallas handed his spear to the driver, another of his sons fitted on his helmet of engraved and gilded bronze, its plume rising as a jet of dark smoke. Twelve more of his many alleged sons, all on foot, gathered about the chariot. Here were his elite, his staunchest supporters.

'They've not advanced any further,' commented one of them, eyeing the Athenians who remained still and silent.

'Then we'll do the advancing for 'em!' declared Pallas, stepping into the chariot, taking up his tall, figure of eight shield, drawing his sword then thrusting it above his head as a signal to the rest of his men. Some began to move forward, jibing, encouraging one another while balancing spears in readiness to cast. Some without a shield wore cuirass or corselet of bronze or toughened hide. Most were lightly dressed for agility in the growing heat of the day. Several carried tall shields to protect themselves from head to ankle, others a smaller round shield that would serve to deflect a sword blow or the strike of an arrow. And although a few set out bareheaded, others wore head protection of boiled hide set with short horns while others still favoured helmets sewn with rows of interlocking boars' tusks. Plumes of many colours swayed menacingly back and forth as Pallas' men advanced, shouting and boasting among themselves. The Athenians, little different in appearance of arms and armour though each wearing a white band about his left arm for identification, continued to watch their approach, so far offering no response.

Each side possessed its complement of lightly attired archers, those of Theseus' company, their numbers much depleted, were placed further back, those with Pallas, including the few Cretans already attached to his army, were moving away from their camp and aside from the mass of his footmen.

Pallas' host had advanced only a short distance, aiming verbal insults and provocative gestures at the Athenians when the blaring sound of a horn cut the air. Two sharp blasts arose loudly from amid the Athenians, moments later to be repeated. Pallas slowed his men, puzzled over the significance of what they realised must be a signal of sorts though the Athenians still showed no sign of attacking. Pallas' men quietened. Horses snorted, chariots creaked and a dull ring of metal arose from those footmen walking cautiously on. The tension grew among Pallas' force yet still nothing appeared to be happening on the Athenian side. Then, 'Over there!' cried one of his men, pointing to their left from a chariot close to his leader. Heads turned to see a forest of spearheads against the skyline. Many figures had appeared in the distance over a shallow rise; some mounted on horseback, most on foot – all well-armed.

'Wait!' called Pallas, raising a hand above his eyes to peer at the newcomers. His driver hauled on the reins though his men, having spread out, continued slowly on. 'Whose men are those?'

'They look to be spearmen, not archers,' replied his charioteer, staining to make out the figures descending the hill. 'They cannot be ours, sire,'

'Of course they're not ours you damned fool!' snapped Pallas. 'But whose are they? They can't be Athenians, either – there are too many of 'em!'

As if in answer to his question, a man at the fore of the newly appeared soldiers raised up his spear. Pallas returned his attention to the Athenians in time to observe Theseus raise his own spear high in acknowledgement.

'They can only be men from Troizen,' declared Pallas' driver, wiping sweat from his head.

'Men from -!' began Pallas. 'Most of 'em were supposed to be dead with the plague!'

He glanced ahead to see the Athenian company was moving.

As they started forward, Theseus turned to those of his companions close by. 'See those men – Metion and our allies have joined us! Spread the word quickly! Pallas no longer has advantage in numbers so we settle this now - once and for all!' Again raising his spear high, Theseus called aloud to his men, 'Athena Nike is with us!'

Repeated cries of, 'Athena victorious!' and 'Theseus!' spread loudly through the ranks of the Athenians.

In hand with growing commotion, rumour scurried in different guises throughout Pallas' company. First the approaching strangers were allies of their own come from the harbour - then perhaps they were not. Soon they were assuredly not. Pallas saw nothing to be gained from speculation and spurred his men on with a cry of, 'Be ready! We deal with the Athenians now and we take what's ours!'

The adversaries were drawing close when a bearded soldier stepped forward with spear raised from amidst the Athenians. The man strode past Theseus' chariot, his helmet plume prancing, his round shield slung at his left. Here was a man eager to show his prowess, a man keen to be remembered as the one who struck the first blow – hopefully against Pallas himself.

Those familiar with combat in the field knew that the man at whom the spear was aimed was least likely to notice its deadly approach. It would be a mere speck against the sky, a hovering insect until too late. But Pallas, having observed the Athenian weigh him up before casting, knew he was the intended victim and so crouched behind his shield as the spear hurtled through the air. It was his lightly armed driver, concerned to control unruly horses, whose life was forfeit as the blade plunged into his left side, its point bursting bloodily through the flesh of his back, its impetus hurling him with death-cry from the chariot. Cursing loudly, Pallas, spear in hand, leapt from the chariot as his men closed with the Athenians. Warriors on both sides chose their targets but Pallas, much concerned by the approach of Metion at the head of Athens' allies, determined to reach Theseus quickly, to destroy the one man who stood between himself and victory.

Insults took wing together with challenges to join the swish of spears cleaving the air from one side to the other while the archers also selected their targets. Men fell on both sides – a companion of Theseus being among the first to die as a spear split both helmet and head then passing on to glance against the shield of a man behind.

The men engaged in groups, supporting one another with cries of triumph when successful, with cries of pain or anguish when fortune deserted them. When a man fell, others, friend or foe, moved in to seize his weapons and whatever protection he wore regardless of injury or a surfeit of the victim's blood. Many on both sides stood back issuing taunts, awaiting their opportunity to move in and strike down an opponent with lethal blade.

Aware of Pallas battling his way with grim determination through the melee on foot, stopping often to deal with an adversary or to evade a blow, Theseus continued the fight from his chariot. His spear found its mark when, hurled with all the strength he could muster, it rang through the shield of a loudly boasting, well-armed warrior, through the bronze-scaled corselet, through layers of tough linen then deep into his stomach. The man fell, half buried beneath his weighty shield, quivering, clutching at the shaft, his death cry rising like the shriek of a panicked bird.

Pallas saw this, scowled and cast his own spear to good effect at a younger, less experienced Athenian who had left himself exposed, impaling him through the left shoulder so that he fell kicking to the ground. Protected by his shield but in need of a fresh spear Pallas stepped across to lever the embedded shaft from the side of a newly fallen man of his own company who still writhed in agony.

'I believe I see the cause of our troubles heading this way,' said Theseus, his bronze helmet fixed in place, 'and very soon we'll meet!' He

366

grasped the next spear held ready by his driver, jumped from his chariot then took down his shield in time to stop an arrow loosed by one of Pallas' few but vigilant Cretans. Through the raucous din of brutal violence Theseus edged closer to Pallas, each man well aware he must not press so far ahead as to find himself surrounded by the enemy without support. Men on both sides continued to step forward to offer challenge and insult before engaging in combat as ringing bronze quivered the air.

Amid the tumult, amidst the reek of death, Pallas' archers caused Theseus much concern. Their shafts, hissing in from his right, were doing troublesome work with a number striking men close by, one in the arm, causing him to seek refuge away from the fray, another in the neck, proving fatal as the man convulsed on the ground, retching blood. Two shafts were already embedded in the side of Theseus' own chariot. The Athenian archers carried on their business as best they could but there were not enough of them to inflict significant damage. After inflicting ruin upon Pallas' ships at the harbour their comrades, greater in number, had left unseen to conceal themselves in the forest away from Pallas' camp where they had awaited Metion and the men from Troizen.

Elated by their success Pallas' archers had failed to notice the approach of Metion. Slowed for part of the way by the rocky nature of the ground Metion's company now moved in quickly to assail the enemy archers and others from their left. The ever-vigilant Pallas saw what was about to happen but in those moments of distraction almost fell victim to an Athenian spear that hissed by to pierce the thigh of one of his sons. The man, his armour ringing on the ground, cried out for help but Pallas ignored him, intent once more upon achieving his foremost goal – the death of Theseus. 'Let me get to him,' he growled. 'By Zeus and all the gods, let me at him!'

Metion and his men set about the lightly armed archers with a view to slaughter, ending the lives of many in bloody violence, scattering the survivors who fled in panic for the protection of the trees, the few Cretans among them stumbling in the direction of the harbour where they thought their ships would be waiting. With the archers no longer a threat, Metion and his band turned their attention to the left flank of Pallas' soldiers, dashing in with spear and sword as a blizzard of vengeance. The Athenian archers, having held back until assured of their own safety by Metion's arrival, emerged at last from the trees and hurried to a point where they also were able to inflict much harm upon the unprotected rear of Pallas' company. Pallas had all but lost his advantage in numbers and he saw victory slipping from his grasp.

Where the opposing bands were most heavily engaged there continued a disordered clamour of shouting and screaming, hardly dimmed by the clash of bronze against bronze or shield. Men dodged here and there to drag arms or armour from the fallen or attempt escape when wounded. Others with spear hurled or sword broken or with no other weapon at hand would seize a rock from the blood-spattered ground to swing high, to heave into the ranks of his enemy or shatter the skull of an opponent. Dust clouds had risen from dry earth to hover above the arena of battle, swirling, coalescing, appearing to many of Pallas' men as the spectral image of a grinning skull.

Theseus fought his way through the tumult until suddenly, as though sensing what was to happen, men began to back away, leaving open ground occupied only by the dead and dying, with at its far side, not twenty steps from them, a bearded, florid-faced, metal-clad image of vengeance: Pallas. Sunlight glinted on gore-spattered armour. Clustered about him were five of his wrathful, jeering sons, all flaunting weapons, each with shield at the ready.

The turmoil of combat had eased but not altogether stopped. Pallas fixed a dire gaze upon Theseus, seeing within his reach, the man he scorned as a cosseted usurper yet the one who strove yet again to thwart his ambitions. This man would now pay the ultimate price. Pallas' mouth bore a twisted grin of triumph as he tested the balance of his spear.

Theseus eyed him, balancing his own shaft in readiness to cast, the words, 'So here we are at last, my boastful friend,' passing as a whisper from his lips. He uttered no further word but watched calmly as Pallas judged his distance.

Swinging his shield aside, its base resting on the ground to give him support, Pallas raised his spear high, hurling the weapon at Theseus with the insult offered once before, 'Bastard son of a bastard king!'

But Pallas' aim was provoked as much by hatred, as much by his urge to strike first as it was by cold calculation. The lance sped close by its intended target to glance off the shield of another man, knocking him to the ground by its impetus but inflicting no injury. Theseus, allowing time for calmer judgement, launched his spear on a truer course but Pallas, long practised in the ways of the battlefield, lurched aside as it sped close by his black-plumed helmet with lethal hiss. Fate chose the man standing at his rear as its victim, yet another of his sons, when the blade, flashing above the top of his shield, struck the man's cheekbone to slice away a portion of his face, hurling his boar's tusk helmet over the heads of his companions. His blood-drizzling scream rose above other men's shouts, striking dismay into those close about him who at once stepped back. Pallas swore aloud and promptly seized another man's spear. All other fighting had ceased.

Theseus, too, was handed a fresh lance then stood alert to await his adversary's next move. Pallas, anticipating his sons' support, was about to attempt a second cast when Theseus, staying his own companions who stood poised and ready to launch their own spears, stepped forward. 'Pallas!' he called. 'You and I must settle this matter between ourselves! Enough men have died already! Are you willing to step out or do I come for you?'

Pallas, too, strode forward exclaiming, 'Oh - come for me, will you! I'll take you apart with my bare hands if needs be you fucking upstart!' His great shield scraped the ground as, gazing with baleful eye upon Theseus, he tested the balance of the spear in his right hand. Four of his sons moved forward behind him, suspecting Pallas might be

370

overwhelmed and cut down by a surge of Athenians. Four of Theseus' companions advanced likewise though none on either side stood too close to his leader. Other men backed away to occupy less hazardous positions.

Soldiers on both sides were aware of what was to happen. Like ripples spreading outward on a pool, men began to murmur. Word sped from one to another, from friend to enemy, that events other than mortal combat were about to determine their fate. Men who would a short time before have cleaved or pierced one another with cold metal stood together in silence, their weapons lowered. Still could be heard the cries of the wounded and dying as each leader of men prepared to make his fateful move.

For a second time Theseus and Pallas faced one another other directly in combat. Each understood that at this distance, with the skills they possessed, a well-aimed spear was unlikely to miss its mark and both knew that no shield a man could carry would be robust enough to stop it. Theseus was well aware that the ploy he'd used to protect himself at their first encounter would this time fail if Pallas aimed low.

As before, Theseus waited for his adversary to make the first move. Pallas, deducing hesitation to be the uncertainty of a less experienced opponent, strode forward with a cry to launch his spear. Fewer years' experience of real battle the younger Theseus may have possessed but quickness of wit plus the agility of youth were his allies. Hardly had the shaft left Pallas' hand when, letting fall shield and spear, Theseus leapt aside to avoid the missile by less than a hand's breadth. The spear cleaved only air, speeding between his spaced out men to strike loudly against a rock. Even before it tumbled harmlessly to the ground, its blade rendered useless, Theseus was bounding resolutely forward, his hand about the hilt of his sword, the blade hissing clear of its sheath. This was the sword of grey metal given him by Daedalus, the sword with which he had slain then butchered the beast of the labyrinth. He saw now in front of him not an armed warrior, not a man of this sunlit world but another Asterion, another beast; a loathsome creature of darkness that had to be destroyed.

'Athena is with us!' his men cried as Theseus closed upon Pallas who, with hand falling to his own sword but encumbered still by his shield, was fired by an all-consuming urge to kill. But Theseus was on him as a swooping eagle. He seized Pallas' shield, wrenching it aside as the other snarled blind hatred. Pallas' weapon had hardly quit the comfort of its gilded scabbard when Theseus struck hard with a cry of, 'Here is a gift from Athens!' His blade thrust beneath bronze plate, sliced through boiled hide, through layers of linen to penetrate deep, to pierce the spine of the beast that craved to devour his kingdom. Pallas, his face almost touching that of his adversary, gasped in open-mouthed, wide-eyed disbelief then stood motionless, making no other sound than the long, wheezing sigh of a departing life. Theseus wrenched his blade clear to a screech of metal against metal then stepped back. Time seemed to freeze in those charged moments. Pallas remained quite still, eyes gazing directly ahead. He swayed, the sword dropped from his hand then he toppled to the ground like a slaughtered ox, armour ringing as his own weighty shield clattered across him.

Theseus stood astride his fallen adversary, coursing his bloodied sword from side to side, levelling it at the dead man's followers who, having started forward, now hesitated. The plume swayed proudly above Theseus' head to announce, 'I have conquered!' Sunlight glinted harshly on helmet and armour as he declared, 'Here lies the man who would lead you to ruin! Who will join him? Come now – step forward!'

None of Pallas' companions moved to offer challenge. Nor was the ominous presence of Metion and his company at their flank lost on an enemy rendered leaderless, an enemy facing bloody annihilation should they wish to carry on the fight.

With the prospect of violence receding, Theseus' driver brought up the chariot for his gore-spattered master. Theseus clambered aboard, removing his helmet to stand with sword raised in full view of friend and foe alike. 'The gods have deserted you!' he declared to Pallas' men. 'You fought with courage – now take up your wounded, lay aside their weapons and armour and go!'

Tension gave way to uncertainty then the warriors of each side began to move about. There was little conversation. They were concerned only to identify their dead and tend the few fallen who remained alive. The arms and weapons of the enemy would be trophies only for the victor.

Metion stepped over to Theseus' chariot. 'You have won a great victory, Lord Theseus,' he declared.

'No, Metion, *we* have won a great victory - you, me, the men of Athens and our allies. We all must take credit for this.'

'Which of these, I wonder, are his sons,' Metion remarked, surveying the corpses strewn about in grotesque disorder close to Pallas' body. 'Will those still living not contrive to avenge their father?'

'I doubt even Pallas himself would have known who was who,' replied Theseus. 'But it hardly matters. They came here to destroy us. They came with appetites whetted by the promise of Cretan gold but found instead the bitter taste of a lesser metal. If they want to try again we'll be more than ready. Meanwhile have our men strip the arms and armour from their dead then we take care of our own.'

As they returned to Athens the driver of Theseus' chariot turned to him. 'Lord Theseus, who were all those men led by Metion - was Troizen not stricken by plague?'

'Plague? No - there was never a plague. That was born out of rumours spread about on my orders. If Pallas had any informers in Troizen all would have seemed normal to them until it was too late. Metion and a few others knew of it but the rest of our people had to believe it was true because of spies about our own city. In his certainty of overwhelming us with numbers, Pallas never delved further into the matter of Troizen. Pittheus no longer had the strength to ride with his men so Metion and those of our men serving under him met up with them to take charge.'

Chapter 13
The VISION of THESEUS

The sun was low in the west when, after the carnage of that day, Theseus sat with wine goblet to hand in the soothing company of Haemon and his lyre. 'Tomorrow,' he sighed, 'when the sun rises, we will dedicate the weapons taken from our enemy at Athena's shrine. Tomorrow will be a new day for Athens now the shadow of Pallas is lifted.'

'You are a hero to all the people of Athens,' said Haemon, laying aside the lyre. 'In the nature of things, heroes live forever. Your name will live in the very stones of our city. It will soar like the birds above this land, and yes, over lands far beyond as does that of Heracles. This I most humbly foretell.'

'Oh, like Heracles,' smiled Theseus. 'No, I seek no glory for myself. I have freed our city from the shameful retribution imposed on her by Knossos and ended the greed of a conniving tyrant. I believe it was what the gods meant me to do. Not even Minos will care to scheme against us again, though I imagine he'll replace his losses in men and vessels soon enough. But I will make our city strong – stronger than she ever was – stronger even than Mycenae.'

Theseus drank from his goblet, gazed down in deep thought then said, 'You know, when I first set out for Athens I considered myself a grown man because of all the training that had made me strong and fit. Only now, only after the marvels and the horrors I've witnessed can I come to terms with the fact that I was still no more than a boy when I left

Troizen. I could never have imagined the challenges that would confront me. There are many truths to be found in mortal danger and in the tumult of battle. But Haemon my friend, there is another more pleasant task ahead for me. I must have a wife – one with good looks and a fine figure, naturally. I must have an heir to maintain the confidence of our people and the security of Athens and I don't intend to go through the troubles that beset my father in doing it. Then I think of the household running Knossos – yes, like that of Mycenae, a truly blighted family apart, it seems, from Deucalion. Yes, Haemon, it's something I need to think hard about.'

***

Many days had passed, the seasons were changing, the days and nights becoming cooler. Wild birds crossed the skies in greater number on their cryptic journeys. The public rejoicing, the ceremonies, the sacrifices at the shrines – all were by now a memory.

Theseus, in white tunic, with the sword of Knossos at his side, strolled with Metion, two guards and two of the city's elders in the agora. There were the usual traders with wares or samples on display but one group in particular caught his attention. Several men, women and children had congregated about a stall, one of them Theseus recognised as an important ivory trader based on Sicily, another from Cyprus whose copper ingots would be waiting among a diversity of goods in his vessel moored at Phaleron, where no trace remained now of earlier conflict. Others were crewmen and travellers from various shores.

There was something about the gathering, about their conversation, about the manner in which they gesticulated that hinted of an unusual event – perhaps something Theseus might do well to know about, especially as he had heard them mention Crete and Knossos more than once. He and his small company approached amiably, not wishing to quell their conversation. On seeing him, one of the merchants lifted his hands then gave a short bow, saying, 'Ah, Lord Theseus – our congratulations upon your victories. We are as always at your service.'

The rest, showing equal respect, fell silent.

Theseus replied, 'And as always you and the goods you bring are welcome here in Athens,' yet he wondered also if the man would have addressed Pallas in like manner had victory been his. 'What is it that enlivens your conversation today?' he asked. 'D'you have news from Crete?'

'Lord Theseus, these sailors have a great deal to say,' answered the trader with a sweep of his hand. 'They have news of events you may wish to hear about.'

'Travellers from Crete tell a strange tale, my lord' began their ship's captain, 'one so strange that I would hardly have believed it except that -.' The man hesitated as if in fear of ridicule.

'Except what?' Theseus asked.

'Except that by and large the accounts all agree. They're accounts given by men of different nations who trade with Knossos - men who speak different tongues with one never having known the other. There were many ships berthed at the port of

377

Amnissos. Many men claim to have witnessed the strange event of that day.'

'But none of our own vessels were present, naturally,' remarked Theseus with a hint of impatience. 'So tell me - what exactly *did* they see,'

The captain took a deep breath. 'Lord Theseus - they speak of two men flying westward over the sea from Knossos! Yes, two men in the sky with wings – wings like those of great birds!' As others nodded in agreement the man held out his arms as if to reinforce the statement. 'Two men gliding through the air like – again I say, like birds! One, they say, was older and bearded – the other young and fair.'

'Is this tale to be believed?' asked one of the elders.

'After what I saw in Knossos,' breathed Theseus, 'I'd believe almost anything.'

'They must have been gods,' added another man, 'gods that have deserted Knossos. That's what people were saying.'

'Gods you say?' responded Theseus. 'No, they were not gods. Now you've said this much I can guess who they were.'

'These were men you knew?' queried the elder.

'Aye, they were - Daedalus and his son Icarus, men of imagination and the means of expressing it. I met them at Knossos and I tell you, without their aid I would never have returned alive to Athens. Now you'll have me wondering day and night how they did this and what became of them.'

'Ah,' continued the captain, clasping hands at his front, 'I'm afraid, My Lord, there are yet more tales – less agreeable I have to say. When we were ashore at Pylos, in the Peloponnese, the men of other vessels we spoke with reported how one of them – the younger of the two – fell to his death from the sky. They say he soared - they say he circled about reckless in the pleasures of his freedom and in his desire to explore the sky above. They tell how he flew too close to the heat of the sun and how it destroyed his wings. Yet others, sailing far to the west, from close to the shores of Sicily, claim they observed only one man on this strange voyage through the air above.' The captain hesitated nervously, then added, 'I - I fear, My Lord, this news is not to your liking.'

Theseus stared at the sky a while then looked down in sadness. 'If all of this is true then, yes, it's news I wish never to have heard. Icarus – yes poor Icarus, a light that has gone from this world. What I have learned today will haunt me as surely as those memories of the labyrinth.'

Other vessels, other travellers came and went from Athens, bringing with them other, more down to earth tales. Theseus ordered the reporting of every one of these directly to himself so that, in time, a picture of events beyond Attica became clearer in outline if seldom in detail. One evening, when the nights were still cool, he sat with flagon of wine by an open fire, reminiscing, relating what he knew to Haemon.

'Gossip and rumour weave their way like passing birds but bringing them together offers a strong enough thread of narrative upon which to hang credulity. It seems Minos was so enraged at the escape of Daedalus he sent out men to find him. After hearing the same reports we were given, he himself took a shipload of armed men to Sicily.'

379

'Minos himself?' queried Haemon. 'And they claim he went all the way to Sicily?'

'Yes, he'd been convinced Daedalus had offered his services to their king, Cocalus, and so headed straight to the palace to demand Daedalus be returned into his hands. Apparently, Cocalus wasn't keen on the idea of giving the old man up. Daedalus himself wasn't keen on it either but Minos insisted and no doubt threatened reprisals. As to what happened next – well, some maintain Cocalus wined and dined Minos then had him murdered in his bath, others say he drowned when drunk and that his death was an accident.' Theseus drained his goblet, adding with a wry grin, 'Either way, it seems he came to a clean end.'

Haemon reached to refill their goblets, saying, 'If that is true then it's still an ignominious end for such a great and powerful king. And in spite of how you found him, he was long regarded as one of the wisest of rulers, was he not?'

'Yes, I'd heard that said often enough when I lived at Troizen, mainly by people who I recall had never been to Knossos. Maybe it was his obsession in later years with Asterion – perhaps it was the very presence of that creature beneath his palace that unsettled his mind. But I assure you, my friend, the female members of his family would also have tested the wits of any man. I note as well that in spite of the many tales that have passed through this town since my return from Crete, there's never been mention of Ariadne, not a hint of her fate. I can't help but wonder, even now, what became of her.'

'Perhaps she tried to find her way back to Knossos by sea and drowned when her vessel was lost in a storm,' suggested Haemon, setting down the flagon. 'But as you yourself pointed out, we may never know,'

'True, we may never know. Now yesterday I received advance news of envoys soon to be on their way to us from Knossos. This was reported by traders from Mycenae who had been charged to inform me about it. Why they're coming here I have no idea,' said Theseus, 'but if it's more demands they're intending to hand out then I'll send each man back with his staff of office inserted somewhere not so diplomatic.'

'There can be no more demands now Minos and that creature are gone,' responded Haemon. 'And who would make them? Not his widowed queen, surely.'

'I think not,' agreed Theseus. 'I hear Deucalion has taken the throne and from what I know of him, he'll behave very differently than did his father in later life. No, I doubt Pasiphae will any longer have a say in the affairs of Knossos. The Cretan vessel is due at our shores the day after tomorrow - then we'll know their purpose. There was a prophesy I heard before our final confrontation with Pallas - "One ruler will triumph. Two will die. Two will gain their father's throne." After all that's happened, it appears to have come true. And yet…'

Haemon waited as Theseus, eyes closed, remained for some time deep in thought. Then he spoke again. 'Haemon – I slept deeply last night, more so than I usually do, then I lay half-awake before sunrise thinking about the Minotaur, about the beast I slew. I wondered, almost, if it had been a dark dream. I wondered, that is, until I was fully awake. Then I wondered if the beast really ever goes away. It seems that however many times it is destroyed, it will always return in different guise. The beast will always be there, waiting to rise again.'

'That may be so, My Lord,' breathed Haemon, 'and it may be the wish of the gods. But it must also be their wish that one such as yourself will arise as surely as does the sun to confront and defeat such evil, as indeed you have.'

'Reassuring words, my friend,' smiled Theseus, lifting up his goblet. 'Words I'll drink to.'

***

Metion with an armed party escorted the two envoys from the restored jetty at Phaleron, along the track to the western gate and into the city. They were ushered across the agora much to the disgust of those citizens who recognised their Cretan attire and the staff each carried bearing the gilded double axe. The envoys well understood how much at risk their lives might have been were it not for the presence of the guards. Having climbed the steps to the acropolis, having entered the palace, they were allowed rest and refreshment before being conducted to the great hall. There Theseus sat in Aegeus' throne with Haemon, the priests and elders of the city gathered close by. Theseus wore his father's purple robe. It was one of the few occasions when he would wish to appear in regal attire. His sword, nevertheless, lay concealed beneath.

Flames danced brightly in the circular stone hearth, timbers spat glowing motes into the smoke, male and female courtiers stood about the hall in anticipation. Why after all that had happened, they asked one another, had the Cretans made this journey?

'Athens offers you welcome,' declared Theseus, noting that these were not the same men who had confronted him on the occasion of those onerous demands made upon Aegeus. 'Tell me the purpose of your visit.'

'We thank you for your hospitality, Lord Theseus,' replied the younger envoy as both gave bows of respect not previously offered by Minos' nobles. 'We appreciate we are not welcome here but please be assured we intend our visit to be for the benefit of Athens as well as for Knossos.'

The older envoy spoke next. 'Lord Theseus, you may be aware that our king has departed this world and that his noble son, the peerless Deucalion now sits upon the throne at Knossos.'

'I am aware of that. Please continue.'

'Lord Deucalion sees the world differently than did his father. He intends there will be great changes at Knossos. He wishes to promote good relations with all his neighbours in the islands, in the Peloponnese, throughout Attica and in particular with Athens now this unfortunate affair between us is ended - provided no other party interferes with his trade or his overseas interests, that is.'

'Not Athens nor any other power I know of has sufficient strength at sea to threaten the navies of Knossos,' responded Theseus, 'nor have we need to do that. We have trading enclaves of our own though not spread as far abroad as are yours.'

'No, Lord Theseus,' continued the envoy, 'and that is what has brought us here. There is danger growing far to our north and east. Our sailors return with tales of countless peoples on the move – not just warriors but whole families with oxen and carts loaded with their possessions. It's said there are whole nations of landless wanderers. We do not know why this is happening but already some of the more distant kingdoms visited by our traders have been attacked, pillaged and yes, even laid waste by what their people, those who survive, describe as savage hoards. These barbarians may never reach Crete nor even Attica but that does not mean we should ignore the problem by continuing to quarrel amongst ourselves. The well-being of our trade, our colonies and yours may sooner or later be under threat.'

'We've heard such rumours here in Athens but we have little knowledge other than that carried by travellers - and now by yourselves.'

'Then let us assure you, Lord Theseus,' continued the envoy, 'Lord Deucalion considers it important we become allies rather than continue as we were. He understands you yourself have no consort and as yet no prospect of an heir to your throne. He therefore offers you his sister, the lady Phaedra, in marriage to secure our good relations, if this is acceptable to you. The lady has assured us in person and without duress that she considers the prospect most agreeable.'

To the initial discomfort of both envoys, Theseus began to laugh. 'Phaedra! Yes, she's a beautiful woman - like her sister, Ariadne. Have you, has anyone knowledge of *her* whereabouts since she disappeared on Naxos?'

The envoys regarded each other blankly. 'Lord Theseus,' began the younger of the pair, 'no one at

Knossos has knowledge of her fate, nor do they at Naxos where other envoys from Knossos made enquiry some time ago.'

'No,' responded Theseus, 'I didn't expect anyone would. But I'll not delay matters for the sake of it and I agree this alliance would be of benefit to Athens.' Theseus laughed again, adding, 'And I assure you taking Phaedra to my bed would be no hardship whatsoever. I rather look forward to doing so provided she otherwise behaves as a queen ought to behave!'

The courtiers laughed also and the envoys were much relieved as Theseus continued, 'After you've rested here for the night you may sail back and inform Deucalion that before I agree to this union, any tablets bearing the terms of Athens' shame must be brought here and destroyed before my eyes.'

'Your request, sir, was anticipated before we left Crete,' responded the older envoy. 'Those tablets are on board our vessel at Phaleron and will be delivered at your convenience.'

'Then we must take wine together,' smiled Theseus, 'and discuss the finer details of this proposed alliance – oh, and the arrival of the good lady.'

***

'I wonder how he'll make out with her,' grinned the younger envoy as they later sat alone in their allocated chamber. 'She'd be a handful for any man - or men, if she lives up to her reputation.'

'As demanding as her mother and her other sisters, I'd say,' responded his companion. 'He must have some idea of what he's taking on.'

385

'He ought to if he spent any time with Ariadne as it's now claimed he did. Yes, this alliance can only be for the good, unless she wears him out.'

'Well,' yawned the older man, gazing out at the night sky, 'we leave for Crete tomorrow with good news for our new king. What other news we pick up on our way back or what will greet us on our return is in the hands of the immortals. There is trouble abroad, that we do know.'

***

She sat in a place of honour by his side, a goddess in soft-cushioned comfort, her firm breasts, nipples rouged, proudly bared above the sleeved bodice of a brightly coloured flounced dress. Gold bands held her ringletted hair in place, firelight glinted on her precious earrings and on her finely wrought bangles of Cretan gold. Close by waited her personal slave, Hylas, together with two of her more plainly dressed serving girls, both as slim, both as sensually full-lipped and full-breasted as their mistress. Haemon, a look of contentment on his face, sat aside strumming gentle notes from his lyre.

Recalling the family situation at Knossos, Theseus would not be caught unawares by Phaedra's promiscuity; she would not become another Pasiphae. Soon enough he expected he would find good reason to return Hylas to Crete while the maidservants would serve him as side dishes to Phaedra's main course. Kingship had its advantages.

Phaedra, sitting by his side, missed the luxuries of Knossos but was determined to introduce them whenever and wherever possible throughout

Theseus' more modest estate. As days passed, Cretan ships arrived at the harbour bearing palace luxuries never before seen in Athens; furniture, wall hangings, vessels for the dining table, rare perfumes and pastes for the new queen's personal adornment. There, also, were artists to decorate the palace walls in the manner of those at Knossos. Courtiers chatted, children stood in obedient silence, as slaves passed about with flagons of newly imported Cretan wine.

But other ships brought reports that, backed by the oracles of Athens' own shrines and by those delivered from Delphi, had Theseus one day call together Metion, all the elders and the senior priesthood of Athena's and Zeus' temples. They assembled in silent expectation before his throne in the great hall.

'A tide of ill fortune approaches Greece,' Theseus began. 'For months it has been rumoured, the oracles have predicted it and it is looming ever closer. The people of Troy far to our east control trade routes to and from the Euxine Sea. Priam, their king, seeks to regulate our trade and impose taxes on our vessels to enhance the power of his own arms in the face of these dark forces. There has for some time been talk of an expedition against Troy under the leadership of King Atreus of Mycenae. He desired to secure those trade routes with the help of his allies but his house has seen too much disorder these last years for him to act. Now it will more likely fall upon his sons Agamemnon and Menelaus to fulfil that task. Whether Athens is a part of this or no, our city must be made stronger still. Our defensive wall will be enlarged and the acropolis strengthened to render it impregnable. Since the defeat of Pallas we hold most of Attica. To enhance our security I intend Athens will soon bring under her control all of this territory. Its towns and its ports.' Theseus rose to his feet to declare, 'The beast is never far away. It did not depart this world with the death of Pallas and his kin. Always it is there, waiting now as a thundercloud to spread darkness over our world. Athens must stand as a bulwark against an affliction that threatens one day to sweep through all of Greece and beyond. The oracles predict our city will be a beacon in that darkness, a beacon to guide future generations through mists of desolation to a greater light. A light that will one day shine through all the ages of mankind. I, Theseus, am sworn to make it so!'

***

There was another of less elevated status with a mind to secure his own future. After a beating and remonstrations by his parents over his not having joined them for the evacuation north when invasion by Pallas was looming, the mop-haired shepherd boy had bided his time. Now all seemed right for him to make his move.

It was a chill dawn when he arose in silence to find the sky barely lightened. He trod quietly, a shadow amidst shadows, the only sound the rough snoring of his father, the soft murmuring of his mother in their fetid bed. Pulling his father's heavy woollen cloak about his shoulders he left the dwelling on a whisper of air. No longer for him would be the grimy hovel where tiny pests of the night crawled out to bite while unseen creatures scrabbled in dark corners. This time he was not setting out to tend the goats. In half-light he hurried to where the precious gold object lay hidden, to the gnarled pine tree that stood as its marker.

Members of his oafish family had failed to agree, in spite of heated arguments, on how its value could be realised whilst all the time fearing it might be stolen. The boy dug with bare hands into the soil, glancing from side to side, fearful of being seen. There at last, wrapped in cloth, was the cup – his cup. He shook away the dirt then, having replaced the earth, set off at a trot to the harbour of Phaleron, his prize concealed together with fruit and dried figs in a shabby leather bag slung over his shoulder.

There were two Cretan ships moored at Phaleron – he had watched them sail across the bay and into the harbour during that previous afternoon. They had already taken on cargo so would cast off at sunrise. On board the larger of the two there ought to be room enough to hide until the vessel was out at sea – too far out for her captain to wish to return. The ship would take him to the wonderful Knossos he had heard so many people speak about. There he would make his way along broad, gilded streets to that fabulous palace of light. There he would present his treasure to the magnanimous new king. There he would serve. There he would be safe and well fed amid the luxury of its halls.

Once at Knossos he would be away from the looming troubles of this world. That was what he told himself as he hurried down to the harbour.

THE END

CREDITS

I thank Lynda Buxton for her care and attention in checking through to correct my numerous typographical and grammatical errors

Also by The Author

THE MAN WHO SOUGHT ETERNITY
RETRURN OF THE HERO
THE DEVIL IN EDEN
THE SINGING STONES

Further works by Jeff Clarke may be found on
www.jeffreypeterclarke.co.uk

And on his author page at:
https://fiction4all.com/ebooks/a1549.htm

.

www.ingramcontent.com/pod-product-compliance
Lightning Source LLC
Chambersburg PA
CBHW072302020726
47501CB00002B/355